7/01

12/8/02

Hard Bottom

Also by G. F. Michelsen

To Sleep with Ghosts

Hardscrabble Books—Fiction of New England

Sarah Orne Jewett (Sarah Way Sherman, ed.), *The Country of the Pointed Firs and Other Stories*

Lisa MacFarlane, ed., *This World Is Not Conclusion: Faith in Nineteenth-Century New England Fiction*

G. F. Michelsen, *Hard Bottom*

Anne Whitney Pierce, *Rain Line*

Kit Reed, *J. Eden*

Rowland E. Robinson (David Budbill, ed.), *Danvis Tales: Selected Stories*

Roxana Robinson, *Summer Light*

Rebecca Rule, *The Best Revenge: Short Stories*

R. D. Skillings, *How Many Die*

R. D. Skillings, *Where the Time Goes*

Lynn Stegner, *Pipers at the Gates of Dawn: A Triptych*

Theodore Weesner, *Novemberfest*

W. D. Wetherell, *The Wisest Man in America*

Edith Wharton (Barbara A. White, ed.), *Wharton's New England: Seven Stories and* Ethan Frome

Thomas Williams, *The Hair of Harold Roux*

HARD BOTTOM

A novel by

G. F. MICHELSEN

University Press of New England

Hanover and London

Published by University Press of New England, Hanover, NH 03755

© 2001 by G. F. Michelsen

Printed in the United States of America

5 4 3 2 1

F MICHELSEN

Library of Congress Cataloging-in-Publication Data

Michelsen, G. F.

Hard bottom : a novel / by G. F. Michelsen

p. cm. — (Hardscrabble books)

ISBN 1–58465–081–8 (alk. paper)

1. New England—Fiction. I. Title. II. Series.

PS3563.I336 H37 2001

813'.54—dc21   00–012282

For Alexandre

Acknowledgments

My heartfelt thanks to Joe Amaral, Chris Armstrong, Molly Benjamin, Tom Cook, Margo Fenn, Bob Jensen, Eric Palin, Pete Sessa, Richard Walters, Dana Hornig, and others too numerous to mention, whose generous and expert advice guided me on various aspects of the novel; responsibility for how the advice was used, or ignored, rests with me alone. Part of this book was written with the financial assistance of a grant from the National Endowment for the Arts, and in workspace provided by The Writers' Room, and I am grateful to both institutions for their help. Chapter Two was first published in the spring 1999 issue of the *Notre Dame Review* and appears here by permission. Last, but far from least, I wish to thank my wife, Elizabeth, and my children, Emilie and Alexandre, for their loving and uncritical support.

Prologue

From the second floor of the Hill I watch the bay change textures as the light dwindles and returns.

I never noticed so many textures before I was locked up in this cell.

In the morning the water goes from the deep matte of velvet, to the grain of worn dock pilings, to surfaces harsh as number two sandpaper.

Later the textures run back down the spectrum. They start with the rough edges and travel through a complex surface like the braided silver Caitlyn's necklace is composed of. All the way to that indigo velvet, and then night, when you cannot see the bay at all because of security lights.

I am making a big deal of not much since even in the morning most of the bay is obscured by oaks and the bulk of the Superior Courthouse where they will arraign me later.

Gates clang and the deputies come through calling men

for court. Silva yells, "Cahoon, you on deck." The deputies have to treat us carefully because in J.D.-1 we are all on sick list. Still it takes little time for Silva to fold me into a wheelchair and snick one cuff on the frame and the other around my left wrist. Then he rolls me down a ramp and outside.

The fresh air tastes good. The flavors I make out in one sniff include applejack, maple smoke, car exhaust. Cold, and dust from piles of leaves that children kick through and cars scatter in their slipstreams.

I breathe as deeply as I can against the bandages, the little spikes of pain.

It always smells this fine, leaving the Hill.

Traffic cones block the back entrance of the courthouse. Silva wheels me toward the front. The back hall was flooded in the storm, he says. The reason I am being arraigned in the old courthouse is this: The nor'easter dumped three inches of rain in Orleans and it leaked through the roof of the new Second District Court, where Chatham cases are tried. That was a state contract, and it went to Kiernan Concrete. Kiernan always lowballs the bid and buys cheap materials to pad their profit margin.

In a weird way I am also here because of a storm. Because the kind of cheap materials I am built of were not able to keep me together in the strain that high winds bring.

The clock reads twelve minutes to eight. The morning crop of OUIs slouches from a line of rusted sedans across the bitter asphalt. Men, mostly, in windbreakers and work-boots. Their eyes are bright with Visine, their breath sharp with mint. Most of them have gone this route before. The women laugh too loud and carry handbags that are plastic imitations of what TV actors carry. They fire up butts, sucking the smoke from Merits and Kents deep into the cave of hangover. Every angle of body screaming for beer.

I wouldn't mind a beer myself. Or a Kent.

We follow them around the building to the front lawn.

The lawyers already are shoaled there in camel's-hair coats between an antique six-pounder cannon and a statue of James Otis.

I think it appropriate that a lush like Otis should have a place of honor among these Cape Codders.

The breathing of the lawyers creates short-lived silver fans in the chill.

They wear loafers, like summer people.

The doors are not open yet. Silva shunts me up the wheelie ramp to a position beside one of the columns holding up the courthouse cupola. In the OUI crowd I spot a guy I know. He crews on Elliott's gillnetter. When he sees me, he turns away.

I am cold; the sun has not reached the courthouse. I touch the column, expecting a deeper chill from stone, but it is the same temperature as the air. The gray material sounds hollow when I knock on it.

They built these columns out of wood, fluting and painting them to look like granite.

I see Grealey first. Grealey, the Volvo-people's lawyer. He moves with the same smugness as the other lawyers only more so: like a tanker bearing down on a fleet of mackerel seiners. The weimaraner lopes up from behind, overtaking, a black and fluid force—towing Skull, Thatch's accountant, on a long lead.

Thatch Hallett walks behind.

All three catch sight of me at the same instant. Grealey pretends not to. He hauls out a cell phone. The accountant looks at Otis. The dog scratches its stomach. Thatch, who is tall enough to see above the crowd, stares at me without blinking. That is when it comes back to me, how hard blue can get: harder than the North Atlantic in winter.

The last time I saw Thatch Hallett he was staring at me down the sights of a thirty-ought-six. It is those eyes that pressured me into the fists of the storm. It is they that direct a force bound to crush what I love to dust. My stomach loses mass. I find this odd. Eyes that hard should make everything they touch gain weight, become more rigid.

The December air has roughened Hallett's nose and cheeks, turning them a light maroon.

Cold always changes the textures of things. I remember this now. Cold alters trees and skin in ways I do not expect. It changes the feel of my gut, the very mass of me, and no way of telling if that leaves me with more weight or less.

A van parking at the foot of the Hill blurs my line of thought. It bears a satellite dish on a boom and the words CAPE ELEVEN NEWS. Two men stack relays on the lawn.

Thatch's lawyer submerges in the school of other lawyers. Thatch himself is dressed in a houndstooth jacket. He wears the same paratrooper beret he always wears. That green jungle-pattern stands out against the fractal branches, shifting as he tells jokes to Skull. He loves doing this because he knows, everybody knows, Skull never laughs.

A woman skirts the lawyers, peering nervously right and left. She wears thick eyeshadow and a worn kaftan. Her lips are painted, and ridged like a fuel filter. The crook of her elbow shelters a tangle of brindled fur.

I shift uncomfortably. I haven't got a lawyer and Harriet's presence with the cairn terrier too will only make things worse in the narrowed vision of a judge.

Grealey moves back into view around the OUIs. The courthouse door opens. A guard yells, "Upstairs for Superior and Grand Jury, downstairs for Second District." Noise of shoe soles, "Take-it-easy's," "Hang-in-there's." The OUIs turbo down final drags of their cigarettes. Grealey climbs the steps and stops in front of me. He does not seem to like the wheelchair; he lifts his nose and stares down the ridge of it.

"You're not represented by counsel," he says. It is not a question, so I don't answer. He peers at the wheelchair again.

"Why don't you make him walk?" he asks the guard. "It's just a tissue wound."

"It's the rules, Mr. Grealey," Silva says. "Insurance." He shrugs.

"He's trying to look like the victim," Grealey continues, "in court. But it won't work."

I peer at him. I barely register what he is saying because all the different surfaces and weights in my chest are pressing against the bandages holding them in and it kind of aches. Thatch strolls down the slope of lawn, turns seaward. The dog stampedes a squirrel. "Jesse," Thatch calls. His voice is strong as a radio announcer's. Grealey leans over and taps me on a bandage.

"It won't work, Cahoon," he repeats. "And you know why?"

I follow Thatch's gaze. A wedge of bay is visible between Barnstable Marine and the white dunes of Sandy Neck. Grealey was an assistant DA the first time I was in court, thirteen years ago. He doesn't look any friendlier now than he did then.

"Because this has to do with events," Grealey continues. "What happened to my client's real estate, as opposed to what things *look* like. Facts," he adds, as if I hadn't understood him right. "Convicted felons should have some respect for facts."

Set like a gem in that chink of ocean, a fishing boat with a white superstructure runs slowly to the east. It is three or four miles out so I cannot be certain if it is a dragger or a gillnetter. It moves steady and slow so it probably is a dragger; and, while I never really liked dragging, the sight of that boat creates a feeling in my stomach so powerful that it fills my gut and drowns out other pressures.

It feels like when I was in high school and I would walk to Casey Ryan's garden at night and she would change into her nightdress at the lemon-colored window and know I was watching.

It feels like I drank a gallon of Might-E-Foam with a pint of catalyst and the chemical is expanding to a hundred times its volume in my leaky chest.

Grealey checks his watch and looks at Silva again.

"The wheelchair won't make a difference," he says. "It's his *motive* for what happened six days ago that's important. Not the wheelchair."

I stare at the fishing boat, trying to breathe against the bandages.

I want to tell Grealey, this has nothing to do with events.

This has to do with textures; the textures of what we feel, and how they rub against the surface of the outside, and what results from that friction.

I am conscious of keeping my mouth shut and even. I watch that small window of sea.

The dragger hauls her net east, chasing a shoal of black-back flounder, or fluke or whiting maybe, into the brass reflection of the sun.

NOAA Weather Forecast

This is the December first extended forecast for waters from the Merrimack River to Chatham, Massachusetts, up to twenty-five nautical miles offshore:

The jet stream continues to curve southward from Ontario to Maine. A high pressure zone currently over New England will move offshore by late Sunday. A weak low pressure zone is expected to move out of Pennsylvania into the area at that time.

Offshore forecast for New England waters from the Northeast Channel to the Great South Channel including the waters east of Cape Cod to the Hague Line:

Winds north, twenty to twenty-five, becoming northwesterly, seas three to six feet. Tomorrow, winds shifting south and southwest, diminishing to fifteen.

Reports from offshore buoys:

Isle of Shoals: air temperature thirty-one, wind northerly twenty-two, water temperature forty-two, seas five feet.

Southeast portion of Georges Bank: air temperature thirty-three, wind northwest nineteen, water temperature forty-four, seas five feet.

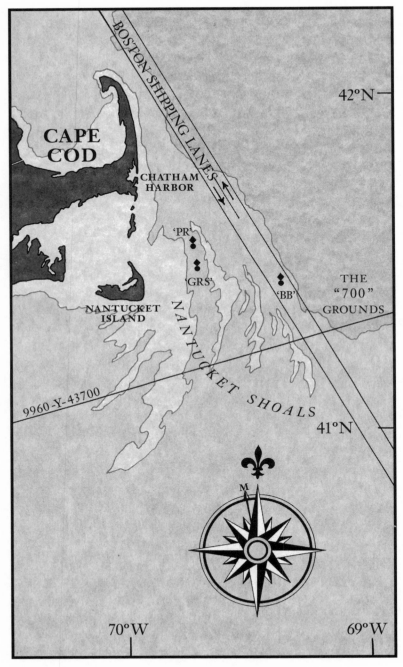

FISHING GROUNDS, NANTUCKET SHOALS

Chapter 1

The 700 line

41 degrees 10'N; 69 degrees 04'W

On the day everything starts I am forty-four miles east-southeast of Nantucket, looking for gray sole on the western edge of Georges Bank.

I pull back the throttle to 900 r.p.m. and check the Loran. The set has been giving me trouble. It skips off the ranges it is supposed to show, then locks onto bearings in the Gulf of Mexico, but right this minute it holds to the 700 line. On the fishfinder a thin scatter of blue cartoon ghosts pulses at 49 fathoms. I would like to think these are sole but they are probably shrimp.

Throttle back some more and the diesel grumbles lower. The boat rolls hard. My boat is a fifteen-year-old, fifty-foot Bruno and Stillman lobster boat with a customized Gardner 380 diesel engine. The swells rise four or five feet from a high-pressure zone that came through two days ago out of the northwest, driving winds of thirty knots before it.

The VHF rips into run-on.

"This is Coast Guard Brant Point Massachusetts Group, Coast Guard Brant Point Massachusetts Group. The following is a list of areas closed to fishing by the Northeast Regional Fisheries Management Council—"

"Pig!" I yell. Pig is my mate. An object hits the deck below. It's a *Penthouse* double issue. I can tell by the thud.

"We're on the fish," I tell him.

I hope we are on the fish. My echo sounder is old and sometimes the ghosts you see on the screen are just that. Electric ectoplasm, the echoes of echoes bouncing off layers of till or other glacial garbage under the seabed.

Pig comes up the hatch. He smoothes his moustache with his tongue. He pulls on boots and gloves, warm from being piled against the radiator, and leaves through the after door. I press the autopilot switch, wait to make sure it is tracking, grab my gloves and follow.

My boat used to be a longliner. In those days the long afterdeck was clean except for tub trawls and a row of buoys lashed against the wheelhouse roof.

Three months ago, however, I bought a winch, an H-frame gallows and hydraulics from Ted Angstrom. Ted had sold his boat to the federal buy-back program but he had not sold his spare gear. I got a second mortgage from Chatham Bank and Trust and went to New Bedford and bought two otter trawls. I also bought extra ground cables, rollers, buoys, and hydraulic hoses.

Then I turned my boat into a dragger.

Sim Pierce helped but it took a long time to get everything running right and I still have not got the hang of all the equipment. So Pig and I work slowly, checking twice before we shoot this gear into the unforgiving ocean.

When everything seems okay I crack the valve to get power on the main winch. Then I release the brake on the reel. The reel squats in the middle of the H-frame, on the stern. It carries the net wound up in an aluminum spindle like a skein of coarse orange knitting.

Waves loom up on the port side, swing the hull through a two-step, rush off to find another partner to starboard. My senses fill with sour exhaust and the spunk of salt and fish-guts; with rush of wind and the endless whiskey voice of the engine; with fingers numbing and the herring gulls crying as they cut circles in the updrafts, and me and Pig bracing against the motion and closing our ears to the noise and stamping our boots against the cold and hanging on with one hand as we work.

Back in the wheelhouse I peer around to make sure we are not going to run into anything. A car carrier looms on the western horizon, flat and static as a rifle target, although it is actually running north at fifteen knots in the Boston shipping lanes. Farther east, the black "T" shape of a Chevron test rig perches spindly as an egret over Little Georges. The drilling rig reminds me of something; I have no time to track the memory down.

The radar, on ten-mile range, shows a couple of foxfire dots to the northeast that are two Gloucester draggers we passed earlier.

I check the fishfinder. We are still on the echoes. I look at the chart, because I want to follow the chamois bottom here, soft sand with no rocks or wrecks at all. I adjust the auto to the course I want, jot down the Loran bearings and pull the throttle back a touch.

Then go aft once more.

Things speed up now. I ease the winch brake loose and the cables start to run. The cables are shackled to two "doors." The doors are six-foot slabs of steel weighing three-quarters of a ton apiece, one on each side of the gal-lows. They work like fins underwater, pushing different ways, dragging open the net's mouth. The doors drop into the hissing foam. They sink too quickly, not enough tension;

I put pressure on the brake. The doors check, and subside under the wake, one pulling port, the other starboard. The tarred steel cables run smoothly through the blocks. The cables are called legs, in the trade, and they always remind me of the smooth-oiled legs of a woman spreading gently as the slow sex of sea pushes the doors outward, thrusting into the open net with all the funkiness of benthos, the whole circle of conception and hunt, birth and murder, wrapped into that acceptance—

I push that image out of my mind.

Caitlyn used to say, I could have been a poet, if only I'd been able to write.

Anyway, down she goes. The ratio of depth to leg should be three to one. I watch the cables unwind off the drums until they reach the one-hundred-and-sixty-four fathom mark. Then I screw the brake shut. The cables thrum and throw sprays of water as they tighten. The boat slows, yaws a little. She hunches into the water, puts her shoulders into the load like a Percheron dragging a plough.

And we are fishing.

I return to the wheelhouse, open the throttle a bit, unhook the autopilot and steer 170 degrees. On this section of western Georges the bottom slopes lazy to the north. At three knots we will run two miles in forty minutes as long as we don't get hung up. So we'll haul back at eleven-thirty.

There is not much to do now. Pig takes the wheel. Grabbing a flashlight, I descend the companionway. *Penthouse* lies splayed on the deck. I pick it up, peer at the centerfold and feel a rapid and expected lust. The pink forms seem full of liquid smoothness in a world so hard you have to drench everything in oil to make it run.

When I open the hatch to the engine compartment the roar of diesel is loud enough that I can feel it tremble on my skin. I crawl into the compartment to the starboard side of the engine and check the fuel injection pump. This has a tendency to run rough, but right now it is cool to the touch.

I move aft, still crouching, through a bulkhead into the chill gloom of fishhold. Twisting under a locker, I shine the flashlight upward, between bulkhead and hydraulic lines, to the flange where the fiberglass hull joins the deck. These old Brunos have a problem with the balsa core between the layers of fiberglass. The core shrinks and forms voids and then water seeps in through the gelcoat. In winter the water in the voids can freeze and split the hull and this process usually is visible first at the flange.

Everything looks intact.

Up the fishhold ladder, into a curse of wind.

Pig smokes in the lee of the wheelhouse. I ignore the lust that flick of tobacco brings. The autopilot is on. I go back down the companionway and refill my mug from a twelve-volt coffee maker fastened by the galley stove.

In the wheelhouse I take off my outer gear and perch on the pilot stool. Cut the auto. Sip coffee, watching the tip of the harpoon, lashed to the tuna pulpit, swing back and forth, measuring in small arcs the steel indifference of horizon.

Mumbled verse of engine and seawash. The VHF rips harsh urban stanzas into the rhythm of it.

"Tommy, Tommy, you around?"

"Back o' Stellwagen, his wife said he'd be there all day."

"You believe what he told his wife?"

"Channel twenny-one."

"All stations, this is U.S. Coast Guard Brant Point Massa-chusetts Group."

Back to the chart.

The fisheries management council closed different parts of the Georges Bank grounds, either because they are spawning areas or because there are just not enough fish left there. Other areas are shut for part of the year for some spe-cies and closed year-round for different fish. With all the shifts in time and space it is like playing Twister with boats to figure out which places are safe to soak your gear.

The closed area for this section of west Georges extends

through December 31st as far as 69 degrees west, but that leaves me a wedge of the bank where I used to see a lot of mixed groundfish when I was hooking.

This course of 186 degrees sneaks me right down the east side of the closed area, about a third of a mile off. I will have sufficient margin for error as long as I am careful. Jackie Blish got busted for being only an eighth of a mile into the haddock spawning area. The Feds spotted him and fined him five thousand dollars and tied up his boat for six months. Then the bank took it and now he is working for the town.

I do not want to work for the town.

The Loran says I'm on track. I top up my mug, look through the aft window. Gulls write songs of loop and plane on the frothing sheet music of wake. Pig comes in for coffee.

This is a time when I have to say I am pretty content. I have been up since two A.M. and my brain holds a kind of wash to the edges that comes mostly from sleeplessness and a little from the Rolling Rocks I drank last night. The diesel has a bad injection pump and the hull is getting set to crack itself apart.

And Caitlyn won't talk to me. The only subject she will discuss is Sam's hockey practice and everything she says about hockey is polite and so cold it feels like we are breathing in a freezer. Sometimes I start fights just so we can say something personal to each other again.

The fish are scarce enough that I will be lucky to come home with five boxes.

I am behind on the boat mortgage as usual.

But to go fishing you have to be an optimist or a gambler, if that is not the same thing.

So I hold back the urge to hit something hard enough to bust either my hand or what I hit. Instead I concentrate on how the Gardner is running fine and the sun is up and throwing itself in a billion bayonets of glass on the sea and how I have not had a cigarette in almost two months. Out here it is impossible to see land and even my wife seems abstract, like a navigational problem I will have to deal with later, but not on this circle of ocean.

The brew in my mug is hot and sweet. The next haulback could give us three hundred pounds of medium gray sole. At three-twenty a pound that comes to over nine hundred bucks.

Although judging by how *Hooker* moves in the waves, that net is not full.

Eighteen minutes later I throttle back. Pig takes the wheel and I go to the winch. The legs wind aboard dripping and then the doors clank-slam up to the blocks, where I hook them in. This is tricky work. I have one good arm that I need to hang onto the H-frame with, and one arm a little weak for the job.

Pig puts her in neutral. He takes the idler-chains off the doors and hooks them into the reel. Then I wind the reel till the mass of net, like a monster drawn in orange crayon by a child, crests the somber waves. Keep on rolling till almost all the net is wound around its spindle, steaming and dripping over the stern.

The cod end of the net comes through the open gate of the transom and is dragged into the air. The tail, swaying dangerously over our deck, bulges like an old sock stuffed with pennies.

Fins and claws poke through the mesh, shuddering and waving in trauma.

It is not a great haul. The cod end contains a hundred pounds of good fish maybe. The rest is weed, rocks, and skate, which sells to the Asian market, but not for much. Pig shuts the transom gate. I lower the cod end a foot, step carefully near the bottom of the sack, and pull loose the nylon twine that ties the opening.

And it all spews wetly out, the sea's glutinous afterbirth, splatting on the rubber mats I glued on deck to bear the shock; ten skate, four gray sole, an undersized lobster, a half-dozen cod. Hundredweights of mud, sea anemones, and shells are mingled in with the fish; so are a rotted wooden lobster trap, sputnik weed, cans. Pig comes aft and we gaff the skate and sole into the open fishhold. I reopen the gate and shovel and scrape everything else into the gray-green flank of waves until only the six cod are left.

One is a two-year scrod; four are "market" cod, under limit. The sixth is a whale cod, easily forty-five or fifty pounds in weight. They lie gasping, throwing up what they just ate. Automatically I look at the vomit; if I know what they are eating I can go where their prey tends to school.

They have swallowed sandlance mostly, and crab; a juvenile sea scallop, moonsnails.

The goatees on their chins give the fish an absurdly intellectual look, like humid Ho Chi Minhs.

Already the wide, banner-like fins droop; their silver-brown scales turn matte in the sunlight. The whale cod flaps its tail weakly. He is probably twenty years old. Few cod of that size are left in these waters off New England.

Pink bubbles pop at the cods' gills. They are placid, nonemergency fish and do nothing in a hurry, least of all swim toward light. Being yanked upward ten atmospheres in four minutes is something they were not designed for. The fast change in pressure busted their swim bladders on the way up.

The fish will die, one way or the other. My fishing permit allows me fifty pounds bycatch of cod. If we keep them on board and the Coast Guard inspect us I could cop a fine like Jackie's.

Pig keeps the whale cod, and scrapes the rest with the edge of his shovel into the sea. The gulls swoop low. One of them dives, then rises, squawking, a wedge of pale flesh dangling in its beak.

Look at the chart again. If this area is so bare it probably means one of the New Bedford draggers was in here. We will have to steer into places the big boys avoid. That means dragging on rocky bottom and close to boulders and wrecks no one wants to mess with because they tear up the nets. But if that is where the fish are, we do not have much choice.

I toy briefly with the notion of staying on real dragging ground. We could do another three smooth haulbacks until we are sure.

I crush that fantasy all the way, like stamping on a cigarette till it does not even smoke.

The truth is, we always fish hard bottom. It's the only fishing left. My trawls are set up for it anyway with thick rubber rollers and ticklers on the groundline and tougher twine on the belly. It was only optimism that made me try the soft ground today, and I got what I expected.

I pick out a stretch of mud and rock, about half a mile from the closed area, running up to a couple of bigger rocks and a wreck on the 706 Loran line.

There are two half-gyres of current that run things around here: a big, clockwise, three-quarter circle that enfolds Georges Bank and Little Georges; and a smaller arc, same spin, that curves around Nantucket Shoals and then shoots off south. I look at the arrows of tide now pushing southeast to Little Georges and put in a small prayer that the Loran does not fuck up. Otherwise we will drift into the southern rocks before you can say "three thousand bucks," which is what a new otter trawl costs.

It takes me ten minutes to unhook the extra ground cables you need for soft bottom. Then I push the throttle to 2000 and swing the boat around toward the northern wreck.

Chapter 2

Ghosts

41 degrees 12'N; 69 degrees 01'W

We make three tows without trouble, quartering into a southerly swell, corkscrewing back on the reciprocal.

Pig and I switch jobs every tow, one of us steering while the other guts fish and hoses down the deck. We do not have to work hard at the gutting because we are not catching much fish.

Around noon the light cirrus that earlier Saran Wrapped the sky disappears. The light sharpens as it crosses the zenith and the air, as if prodded by that light, turns very cool.

I stand, one lobe of my ass on the stool, steering with a boot on the wheel.

Pig goes out for a butt, pops back in. It is during one of the times he is in the wheelhouse that the call comes through.

". . . day, Mayday. This is *Commando*, the *Commando*."

Pig turns the volume up. Looks at me without saying anything.

"... open now. Repeat ... seacocks—

"... *down?*"

The white noise rises. The transmission has a rhythm to it, a clear crackle and fizz and crackle again, like music broadcast from a distant station.

I check the VHF is on full power. I adjust the squelch and white noise only comes in louder.

Silence, but for the emphysemic rumble of diesel and the wind and the hiss of wake, which seems greater, colder than before the call.

Brant Point Coast Guard breaks in, demanding a repeat.

"Fuckin' asshole," Pig says. It's not clear who he's talking about.

We are coming to the end of our run now and cannot hang around listening to the radio or we'll hit a piece of rock that could tear the trawl's belly out. We haul back on half a box of skate and another of pout. The net has a three foot gash in one of the side panels. Pig winds nylon twine back and forth bare-handed to stitch the hole shut while I fill out the NMFS catch sheets. As I write I find myself listening to the waves once more, the hard lisp of wind, the orchestra of water. The waves mouth vocals in no order, they lick and tongue the keel. My brain projects movies against their noise, as on a screen. Without trying to, I imagine the wrecks broken on the rocks fifty fathoms below. Eel and lobsters hang in the dark corners of their bulkheads.

Microcircuits rust together, radio dials are encrusted with barnacles, the fine stitch of coral knits hand bones to VHF mikes. I think, that message cannot be from *Commando*.

The *Commando* disappeared almost six weeks ago, somewhere on Little Georges.

There is no living human for eight miles in any direction, unless you count Pig.

He comes back in, holds his stiff hands to the heater.

"Hear anything?" he asks.

"You know what that was."

"Fuckin' asshole."

"It's kids," I say, "they get hold of Daddy's radio—"

"Didn't sound like a kid."

"Fourteen, fifteen years old?"

Five minutes later Brant Point Coast Guard warns all stations that anyone who puts out a fake distress call on channel sixteen is committing a Class D felony punishable by six years in jail and fifty thousand dollars fine, not counting costs.

* * *

We shoot twice more and the second time, on our sixth run, we hang up.

I circle *Hooker* around at dead slow and get the net in without much trouble. A piece of petrified root, from thousands of years ago when Georges Bank stood above sea level, is twisted in the mesh.

So is a hunk of red-rusted iron, part of a younger dissolution. The metal tore a four-foot rip in both belly panels, which is not too bad.

But while I am hauling back, the engine changes rhythm. I should have known. We were starting to take that rhythm for granted, in much the same way as you don't notice your pulse until something happens to interfere with it.

The Gardner's beat dips and speeds up, dips and speeds again.

When I go below the fuel injection pump feels hot. I whack the machinery with the heel of my right hand, catching one knuckle on the lock-nut of a fuel injector. Blood from the cut looks black in the poor light of the engine room. It drips on the grease-stained mat of the Bruno's hull.

I have no spare fuel injection pump. *This* is the spare that replaced the last pump when it went south.

I lick the cut on my right hand. It tastes of salt and rust, like the iron wreck below us.

If we go in now, what we have caught so far will barely pay for the fuel.

If we do not go back, and the fuel pump goes south for good, we will be paying the Coast Guard for a tow home.

It's not so much the money as the humiliation. One of the reasons I fish is, I can take care of myself. Frankly, I feel contempt for the fellows you see getting towed back over the bar into port. Even though I know it has got to happen to everyone at some point, it has never happened to me. Each time, I think, Dumb bastard didn't check his oil, or his water filter.

I always check both before heading offshore.

I climb back topside to tell Pig we are going home.

The day yellows. While Pig hoses down the deck and shovels ice in the hold I punch up the way station on the Loran. This tells me what course to steer to the Bravo buoy in the ship channel. I check that course against our position on the chart because the Loran gives you blind direction only. Its circuits are unacquainted with the ground and for all they know the course to the next way station could run over solid land.

You can buy satellite navigation systems now that show the ground you are on and beep if you head for rocks. But *Hooker* cannot afford such gadgetry.

Pig goes below and makes sandwiches. The turkey, mayo, and cranberry sauce taste all right, although nine days after Thanksgiving we are both sick of turkey. A Coast Guard Falcon whistles overhead, circles once to get our numbers, then heads into the sunset.

I think of Caitlyn again. Maybe it's because we are going into port, the hard ties of land reaching out as we approach.

The trouble with thinking about Cait is that I have no clear idea of what is wrong with us. I cannot deal with a vague and permanent coldness the way I replace a fuel pump. It does not hurt as much as something specific would—if she left me, say. But in a way it feels worse.

Because knowing what is wrong and how to fix it is anesthesia of sorts. Whereas there is no defense against a trouble whose logic is foreign to me.

Pig washes dishes in the galley, whistling *Margaritaville*. Light is drained from the sky by a hole in the east. Darkness pours in to replace it, filling the troughs between waves, rising higher and higher in each of the thousand swells till it overflows the horizon. The sky thickens from royal blue to lapis; but this is a thickness that in a reverse kind of way actually creates translucence, so planets can shine through the color of it.

It is 18:20 by the time we are abeam of the "BB" buoy.

Around 20:30 I spot Chatham Light winking its double ten-second flash against the horizon. The light is not as bright as usual. Something else, a glow like phosphorescence, climbs the sky's northern edge. The shine of it does not go away but flickers and blossoms and falls. Colors that should not be there shimmy against the dark; purple and pink, yellow and aqua, like ambulance lights in a fog, or the glow of a TV seen from outside a house, shifting and changing with the commercials.

"Pig," I yell, "get up here."

Penthouse thumps. He comes up the companionway, zipping his pants.

"Northern lights," I tell him.

"Seen 'em before," he grunts.

"Mister *cool*."

He chews his mustache.

"Gotta ask yuh, Ollie," he says after a beat. "How many boxes we got back there, yuh think?"

"Maybe a quarter blackback," I tell him. "Two boxes of slime eel and conger. Thirty pounds yellowtail. Three lobsters, bycatch. Some skate, some pout, one cod."

He keeps chewing.

"What's the price on that?" he asks.

"We'll see tomorrow, I guess."

"Yuh know what I'm saying."

"If flounder's still at two seventy, maybe three ninety?"

"And what's my share?"

"Shit, Pig," I tell him, "you know you don't get squat. Neither do I. The first three hundred goes to the boat."

"It ain't enough."

"Tell me about it."

"I mean, I don't reckon I can do it anymore."

I turn to look at him. In the gleam of the controls, with that lampblack mustache, he resembles a killer from a comic book.

"You quittin' on me, Pig?"

"Hey, my friend Charlie Loomis is head chef at a restaurant near Mad River. He says he can get me a waitering job, clear five hunnert a week tax free."

"You know how to ski?"

"Finestkind." He looks at me indignantly. "Well, some. I'll know by the time season's over, I guess."

"I'll give you an advance," I tell him.

"On what?"

I shrug. The irritation that first surged in me when the pump missed returns.

It hooks up with what I was thinking earlier about Caitlyn.

I hold the wheel tight to keep it all down. The cut in my right hand throbs. My jaw is set so hard that my teeth ache.

I do not want to look for another mate this time of year. I do not want to train a shucker.

But Morris Island is visible now. I jam my face in the Furuno mask. The phantom world of radar opens around me, the green blips that are traffic or buoys or just big waves, glowing and waning, glowing and waning, as the scanner touches them with its thin electric feelers.

The first of the small buoys marking the channel over Chatham bar is a half mile off. The water over the bar is only seven feet deep at half-tide. The bar, using arcs and cords of shallows, the fast current of tide, and long swells cantering in from the Atlantic, conjures up seas that are of really weird shape and also dangerous. I have seen breakers in the form of pyramids and castles and grasping fists as I went through that channel. I have watched the water go from ten feet deep over a swell to so shallow in the trough you could count the scallop shells lying on the sand.

So I have no time now to think about Pig or anything except getting us over the shallow ground in one piece.

I straighen my back, take the helm off auto, and stare through the windows till my eyes are used to night once more.

Fish

from *Notes on the Ecology of Cape Cod* (Salt Marsh Press, Falmouth)
by Irwin E. Zeit, Ph.D.

No reliable estimate exists of the numbers of codfish before scientific
surveys were initiated by Bigelow and Schroeder in the early twentieth
century. However it is safe to assume, from eyewitness accounts, that the
waters of Cape Cod teemed with them.

The man who gave the Cape its current name, Bartholomew
Gosnold, in referring to the numbers of cod, said "In the months of
March, April, and May there is upon this coast, better fishing, and in as
great plentie, as in New-found-land. . . ." The Newfoundland banks in
those days were thought to be so full of cod that you could walk on water
there by stepping on the backs of fish.

The Wampanoag Indians were too few to put a dent in the numbers
of codfish. Only an industrial fishery could do that.

Curiously, the leading industrial nation of the twentieth century did
not care for seafood. Meat, the food of the rich in Europe, was cheap and
readily available in America and these refugees from Europe, with some
exceptions, wanted to eat what the rich ate. Because of low demand, the
New England fisheries had no great incentive to invest in new
technologies available before and immediately after World War Two;
thus they remained largely in an artisanal state of innocence. The
Chatham longliner, the Gloucester side-trawler were excellent fishing
machines in their way, but they were unable to reap the kind of vast
harvests that could decimate a fishery.

This did not mean there was no concern. Cyclical changes in cod
stocks in the 1870s prompted warnings of doom. Editorials claimed that
the blocking of alewife-spawning runs by dams was in turn starving the

cod which (so it was inaccurately believed) depended on herring for food. Schooner fishermen complained that the otter and steam trawlers, which appeared in the early 1900s, would wipe out the resource in a matter of years. Yet U.S. landings in 1939 were roughly equal to landings in 1913.

The Second World War altered this rough equilibrium. Wartime restrictions in meat supply forced consumers to eat fish and like it. By 1945, U.S. demand for groundfish was 54 percent greater than in 1939.

The war had wrought many greater changes. Now U.S. foreign policy called for injecting large sums of money into European economies to fend off Communism, and much of those monies went into subsidizing foreign fishing fleets. To the same end, the fishing grounds of Georges Bank were thrown open to outsiders, while tariffs were skewed to favor fish from abroad. Meanwhile, American fishermen were banned by law from organizing, or obtaining subsidies, or buying cheaply built foreign boats.

By 1960 the Europeans had built fleets of stern trawlers so large and efficient they could virtually clean out a fishing ground in a matter of weeks. A large dragger might land ten thousand pounds of fish in one run, and a factory ship, like the Russian *Pionersk*—for greater Cold War concerns had resulted in Communist ships also gaining access to U.S. fishing grounds—could process up to 800,000 pounds in one day. The U.S. market for fish, totally satisfied by American boats before the war, by 1976 was 93 percent supplied by foreign fishermen.

What happened to Georges Bank haddock was illustrative of these trends. American fishermen had averaged catches of 110 million pounds a year prior to 1965. Then Soviet fleets began "pulse-fishing" the resource. Total landings immediately jumped to 283 million. By 1974, U.S. landings were down to 6.5 million, and local haddock were in danger of extinction.

Following years of severe overfishing, the U.S. government reacted in 1976, passing the Magnuson fisheries conservation act, which effectively barred foreign fleets from Georges Bank and other U.S. fishing grounds.

Americans had learned a lesson. Unfortunately it was the wrong one. The high price of fish enabled them to invest in large European-style draggers. The stocks of groundfish enjoyed a brief respite after 1976, while the big U.S. trawlers were being built; then they plummeted again. A haphazard conservation system run by federally mandated local councils was largely unsuccessful in protecting the fisheries from the otter trawls of bigger American vessels.

In 1995 the federal government stepped in again, forcing, in New England, the imposition of Amendment Seven, which added to a lengthy list of grounds closures a stiff reduction in working hours. As the twenty-first century loomed, allowable fishing hours were once again reduced, so that Cape Cod groundfisherman could work only 88 twenty-four hour days, or 176 twelve-hour shifts, over the course of a year.

Chapter 3

The fish pier

41 degrees 42'N; 69 degrees 56'W

It is almost eleven when we get to the fish pier.

A couple of boats have come in before us and lights glow in the Down-Cape culling shed.

Down-Cape is a fish wholesaler. After the Chatham Fishermen's Cooperative went belly-up, wholesalers started renting this pier from the town.

It did not work well for them because shortly afterward a storm smashed a hole in the barrier beach that protected Pleasant Bay. The tide washed sand straight into Aunt Lydia's Cove, where the fish pier is. The cove shoaled up so badly that now you can only worm in at half tide or better.

It is a little better than half-tide at this point and the Bruno does not draw much water and still we scrape bottom twice.

The only usable berths are taken by an inshore dragger more beat up than *Hooker,* and Ojala's antique, and Phil

Amaral's gillnetter, the *Crazy A's*. The *Mary Anne* Project barge is anchored hard by the *Crazy A's*. The rust is clearly visible on the barge's pipes and housings in the glow of our starboard running light.

Pig puts out bumpers. I ease *Hooker* in around the barge, soft as polarfleece, forward of the gillnetter, where the Coast Guard rescue boat used to moor before they sent it to Provincetown.

I call the federal fisheries service, as I am supposed to do, from the outside pay phone, to tell them our fishing day is done.

Then Pig wants the phone and I go looking for Johnny Norgeot, the dockmaster.

I find Johnny in the culling shed along with Amaral and Sim Pierce. Sim is a pal even though he is a gillnetter. Wayne Ojala and his mate, who do not talk to me or Amaral, stand to one side. Bill Gilbert, a born-again Christian who speaks only to the Lord or other Christians, of whom there are two in the Chatham fleet, stands a little separate. Six men slouching at various angles to each other and a dozen boxes of blackback and three tubs of late-season dogfish in back. Six unshaven and smelly men in sweatclothes, oilskins and bad light, who ignore the guys they do not get along with and bullshit the ones they do while Johnny tags the boxes and talks to everybody, partly because that's his job, and partly because that's Johnny.

"An' if flounder don't get any better." Amaral wipes snot on his glove. "Oh I say the hell with it, I'll lay her up and go quahogging till tuna season."

"Place called Ned's Marine Motors, in Scituate. But what they really handle, I guess, is hot diesel parts."

Johnny notices me. He lifts his chin and the others look around. Then they go back to talking.

It takes them a while to retrieve the rhythm. Everybody waits just a hair too long to answer. When they speak, their comments lack force.

"Won't need ice, Johnny. Anyway."

Boots squeak on concrete.

"You spendin' time on the penny-ante," Ojala says, "I got three boxes of pollock and windowpane waiting."

"You callin' me penny-ante?" Amaral snaps an oilskin strap.

"One whistle, Captain," the VHF comments.

A dogfish, waking up in the tub, kicks its tail. Brine splats on the wet floor.

"It's just," says Ojala's mate, "he didn't make no mention about it. Or nothing."

"It's a hoax call," Gilbert says, "it coulda been any of the fishermen around here."

Johnny looks at him and says, "I got no problem with you layin' Jesus around, Bill, but you don't say that shit 'bout guys around here."

"His shit don't stink," Amaral says.

"He came 'cause the Coast Guard called him."

"For a hoax?"

"They can't know for sure."

"Six weeks!"

Spit hits the floor, loud as a small caliber shot.

"But he hung around to see him," Ojala adds and this time he jerks his thumb at me.

Gilbert glances at the partition that blocks off the dockmaster's cubicle.

I edge past the tubs of dogfish to peer around the chipboard. A big fellow with chrome-blue eyes and gunmetal hair sits in Johnny's castered chair. A large weimaraner is coiled asleep at his feet.

Beside him stands a man who is thin as a snake and almost completely bald except for five or six strands of hair glued to scalp-shine.

He is dressed in an Antartex coat with a wool lining so thick it keeps his arms from folding. He holds his clipboard almost horizontally, like a stick-figure.

Skull. Thatch Hallett's accountant.

And Thatch himself.

I remember now what the Chevron rig reminded me of. Two months ago Thatch asked for permission to test drill the aquifer on land he owns but to which me and my sister, through a deal Frank arranged, hold mineral rights.

We gave him permission.

That's the last time I saw the man.

Thatch is on the phone. When he sees me he puts the receiver down and unwinds his legs. The dog stirs, opens one eye, takes me in, closes it again.

Thatch wears his camouflage beret pulled down on the left, as if he were in Airborne or something. His face is tanned. He has on wide-wale corduroys, Bean hunting boots, and a leather flying jacket with a silk scarf.

"The Red Baron," I say.

He pretends not to hear.

"Ollie," he says, "how you doing?"

I lean against a dogfish tub. This is a plastic container, filled with seawater to keep the fish alive, barely. Dogfish should be eaten fresh because when they die their blood starts to release uric acid, which turns the flesh bitter. But nobody keeps them alive for that.

The reason these fish are still breathing is, Amaral signed a contract with Marine Biological Laboratory in Woods Hole to bring in live dogfish. Amaral claims the researcher cuts out the live rectal glands and distills out of them a chemical marker that will tag the damaged cells of nerves.

"I been trying to reach you, buddy," Thatch continues. "Didn't you get the messages?"

I lick my cut knuckle.

"You heard about the transmission?" I ask him.

Thatch's irises turn pale.

"Flickie's wife called me."

Flickie was mate on the *Commando*. The *Commando* belonged to Thatch Hallett. Thatch is a developer, not a fisherman, but he bought the boat two years back as a tax write-off. Lots of people did that; they made great write-offs.

The door opens. A tall man comes into the culling shed. He wears cowboy boots and a leather jacket and a baseball cap. The cap reads *"Mary Anne* Project." Thatch shakes his head at him. Now he looks to where Amaral is carefully watching Johnny Norgeot ink out a slip for the dogfish.

"Let's go outside," Thatch says.

"Cold out there."

"It's not private here."

"Far's I know, I got nothing private to talk about with you."

Thatch shrugs.

"Marston's Hollow?"

"We got nothin' to talk about," I repeat without raising my voice.

He stops smiling.

"You only own the water rights," he says. I shrug, imitating him. But Thatch is not going to let go of this. He checks his watch, as if he had to be somewhere in a hurry. Then he says, "Maybe you ought to think of your family, Ollie."

The culling room goes silent.

"What are you talking about?" I ask quietly.

"Your sister. She owns half the rights. And Caitlyn, and Sam too—"

"I know who my family is."

"In that case." Thatch spreads his hands wide, as if he had scored a point. "Don't you think you should ask—"

"Thatch," I interrupt. "It's none of your fuckin' business."

His eyes track mine without a waver and he smiles again. It is a pleasant smile. He has a big, droopy nose and chin and cheeks and his smile uses all the raw material and makes something bigger than what you're used to.

I push myself off the dogfish. I look down at them, out of habit; they always held a kind of reverse interest for me. Toothless sharks, three to four feet long. They carry their young inside, like humans. I have seen the babies come out under the stress of being hauled into a boat, six or seven perfectly formed little sharks with gills and tiny dorsal fins. When I was longlining for cod, when the fishing was good, I hated nothing more than to get a lineful of dogfish.

Now men go looking for them.

"Look," Thatch begins again, "you can—"

"I'm not interested."

"You don't take the offer now, it might not be around later."

"Thatch," I say, "You wanted to check the water table, you checked the water table. I got nothing else to offer so just stay the fuck away from me, okay?"

I shoulder roughly between Thatch and the bin and step on a juvenile dogfish that fell out of the bin. Both my feet skitch out from under. I hang onto the fish bin but it is on my left and my bad arm cannot take the strain.

I crash onto the concrete floor, smacking my head on a caster.

Thatch bends to help me up. The dog whines behind him. I shake off Thatch's hand and lurch to my feet. "My family does just, just fine," I hiss at him. "I'm not gonna sell those rights."

Bill Gilbert giggles. A dogfish freaks out. Its tail kicks the water hard enough to spray me. I pick up my watch cap and stomp out the door, back to *Hooker*.

My boat looks real good to me now. Her hull core may be sodden and the decks scarred and the wheelhouse paint chipped. But I know her flaws and she knows mine.

Pig is listening to WOMR in the cabin. As I pull off my seaboots he says, "I just called my friend in Vermont. That job's open."

I unlock my jaw to talk.

"I don't need this."

"It's regular money."

The right boot does not come off easy.

"You wanna quit," I grunt, "just say so."

"Shit, Ollie," Pig says, "you're a pal 'n everything but—"

The boot pops loose, taking the sock with it. I lose my grip on the rubber and it bounces off the kerosene lamp on the galley bulkhead. The lamp's chimney hits the deck and smashes into tiny pieces.

"Jesus, man," Pig says sadly. "Take it easy. Yuh can get another mate—"

"I know I can get another mate!" I yell.

"Yuh know," he continues in a gentle tone, as if he was soothing a puppy, "It's an early season this year. They're making snow already, in Sugarbush. Gary says the cabin's got plenty of room. Whyn't yuh take a couple days off, go skiin', do yuh good?"

"Skiing." I look at him and wonder if he is joking. But Pig doesn't tease much.

"Yeah." He's enthusiastic now. "Powder snow. Roaring fires. And pussy." Closing his eyes, he runs his tongue over the moustache. "You should see snow-pussy, man—tight bellies, tight little asses—"

"You're still working for me," I tell him, "while the boat's loaded. Why don't you get on deck and start hauling those fuckin' boxes?"

"Man." Pig opens his eyes. "You're just a fuckin' animal, man."

And he stomps topside.

Chapter 4

Home

41 degrees 44'N; 69 degrees 58'W

Once Amaral has moved his boat clear we haul the boxes and get our slips.

Pig splits, for good I guess.

I jog the boat back into the midnight darkness, touching bottom only once. Pick up the mooring, shut down. Sweep up the broken glass in the saloon. Row the dinghy through the dark, through the chortling, invisible water, back to the pier, where my truck is parked.

My truck used to be a '93 GM pickup painted dark red. It is hard to tell what it used to be since it is so badly rusted and has been fiberglassed so often that the contours are indistinct.

I bolted in two-by-fours so I can carry nets in back because the bed is rotted. My dog ate the upholstery in the cab. This does not matter because the cab is so full of boat gear and junk-food wrappers you can barely see the seat.

The valves sound like a tap-dance routine. The muffler is

fifty percent hole. The inspection sticker is four months out of date.

The truck suits me. When I am ferrying quahogs as I did three winters ago or other cargo that drips salt water, I do not rust the bed since it no longer is there.

If my trawl doors dent the body when I drive them to the welding shop for repair, it does not matter.

My son can tell I am coming from a quarter-mile away thanks to the noise this muffler lets through.

Among all the junk in the cab I usually can find a piece of wire or a fuel filter or whatever I need to keep the truck running long enough to get to the next place.

Tonight the shitheap won't start. All my excuses wash away like chalk marks in rain. I dig around until I find a can of starting fluid. I prop the hood and spray so much ether into the carburetor that my head goes light. The cab smells like a doctor's office when I climb back in. After four attempts the engine fires.

Enough time remains for a beer at the Squire before closing but I am too tired to think of anything but bed. I fetch a Rolling Rock out of the back and suck in its cold foam. I find a tape in the ashtray and slot it into the deck.

The Ramones call for sedation.

My house lies down a dirt track just before the Harwich line on the west side of Route 28. It's next door to a development, and the project's lights paint our driveway orange. Caitlyn's car is not there but a black ZX is parked behind the stack of longline tubs. So is a 1985 vinyltop Ford sedan in good shape although it has different-colored rocker panels.

The ZX belongs to Billy Sturges. Caitlyn's brother.

So the Ford belongs to Fleetwood.

Eb jumps me when I walk in the kitchen. Eb is a Cape Cod Black Dog. He is stringy and long and has a thick purple tongue. Eb likes me well enough but what he really likes is these activities: rolling in dead seabirds, rescuing stones out of ponds, and running.

He will run all day if he gets loose. He usually winds up three towns down, in Eastham.

Over the dog's floppy ears I see Billy propped on the brown couch. Fleetwood is curled in an armchair beside him. Bags of corn chips and a box of frosted chocolate doughnuts are conveniently racked on a collapsible dinner tray between them. A blue cooler lies at the foot of the couch. Twin columns of purple-gray smoke rise from a Captain Morgan ashtray into the TV light.

The smoke reminds me of the northern lights when we saw them west of the Bravo buoy.

"I don't know, dear," Fred Gwynn replies. "All I did was show them Aunt Ethel."

Laugh track. Billy takes a deep drag of his Merit. He cups his cigarette as if to protect its small flame, holding the tip inverted in a cave of fingers. I stare at the butt. The longing is a Dracula in my lungs.

We slap palms.

"When ya gonna get that muffler fixed?" Fleetwood asks.

The message blinking on the machine is from a woman at Visa's collection agency.

I check the fridge. My Rock 'n Rolls have gone. In the alcove, Caitlyn's computer terminal is on but it shows only her screensaver, a schematic lozenge endlessly rolling on its diagonal axis.

Billy waves toward the cooler. I open it; it's half full of Coors Ice.

"No thanks," I say. "Where's Cait?"

"She went out. I'm babysitting."

"Uh-huh."

"Sam's asleep. I read him *Alien Power-morphs*. He liked that."

Fleetwood leans over and opens the cooler. She scoops out a can, pops it, swigs. This is a reflexive motion, of the sort someone would employ to scratch his forehead.

"Ollie." Billy leans forward in the smoked light. His bag

of welding equipment slumps on the couch beside him. "I went to New York City."

I sit at the kitchen table. The new J. Crew catalogue came; I have a sex life again. A bunch of Caitlyn's magazines —*Wiccan*, *GyNET Monthly*, *Cosmo*—are piled by the phone.

An etching of a whaleboat hangs on the wall above the table. My uncle Manny gave me that. Manny's father—my great-grandfather—worked as a cabin boy on a New Bedford whaling ship.

The boat in the etching is frozen, the sea petrified, the men paralyzed in the act of hunting a right whale frozen before them.

That is kind of how I feel when I get off *Hooker:* wind and diesel and ceaseless motion all frozen inside my head till I grow accustomed to shore again.

Today's *Stranded Times* carries on page one an article about the Price-Shoppe development. I open a stack of pizza boxes. The bottom layer holds pepperoni and onions. The mozzarella has congealed to the consistency of silicon compound.

". . . for some Jewish guys in the Bronx. They needed someone could weld stainless. So I take the subway to Manhattan . . ."

I switch off Billy again. I should read this article. A stench rises from beneath my feet. Eb hunkers under the table, watching me, attentive as a scout. A piece of half-chewed pizza crust lies by his muzzle. One paw rests on a worn tennis ball. I don't like it that Caitlyn just left Sam with Billy like that.

I do not like it that Billy is here at all for that matter. Last time, he arrived for Labor Day weekend and was still here Columbus Day.

Billy is okay. He would never leave Sam alone or do anything bad. He pays cash for what he eats and drinks. What is really annoying is that he smokes and I have been trying not to and that makes it tough.

Also, Caitlyn and I have been clawing at each other a lot recently and he gets in the way of our routine.

"Near the United Nations," Billy continues. "An' I seen him!"

Billy also has strange ideas.

"Fuckin' president of France!" Inside one fist Billy's Merit hoards its sacred flame. The thumb and two fingers of his other hand grip a Coors; the other digits grasp corn chips.

I stare at Billy. I get a softened feeling, as if my muscles suddenly had relaxed, like frozen pork chops in the Radar Range. This is what home means to me: beer, dry warmth, and conversations uninvolved with staying afloat.

I eat another wedge of pizza. An article next to the Price-Shoppe story describes how the state will double-barrel Route 6 between Dennis and Orleans so we'll get twice as many tourists in the summer as we have now. What we get now sucks the town water supply to drought levels by August. Billy keeps ranting. I barely finish the headline.

"I couldn't buh-*lieve* it."

"Turn the channel," Fleetwood says, "I hate *Bewitched*."

"I will, you get me a beer."

"Get you two, I'm four ahead."

I check on Sam. His room is over the kitchen. He lies sprawled half on, half off the bed. An Alien Power-morph toy lies strangled in his left arm. When I try to pull it from his elbow he mutters "Mom" and "pigeon!"—something like that. The stuffed kangaroo he has carried around since he was two is crushed beneath his back. Sam has dark hair and perfectly round cheeks and a nose that is starting to lengthen to a shape that resembles mine.

Drool spills down the slope of his cheek. I cover him with the quilt.

A book is propped open beside his bed. I pick it up. It is called *Children's Tales of Olde Cape Cod*, by Wendy Rose Adams.

Caitlyn has been reading him stories that contain no aliens.

I wonder where she went. The feeling of peace vanishes. I open Sam's book to kill the question. Its illustrations show pirates, men in frock coats, Indians. One drawing depicts a brown woman who is half fish.

She is not a mermaid. Mermaids are always white and, unlike any other such drawing I have ever seen, this one has no arms; the scales reach all the way to her neck. I start to read out of an unwillingness to face other matters.

Ahzoo and the Big Bluefish

from *Children's Tales of Olde Cape Cod* (Olympia Imprints, Yarmouth Port)
by Wendy Rose Adams

Many years before the white man came to Cape Cod there lived among the Wampanoag tribe of Santuit a young woman named Ahzoo.

Ahzoo was not a pretty woman. Her body was the shape of a kettle, her mouth was too big for her face, and her nose was large and misshapen. Her eyes were small and set too far apart. On top of all this, Ahzoo was lazy and sharp-tongued. She had few companions, and none of the men wanted her for a wife.

Ahzoo did have one quality. She could sing. Her voice was so sweet and true that when she sang people forgot how ugly and lazy she was and dropped what they were doing to come around her lodge and listen. Her songs were about love and hunting and the strange spirits that filled the woods and bays around her. She liked to sit beside Cotuit Brook where it fed into Santuit Pond, after the sun went down, and sing. When she did, the birds and animals stopped searching for food to hear her better. Even the fish in Nantucket Sound schooled by the mouth of the brook to listen when Ahzoo sang after dusk.

One day the chief of the bluefish, hearing of Ahzoo's reputation, swam all the way from Long Island to listen to her. He was the biggest and fiercest of the bluefish, as large as a small whale and handsome too, but as soon as her first song rose over the oak trees and beaches he fell in love with Ahzoo. He could not see how ugly she was. All he could hear was the sound of her voice. He tried to swim up Cotuit Brook to find her but he was too big, and kept running aground. The big fish told his friends that he was sad because he had fallen in love with a young woman. He was not human, and she was not a fish, so they could never be together.

But the chief of the beach spirits heard what the big bluefish said and felt sorry for him. One night he changed Ahzoo into a herring and put her in Santuit Pond and told the chief of the bluefish what he had done.

So that night the big bluefish swam all the way to Nantucket to get a running start. Then he finned as fast as he could for Cotuit Brook and plowed his way inland. He plowed and he plowed through the shallows and finally he reached Santuit Pond but by that time he was so exhausted that he died. And Ahzoo, seeing him there, dead of love for her, felt her heart break the way his had, and she died also.

The Wampanoag buried the two lovers in a mound called "The Fish Grave" by Santuit Pond. And they noticed that plants grew better on the mound, especially maize and beans. From that day forward they buried bluefish and herring with their crops, so the plants would grow big and strong and feed more of the people through the harsh winters.

Chapter 5

The Ballet

41 degrees 44'N; 69 degrees 58'W

After I finish Sam's story I take a shower. The blood of the
fish we killed washes off me and mingles with the fragrance
of Caitlyn's calendula soap. The profits from this soap go to
protecting all species endangered in the Guyanan rainforest
but not the endangered species her husband hunts offshore.
The water backs up around my feet, smelling lightly of
flounder.

The cesspool is full again.

My stomach gurgles from pizza.

The bedroom TV is on when I get out of the shower. Ath-
letic people dressed in eighteenth-century army uniforms
fill the screen. They dance to mannered horns.

Caitlyn sits on the bed, pulling off red cowboy boots.

"Oh," I say. "Hi."

"Hi." She throws the second boot in the corner. "When
did you get back?"

"Half hour ago." I dry myself. She does not look at me. She has no interest in seeing me naked anymore.

I pull on a pair of Randy Travis sweatpants that I bought at the thrift shop. Caitlyn wears a red blouse with lace ruffles and a long, old-fashioned black skirt that she also got from the thrift shop. The wicca necklace she bought in Salem curves snugly across the culvert of her breasts. Her belly sticks out. When she takes off the skirt she has a red weal across it from the elastic waistband. Her buttocks are a little soft but she still has a nice figure.

I peer at her face. Her lips are coral. Max Factor did the corners of her eyes. Her teak-colored hair always looked like someone set off gelignite in the middle of it. Tonight it contains more frizz than usual.

On TV the *Nutcracker* soldiers dance, deliberately stiff, trying to regain control over a world of toys.

Anger builds in recognizable ways when it is aimed at someone you have lived with for ten years.

It is like a tide that knows all the channels and rivers in a wide bay and it gurgles in fast, covering the sandflats in ways you can predict but not affect.

I fight it anyway, trying to say what I have to say foamy, light. It does not work.

"So, where'd you go?"

"Oh, Christ," she says.

"What?"

"What is it—" she swings around, jerking her curls to the left, out of her eyes—"go on, what is it?"

The words we use are precise, as suited to their purpose as the cutting claw of a blue crab.

They trigger in the other person, not the answer sought on the surface, but the exact note of insecurity you were probing for in the first place.

For a long time we went to a counselor, to avoid these fights.

Doctor Hinckley was a woman who believed in miracles

and angels and something called "deep sharing." She urged us to channel our anger in positive ways. She wanted us to free the children locked inside of us but with me that did not help because the kid inside was more pissed off than I was.

Our brawls did not diminish in frequency or pitch.

We slip into them easier than we avoid them now, like old slippers that fit perfectly around the foot.

* * *

A thin woman in a lacy outfit has center stage on the TV; the toys fall in behind her, marching seriously nowhere.

"It's 'cause I went out," Cait begins.

"It's not that," I say. "Not that you went out. But you just left Sam with Billy—I mean, he just shows up, what do you do, boom, 'Hi Billy, here's the kid, I'm going out'?"

"Billy's okay."

"Billy is *not* 'okay.'"

"He's around more than *you*." She pitches the last word like a softball.

"Don't give me that."

"Don't give me that 'I'm a *fisherman*' shit."

"So?" I say. "It's what I am."

"It makes no difference to Sam, what you do when you're not here."

I want to get back to the previous topic now but arguing with Caitlyn is like laying a straight course when the tide is running hard; you'll never end up where you think.

"Billy's a lush," I tell her quietly. "I would think, you of all people, you'd—"

"He's *not* a lush."

"You just don't want—"

"You don't want me to have a life!" She is almost yelling now. She punches air with one fist, marking the beat of her words.

"That's not the point—"

"You don't see it." Her voice drops. "You go out for two

days, fishing. Okay so you haven't been out much lately 'cause of the gear and the restrictions and everything—but you go *out*, it's like a *change*, a change is as good as a vacation—"

"Well, *you* work."

"Three days, I mean, come on—"

"You could do more—"

"There *isn't* any more, Ollie. I called the numbers in the classified. You know what kinda jobs they have for women. I mean, what're you saying? My God. If there was more work God knows I'd do it, don't you think I'm *sick* of this shit house our *shit* cars—"

She whips off her blouse so fast it rips the lace. She stares at the torn fabric. I know she is thinking, This is a forty-dollar blouse from Filene's Basement and now she will have to drive to Hyannis to replace it and she won't be able to find it anyway because they change the inventory weekly.

"I'm just sick of all the shitty things in my life," she continues. "The cars, the collection goons. The things that don't work."

"You used to laugh, because of the cars."

"That was a long time ago, Ollie."

She wads up the blouse and throws it after the boot.

"You used to think it was funny."

"We haven't had health insurance in almost two years!"

I say nothing, because it's true.

"You could make it better," she picks up again. "You could do the retraining, the federal thing—"

"I don't want to retrain."

"Well, you could sell the rights to the Hollow—"

I sit on the bed. The door opens. Eb creeps in, expecting to be shooed away. He drops his tennis ball and crawls under the bed. One paw pokes out and drags the ball in after him.

It's a measure of her unhappiness that Cait does not react. She does not care for Eb at the best of times.

I stand up and move to the dresser and lean my ass on it. Not looking at her.

"You going for somebody now?" I ask.

"No."

"Well where were you then?"

"None of your business."

My jaw is so tight it draws pain like white flame from a molar.

"I was with Ellen," she says, "at the Squire."

"I thought you had no money."

No response.

"So you saw Bucket?"

"Sure. He works there."

I can see the dead trees in the security lights from where I stand. The wind rocks them back and forth. The chimes she nailed outside the window jangle, little stars and moons and witches, spin hapless in the gusts.

The warm front is approaching.

"You even thought my truck was funny. You said it was like me, it was fucked-up but the engine was good."

I pick up one of the glass ornaments that occupy most of the dresser's surface.

"You have to speak the same language," she says, "to get the same jokes."

"What are you talkin' about?"

"Exactly."

We both hear Eb in the pause we leave, licking his balls under the bed.

Something that once was whole grinds in my right fist. I open my hand. A small glass lozenge lies, one pane snapped, on my palm.

Silver wires run from each inside corner to a shape that is meant to represent both a heart and fallopian tubes. It's the symbol of GyNET, an online retail network for women. Caitlyn works for GyNET, at their office in Orleans.

Blood from the cut the glass made rims the shear-plane.

I close my hand again, move to the bed, and sit once more.

"Cait," I say quietly, "what is going on?"

She fishes the blouse off the floor and places it tenderly on her dresser amid a couple more GyNET lozenges and seashells and a glass harbor-seal and a little sign reading "The Goddess is IN." She did not see me pick up the lozenge; she does not notice its absence.

When she speaks next her voice is softer.

"You come in and you talk *boats*. Even when you talk about other things. You see everything like a fuckin' long-liner, in nautical miles and, like, boxes of *fish* and how you can get out again as soon as possible—"

"I'm a fuckin' draggerman, now."

"See what I mean?" she says. "It's just denial you—"

"Talk about other languages," I tell her.

"The language we use," she says, "comes from what we're invested in."

"See what I mean?" I repeat. "Anyways we never talk about other things, we only talk about Sam's hockey."

She picks up a shell, puts it back in a more perfect relationship to the others. She is not really watching what she does.

"I want to talk," I tell her, "without fighting. I just want to talk about something different."

"Sam's hockey," she replies, "is a big part of my life." What she means is, she spends six hours a week driving Sam to hockey events and this is yet another cross she must bear.

I was the one who wanted our son to play hockey.

"I used to think it would be okay," Cait continues. "I don't think so anymore. You know?"

But I don't know.

The dancers on the TV screen bow, retreat. A loud voice compares breakfast cereal to flying.

She uses the john. I put the broken lozenge in my underwear drawer. We take turns at the sink, brushing our teeth, spitting foam at cracked enamel. A crucial solitude has formed between us, like oil in a crankshaft, allowing us to move together with less friction.

When I get into bed I feel the heat from her radiate under the blankets but I make no effort to touch her and Caitlyn does not touch me either. My palm stings where the crystal cut it. My head aches and the sea washes back and forth in my inner ear and the bed feels like it is rocking.

From this house, with the wind out of the east, you can hear the surf as it rolls against Nauset Beach.

I close my eyes. Through the lowered defenses surges the single, numbing fear, that if this all comes crashing down I could lose Sam.

This is something I cannot think about even.

I flip my eyes open, watch the branches make Halloween shapes against the window.

That brings to mind the VHF, the thin voice from a boat that had already vanished, while the static howled and the cold sea washed bone-clean below.

Don't want to think about that either.

Finally I turn my mind to the *Hooker*, as I usually do.

I cannot keep her going at this rate, not with the engine crapping out and the fish so scarce.

Not with late mortgage payments and a total of seven hundred and twenty dollars in the bank.

With boats, though, you can always focus on tiny things.

For instance: I wound that mooring bight tight around the bow bollard and tied it down for good measure.

And I checked the chafing gear around the warp—made sure she was safe as she lay at the mooring, alone and obedient, her bow intimately stemming the cold and sand-filled tide while her Loran antenna hummed in the wind like an old cello.

Eventually, while thinking about the float on the backup bilge pump, I am ambushed by sleep.

Chapter 6

Bad Bearings

41 degrees 44'N; 69 degrees 58'W

When I wake up the sun is mainlining light into the glass ornaments on her dresser. They shine as if lit by grace.

The sun has to be almost due south for light to hit from that angle.

I go downstairs. The house is freezing. Fleetwood, wombed in her sleeping bag, snores on the brown couch. I guess she won the drinking match; she usually does. Fleet hauls coal for PJ's Firewood and the fact that she is still in my house reminds me, this is the weekend.

No one else is around. The woodstove is cold. I take the last two logs from the box in the living room. Normally I would be cursing Sam because it is his job to keep the woodbox full but I still have sleep inside me, working the clutch, disconnecting me from the gears of anger.

Crumbs of dream float on that disconnection.

I was a passenger in a giant aluminum seaplane. It was full

of recessed light and crystal. A band played show tunes in the saloon. A woman in a long green dress spoke in a hoarse voice; "*Commando*," she said, or I think she said that. "The *Commando* lives." The saloon stank of danger; the plane was going down.

New flames from the open stove braize my cheeks. The TV says, "Nothing like the Bechamel he made when he was a *bigamist*." I bank the stove, click to the weather channel. The announcer claims the incoming low slowed over Pennsylvania. Southern New England can expect flurries and northeasterly winds, becoming easterly at fifteen to twenty knots. Swells four to six offshore. It's decent fishing weather, but I can't go out without a deckhand.

I fetch two-part epoxy from the mudroom and cement the broken side of Cait's lozenge. It does not look too bad; just a thread of white across the pane. I replace it among the seashells and happy signs. The black imaginings from last night come galloping back.

I grit my teeth. Look for clean underwear. Eb drops his tennis ball at my feet and stares at me as I get dressed. The Visa woman is on the answering machine again. The phone rings as I am listening to her message. I let the machine answer but turn up the volume, thinking it might be Doomo. Pick up the J. Crew catalogue and flip through it, looking for lingerie.

A woman's voice. Visa, I guess, but I am mistaken.

"Hi, this is Michelle Meyer at Cape Eleven News. Uh, Mr. Cahoon, I wanted to ask you a couple questions about the Price-Shoppe hearing at the conservation commission Thursday, I mean the hearing is Thursday." She giggles. "I've been trying to call you but—anyway, I have a source who, uh, who says you and your sister own some kind of, like, rights? He says they might—"

The machine cuts her off.

"Doomo phoned," a note from Caitlyn reads. "He'll see you at the fish pier at 2." The clock says twelve fourteen.

The linoleum is covered with Power-morph toys that Caitlyn confiscated from Sam's bookbag.

I stuff the J. Crew catalogue in my pocket without thinking about it; put on my watch cap and leave.

The air outside is clear and cold as Mercury. The temperature is heavy in my fingers, on the tip of my nose.

Next door, bulldozers snort up and down the diesel scale, digging cellars for a development. They have to dig deep because it's the kind of development where the houses are half buried and covered with weathered shingles, or live turf even, to conserve heat, to not stick out of the landscape.

Frozen puddles from the gale four days ago crunch like ribbon candy underfoot.

Lilac blossoms are dying between the longline tubs and the northern addition. They have no business being around this time of year. What happened was this: The tail end of Hurricane Gisela passed through in late October and the winds reached eighty knots and badly stressed the plants. The stress disrupted the plants' seasonal clock, causing them to assume they had been hit by a harsh but short-lived winter. Unusually warm weather for a time confirmed that assumption.

A month ago we had daffodils and crocuses by the side of the house. Only lilacs and forsythia are left now to recall this doomed attempt at spring.

I look back at my house, thinking of Caitlyn—somewhat amazed that after our fight last night it stands the way it always did, with no visible damage. The house consists of two graceless additions nailed onto a tiny prewar cottage and covered with vinyl siding of a faded turquoise color. The needles from tall pines behind have accumulated on the kitchen roof and rotted the wood so it leaks in a southerly wind. But we have been renting the place for so long that we are used to its problems.

Besides, the rent is low.

These are chores I could accomplish: stow the longline

tubs in the cellar, get rid of bags full of beer bottles on the porch, rake the drifted pine needles before real winter arrives. It would please Cait if I did them.

There is no time today. With all we have to do to keep things running even at survival level there is never any time.

* * *

My truck starts without ether. Eb leaps in and gnaws at the dashboard padding and I whack his ass with September's *National Fisherman*.

I pick up a sandwich and a coffee to go at Larry's PX. I don't talk to the guys I know at the booths. Then I head back to the fish pier, down Main Street.

When I grew up, Main Street and the rest of the town for that matter was pretty much deserted after Labor Day, except for locals.

Then, in the eighties, the retirees arrived. In the nineties young professionals with fast modems moved in so they could raise their kids far from crime and other attributes of lower income.

Swedish cars line the sidewalks. Young men in grouse-shooting pants buy belts depicting sperm whales. Their wives wear clothes of the same hue as tropical fruits. The wives are powerful and well maintained, like the cars.

I glance at Eb. He has his head stuck out the half-open window. He does not notice humans. All he wants to do is run.

Nobody looks at me as I drive between these people. I stare at the Christmas decorations. Every December, Chatham dresses up for a weekend celebration called "Down-Cape Yule." The Christmas finery the shops put up makes me feel good.

The Rose Crowell Shop, which specializes in shuffle-board apparel, has strung up garlands of white pine with hundreds of gilded bells and scarlet ribbons. Large glowing angels and candy canes made of plastic sway in the easterly breeze over the street itself. Forests of decorated firs, clouds of white lights, regiments of scarlet elves line the Company Store arcade. Bells jingle and electric choirs sing whenever a door opens.

I am blind-sided by the urge to see Sam.

I can't; he's at hockey practice.

At the fish pier I let Eb run down the beach. This would be a risky move except that he usually gets so interested in beach smells that he forgets about Eastham for awhile.

I row over to *Hooker* and check engine and crankcase oil and water filter and open the saltwater intake. The Gardner starts readily. I drop the mooring and putt over to the pier.

After I have tied up, I unwind the net till the ripped section is exposed. Then I get out twine and shuttle and set about mending it.

Hook, loop, retrieve.

Hook, loop, retrieve. The rhythm is automatic once you have done a few rows of mesh.

The engine, still running, makes believe it is reliable, competent. The wind picks up off the outer beach and my fingers stiffen. Once in a while a gust bats exhaust into my nostrils. I have to tuck my fingers periodically into my armpits to melt them so they can bend again.

Doomo arrives early. He has a big job in Hyannis and wants to get mine out of the way.

Doomo is the only diesel mechanic on the Cape who makes appointments and then shows up. The rest of them, possibly buoyed by independent incomes, avoid work like it might hurt them physically.

He lugs his tools below. The Gardner revs up and down as I finish the repair and wind the net back on its reel. I go below and find his tools spread like courses of silverware at the entrance to the engine compartment.

Doomo is built like a steel boiler. He has broad Finnish cheekbones, Trotsky glasses and a giant beard like a bayberry bush tinted with diesel fuel. He wears a Marttinni knife on his belt. He lies close to the Gardner as if figuring out how to cut its throat.

"Got a beer, Jack?" he asks.

I fetch him a Rock 'n Roll from the ice box.

"Latrobe Brewery. Used to be good, till they got big," he tells me.

"So," I say evenly, "what's goin on down there?"

"Brits used to make good engines. Now? Piece o' shit. Ever since the war, they—"

"I know what you mean. What about the injection pump?"

He is annoyed because I cut off his sociopolitical analysis and does not answer.

"I need a new pump?"

Doomo hands the empty bottle out the hatch. I get him another.

"What *you* need is a new engine."

"Ah, come on," I reply in a bantering tone but my stomach sinks under the weight of what he said.

Doomo crawls backward out the hatch. He drags a black twin-valved hunk of metal after him. The smell of diesel fuel is strong. The Finn's political predictions are useless; he swore Bush would beat Clinton and that letting Poland into NATO would trigger nuclear holocaust; but on engines you can trust his judgment.

"This new pump unit you put in," he says, "yah well it's got exactly the same defect as the old one. The drive gear is crooked." He lathes the fitting with his thumb. "That's because the cam that *drives* it is bent, an' that retarded the timing, so the whole engine ran hot.

"So what you got now," he continues, "is bad bearings."

"I don't get it."

"It's a circle, Jack," he explains patiently. "The first pump bent the timing cam. With the timing bad, the engine got too hot, and so did the main bearings. Then the heat prob'ly warped the cam even more. Now, even with a new pump, that cam will twist the gear sideways, see? And the whole thing starts again. It fucked up this unit, and it'll fuck up the next pump you put in.

"Diesel's like anybody else," he continues pompously, touching his knife. "What's important is, the timing. Guy has good timing—like in making money, or meeting women, or drinking—he'll be okay. If he don't—"

He chokes off the engine. I climb to the wheelhouse to shut the ignition. I do not need Doomo's philosophy. The tide tables, the snapshots of Sam and Caitlyn pinned over the chart table, flutter in the draft. The instruments are all shut off now and the starboard windows stare out over the pier.

This wheelhouse normally gives me the illusion of power, because from it I can see where I have been and what the weather is and where I have to steer to get out of trouble. I can look at the radar and spot traffic before it comes close. The depth sounder tells me how much water lies under my keel.

This trouble, though, threatens my wheelhouse. It is a virus in navigation itself. With bad bearings, that engine will die. Because a boat is a machine for moving, no engine means no boat.

No boat, no wheelhouse.

A circle, as Doomo said.

"Hey," I call down the hatch, "how much time I got on this?"

"Whaddya mean?"

"Running hours, I guess."

"Running hours?" The sanctimony of the expert gleams in his voice. "Theoretically you got maybe twenty hours running time I would say Jack.

"On the other hand," he continues, and I hear the sneeze of another bottle opening, "you might run this bitch till Easter before she went south. Yah, well, another thing—I been lookin' at that hull flange."

I believe there is no such thing as bad information, as long as it's accurate. However I do not want to hear what Doomo is about to say. I can take only so much bad news today.

"One thing you can do on these old Brunos," he continues, "is Might-E-Foam inside the core."

"Might-E-Foam?"

"Yah know—a chemical foam. You put in the catalyst an' it expands fifty, a hundred times its volume. It'll fill the voids in the double-hull. Only thing," he adds, "make goddam sure you drill holes all along the lining, or it'll crack your hull apart. That stuff will blow up steel, you don't give it room."

We agree he will buy a new pump and replace the shot one tomorrow. He puts the bad one back for now.

I write him a check that I believe will not bounce, and steer *Hooker* to her mooring.

Back on shore I waste ten minutes whistling for Eb. When he finally shows, grinning and drooling like he was just around the corner the whole time and what's the fuss, he has a stink on him that would turn vinegar.

* * *

I drive with no direction. One hand picks at a rip in the dashboard. My teeth gnaw on one side, pulling my mouth that way. This reminds me strongly of someone I can't recall.

I avoid Main Street. Blueheads going 10 m.p.h. are clogging Barcliff so I turn left on Route 28. The big plate-glass windows of Dorene's Bridal Apparel are brightly lit. Most of the mannequins inside wear white and a couple are dressed in wide robes of violent color.

A white Subaru sedan slows down making the turn at the corner of Depot. The driver has a big head. Much too big. The head has a fat yellow beak and red feathers. The driver swivels to look at me as he drives by. It takes me a second to realize it is a human wearing a chicken mask. I twist around in my seat, watching it go. Seeing that chicken for some reason makes me need a cigarette. If I had a pack in my pocket there would be nothing I could do, I would light up right now.

I drive down Depot Road to the Cape Fisherman's Supply because I need more propane so I can cook something besides sandwiches offshore. Maybe I will check out the price on Might-E-foam. The sight of the ugly brick and vinyl building that houses the shop brings out this ridiculous nostalgia, of future missing, like before Sam goes on a school trip. My stomach feels hungry, as if something had been subtracted from my gut. The Fishermen's Supply, Larry's, the pier—they all stink of fishing to me.

I cannot imagine my life without these things.

At the last second I do not stop. There is an emergency solution to all this. I take a right down Main. My teeth grind harder on the left. It feels like the brake linings wore a little on that side of my mouth.

Without actually making the connection I get a feeling for Caitlyn, her mouth tensed in a backwater of memory.

I reach Fuller's Landing kind of before I mean to, which is how I usually arrive there. Fuller's Landing is a long strip mall torn from the side of Route 137 where there used to be nothing but scrub pine and a little piece of water called Shubael's Pond.

The mall was built by Thatch Hallett. Thatch named it after his son, Fuller. Fuller was killed in a forklift accident in East Boston. Thatch's theory was, if he built enough shopping areas on the Cape there would be jobs for kids like Fuller. Then they would not have to go and die in sub-code warehouses in the city.

The strip mall was built to look like a New England village: to blend into the land. That's fine if you think New England looks like white vinyl "cottages" four stories high and eighty yards long with a food court and discount jean stores in the basement.

I made Eb get in back, because of his smell. Now I tie him to a two-by-four with a length of yellow potwarp.

The Chatham Bank and Trust occupies a freestanding building on an island in the development's center. This structure looks like a lobster shanty, only twenty times bigger and with Andersen windows. The hallways are upholstered in plastic lobster buoys, reproductions of schooner prints, and green rayon carpeting. I walk on silent pile to the consumer loans room to talk to Mrs. Snow.

I got my first savings account from Mrs. Snow when I was eight years old. My uncle took me. That was when the bank occupied two rooms next to the movie theatre on Main Street. It is almost four o'clock but she goes right in to see Steve Vaitsos. When she comes back she fashions a conspiratorial face and whispers, "Just five minutes now." She offers me a fresh apple. I shake my head, sit down where she points. I am very aware of my jeans and workboots in this room where every surface is protected by polyurethane and disinfected nightly.

Color photos of the bank's five directors hang over the schooners. Thatch Hallett's face is square in the middle. That photo is the only place I have seen him without his beret. He always wears it, even at meetings of the Chatham town finance committee, of which he is a member.

People tell this story about Thatch. A kid from Mashpee broke into his house one night. The kid had a .22 pistol. Thatch had a hunting rifle. He flipped on the lights, aimed his rifle at the kid, and ordered the kid to put his gun on the floor. The kid put the pistol down. Thatch shot him in the heart.

It's just a story but, if it is not true, it should be. Thatch is like that. He rides horses and hunts deer and calls his house "The Alamo." I wonder how he likes having his mug framed among all this plastic and without his beret to boot.

* * *

Steve Vaitsos is roughly forty and extremely handsome. He has brindled hair and and brown eyes with healthy white all around them. He wears blue suits cut to fit his health club pecs. He seats me in front of his desk and wants to know what he can do for me.

So I tell him, and he never says no.

What he does is this. He opens my file on the table before him, pulls out printouts one by one, and presses down on them with all his fingers.

"One twenty-year balloon note on a 1974 Bruno & Stillman 50," he begins, "payable at eleven point four percent. October twenty-fifth was the due date on the latest payment?"

I nod, though it was not a question. He looks down again.

"One personal loan on a principal of six thousand dollars at twelve point two. Maturing in May of next year.

"One twenty-year equity-owner's second mortgage, with the collateral we arranged on water, mineral and bottom rights at the Marston's Hollow property? Erin Cahoon is cosigner on that. Which you used to reequip the Bruno last month."

"September," I correct him. "What I was thinking was, maybe I could add a loan onto that one to—"

"Yes." Steve sucks air through his teeth. He taps his fingers on the personal loan.

"What kind of engine were you thinking of?" he asks.

"A GM," I answer immediately, "a 371." Suddenly my heart beats faster. You know you have hooked them when they start talking details. "They're the most reliable. With power take-off and—"

"The only way," he interrupts, "would be a third mortgage on the Marston's Hollow rights."

"That would be okay," I tell him. I am trying to sound cool. As if I negotiate third mortgages the way I buy six-packs. "Rin wouldn't mind, depending on the terms of course."

"Unfortunately." He bows his head briefly. "Oliver?"

"Yes?"

"The sum on Marston's Hollow already is two percent over our guidelines here."

I stare at him.

"It would be hard to do," he goes on. "In fact it would be impossible?" He nods, agreeing with himself.

"What about a boat loan?" I ask him.

"We don't do boat loans."

"But you used to—"

"I know. Not any more. We had too many problems. You know."

I nod. You can't really blame him on that one.

His fingers are starting to bug me. When he presses down the tips of them go white and the tops of his nails turn bright pink.

"Trouble is," I say, "I can't fish without an engine."

"I'd like to help you," Vaitsos repeats. His eyes look at me straight. He makes me believe him. A picture of a woman and two kids stands on his desk, angled so I can see them. The woman is plain but she has a kind smile.

"Just tell me what I need to do to get a mortgage. I'll do it."

"I wish I could help you. It's not my job to get you into trouble?" His tone is light, phrased as a question. "Don't get me wrong. But maybe you're finding it difficult to make the payments you already have?"

I hate that way of speaking. As if phrasing everything as a question absolved him of responsibility for what he said.

"It'll be a lot harder to make payments when I can't work 'cause my boat doesn't have an engine."

He presses on the documents again.

"You may want to think about selling those rights," he says. "You don't own the land so it's useless as a capital investment. But the rights you own *are* valuable? Someone could fix up that cranberry bog and clear thirty thousand a year . . . Even after paying off this note, you would probably have some cash in hand."

I stand up. Vaitsos asks a few questions about the fishing and I answer politely enough considering the feeling of missing just expanded in my stomach.

Before I go I ask him how much extra money I would get by cashing in the rights on Marston's Hollow.

Vaitsos takes his fingers off the papers entirely. The tops of his nails pale once more. He warns me that this is all "ballpark." Then he quotes a sum that even after I split it with Rin would buy a used GM and pay off half of what is left on the Bruno note.

When I return to the truck I find Eb has slipped his rope. I whistle for him for five minutes then get back in the truck. He is probably halfway to Eastham by now.

I turn the wrong way in leaving and end up in the central parking area. A bronze statue of Thatch's son stands on a cracked concrete plinth in the middle of the lot.

The statue is eight feet tall and cast in a rough style that is supposed to be artsy but just looks amateurish, as if the sculptor never bothered to finish it off. He stands with his hands empty and one shoulder kind of hunched like Quasimodo.

Only his face is smooth. The expression is kind of wistful, as if he had lost something important and could not remember where he put it.

I went to high school with Fuller Hallett. He didn't look anything like that.

I have to drive around a one-way system for three minutes before I can find my way back to the main road.

Chapter 7

The Squire

41 degrees 42'N; 69 degrees 57'W

No one is around when I get home.

A note on Caitlyn's calendar informs me Sam is at hockey practice until six.

No sign of Fleetwood or Billy. The fridge is empty. A single Coors Ice remains in Billy's cooler. I drink the beer. It tastes like club soda with hops flavoring. It has about the same effect.

The woman from Visa left another message on the machine. She sounds more pissed off than ever. Barry Ames from the fuel company says, It's C.O.D. from now on. He won't do another delivery on credit.

The weather channel calls for winds veering westerly, ten to fifteen knots. The front is overhead. The barometer reads 29.45.

The house always seems too quiet when Sam is not home.

I get back in the truck. I find a cold Rolling Rock hidden between a junked alternator and a sacrificial zinc.

Head for the boat.

It takes a long time because on Route 28 I fall in behind the Cape Cod Coma Club bus. That is not its real name; it is a yellow schoolbus that ferries the paralyzed and those in a persistent vegetative state from nursing home to hospital and back and you are not allowed to pass until they crank down the patients and roll them into the home to shut them away with their I.V.s until next week.

I think of Shubael's Pond while I sit in the growing line of traffic. I used to go there with Caitlyn, the first summer, when I was still engaged to Casey Ryan. We would drink beers at the Squire and maybe a peppermint schnapps.

After a few more schnapps we would find ourselves sneaking separately out the back entrance and into her Dodge. And through the streets we would travel, down the dirt road to the pond.

It was not always by moonlight but I usually think of it that way, under a moon that made the unassuming scrub oak and pine resemble myth trees, the kind wizards turn people into. The pond at night was so smooth it was a magic thing that would change you forever if you touched its black water. We took off our clothes, dropped them carefully away from poison ivy, and walked in. The air was sweet with white-pine needles. Everything was so full of danger and possibility that in the red alert of my senses I thought I could hear the sound of the dark as it hummed to itself like a dynamo. The water felt like old, warm flannel. Caitlyn and I held each other in the shallows, trying not to make love, knowing we would fail in the attempt.

The pond is still there, what's left of it—the town would not let them fill it. But it is in the middle of Fuller's Landing now, surrounded by gravel banks and ATMs.

The Rolling Rock was empty three minutes ago. I don't feel even the first hints of a buzz. I need another beer. I do not want to go to the Squire because Bucket is there. I have no choice, however. It is the only bar not full of Volvo people.

I pass the fish pier turnoff and continue into town.

The Squire is on Main Street but it's not like that. It is a relic from another era, a Victrola in a showroom of CD players. The front bar is brown and dim and vanity plates cover all the beams. The room behind is dimmer and lower and devoid of tags and the back room is so dark that clients sitting in one booth are almost invisible to those across the aisle, which suits the inhabitants just fine. A bleached fresco of Chatham, the way it looked before the golfing shops and cookie-cutter half-Capes, covers the walls.

A Power-morph video game makes laser beeps in the second room.

No sign of Frank, which is how I like it.

I perch at the front bar as far away as possible from Al Teixeira, who sold his gillnetter last June. Al now lives off a wife who owns a boutique that sells lace-fringed pillows.

Bucket comes down the bar toward me. He doesn't look any different than he did before Caitlyn spent the evening at his bar. He does not act any differently either and I figure we will play it this way for a while. It's the way guys tend to play it when the problem is women and the choice is either ignore it or hit each other over the head with a tire iron.

He pops me a Rock 'n Roll. The beer goes down without fuss. A mild kick of buzz flails around inside me but things are battened tight in there and it fades fast.

I order another.

Pool balls snick in back. Someone says "Go baby go!" and another shouts "Awright!," then groans. A soap opera shows on both TVs.

I strip off the bottle's label with my thumbnail. A man with a "101 Airborne" tattoo down the bar brags about how much money he is going to make growing sea urchins for the Japanese market in tanks near Oyster River. Bucket is listening to him because this fellow got federal money to buy the tanks and everyone listens to a man when he got federal money. It's like he figured out the great American scam. And maybe he did.

I wish there was federal money for used diesels but the grants are all aimed at getting you out of fishing, not back into it.

I did other jobs besides fishing. Landscaping, banging nails. They did not teach me anything I wanted to know yet they left me so tired by the end of the day it was all I could do to watch TV. Usually I quit.

Twice, I got fired.

The sun rams beams of yellow light horizontally down Main Street. The beams turn orange, then retract, and nothing is left but shadow. The black-Indians come in and sit in the black-Indian corner. A blues guitarist known as Cryin' Jimmy sets up his mike in an alcove off the pool room. George Peters sits beside me and buys me a beer.

George says nothing. This is one of the things I like about George. We have been friends since fifth grade and he never made small talk to me unless the Red Sox were winning and then the talk was not small. George is a contractor but unlike the rest he is picky about what he builds. Right now he is putting up the development next door to my place where the houses are half-buried and clustered too so that most of the woods around them are preserved. The fact that George is a black-Indian and he can still be picky in this white-bread town gives you an idea of his skill.

Skull comes in and hunkers in the second room in the booth where his buddy, Swear, holds court.

The beers in me start to fizz. A second high surges in my chest but it is small and edgy like a rat and I know it will disappear as soon as I slack off the drinking. This edge makes me want to examine Bucket's face for signs of stealth.

To avoid doing so I walk to the juke and punch in E-3. The Sex Pistols fill the second room with psychosis in three chords. "Ah fuck you Ollie," a woman calls but not seriously. It's the wife of Flickie, who disappeared on *Commando*.

She got $100,000 from the insurance, Sim Pierce said.

Another rumor has made the rounds in town: that Flickie and his mate scuttled the *Commando* on purpose. Then they split the insurance money with Thatch and moved to South America.

Plenty of people have scuttled boats for the insurance, but everybody knows this rumor is just wishful thinking.

On my way back I spot in one of the booths a wedge of Clairol-blond hair spiked every which way. Underneath, mauve glasses and blue lipstick. Large breasts squeeze like toothpaste out of a tube dress. My sister Erin leans over a car seat, tempting her kid with the hard brown teat of a Bass bottle.

I slide in opposite. She glances up, then goes back to feeding my nephew ale.

"What's going on?" she says.

"Not much."

She looks at me again.

"Caitlyn?"

I shrug.

"Bitch needs to loosen up."

The defense is automatic.

"She's at the end of her rope, Rin. I just figured it out—"

"We're all at the end of our *rope*."

She places the Bass on the table. I filch a swig. A thin figure stalks in rubber boots and a lumber jacket through the second room. His skin is the color of tobacco juice. His ax-shaped nose sweeps back and forth, sensing solid objects through the fug. When his head swings the cloud of gray hair behind sweeps in the other direction. His scrawny neck is wrinkled from the torque of a polyester tie cinched too tight. He looks like a cross between a radar scanner and a marsh heron.

Swear shouts, points at his watch.

"Uncle Manny," Rin comments, "is late."

Zappa gurgles and says "Oglala." Rin wipes drool off the bottle neck.

"Sioux," Zappa says.

"Did you hear that?

"Ollie."

"He said, 'Oglala Sioux'!"

"Dead radios?" Manny shouts. You hear bits of talk that make no sense in any bar but in the Squire you hear more than most. "You don't have to believe in dead radios."

I pick up Rin's Merit fuming on the ashtray and suck in a hit. The smoke is thin, like a razor concealed in a chemical sheath. My lungs love the cutting; I hold the smoke in, worship it in bronchial passages. Rin avoids looking at me. I replace the butt.

"Nothing's working anymore," I tell her. "Is that what you want to hear? Nothing's working. Caitlyn she's, I think she's seeing Bucket. And there's no goddam fish left anyway."

I lean over and stare at Zappa. He has large hooded green eyes that come straight from Rin. He is five months old. He opens his pea-sized mouth and blows a bubble which I pop with one finger. Rin grabs me around the neck and squeezes, bringing my nose into the valley between her breasts. These are as pretty as they were when I was fifteen, and twice as big now she is nursing. I yank my head away and my watch cap falls off. Leaning over to pick it up I bump someone standing behind me. Beer rains on my sweatshirt.

A tall man looks down at me through a pair of oily Ray-Bans. He wears a military-style baseball cap. The words "*Mary Anne* Project" are printed on it in gold.

"Sandy," Rin says in a tone much nicer than she uses with me.

Manny winds into something in the old men's booth. I can tell Manny is winding because he uses more and more Portuguese words. Manny, though we call him "uncle," is our great-uncle. Since my grandfather died he is the only Cape Verdean lush left in town.

My great-uncle seeems to think this makes him a hot shit.

I stare at the tall man. Then I glance at my sister. She smiles at me as if it's none of my business which of course it is not. She has a big gap between her two front teeth that gets wider when she smiles. "I told her," a guy in the next booth says, "it had nothing to do with the bullfrog."

I walk back to the front room. A gillnetter falls in slo-mo off his stool. A brief period of confusion ensues. Empathy also, of shorter duration. I notice George hunched across the counter, twisted and uncertain as a hermit crab who lost his shell. A broad man in a "Blue Devils" jacket leans over him intently.

". . . with the Bruins," he's shouting, "defensive mess . . ."

Amid the white noise a girl's voice says something like "Witches dancing around the apple tree," followed by "moon." I peer into the knot of people this came from but they are laughing like a beer commercial. I am not certain I heard it right anyway.

The broad man's name is Jack Sibley. He swings a hand around. I shake it without enthusiasm. Behind him the half dozen nailbangers who work for Sibley talk loud and gesture big because there are girls in the bar now.

The beers simply will not cut it if I have to fend off Jack Sibley. I yell "schnapps" in Bucket's direction. George glances at me. I smile at him without indulgence.

Sibley leans deeper across the bar, including me in George's reluctant orbit.

"He's gonna *want* big D," Sibley adds, "at the Price-Shoppe hearing."

"Who?" My mouth gapes. For an instant I get the feeling people in the Squire are talking a spy language of which I am completely ignorant.

"Whaddya mean, who?" Sibley asks. "Who I been talking about? Thatch Hallett."

I take a sip of my schnapps. I remember now: Thatch played hockey for B.U.

"You going to the hearing?" Sibley asks George, who shakes his head. "Ah, come on guy." Sibley slaps his shoulders. "Ollie's goin', right? He's an abutter or something."

"He's more 'n that," George says softly.

"That's right." Sibley nods. "You got the water rights next door, what's the place?"

I don't help him.

"Marston's Valley? Marston's Pasture?"

"Marston's Hollow," George says.

Cryin' Jimmy pulls a minor chord from his slide guitar. People in whale pants start moshing by the juke. I finish my drink. Bucket comps a strawberry blonde a beer. He leans over the counter, showing off his wrestler's muscle. I try to imagine him and Caitlyn talking close, their bodies learning how not to be surprised.

For some reason I cannot see this clearly.

The schnapps rub against each other and make heat where my belly is. The heat feels necessary, somehow. A draggerman who used up all his fishing days three months ago walks unsteadily toward the door. Sibley walks around the draggerman and grabs my good arm in one fist.

"You're a stand-up guy, Ollie," he hollers. "You gonna do the right thing. I know it."

He has a square Irish face and lips pinched together like a pollock's. The whites of his eyes are pink. His hands are big and the pressure hurts a little. The pink of his eyeballs reminds me of Vaitsos' nails.

"I always do the right thing," I tell him.

Sibley's smile is wide open and so are his eyes, usually; but as I watch they narrow a little; they take on a flavor of concealment.

"So you gonna sell the rights."

I smile back at him. My hand tightens around the empty glass. The left side of my mouth is pulling again.

"Now I think that's my business, Jack."

"It's *not* just your business."

Sibley's smile dies a slow death. When I look at his eyes now it is as if the channels had changed. I see cool, empty, wet spaces, drenched with wind. Sibley's wife left him for a woman last Christmas and they moved to Wellfleet. I wonder if the wind was caused by that, or if it was the other way around.

"It's everybody's business," Sibley says carefully. He raises his voice over the last chords from Cryin' Jimmy. "If Price-Shoppe don't get the rights then Thatch can't finish it. And if Price-Shoppe don't get it finished then we're fucked. Me and George here and every contractor in town, we don't get a chance at the interior bids, and that—that's all because of you."

"What the fuck's the rights got to do with it?"

"You know."

"I don't know what," I begin, but Sibley interrupts me.

"You're gonna sell." He forces the smile back in his voice. It takes all the crank he has got and no juice is left to change his eyes. I remember his wife now: a quiet woman who kept ferrets. "You're just jerkin' us around."

"It's none of your business, Jack," I repeat softly. "Back off."

He stares at me for a second or two. "Talk Too Much" finishes. People in the second room clap.

"I can't believe it," Jack says finally. He says it in a normal voice but normal for him is like a bullhorn. Also it comes in that space between the applause and when everyone picks up the conversation again, so it sounds louder. "One cripple Portygee hook-fisherman. An *ex-con* hook-fisherman, an' his slut sister."

I put down my glass. I turn slowly to face him. I have been trying for ten years to keep from doing what I am about to do but the effort requires thought and Sibley gave me no time to think about it.

I kick him in the balls.

The balance is right and there is good speed and momentum behind my work boot.

Some might call that cheap but I grew up skinny and not very tall and with one bad arm and I learned how to get my licks in first.

Anyway Jack Sibley doubles over, saying "Hoop, hoop." His beer crashes to the deck. I smack him in the ear with my good arm, just hard enough to topple him so he can't come back at me right away. Stools fall, glasses break. A barroom is an amazingly fragile place, when you think about it. Bucket sprints around the back of the horseshoe to come at me from behind. I get a feeling that the whole reason I came to the Squire was so Bucket could run at me like that. The nailbangers slam down their beers and move toward me. Only George is in the way.

He stands up in front of the nailbangers.

"George," I yell, "stay out of it." A hard jag is in me. I want to fight these guys myself. Mostly I want to beat the shit out of Bucket and get beaten, if necessary, in return.

There is no doubt about that last possibility. The odds are too long. Bucket gets his elbow around my neck, so I am busy. George goes down under three of the nailbangers. Two more take their place. "Dickbreath!" George grunts. It's his only insult, just about. "Ah fuck you *dick*breath!" Rin roundhouses a nailbanger with a diaper bag. He goes down like a shot quail. Someone punches me in the stomach, so I breathe like Sibley. Swear stands on a bench in the background, handicapping the fracas. Close up in the ranks of crowd, Manny shouts in his odd descant, "Abomination! Not like da ship—"

Meaningless.

Cryin' Jimmy shouts "It's all ovah folks!" into the mike. But Manny's flywheel has only just begun to spin.

"Look at him, he go wit his radio an' his radar on the sabbath even, and tinks he's brave like the man in sailing ships! The dangers of *mar*, ya. Look!"

Sirens gulp down the scale outside. George rages again: "Dickbreath!" Splashes of blue light wet the ceiling. I can see this with ease because I am on my back on the floor now with Bucket's knee in my stomach and one of Sibley's carpenters leaning his boot on my cheek.

"Yeah, Godstorm." Manny points at me. "Feed him to the *bacalhao* he catchin'!"

People grin nervously. A pretty girl pulls back in a rush, lowering her head from the strangeness of him. I am used to Manny's strangeness. Even if I were not, I am too full of the rage from what Sibley said and the anger in me anyway and the heat generated by the schnapps to pay much attention.

A man with hooded green eyes and a jaw thrust out stands behind where the girl was. Frank has his hands in his sweatshirt pockets and a butt screwed into the leading edge of his lips. His eyes when they look at me do not blink or alter even by one degree. The jaw cannot alter because the lines around his mouth are so long and they clamp it down so hard. He looks exactly the way Rin does when she gets mad. This is not surprising since Frank is her father, and mine.

Radio noises and pockets of cold air enter with the cops. It's Ricco and Van Fleck; I can tell by the way they use a form of choke hold right off the bat. Ricco finds my bad arm and twists it hard. Van Fleck knocks my watch cap to the floor. Bucket and the nailbanger lurch warily to their feet. George calls the cops "dickbreaths."

A chill of night in Spanish metal around the wristbones. Ricco pretends I head-butted him and rams me against the wall so my brain rings.

Van Fleck knees George in the stomach before cuffing him. The anger in me turns the landscape brown. Bucket's knee is within range. I want to kick it so the bone cracks and the cartilage snaps backward and he can never walk again without limping.

I don't do it.

Every atom in my head wants to hurt him but this time I close my eyes and turn the atoms back, one by one, the way I taught myself in jail, until the moment passes.

An EMT I went to high school with comes in holding his

First Aid bag. He kneels beside Sibley and unzips the contractor's pants. This guy always wanted to be a surgeon and he wants to operate now. Sibley pleads with him. Rin, watching from behind blue uniforms, grins. The gap in her teeth is wide.

Eventually I am hauled backward, through the crowd. The salt wind reaches out to pull me in. Hands preserve beer from our passage and the faces watch without compassion.

My father's no longer is among them.

Chapter 8

George gets bailed out at four A.M. I hear the clanks as they unlock the door and he yells "Yo, Ollie?" before one of the cops pushes him into a wall.

They love doing that.

"Dickbreath," George mutters, glumly.

I made my single phone call but the answering machine at home ate it and Van Fleck refused me another.

The cop station is modern and the tank is about three times bigger than they need for this town, even in the summer. I can hear the low murmurs of men in other cells. A woman sings, in shaky soprano, a Beatles song. I feel incredibly alone—much more so than I feel at sea with my instruments.

The smell of cherry disinfectant is pervasive and strong as guilt. I wonder if all jails order the same brand of disinfectant so that no matter where you are locked up, from

MSI-Concord to Thomaston, Maine, you will know you are in prison every time you draw a breath.

Anyway I lie sleepless on the stainless bunk till the morning shift comes on. I figure George phoned Caitlyn when he got out but nobody comes for me and I get shipped straight to court with the night's catch of OUIs.

This is Second District, the usual courthouse for Chatham. It is the brand new building with a bad roof just off the Orleans rotary. George, dressed in his Sunday suit, sits in the main body of the room. He looks OK except for a bandaid on his forehead. Paula, his wife, looks tired. Their lawyer whispers in her ear and grins. I sit on the defendants' bench for an hour or so while the clerks, like leaf-cutter ants, carry papers back and forth. I don't mind the waiting so much; at least I can see George and Paula.

I recognize the judge as soon as he comes in. He has thick wattles and a rufous, water-buffalo neck.

Nickerson. Just like last time.

George finds my eyes. Neither of us shows expression. The judge deals with old business. Caitlyn walks in and sits in back next to Paula. She does not look at the defendants' bench. She opens a magazine and reads it intently.

The judge goes down the docket. Three OUIs are processed at speed. Then he gets to me.

"Cahoon," he growls, "Peters. This the same incident?" Staring at me now.

The DA-cop liaison looks it up, then says, "Yup."

"You two never learn, do you," Nickerson grumbles.

He wants to throw the book at us but Sibley's lawyer did not show so all he can process is a misdemeanor. Also, Nickerson is a hard-ass but even he has better things to do what with some of the drug crime creeping down here from Boston and Providence.

I plead nolo. This is what you do when the crime is small and you don't have a lawyer. He continues the case without a finding for six months. I will have to pay court costs and a hundred and fifty dollar fine. George's lawyer opts for the same deal.

I try to find George's eyes again. The last time we got into trouble together I asked Frank for money for a lawyer. He refused. He told me that if I got caught fair and square then no lawyer on earth was going to help me. "Plead nolo, and kiss the judge's ass," was his advice.

This is not a bad deal. There is no reason for me to feel as if I have permanently lost my drawing rights on sunshine.

George leaves without looking at me.

I go to the clerk's office and sign papers. Caitlyn is waiting on the steps when I come out.

She looks good. After the tank she is something bright and clean as a northern landscape. Her long explosion of dark hair has been contained and trussed with a leopardskin tie. It shines in the cold sun like spun anthracite.

Caitlyn has a big face; wide mouth and airfoil lips and a fine straight nose except for a little bend she got playing field hockey as a kid. When she is angry her features seem even bigger but they keep their proportions.

The left part of her mouth drags downward. It amazes me that I never picked up on this detail before.

She wears a red sweater. Her jeans streamline the arc of her lower body. I follow her to the car. The second Cahoon automobile is a 1983 Olds Custom Cruiser wagon, painted taupe. The paint job is marred by rust tumors that I disguised with antifouling paint. Cait has pasted bumper stickers on the rear window: "DON'T HONK: This car is driven by a WICCAN!"; "Mom's Taxi;" "GyNET [Web of Women]." Our vehicles tend to define themselves by what they don't do and here is the Oldsmobile list: The driver-side power windows don't roll down, the points don't quite meet, the carburetor float doesn't always come loose, the right brake light won't shine.

Caitlyn drives fast and rude. When she is mad she brutalizes tourists and blueheads. She cuts off a Florida plate at the Route 28 turnoff. I reach up to pull the watch cap tighter over my head. That is when I remember Van Fleck knocked it off, in the Squire.

At the Main Street lights she turns to me and says, "Sam asked where you were last night."

"What did you tell him?"

"I told him the truth."

"Well, that's what he should hear."

I squint my eyes against the sun. My head is tight and my stomach feels both hollow and full of reverb from peppermint schnapps.

"Did George call you?" I ask.

"Yeah."

"An' you didn't bail me out?" I can feel my lips tipping. I make an effort to keep my mouth straight.

"I wasn't gonna leave Sam."

"What, Billy's not good enough now?"

"He wasn't home. Goddam you anyway, Ollie."

The lights change. She looks straight ahead and speaks softly as if she were talking to someone inside her as we accelerate.

"I been *tryin'* to understand. Tryin' to see what *happened*."

She fishtails a retiree. His horn dopplers into background.

"Like I said before," she continues, "it's a failure of language."

"I smell shrink."

She ignores that comment.

"It's like I'm watching a bad comedian, he forgets the punch line and anyway he's talkin' in *French*."

"What, us?"

"You."

"Oh," I say, "that makes me feel better." I can't move my jaw well when it is straight like that.

"It's always yourself you worry about, you know that? Always how *you* feel."

We stop again at the Eldredge Park Way intersection.

She stares at the light as if it had changed against her for personal reasons.

"What I been trying to say, Ollie. I think you should leave. Go somewhere else, just for a while. So we can, like, *think* for a while."

I look at her profile. I am hung over enough that everything, the sunlight, the car, seems painted like a cheap theater backdrop. I could easily pretend Caitlyn did not say what she said except for the way my chest is compressing into a lump, which tells me she did.

"You know," she continues. "I don't know. A trial separation?"

We do not speak for ten, fifteen seconds.

"What about Sam?" I say.

"It's better for him—"

"That's easy for you—"

"Shit, Ollie. You seen his English grades? You seen his teacher comments?"

"You can't tell me that's just because of us."

"Of *course* it's because of us."

We are off again, a tad early. Caitlyn always uses both hands for driving which means she cannot use them for emphasis, so she pounds on words instead. "Of *course* it is."

She takes a deep breath and it comes out shaky.

"The other day, well, a few weeks ago—when I was expecting you home—you know, there was that thunderstorm. I didn't tell you. I was roasting the chicken and I remembered the first chicken I ever made for you, at the cabin.

"I got, like, this rush of feeling. I thought I'd make everything nice. I went to Stop 'n Shop and bought cranberry sauce, and butternut squash 'cause you like that. And I bought some Rolling Rocks."

"Caitlyn—"

"I know it wasn't your fault."

I rub my face with my hands, hard.

"Cait, it was the first day we got the trawl working right. I wanted to get a good day in for a change."

"I know. I *know*."

"I come in for the important things."

"Sometimes. Anyways. D'you want to hear what I thought?"

"Not really."

"I thought, this is like what you always say about boats. It's the little things that sink you. The *accumulation*. I thought, Finally it's a *chicken* that's gonna sink us. And right then, there was a big clap of thunder. It was like a movie, only it wasn't. It felt like the storm was *agreeing* with me."

"It wasn't the chicken."

"Whatever. But I can't deal with it anymore."

I watch the trees flit by. We are a quarter mile from our road now. She puts a hand on my knee, takes it off again. I get a weird flash of her doing that to Sam when he was young, in comfort, in reassurance.

I feel defenseless now. I feel as if some cheap Marvel Comics hole-to-Hell is opening under me. Like the sense of loss to come I got outside the Fishermen's Supply, only bigger.

I fight to line up my mouth again and get the throat to open. Turning down our road, she hits every pothole, and parks the Olds next to Billy's Datsun. I close my eyes so I don't see our house or anything.

The wagon is preigniting. Caitlyn yanks the gear shift back into drive. The V8 stalls. In the sudden silence she sighs, hard. The insides of her palms are white on the steering wheel.

"It's only—" I begin.

I close my hands into fists and start again. "It's only, what we have is a family, it doesn't work separate. It's like a fuckin' bird or something. You—you can't pull a wing off it and expect it to fly!"

"It's better this way." Her voice is calm now. She likes it

when I get upset—she says it means we are communicating. I am beginning to think she just likes it.

"I still love you," I tell her, wondering if I do.

"What we have isn't love," she says, "it's myth-partnership."

"You swore," I say, and though I do not mean to increase the volume it comes close to a yell. "You swore you wouldn't use that, that GyNET bullshit."

Now I am getting to her. Her cheeks grow pink the way Thatch Hallett's did.

Her mother was a cousin of Thatch's.

She looks through the windshield as if she still were driving. I notice that the skin under her eyes is puffy. The morning light emphasizes the vertical wrinkles between cheeks and mouth. She looks middle-aged and vindictive and for a second there I feel that I do not love her anymore; no, worse—that I hate her and all her petty concerns—that I have been fooling myself for years by trying to save something out of this shipwreck of a marriage when there was nothing worth saving anymore.

I hit the dashboard with my fist, once. It is not so much anger that makes me do this, but the idea of waste. The padded naugahyde is dented where I hit it. The cut her lozenge made smarts inside my grip.

She shakes her head, satisfied, and gets out of the car. I follow her into the mudroom. She turns to face me, as if not wanting me to come into our house.

I look away from her; at the shelves of the mudroom covered with four or five hundred dollars worth of hockey gear that Sam grew out of; at the rose food and old glue and flea powder and boxes a quarter full of soggy detergent also stacked there. I put those shelves in a year ago and already they sag between the braces with all the junk we do not use anymore.

"I need to think, Ollie," she says. "Please?"

I look at her again. The quick hatred that came out of nowhere a minute ago has gone back to nowhere.

But I have to admit, right this instant, I would not mind leaving here. I wouldn't mind not fighting every five minutes—skipping the skirmish of our life together.

Not moving around each other. Not doing the dishes. Not riding herd on Sam.

This is a Frank kind of feeling.

It lasts until I get upstairs. Sam's door is open and the sight of his "Thomas the Tank Engine" collection and Chessie System posters and the bald kangaroo and Powermorphs makes the hollowness in my stomach worse. I am too tired and hung over to withstand such void.

The tears surge, hot and fatty and without warning.

I collect some clothes. Most of my work stuff is on the boat. I search for something to distract me later from thoughts such as these, and find a book Cait gave me last Christmas. The book is about the ecology of Cape Cod. I already read the chapter on fishing and it contained little I did not know so I put it down. But reading, even reading stuff I know, is better than thinking.

Tears leak out of my squint twice while I pack. I think of Bucket and wonder why I did not bring him up while we were fighting. Surely betrayal is the sharpest weapon I have to hand? Yet even under the deep weight of hangover I sense that if she cheated on me with Bucket it was only the last in a line of smaller treasons, and I had as much of a hand in these acts as she did.

Anyway I have no proof, about Bucket.

I throw my bag in her car. My left shoulder aches where Ricco twisted it. I am feeling bad, because of what I thought earlier about hating her. I don't hate Caitlyn. She is kind, deep down, and she takes care of Sam. If I don't love her anymore it surely is a failure of mine, for letting go of the constant shaping that a marriage needs to survive; for not giving my family the predictable home life they both deserve and need.

I go back inside. She makes me a cup of coffee. I want to refuse it; I need to drink it. I am cold. I swallow the brew, not looking at her. It sucks. She never made good coffee. Things almost seem normal.

We agree I will take Sam tomorrow or, if I go fishing, whenever I get back. She gives me a ride to the Squire parking lot.

I do not look at Caitlyn when I get out. She drives off without looking at me either. As soon as the wagon disappears I realize I forgot to ask if Eb ever came home.

He was not back when I was there, but he could have come and gone.

Rock

from *Notes on the Ecology of Cape Cod* (Salt Marsh Press, Falmouth) by Irwin E. Zeit, Ph.D.

It is a curious pastime to look at yellow bulldozers scraping at the sandy topsoil of the Cape for new housing, and reflect that this activity, which at the beginning of the twenty-first century has so thoroughly altered the character of the peninsula, constitutes a scale model of how it was created.

The Laurentide ice sheet began to form 75,000 years ago at the dawn of the Wisconsinan glacial stage. Approximately 25,000 years ago the vast glacier churned into New England, and 4,000 years after that it reached the area that is now Cape Cod.

At that point the ice sheet consisted of three distinct lobes that acted together, like bulldozers working line abreast, ploughing up the igneous rock they traveled over and shoving the pulverized debris forward, exactly like a blue-green grader the size of Austria.

At what is now Nantucket, the glacier stopped. Melting water from its compressed ice created braided outwash plains, a form of mineral centrifuge that dropped heavy rocks near the glacier wall, and finer and finer deposits, farther and farther out.

Then, as the climate warmed, the glacial bulldozers switched into reverse, lifting their harsh icy blades, leaving the piled up rocks behind in great mounds; the Buzzards Bay moraine, that forms the north-south high ground of the Elizabeth Islands and western Martha's Vineyard and Falmouth; and the Sandwich moraine, running east-west from Dennis to the canal, which provides the Cape's meager altitude from Scargo to the hill of the County Jail in Barnstable.

The rest was outwash plain, glacier refuse, pocked by boulders or chunks of harder ice. And it extended much farther out, across the Nantucket fishing grounds and Georges Bank—swampy sub-Arctic tundra where mastodon and sabre-tooth roamed until water released by the melting of glaciers raised the level of the sea.

And the sea rose, and rose again, flooding Georges Bank and the many-layered tundra it once hosted. Moved cyclically by the moon, the currents cut great cliffs in the till plains and piled them up into Provincetown's heights, Monomoy's dunes, Tom Nevers Head. Trapped between the semi-diurnal requirements of tide and the circular ramparts of Georges Bank and the Cape, the ocean found itself twisting there in a clockwise pattern, concentrating its minerals and aquatic life in a great and fecund gyre, while underneath the fishing banks the submerged moorland rotted into gas and oil that one day would be tapped by man to run the bulldozers that he used to alter what the glacier originally had built.

Chapter 9

The truck starts. Now of all times, when none of the things in my life should work, the truck fires right up. So I drive to an ATM and take out a hundred bucks.

Cash always makes me feel less hung over.

Then I go to the fish pier. I hump my bag to the dinghy and row with the slop to *Hooker*. My left arm aches worse than before. I throw the bag in my bunk and set the coffee maker running.

When the coffee is ready I climb to the wheelhouse and switch the VHF to weather. Sitting on the pilot stool, letting the coffee steam warm my cheeks, I wait for the area forecast.

When it comes it is more of the same. The high pressure system currently over New England should dominate the area's weather pattern through Tuesday.

30.11, the barometer reads.

The wheelhouse is freezing. I fetch a spare watch cap

from the gear locker and jam it on my head. I start up the Gardner and get the heater going and it is still cold.

I look out the side window and notice Joe Santos's gillnetter anchored by Laflin's Landing.

Joe is taking his boat to Pemaquid, Maine. He claims he can make a living off the whiting fishery there.

Far against the bluff of Minister's Point I catch a dash of movement.

Through the binoculars I make out the blue gleam of an ocean rowing shell. Harriet is practicing, as she does daily, for the annual critter row. On December thirteenth my mother will push that kayak all the way around Pleasant Bay. What money she raises from the stunt will go to the MSPCA.

Now she is coughing out the tailings of Old Golds and vodka in a purple exercise suit from Tern Island to Nickerson's Neck.

The wind blows hard from the northwest, probably twenty to twenty-five knots like yesterday. The tide is just past the ebb and *Hooker*, rocking a bit, turning her bows to the greater force, confronts the low chop of Aunt Lydia's Cove.

The break in Nauset Beach lies off my port quarter. The incoming tide gets a rise from the westerly wind. The water rears up, cold and white in the distance, smashing at the shallows with thin fists of foam.

The sea beyond the surf has a dark, hard sheen, as if it had gone through an annealing process, was smelted in the low temperature, in the Bessemer force of the front that just blew through.

Channel nine on the VHF. A voice says, "If I'd come in Friday, like I said, she'd never of even *seen* Tim."

I am shivering, despite the coffee. To keep my mind off temperature I slip the mooring and run *Hooker* to the fish pier to wait for Doomo.

I am halfway across the cove when I realize I forgot to check the oil and fuel levels as I always, and religiously, do.

* * *

The new pump is installed by four in the afternoon. It was not cheap. Doomo says the Boston dealers do not stock that model anymore and he had to pay extra to ship that one overnight from Newark.

He also says I can pay him next week, which is pretty cool. I pick up refilled LPG tanks at the Fishermen's Supply. They have not closed my account yet although I am over two months behind. On impulse I charge up three five-gallon tubs of Might-E-Foam. The Ames tanker comes by the pier and takes all my cash in exchange for sixty gallons of diesel fuel.

I run the *Hooker* back out but the combination of VHF, and wind, and the rumble of the Atlantic always trying to carve off and eat the southern beach, begins to get to me.

My thoughts are light and hard to pin down. I leaf through *Notes on the Ecology of Cape Cod*. My eyes are too tired to follow the close print. Sometimes I have to shut them hard to keep my thoughts from floating toward Caitlyn and what just happened.

Once, with my eyes closed, I see a brain photo of *Commando*, canted over on the rocky bottom. Flicky's skull shines as he keys the mike again. The querulous questions of the dead are snapped from his teeth into the gyre of current.

To keep from thinking I get the Makita, screw in a quarter-inch bit, and drill holes in the ceiling. The ceiling is the inner skin that separates the hull's balsa core from the cabin. I punch a hole every three inches in a three-foot radius fore and aft of the fishhold bulkhead and half the time the drill hits thin air. I cover the holes with masking tape and mix up a tub of Might-E-Foam and catalyst as the directions indicate. When I pour the Might-E-Foam into the flange I hear it glugging nicely through the channels where the original core has shrunk.

But within five minutes, as Doomo predicted, it goes

crazy, squirting through the masking tape, pouring out of the holes I drilled. I watch, amazed, shocked even, as I tend to be when something I did achieves an effect far greater than what was foretold. It's not that I didn't believe Doomo but I sure did not expect the stuff to be this powerful. The expanding foam jets out in thick yellow horizontal streams like banana frappe and piles up a foot deep and hardening between the coamings.

Twenty minutes later the puddle has solidified into a very dense styrofoam that I can carve away with my filet knife.

I am going to buy more Might-E-Foam, I think. With enough of it I could reline the entire hull.

I throw the excess foam in garbage bags, and sweep away the residue from cutting. I hook up the new LPG tanks. Make more coffee and walk around the saloon, sipping. My headache is back. I am hungry. I don't feel like sweet corn, lima beans, and cheddar potato chips, which is all that remains in the galley lockers.

I row ashore and get in the truck.

I know, without thinking about it, where I am going.

* * *

"The Kitchen" is what we called it from the first, when Frank split and Harriet moved back here from Forestdale.

It is way the hell on the west side of town, in a patch of woods by Queen Anne's Road: a small, undistinguished farmhouse, late Teddy Roosevelt. Warp-eaved, gap-shingled. Paint the color of squash pulp peels in curls from the trim.

Behind it, a barn, a chicken house and a tar-paper garage straggle back into the honeysuckle like a failed ambush.

A Victorian cottage restored by a dermatologist from Brockton stands on one side; on the other, a late-eighties half-Cape with a lanai and a swimming pool.

I run the truck up the driveway's slope and brake hard at the top. Always some cat or cairn terrier is escaping into the ruts and if anyone hits it Harriet will have hysterics for a week. My headlights wash over Uncle Manny scuttling like a fugitive into the chickenhouse. His lamp makes broken patterns against the smashed frames of the coop.

The Kitchen hits me in the senses as always. Smells come first: laundry detergent and Portuguese sausage. Terrier piss and Old Golds. Heating oil and mildew.

Then the sounds. The dryer goes whop-creak-gush, whop-creak-gush. Lost pennies rattle rhythm behind. Heat pipes clank, bass thumps. Mel Torme sings Irish ballads on the living room stereo. Over and under everything else burn the treble neurotics of television.

To get to the kitchen proper you wind around the laundry room and a crooked hallway like the wings of a stage and this is appropriate because always you can expect some form of cheap psychodrama to be playing inside.

Here is what's showing tonight. Rin scrubs a pan with Brillo. Zappa snoozes, furled in a serape, his lips just touching the elongated mauve nipple of his mother's right breast.

One of the cats is stretched on the stove's grill section. A cairn puppy and a mutt Rin picked off the streets streak from under the table fast as those BOMARC missiles they used to keep at Otis Air Force Base. As the dogs recognize my scent, they brake, skid, tumble over each other. The pup pees in excitement.

My own scent after one night fishing and another in the tank must be pretty clear to dogs.

Harriet sits in an armchair at the head of the long table, filling out the crossword in *Parade*.

"Hey," Rin says, softly so as not to wake the baby, "it's fuckin' Papillon."

"Ollie!" my mother gasps. She sits up, newspapers furling. The stack of notebooks in which she adds up bills she will not pay topples into the ashtray. Ashes fly. She winds her arms around me, leaves Prince Matchabelli on my cheek. "They let you *out*. You never *called*."

"Saw you rowing, earlier."

"I told you, Harriet," Rin says. "It wasn't a big deal."

"I did six miles," my mother says shyly.

"I owe you one," I tell my sister. "You bopped that guy pretty good."

"You bopped someone?" Harriet asks.

"With a diaper bag," I add.

"Wasn't just diapers," Rin says. "It had two pints of frozen breast milk in it."

Harriet starts to laugh. It turns into a cough. Ashes gray the air again. She takes a belt of her drink.

"It's not funny," Rin says. "They would of kept me in except they didn't have a policewoman to take care of him."

"They took *you* in?"

"Van Fleck." She grins. "Asshole never got over it 'cause I wouldn't sleep with him in high school."

"Well," I say, "he must have been the only guy in Chatham."

Her face lengthens. She hurls the Brillo at me. I walk around the L to the drinks counter. Zappa whines and goes back to sleep. The crowd handler of Wolfschmidt is not in its usual hiding place under three years' worth of *TV Guide*.

"Randy been around?" I comment.

"It's under the TV," Harriet says.

"You think you can just walk in," Rin yells, "make comments about me, about Randy, like you was lord high fuckin' god of the universe, what the fucksa the matter with you?"

A cooking program shows on channel seven. Nigerian drums pound juju from the cellar. For a couple of seconds the rhythms of Olatunji coincide exactly with those of Mel Torme.

Rin's face is round again. She never stays mad for long; her sense of proportion is too good. Or maybe it's her sense of humor, unless they are the same thing. She strokes Zappa's neck as she checks the stew. She pours herself a glass of Tab.

"You wanna hear something weird?" Rin asks. "While

they were figuring what to do with me? They put us in the tank with this woman, they got her for OUI. Anyway, she's good and high, she pulls out an ole pantyshield wrapper and a ballpoint and starts, like, writing a list."

I sit in a wicker armchair and push my legs out. My feet touch something soft on the floor. I pull them back hastily.

"He's fine," Harriet mumbles, not meeting my eye.

"Anyway," Rin continues, "I ask her what she's doing, and she says, 'I'm writing down the names of all the guys I ever slept with.'

"I don't say anything. But I kind of, like, edge over." Rin sits on the bench on the table's other side. She wriggles her ass sideways, peering over the shoulder of an invisible cellmate. "I look down the list, and sure enough—Randy Walsh! Plain as the nose on your face, halfway down."

Rin's face is long again but her eyes are narrow, the way they go when she feels sorry for someone. I am not sure if she feels sorry for Randy or for the woman he slept with. I hope it's not for Randy, who screwed around when they were married and will not pay child support for his kid and steals Harriet's vodka, when he can find it.

I top up my glass. As I pour I am thinking that this family never learns. We do dumb things with the wrong partners and hope it will all turn out for the best.

The hope is the depressing part. Everybody in this kitchen always hoped and hoped despite all evidence.

If hope was a fuel you could burn like oil, Harriet would never have to worry about heating bills again.

Inside me the Wolfschmidt starts to find its own personal channel. It chills things just enough that I can go back over what Caitlyn said and figure out what she was really telling me behind the words.

This is hard work. I was tired before because of the night in the tank. And fighting with Caitlyn wears me out.

I rub my bad arm, trying to squeeze out the ache Ricco put in. All I can remember now is Caitlyn's tone: how the rough drive of it felt out of all proportion to the incident. Such impulsion could not come from one night or one week of anger. It had to build up over a long time to splinter the edges of her voice the way it did.

That's as far as I get before the stew is ready. I set the table. Rin yells for Manny. Zappa yells for Rin. The juju stops. Walter emerges from the cellar and sits next to Harriet. He carries a bottle of single malt whisky that he keeps hidden in the cellar. Walter looks like the boy next door turning werewolf in a B movie. He has even features, black hair, and skin and denim uniformly dyed with soot from the old furnace.

Rin cooked the linguica with garlic and cabbage and onions and potatoes and vinho verde and it tastes fine. I eat only a quarter of my plate. Manny comes in and fills a mug with vodka. I ask Walter if he wants to go fishing with me, but he says he is too busy with the boiler.

We watch *C'est Si Bon*. "The cuisine of the Vaucluse," Marius Cradingue announces, "is a happy marriage of Mediterranean olive oil and Provençal produce."

Manny glowers at me over his glass.

"Ya done it again," he says.

"Thanks, Manny," I say. "Thanks for your support, at the bar."

"Ya never learn, Ollie."

"Leave it alone," Rin says.

"How can I leave it alone?" Manny replies, shaking his head repeatedly. "Ya wastin' ya life, boy. Drinkin'. Fishin'. And this time ya got your sister in wit ya, too."

He stomps out, still shaking his head. The mane of gray hair bombs dandruff in his slipstream.

"He was wild, huh?" Rin comments. "Just wild."

I call home. Sam answers. When he hears who it is his voice grows odd and cool, not because of me but because he's trying not to get caught between me and Caitlyn, and that takes control.

Control is always cool.

My throat locks up when I hear him.

"Mom said you were sleeping on the boat?" he asks finally.

And I realize it is up to me to explain to the boy what is going on.

For a second a cord pulled inside my head goes so taut it starts to spin and fray. The image I dreamed up on *Hooker* comes out of nowhere. Flicky's skeleton talks underwater on the VHF only this time the smooth white of his bones is striped with blood so dark it is almost black.

The snapshot vanishes, fast as it came. The tension slackens in my head.

I do not want to tell Sam, anymore than Cait did. I do not know how to describe what I don't understand.

Sam's voice is still off-key; that is not what was bothering him.

"Dad—Eb's not here!"

"Sam—"

"He's not with you?"

"No, he—"

"But then where—where'd he go?" His voice cracks.

"He split yesterday," I say. "At the bank. He pulled one of those two-by-fours loose. But he always shows up, Sammy."

"But you always say, he could get hurt!"

"Well, he could."

"So how do you know he's okay?"

I sigh.

"I don't know, Sammy. But Eb's smart. It's just, he loves to run."

"You lookin' for him?"

"Yeah," I tell him, kicking myself because I didn't, "I'll look for him tonight."

My throat does not feel so cramped now. We talk about other things. He mentions an H.O.-scale locomotive he wants me to buy. The trade is implicit. I lost Eb, I owe Sam a train.

After we finally got sick of the Chatham Railroad Museum Sam and I used to go to model-train shows a lot. We seldom bought anything because most of those trains were so expensive, but simply looking at the models run around their thin silver rails satisfied something in both of us that loved to watch little machines go smoothly in a circle.

We have not been to a show in a couple of years.

I ask Sam to fetch his uncle. When Billy comes on I offer him a job. The pay is a mate's share and fifty bucks guaranteed a trip.

This is more than Pig got.

"Ain't got no other work," Billy answers, which I figure means "Yes." I tell him to meet me at Larry's at three tomorrow morning and hang up fast before he can object.

I grab an Old Gold out of Harriet's pack and fire it up with her lighter. It tastes cool and clear like vodka.

"I thought you gave up," Rin says.

"I did," I answer, crushing the butt in my plate.

"Vortigern," Zappa comments, and throws up on Rin's shoulder.

"You hear that?" I ask of no one, "that baby says real words."

"What's real about that?" Rin asks, wiping down her dress.

"He was somebody, I can't remember."

"Seven terms at UMass," my sister says, "all it did was fill your head with things you can't remember."

Rin rinses her Zappa cloth in the sink.

"You wanna sell the rights to Marston's Hollow," she continues, "it doesn't bother me."

"But Frank gave you those rights," Harriet says.

"And they're useless," Rin snaps back, "like everything else he gave us. Not that he gave us anything much," she adds.

"Christ," I say, "everybody wants me to sell."

"I didn't say I wanted you to," Rin replies. "I just said, if you want to I don't care. Sandy told me," she adds, "what Jack Sibley said."

"I don't," I tell Rin, "I don't wanna sell the rights, unless you do. But you watch out for that Sandy guy, he's a flimflam artist."

"You leave Sandy out of it," she retorts, her jaw tightening, "I don't lecture you about Casey Ryan."

"What do you mean?"

"You know, that night." She is getting back at me, I know what she is doing, picking up any stone that comes to hand to fling in my direction.

"That night, what night, we didn't do anything—"

"Hell, when I saw you on the lighthouse bluff last July she was holdin' your dick."

Walter spills his whisky. I shrug, but my face grows hot. Harriet snorts, sending a cloud of smoke into the lamplight. Some people who come to the kitchen regularly say it is like a big smoky womb that my mother keeps warm and tight to lock out the cold world. And others see in it the nexus of degeneracy in West Chatham, with Harriet and Rin and Walter the black slackers shaping its darkness. I guess a little truth resides in both perceptions. When I get back in my truck, however, I feel as if something hard and confusing as surf has washed over me and left me behind in calmer water.

I am not sure if that is because it's my family, or because the Kitchen holds a bunch of memories of people who are close to me or were once, and this cradles the courage a little.

Or maybe it was the boiled dinner.

You must not map relief too closely.

A piece of cardboard from an Old Gold carton, stained with chicken shit, covered in Manny's spidery handwriting, is propped on the truck's wheel. He is sorry for what he said at the Squire. He wants to know if I could loan him eighty bucks so he can take out ads in the *Chronicle* to market his eggs.

I crumple the cardboard, flip it into the honeysuckle.

I drive around town for forty minutes, calling for Eb at his usual pissing posts.

I go down Route 28 all the way to Eastham and back.

I do not see him anywhere.

Chapter 10

Reverse Jonah

41 degrees 13'N; 69 degrees 01'W

41 degrees 11'M;69 degrees 02'W

Larry's PX at three in the morning in decent weather used to be so full of guys in black rubber boots you could barely make out one side from the other for all the cigarette smoke.

Now I count only a dozen fishermen. Still, looking at the counter from the booth I am sitting in is like sighting Monomoy through a June fog. Maybe that is what's really wrong with fishing, I reflect hazily; everybody's profit margins are being eaten up by R. J. Reynolds.

Whereas luck smiles on the healthy, the pneumonically correct.

Then again, I gave up smoking five months ago, if you don't count the half-butt I had last night, and I have been losing money ever since.

Hooker's bunk was hard. My head aches with dozing. I

need coffee the way a junkie needs dope. At least I never turned to smack as many of the New Beizh deckhands did when fishing soured.

At least I never pulled the weekend B&Es, or ran the boat south for square grouper.

My watch reads three fifteen. I am annoyed because Billy is late. Also every molecule in my lungs is repeating "Camel Filter" in a whiney sort of tone.

I signal repeatedly for the waitress to warm up my mug but while she goes to the booth of gillnetters every minute or so she never even glances at my booth. Finally I walk to the counter and Ronie pours me coffee from a fresh pot. Sim Pierce bulls in just then and orders the corned beef special. I slap his shoulder and make some vapid comment about cholesterol. He looks at me and around the beard his face changes the way oak reacts to frost. Then he turns and walks away.

Yeah well fuck you too, I think, and my stomach glows with anger.

Taking my coffee back to the booth I tell myself there is no point in worrying about this. Commercial fishermen are solitary and cranky by nature and the Chatham bunch are worse than the rest. If I had a buck for every feud these guys dreamed up against each other I could buy myself a new GM tomorrow.

But I thought me and Sim were friends.

The anger blows off but the coffee does not taste so good now. I repeat to myself that I should not take this to heart. I pick up the *Stranded Times* someone left at my booth and turn automatically to the court reports. That is what Chatham people do with the *Times;* go to the court reports to see who they know got into trouble. Then the obits, to see if the trouble was fatal. Finally they read the AA listings to choose, from the 313 weekly meetings on Cape Cod, one that best suits their schedule.

"A drinking town with a fishing problem," Casey Ryan once called Chatham.

Sure enough, I find myself halfway down the Second District Court listings. Someone underlined my name twice with a red felt-tip.

CAHOON, Oliver L., 36, 17 Crow's Pond Lane, Chatham: assault, disturbing the peace, Sat. Dec. 2 in Chatham. Continued 6 months without a finding: costs, $50 fine.

I don't see Sim getting upset about that.

Somebody three booths down says, "Well Flickie asked Thatch to replace that EPIRB last spring, but he wouldn't." Somebody else says, "He got all his dough tied up in that development, it don't leave much for radios."

On page eight a fat headline announces the Price-Shoppe hearing tomorrow. I probably will miss it, assuming the weather stays fair and the engine behaves and the nets don't hang.

The article does not say much. The Cape Cod Commission is supposed to deliver a report to the town conservation commission. The report will say whether they are going to rescind their approval of the Price-Shoppe project. The CCC is worried that the mall might screw up an abandoned cranberry bog near the site, or the water table, or the traffic on Route 28.

This last item is a joke, because it would be impossible to screw up 28 more than it already is, in the summer.

The Cape Cod Commission wasn't supposed to get involved in this but the Price-Shoppe people expanded their original plan and the local tree-huggers complained and then the commission stepped in. It is all a lot of small-town fussing, as far as I can see. Erin and I own water and clamming rights next door, but how the hell Sibley and the Cape 11 reporter think that affects Price-Shoppe, I cannot imagine.

Billy shows up as I am putting away the *Stranded Times*. I tell him, Get a coffee to go. The coffees I drank are cavitating in my stomach. Or maybe it's the linguica from last night.

After I use the head I call the fisheries service from the pay phone to tell them we are starting another fishing day. Then I go out to the truck.

As I turn up the heat and clear some of the crap off the passenger seat I find myself wondering where Eb got to. I am so used to him sitting beside me on the mound that not having him there creates a question—Where is Eb?—that has more heat and mass to it than anything uttered by the stiffs in Larry's.

But the thousand tiny queries of a fishing trip crowd in at that point and I forget him again.

* * *

Two hours later we have cleared the bar and *Hooker* is heading east-southeast on a course that should bring us to the 700 grounds in four hours and twenty minutes.

The new fuel pump is running well, although in the paranoia of worry I keep imagining it is slowing down, turning rough.

It reminds me of something Caitlyn said, right after we had Sam, and were lying awake every night fretting about crib death. Listening to the little organism snuffle wispily in his sleeping suit between us.

"It's only when you're listening you hear trouble," she said. "Everything is fine, if you don't listen."

I press down the thought of Caitlyn, and Sam, like drowning it in the billion other possible thoughts the brain might make. It gets lonely enough out here without thinking about them.

My gut muscles cramp up. I want to break the radar housing, crack the window, punch something the way I did when I was talking to Caitlyn in the car.

I jam my strong hand in the pocket of my coat.

The diesel exhaust roars evenly through its pipe.

Billy sleeps on in the pilot berth below.

I concentrate on the instruments, the green glow from

the Furuno, the reddish compass light, the liquid crystal numbers of the Loran. The noise of the autopilot is like the noise of a heart monitor, each click confirming that for now, this instant, the patient is alive and functioning properly.

The various muscles slacken.

Heading 144 degrees. On the radar the GRS buoy smears its Racon signal west of us. An oceangoing tug with a big barge shows clear to the north. The tug's skipper, on VHF, is trying to raise a pal on a Bouchard barge near the canal. The Coast Guard wants everybody to know they are getting incomplete readings from the weather buoy on Georges Bank. They tack on a reminder about the haddock-spawning areas now closed near Cultivator Shoal.

Main gear oil pressure 160, engine oil 35. R.P.M. steady at 2000. Barometer 30.10. The weather report calls for a solid fifteen to twenty northwest with seas running four to six offshore. Through the portside windows of the wheelhouse I watch the waves run at me like hockey players, long black forwards you do not notice till they check you out of the way. The quarter moon, sinking low to the southwest, showers coins in its own image on the swells' shoulders. The spray, as *Hooker* fights her way between checks, shows briefly against the darkness, lime to starboard, raspberry to port as it is illuminated by the running lights. The waves crunch at the bow and hiss at the stern, and the Gardner roars in the background in a rhythm that flirts with chaos but then does not quite touch it; and in that restraint lies safety, and a kind of peace.

The anger is gone, mostly.

It feels good to leave harbor and head for open water.

Now off the port bow something different happens, as if the darkness were posing itself a question. In half an hour it will be the color of a dove's breast as the sun finally commits to the process of dawn.

By seven it is fully light. We are past the ship channel and I roust Billy so I can coach him in the basics. I took him out on a pleasure cruise once but that was before I turned *Hooker* into a dragger and anyway you don't learn shit on a pleasure cruise.

You do not learn anything until you have to do it yourself and make it work.

I demonstrate the winch and how the doors and blocks and chains and reel are supposed to operate. He is not stupid and he takes it in but he also keeps taking cigarette breaks, sheltering the hot tip in his fist the way he always does and finally I growl at him, "Leave the fuckin' butts *alone* when you're working," and he replies "Keep your shirt on" and draws his mouth down just the way Caitlyn does.

Halfway through showing him how to shut off the reel and put the brakes on fast in case of trouble, I hear a strange sound. It's like the long gasping sigh that comes right after someone has held his breath for too long. The sound fades back into the wind as if they were related.

Billy looks to port, the wrong way. I glance at the engine exhaust because that is the quarter from which I expect weird noises. The sound came more from starboard though, and even before I look in that direction the connection is made, the flavor of memory released.

"Wait," I tell Billy. I stand on the starboard gunwale, holding on to the stays and the aft corner of the wheelhouse for balance.

It takes a few seconds. *Hooker* is rolling quite a bit. The swells are real Atlantic here, long green-black geology of ocean, small mountains with ten thousand replicas of themselves carved strongly fractal on each plane, repeating in place the cycles and periods of foreign wind.

Then, amid the solid mountain colors, I catch something even more rock-like, and vast; a low flat island that moves yet does not move in the normal way. It is black and gray-blue with oddly delicate patterns torn on the slope of it—a roughly defined ecology that possesses direction.

It is heading across our bows.

The sea itself looks like it is starting to solidify and turn to muscle as a whale moves on a northeasterly course one hundred yards away, straining through its submerged mouth the microscopic fish.

A feather of steam forms directly above the highest mound of its back, bends southeast with the wind, and vanishes.

A faint rainbow sketches itself overhead; and the sighing sound, which is exactly what it sounds like, the accompaniment to breath, wafts across us a moment later, rich with shrimp.

I run into the 'house and pull the throttle back, knocking off the autopilot with one elbow. *Hooker* is a heavy boat but she is no match for a whale. Joe Hansen hit a right whale once going full tilt for harbor and it split his stem and stove in some planks and he barely made it back to Chatham. My boat floats higher on the swells, absorbing added roll as each wave has more time to affect her.

"Jeezus!" I hear Billy yelling, "Jee-zus!" He stands where I was, a Merit stuck inert in his mouth.

Now he comes forward into the wheelhouse. Before us the whale does not rise and fall as the swells obscure and reveal him but moves smoothly in the same direction he was always going. We do not affect him at all, though surely, with his facile sonar, he knows we are there.

I turn the wheel to starboard, watching the shaft of the tuna harpoon dip across the horizon of his body; wondering idly how whalers dared stand up in the bow of a rowboat, throw a tethered spear into that back, and expect to make the tether fast and be towed across the ocean by a whale and survive. Not for the first time I think those men possessed a type of courage that I simply do not have.

"It's a sperm whale," Billy whispers, "I know it."

Billy has been spending too much time on Chatham Main Street.

"It's a northern right," I tell him. "The plume is V-shaped. Look—"

Well to starboard and maybe three hundred yards off another plume rises, turns to rainbow, and vanishes. Another glimpse of black isle among the sea's hard change. I hand Billy the glasses and goose the throttle back to 3000.

Then the first whale sounds.

The island part of him, now a cable's length off our port bow, arches. His back cracks the crest of the highest swell. "Check it *out*," I breathe, turning Billy manually. The ridges and scars of the whale's hide grow clearer with height. This animal has had close encounters with a gillnet. I can see the distinctive angles where it tore itself through the sharp polypropylene mesh. It was because of those encounters the feds closed the Cape Cod Bay fishing grounds to gillnetters, although in fact most right whales get killed by ship-strike, not gillnets. The scars recede into the perfect cord of his movement, following each other faster and faster into the growing roil of water.

And now the bulk of his weight is deep, and hangs vertically. He curves his tail around to bring the rest of his mass into line. Water cascades off his skin, sounding like a fountain among the wider squish of sea. The flukes twist, presenting themselves in three-quarter profile: two bleached, scalloped billhooks of gristle, each six or eight feet long, sliding faster and faster toward the surface until, in a smack of foam, they disappear altogether.

Forty seconds later we cross the smoothed water and the slight sheen of oil where the whale was. Already the wind is roughing it up. In another minute no trace will be left.

"Shee-it," Billy says. "That was a sperm whale, you can't tell me it wasn't."

"Don't smoke in the wheelhouse," I tell him, and go below to check the engine. I wish to hell Walter had agreed to come with me instead of Billy.

* * *

But everything has an opposite or it could not define itself.

If one postulates a Jonah there has to be an anti-Jonah; a man who brings luck instead of scaring it away.

A lot of people do not believe in luck. I call luck the way things running out of control can fuck you up royally, and touch wood, just in case.

In any event, the first part of that day, I start to think maybe Billy is an anti-Jonah.

He is not a great deckhand. He can handle machinery—he is a welder, after all—but has no clue about the theory of dragging, so all the little details have no matrix to unite them in his head.

All I really need him for is to steer a straight course while we are trawling, yank the throttle back if we hang, push the fish around with a shovel. Billy grew up on the Cape and most Cape boys can do that much.

The first drag, down the 708 Loran bearing, nets us the usual crop of weed, crab and rocks.

When I take her two miles away, by a wreck on the sixty fathom contour, the fishfinder suddenly populates itself with green-blue echoes. I spin her right around—we are far enough from the closed area not to worry excessively about position—and shoot the trawl almost on top of those echoes.

This is rough ground, a lot of medium rocks and shell but no big hangs to speak of, if you exclude the wreck. I goose the throttle when we start to haul, to kickstart the net. Then I slow down to 1800 R.P.M., which translates to three knots, fast enough to pull rollers over medium rocks, but not so fast that it will destroy the gear.

The winch labors and runs slower than normal when we haul back a half hour later. When the cod end comes aboard it is bulging with gray sole.

I release the purse string and our catch fills the deck, a glistening, nacreous mound, from gunwale to gunwale.

I whoop and yell, standing there with the purse string in one hand and fish up to the ankle of my seaboots.

For a moment the land and all its confusion are gone. All that exists is that shivering kicking plenty of fish and a sense of rightness, that after all the trying I finally figured out how the rhythm of this worked.

Whooping and yelling and jumping up and down till my seaboots slip and I have to grab onto the cod end of the net to save myself from falling.

* * *

Billy doesn't even know that gray sole are pale and lean, while ocean dabs are brown and thin; or that pollock are darker and leaner than cod. He rips a market cod, gaffs a pollock out the gate before I can stop him.

The gulls shriek in solid, self-obsessed approval. They form a gray cloud above us and whiten our oilskins with guano.

The earlier joy is gone, dissolved by the responsibilities of such a catch. We have real work to do now, sorting the fish we can keep from those we have to scrape out the gate.

Billy says the handle of the gaff is too rough and it hurts his hands. I hand him rubber gloves. I find myself missing Pig, the way he put his back into it. I even miss his moustache, his porno jokes, the oiled flesh of his magazines.

But in two months of dragging with Pig we never hauled back on a net like this. The dumb superstition returns— maybe Pig was holding us down. Maybe he had to retreat to the mountains for me to catch fish again. It makes no sense but the sea does not always make sense and what people do does not make sense.

If superstition helps me catch fish I will happily believe in Cait's witches, and her women's Internet club.

I slot in the checkers. These are two-by-eight boards that divide the after deck into shallow boxes. Then I leave Billy to sort the rest of the fish. Not into the hold, I tell him, but into the different boxes so I can inspect them later. I do not want to lose sight of this school, I want to haul back on another load like the last.

I pound *Hooker* at full revs back to the first Loran position.

The fishfinder shows a lot of echoes still down there. Setting the auto I shoot the net into the swells. Then I put Billy on the wheel and return to the afterdeck, watch cap pulled down against the increasing bite of northwesterly.

* * *

I go back to the wheelhouse twenty minutes later.

I figure we got almost four boxes, or four hundred pounds, of mixed gray sole on that last run. We got another box of fluke for some reason; I have never seen fluke out here before. Also, one box of skate.

There was a box of cod too, but most of that went back into the drink. My blood circulates a little faster than usual, and I take the wheel from Billy, who is steering slack in waves that are slowly getting bigger.

I reckon the swells are just under six feet by now, coming at us like kine foam-flecked from the long fetch they had from Acadia.

It is starting to ice up on the parts of the deck that don't get washed frequently by waves coming through the freeing-ports. We go outside again to haul back and Billy takes one step and his feet shoot out from under him.

"There goes my Merits," he complains, pulling the crushed pack from his hip pocket.

I dig out the Halite and spread salt evenly around the sheltered patches of the deck.

ORLEANS COURT

BLATCHFORD, Eliza L., 33, Screecham Way, Wellfleet: breaking and entering in the daytime with intent to commit a felony, N. Eastham, Dec. 2, hearing scheduled. Drunk and disorderly, same date, charge dismissed. Possession of marijuana, Barnstable, Dec. 2, hearing scheduled.

CAHOON, Oliver L., 36, 17 Crow's Pond Lane, Chatham: assault, disturbing the peace, Dec. 2 in Chatham. Continued 6 months without a finding: costs, $50 fine.

PETERS, George J., 36, 351 Middle Rd., Chatham: assault, disturbing the peace, Dec. 2 in Chatham. Continued 6 months without a finding: costs, $50 fine.

LARSEN, Lars, 44, 923 Mallebarre Rd., Chatham: assault and battery on a police officer, assault with deadly weapon (beer bottle), Nov. 28 in Orleans, charges filed. Disturbing the peace, OUI, continued 6 months without a finding, anger class.

Chapter II

The Cutter

69 degrees 18'W; 41 degrees 25'N

The next haulback is two-thirds of the first. I certainly would not complain about this. The one after is poor. The fourth is also two-thirds of the first except that it is mostly skate and includes a full box of cod.

The cod are all market and scrod. They puke up small brown crab.

The cod all go out the transom gate.

The ache in my left shoulder grows as I gaff and pitch them out. My good mood dims. This is probably because I am tired now from the physical work. When you don't catch fish you don't work so hard, and fishing is hard enough, from the constant balance and tension in the brain, the braying of the diesel against your ears, the exhaustion of solitude, without having to bend and lift like a stevedore.

But still it is a goddam waste, this dragging game. The

cod sink gently into the waves and half of them do not move their tails as they go.

Longlining was different. With longlines you caught only fish that wanted your bait and could bite on that size hook.

You brought them up slowly enough that the pressure drop did not hurt them and there was no weight of net to crush their smooth strong flesh.

I turn, leaning on the gaff, holding on with my good arm to the port gallows frame. I remember Caitlyn calling me a longliner, as if it was an insult. Sibley called me a hook fisherman too. It hits me with a kind of wonder that I used to be a longline fisherman and now I am not.

I have too much money tied up in dragging gear to go back.

Looking over the waves that are getting high enough to hold a lot of blue night in their troughs, I remember that I used to fish eight tub trawls on this stretch of shoal.

* * *

They were trawls of one-eighth-inch yellow nylon line, twelve hundred feet in length. They carried gangions, three-foot sections of thinner black line spliced in every six feet. On the end of the gangion was a shiny Mustad hook made of Norwegian stainless steel and measuring a half inch between barb and shank. On the end of the hook was a salted sea clam for bait. I hired Cait's friend Ellen and George's brother to work for me three days a week, baiting half the longlines ashore while Pig and I were out setting the other half.

In those days I would drop one end of the line on an anchor with a high-flyer buoy marking that end. I would run the boat up-tide while the line hissed down a stainless steel chute bolted to the transom. When we got to the end I would drop the other anchor with its high-flyer.

Between the two anchors the longline sat patiently on the bottom, five, twenty, forty fathoms down. The fat, slow-moving cod, catching a whiff of clam, vaguely would decide to forgo the sand lance, the juvenile crab. They swam over in the pelucid depths, opened wide their goateed mouths, and ate the bait.

Then, a tide or two later, I would kiss up to the high-flyer and gaff the buoy in. I looped line around the hauler and wound it over the boat's side while Pig coiled on the after deck. The waves reared up to an angle where they became a kind of bottle-green magnifying glass and I saw the flash of belly as the fish rolled and twisted away from the lifting line, their amber eyes resigned, compliant even.

I gaffed them hard, holding the twisting bodies against the chute while the hauler ripped the hooks from their jaws. Then I pitchforked them onto the deck. The bycatch we got in the warmer months was usually skate and dogfish; these went into their separate boxes.

It was not pretty or humane or anything but the fish were kicking and healthy when they came into the boat. You could brake the hauler and free the undersized fish without hurting them much. Even in summer, when you had to cut the gills off the fish you kept because of worms, those cod were clean and sweet.

Things changed. The hundred-foot stern-trawlers out of Gloucester and New Bedford and Point Jude fished with nets so wide and heavy they scraped down all the humps and valleys of good ground, turning it flat and featureless as a parking lot. Northeast of the BB buoy there used to be an area called the Figs that was all hummocks and valleys thirty fathom down. Now it is level and without relief. The same is true of a ground we called the Peaks. Except for the hard bottom, where boulders and wrecks kept the big boys out, the fish could hide nowhere. The nets sucked out the cod and the husbands and daughters and cousins of cod so hard and complete that entire generations were wiped out in a few years.

The government stepped in afterward. They could not

stop the big trawlers that had done the damage because the banks had loaned the trawler companies hundreds of millions of dollars and the banks would get mad.

The government could not afford to anger the banks.

Instead, the National Marine Fisheries Service crafted rules that affected everybody equally. This meant it was the little fishermen, who did not have banks backing them, who went broke. People like the longliners, who fished clean, or the gillnetters, who did not hurt things much.

And now here is my boat, rigged for dragging: sweeping the bottom, in a nickel-dime replication of what the big boys do, but sweeping it just the same. Scraping up every goddam speck of life that will not fit through four-inch mesh on the wedges of ground the big draggers cannot reach.

Winching up the life that seeks shelter beside the boulders and wrecked ships, and throwing back two thirds of it dead or dying.

Going on to the next ground and doing the same there.

I shake myself, as Eb would do. I am cold. My fingers are numb in their rubber gloves. My stomach rumbles again. I let go gas discreetly down the bitter wind.

Ice is building a little on the wheelhouse roof. I need to watch that. Every half-inch of ice built up is a ton of added weight to a boat this size. If I do not pay attention, if I do not hammer it off, before I know it the boat will have five extra tons on top and suddenly she will roll in a bigger wave and not come back.

I climb down to the fishhold and look at the flange but no ice is visible and no cracking I can see.

Maybe that Might-E-Foam made a difference.

Back in the wheelhouse I get ready to shoot once more.

* * *

Eight hours later we have made five more haulbacks with steadily diminishing returns. Night has fallen and no moon is visible but you can tell by the decklights and from the boat's motion that the waves run five feet and better.

The barometer in the cabin reads 30.04. The forecast has changed to small boat advisories, possible gale warnings later.

It is time to go home.

I make sure everything is hosed down and made fast aft and then set the course: 319 degrees and east of the "BB" buoy. After half an hour the boat's motion is getting rough enough that I take her off auto. I get a better sense, by steering manually, of the pattern and threat of the dark ridges advancing on me out of the north.

Billy smokes in one corner of the wheelhouse. I will not make him go outside in this. I breathe the sharpness of tobacco with delight.

The sight of the foam, mounting up the waves' slopes, blowing into their troughs, crashing against the bow, lulls me somewhat. The engine thunders even, solid. My stomach has settled down. In the wash of optimism from those haulbacks I start to think Doomo was wrong. I got two bad pumps in succession but this one is good. I could drive all the way to Portugal if I had enough fuel.

After an hour of steering I get the feeling that this part of me is a dream. Often I feel like this when I have been standing watch for a long time. It's as if a fake Ollie Cahoon does the grunt work of fishing, responding automatically to the brute stimulus of the North Atlantic. The real me is somewhere else, warm, awake. Smoking, playing with Sam.

I used to have a dream, a real dream. It was the cod that reminded me.

I used to dream of the cod I caught. I swam with them ten fathoms down where all colors have been screened out except greens and grays. They were huge; whale cod in fact, almost the size of blackfish. They finned sleek and comfortable among the rocks and wrecks and banks of kelp. I watched them drop their long chins to scoop up a sand lance, gulp mechanically, repeat the process. One of them was three times bigger than the rest. He was maybe twelve feet long. His scales were like half-dollars, his eyes the size of TV screens.

And down where the croupier tides roll men's bones into chance patterns I was kin to that king cod and yet was separate. I understood him and knew how he thought. He knew I was going to catch him and it made no difference because catching was bound up in swimming, and swimming was bound up in the ocean, and the ocean was what gave us both existence.

In the dream, I loved that cod as fully as one creature could love another.

I used to have that dream every month or so, when I was longlining.

I have not dreamed it once since I stopped.

I steer automatically while this ragweed blows through my head. There is not much traffic around. I have seen only one vessel coming up the Boston lanes and that was on radar fifteen minutes ago. For no good reason I get a feeling that he is way too close on our tail. I look at the Furuno again.

Sure enough the blip is big and square less than half a mile off my stern.

It is far too close for this weather and this area. I look through the aft windows and see him immediately, a pattern of red and green running lights and white range light rolling high, with the nightmare loom of ship between.

I goose the throttle and veer east, twenty degrees off our previous course. I fumble for the VHF, my heart running faster than the Caterpillar. Thinking of all the fishing boats that have disappeared around the shipping lanes without warning or Mayday, nothing left but the likelihood they were ploughed under by a big ship on auto and a radar set on too high a range. Reach to switch on the work spots so he can see us, but before I can flip the toggle the after wheelhouse windows go acetylene with light. The illumination is far more powerful than our working lights. I grab the VHF and a voice blares from the speaker before I can key my own mike; like he was reading my mind, I think.

"Fishing vessel *Hooker*, fishing vessel *Hooker*. This is United States Coast Guard cutter *Cape Pogue*, please respond, over."

The blood thumps in my ears. This feels like being mugged. But we are not in the city or Hyannis even. We are at sea in a half-gale and twenty-five miles off Nantucket Island.

"*Cape Pogue*, ah, yeah, this is the *Hooker*. Is that you on my ass there?"

"Switch and answer channel two-two please."

I switch.

"*Hooker* this is *Cape Pogue*. Please heave to for an inspection party."

"You've got to be kidding!"

This is no way to talk to the Coast Guard. But they don't usually board at night and especially not when the waves are running six feet and over.

"Please heave to now sir. Please alter course to 340 degrees and stay on that heading. Party will come up on your left side sir, repeat left."

I wonder why the feds cannot use port and starboard like everybody else.

I change course, bring the speed to slow.

High up and to port the searchlight moves with the cutter's slower pitch, pinning us into the black cordillera of waves.

* * *

Six figures in orange slickers and lifejackets and bulletproof vests come riding like a circus act in a big inflatable down the fire of searchlight.

Four of them leap the gunwale and enter the wheelhouse dripping cold water while the other two veer off in the raft to keep pace on our starboard side.

The chief coxswain in charge is thin and tall. He wears a pistol in his belt. Two of his crew hold M-16s, a little self-consciously. Billy gawps, awestruck and paranoid, at the guns.

There have been a lot of boardings recently, especially around the 700 line where the patrol boundaries of the 122-foot inshore cutters overlap with those of the high-endurance ships. Enough friction built up as a result that the Coast Guard ordered its boarding officers to treat fishermen better. And this coxswain is polite in terms of words but his tone is awful cold. He asks to see my fisheries permit and catch reports and documentation papers. I switch on the wheelhouse lights, puffing in relief because I filled out the catch papers earlier instead of waiting for harbor as I sometimes do.

We stand around, braced against the roll, which is vicious when we are barely under way like this. The coxswain details one of the crew to check my nets, then asks to see the fishhold. I tell Billy to take him down through the engine-room. It is too rough to screw around on deck and I am not leaving the wheel to Billy while we play footsie with a cutter.

The other Coasties stand around, making comments that are friendly overall. I realize one of them is a woman. The coxswain spends twenty minutes in the hold. When he comes up to the wheelhouse again he drags a transparent garbage bag with four undersize scrod lying stiff and slimy in the gut of it.

I say nothing out loud but inside I am yelling. My stomach locks up. I do not even look at Billy. There is no point in throwing him overboard although he dropped those fish in the hold thinking they were conger or fluke or some other fish that bears no likeness to cod whatsoever.

"I got a new deckhand," I tell the coxswain, spreading my hands as if this were all a prank, "he's never sorted fish before."

Billy says nothing. He lights a Merit and the flame of his lighter is steady.

"Could you put that out?" the coxswain asks.

"What?" Billy says.

"The cigarette."

"It's okay," I tell him in an even tone. "He's allowed to smoke in my wheelhouse."

The coxswain looks at me. His small blue eyes have no joy in them, though that could be the poor lighting. I grit my teeth, wishing I didn't say that.

It came out without thinking because I get the same feeling from this that I got from Sibley, and the cops, and Judge Nickerson.

The same feeling I got from Vaitsos at the bank and the Visa woman with the bitter voice.

But I learned long ago you cannot fight those people. You just agree and do what they say and try to survive around them when they turn on you.

He goes back to filling out papers. One of them is a notice of penalty. He looks at the log to check my fishing days. Thanks to changing gear and my engine problems I have fished only forty-two days of the fifty I am allowed this year.

The coxswain calls the cutter on a portable VHF and tells them he is leaving the "subject area." Then he hands me the papers.

"You have been found in violation of the Magnuson-Stevens Act, Section 108, paragraph A-seven. I'm sorry sir. Please fill out that yellow slip. Even though you're under allowable bycatch, you must pay an administrative fine of two hundred dollars per violation. You have three weeks to mail that in. Also, I checked your safety equipment; three of your emergency flares are out of date. What about the mesh?"

He asks the last question of his crew. An armed deckie promptly hands him another official form.

The coxswain closes his notebook with a slap and turns back to me.

"Thank you very much sir. Please continue on this course until the cutter is clear."

The door opens. The inflatable is alongside. The cutter

keeps us pinned with her spotlight for another ten minutes while they bring up the boarding party and haul the boat inboard. I watch in grudging admiration; it takes a certain quality of seamanship to do that well in such seas.

Then the searchlights fade. Now they are just a bunch of yellow decklights, a range light and a dark shape against the blacker canvas of sea.

Five minutes after that the cutter is gone and nothing is left of her but the blip on radar to prove she existed at all.

* * *

I steer 319 again once they are out of our circle of water.

"Shit, Ollie," Billy says after a while, "I'm sorry."

"Forget it."

"But I was the one—"

"It's not your fault, goddammit!"

"You're pissed."

"I ain't pissed at you."

"It's really hard," he complains, "there's so many *kinds* of fish, and they all look the same."

He lights up a cigarette and the yellow flare of his match blows my night vision to pieces.

My stomach aches as badly as it did this morning. I am gripping the wheel like it is somebody I am trying to strangle. I am not mad at Billy. That is a fact. It's the coxswain and the Coast Guard I want to throttle.

It's the big trawlers from Gloucester and New Bedford and Point Judith, Rhode Island.

And, to be honest, it's Caitlyn. I know she has nothing to do with the Coast Guard, but different angers are like cousins, one always reminds me of the others.

Anyway I can feel the angers combine in me and harden into something as solid as a hunk of coal. Like a piece of coal it wants to burn and be translated by fire to the warm life it once enjoyed, and if it has to it will transform everything around it to reach that point of flame.

Those fish were not my fault. I did not put them in the hold. I work hard every hour of my waking life trying to keep my family going yet Caitlyn wants us to separate because what I am doing is not enough.

I grit my molars. The wheel aches in my hands. I push consciously against the anger, its alien rigidity, visualizing it as a presence to be squeezed out by the force of will until not enough space is left inside for the both of us.

You cannot both hold anger and operate a fishing boat well.

But I can see her this time. She is bent over the varnished counter, her black hair banked like starlings around her face, touching the wiccan medallion at her neck. Bucket hands her a Black Russian, the smile slick as goose shit on his mouth.

My molars ache.

My stomach feels like it's bleeding slowly inside.

I concentrate on r.p.m., water temperature, the oil gauges.

I use the head and that helps release my stomach but it is still tense when I check the dead reckoning against the Loran.

My hands use too much force on the controls when I change course for the Chatham sea buoy.

Abeam of the GRS buoy I go below and put a testing finger on the fuel pump. This still runs nicely cool. A picture of Caitlyn shuts down behind my eyes.

I open my right hand and flex tension loose.

Hooker rolls and rises, falls and pitches, galloping steadily for home. Her sharp bow cleanly parts the big waves and her curved buttock lines ride them over and down and over again. The water crashes against the bow, rushes aft, and the wind whisks away its noise at the stern and then the same stanza comes again, always the same—crash, rush, sigh—always different, in its details of texture and scan.

Roughly four hundred and sixty pounds of gray sole and three hundred of ocean dab, sixty pounds of skate and one hundred of pout lie iced in the fishhold.

We should clear twenty-eight hundred bucks, even after the fine, assuming prices hold.

By the time the harbor buoy is abeam I have let go the wheel and put the auto back on. Also I have cooled down to where I can admit that it is only one person I am really angry at.

The fisherman who gets snotty with the Coast Guard. The guy who did not put money aside when most trips long-lining brought in two or three grand.

The asshole who drank it away at the Squire, or loaned it to Manny, which was equally wasteful.

Sam stares at me from the picture tacked over the chart table, passive through the clear gel of Polaroid.

The last crumbs of the coal anger fritter to dust in my head. The only thing in that space now is Polaroid details: the wedge of freckles on each wing of Sam's nose, the way he hitches up his jeans that comes from aping the way I do it.

His love of small trains and gingerbread.

Even in the rose refraction of the compass light you can see he has eyes that are what diamonds would look like if you fired them igneous from chocolate. They are Cait's eyes; in that similarity I find myself unconsciously thrusting my knees against the forward console, trying to push the boat faster, because I want to see Sam, I want to see Cait.

I need to stop this separation.

The boat lines up on the radar path of channel buoys. It is half-tide over the bar and the tide is ebbing, with the wind, rather than against. We should have little trouble over the shallows tonight.

I unclutch the autopilot and guide my boat toward the steady sweeping scythe of Chatham light.

Chapter 12

41 degrees 42'N; 69 degrees 56'W

I like waking up on a boat.

Many people do not. Lots of people come out of sleep all disoriented and don't like to find their bedroom shifting delicately beneath them. But I wake up pretty alert and it makes me happy to open my eyes on *Hooker*'s bulkhead and feel her restless, rocking—waves French kissing the waterline, wind chewing at my radar scanner—afloat and alive all around me while I remain dark and dream-packaged in my bunk.

Dr. Hinckley would say it's a "womb thing" and she probably would be right. But the sea is a womb thing too, looked at on a good day when it is sunny and soft.

Life is a womb thing, if you want to push it that far.

I lie there for a few minutes. *Notes on the Ecology of Cape Cod* rests in the gear hammock beside my bunk. I pick it up but I am not in the mood for reading about plants and fish and quickly put it down again. I have a hard-on, as I usually do when I wake up. This often points my thoughts in a specific direction. I wish Caitlyn were here but she is not and I do not wish to dwell on that so early. Instead I roust through my shore jacket. The J. Crew catalogue is still rolled in the right-hand pocket. I flip toward the rear and brake my thumb among the glossy pages of the waffle-knit woman.

I call her that because I first saw her in the waffle-knit section of the catalogue. She is thin and obviously small, with a fine mouth, bent in a "V," and large slanted eyes. Through all her blonde and clotheshorse attitude she exudes a sense of curiosity, of being interested in you for reasons other than career. She has an ass as lean and mathematically elegant as her mouth and breasts fresh as the first warm day in April, barely visible through the top of the garment she models. I rub myself against the sheet for awhile, staring at her, but odd thoughts keep intruding—did Cait go to work? is Eb home yet?—and the worm of sex cannot twist itself free.

Also this is the Christmas edition and they dressed her up in a Polarfleece that makes her look like one of the Volvo women on Main Street.

I put the catalogue aside. I get up and pile coal in the cabin's tiny heating stove. I have not been paying much attention to hygiene lately, and sweat and the slime of a thousand dead fish are powerful on me. I open the saltwater intake, start the water pump and hop around the head, holding the cruel nozzle in one hand, scrubbing at the worst parts with green soap, yelling "Hoop! Hoop!" the way Jack Sibley did when I kicked him.

The water feels like rods of surgical steel pricking at my skin. When I come out of there I am less smelly and my erection is gone, possibly forever.

I find a pair of jeans and a clean flannel shirt and get dressed close enough to the coal stove for the heat to twist my body hair. I put on my watch cap and make coffee and warm up the cans of sweet corn and lima beans. This food likely will give me trouble later but it's all there is to eat. I start up the diesel and scarf every morsel, sitting on the pilot stool, looking through the wheelhouse windows at the faded grain of sky already blurring into afternoon. Listening to NOAA Weather confirm what I already knew: The wind is northwesterly, twenty-five gusting to thirty-five, and a little too stiff for going out today.

The same is forecast for tomorrow.

It is past three by the time I shut down the boat and row to the fish pier. Johnny Norgeot gives me my check for two days earlier: $364.08. I ask him what the prices are in New York today and he says, about the same. The prices have been pretty good recently because Thanksgiving is over and people are buying fish again, instead of turkey. Also supplies are low because it is almost winter and fewer boats are out. All of this means that the consumer pays $7.99 for a pound of flounder and we'll get two bucks seventy while Johnny gets twenty cents and the Fulton mob pockets the difference. But at least the prices are high.

I call home from Johnny's phone. Cait answers. She did not go to work today. When I hear her pick up, the thin ceramic protection built up around me by all the cares and discipline of fishing simply crumbles. "Hi, Ollie," she says. "How was the trip?"

Her voice is far away as Spain. She could be working for Visa.

The shell forms again around my own words.

"Good. Eb get back?"

"Haven't seen him."

"Can I talk to Sam?"

"He went to Ethan's. They're going to hockey practice together. Where are you?"

"At the pier. Listen—" (holding that protection tight). "I'd like to come over tonight, see Sam—I'd like to see you too," but already she is mumbling, "No."

"We're not gonna be here," she continues. "Ellen said, stop by for a bite when I pick Sam up and I said I would."

"Aright."

"I'm sorry, Ollie. But aren't you going to the hearing?"

I'd forgotten about the hearing, probably because I figured I would be offshore when it happened.

"I guess," I say. Drawing a deep breath. "I just wanted to ask, Cait—what the fuck are we doing?"

No words for a beat or two. She is chewing something, probably Raisin Bran. She eats it with her fingers out of the box.

"I'm not sure," she admits finally. "But whatever it is, we should give it a chance to work. Don't you think?"

"But Cait," I say, "it doesn't feel good."

"It always feels bad," she replies, "that's how you know something is wrong."

"I don't want to feel like this."

"If you want something enough," she replies, "it'll come true."

I snort at that. She asks me to put money in the bank so she can pay the phone bill. We agree I will take Sam tomorrow. I hang up, feeling like I want to go back to the boat and start the engine and go offshore—just head east, for as long as I have fuel, into eventual morning.

Instead I walk around the Down Cape building toward the truck. This route takes me past the back of the ice shack. A splash of graffiti three feet high has been sprayed on the shack's shingles. The words "COMMANDO LIVES" are spelled out in dripped blue letters.

It takes me a few seconds to figure out why that phrase is familiar. The airplane dream, I think, and a little bug steps up and down my spine as I automatically remember the thousand spooky stories told where dreams predict what happens.

Of course it works the other way, too. And I understand that the reason I dreamed that phrase was *because* I had noticed it, at some point, scrawled on the ice shack wall.

I wonder if whoever faked those transmissions painted the graffiti also.

I climb into the truck and it will not start. I get the engine going with ether but it takes almost a quarter can this time. Maybe the carburetor is building up a tolerance.

Once the engine is running I ride sleepily past the millionaires' beach houses toward the lighthouse. Eb might be there, I think. Sometimes he hangs with a pack of mixed hounds on the lawn of the abandoned Coast Guard station——tongues out, waiting for the bitches to pass.

On the way I stop to let a Fuso two-ton maneuver beside the old Blish gallery. The words "*Mary Anne* Project Inc." are stenciled on one side. The *Mary Anne* was a sloop belonging to Black Sam Bellamy, the pirate. It sank in a storm off Nauset Beach in the eighteenth century.

Sandy Southack claims he found the wreck last summer. He certainly found in those dank sands a truckload of rusted cannons and ballast. He is setting up that junk as an exhibit in the gallery.

Some in Chatham say that what Sandy Southack is really good at finding is people to trust him, and give him money. If that is indeed the case, he is so good at what he does that people like my sister will not even listen to those who question him.

No dogs are visible when finally I park at the lighthouse. I lean on the balustrade over the bluffs, next to the wreath the Chatham Fishermen's Association put up in memory of Flickie and the other guys on the *Commando*. I have half an hour to kill before the hearing.

On the lighthouse the neon sign that reads "dangerous bar" is extinguished. The sky above the ocean is burnished hard and bright into the haze that distance brings. Way out ahead of me the frilled surf gnaws at the break in the South Beach, as it was doing two days ago, as it always is doing. The buoys lean crazily west around the dogleg of channel leading over the bar; the tide is coming in. The bluffs below me, undercut by strong currents swirling in from the breach, fall ravaged by erosion gullies into Pleasant Bay.

Farther north, Nauset Beach loses three feet a year to the Atlantic, its lighthouses and shacks washed into the same sandy shroud the ocean wraps old ships in. Someday all the lower Cape will be chewed up and sucked under by the greed of sea.

That does not make me feel bad. No one can stop the ocean so there is no sense in trying, no guilt or anxiety in that defeat. Shame comes only when you know you should be fighting, when your fighting could make a difference, yet you cannot summon the energy.

It feels good to lean on the fence and do nothing for a few minutes except notice what is happening in the harbor. Joe Santos's mooring at Laflin's Landing is empty. I guess he left for Maine. The envy comes unexpected and strong because it would be good to leave like that. Simply drop your mooring along with your past life and take the boat Down East to start again.

Beside Joe's buoy I spot what looks like Elliott's gillnetter covered with tarps.

One more boat with her quota of fishing days used up.

I shift around a bit. That corn and beans is starting to whoop it up below. My gut rumbles, and lies down again. My work boot crushes a dried rose from the *Commando* wreath.

A shutter has come loose behind me in what used to be the Coast Guard chief's house. It bangs irregular in the wind, as if the shade of some petty officer had come back and was looking for attention: looking for things to be as once they were.

A cluster of cottages on Andrew Harding Lane huddle together for comfort, the way sheep do after coyotes have picked off a lamb. One of their number was washed into the bay when the tail end of Gisela whipped through here in October. The owners have piled up sandbags to protect the lowermost. Already the cottages look like refugees, surrender implicit in such poor defense. Only the sagging tower over Swear's house, with its patchwork of paint and its widow's walk covered with flagpoles and banners and at least a dozen antennas—TV, shortwave, VHF, CB—flaunts defiance at the doom-drunk water.

The defiance is just that, an empty gesture, a fist raised against the storm, because with a nor'easter and a high tide the waves will shove in the front door and flood Swear's parlor two feet deep in salt water.

A boy and girl scramble from a gully beneath me. Ducking under the fence they glance in my direction, pretending not to, concealing their cigarettes, their locked hands.

I remember Rin bringing up Casey Ryan out of thin air. Now I am standing where it happened.

I was drinking with George at the Squire and Casey was there and before I knew it she and I were dancing and holding each other too tight for friendship.

An hour later both of us were so loaded the walls were moving and we slipped out the back exactly the way Caitlyn and I used to do when Casey was the one trusting and at home.

It was a drink event, though. The booze let us cut through the eleven years between to find a kernel of how we once were still glowing a bit and orange, even in the fog coming off the sea that night. We smoked a joint. We climbed into a gully protected by eelgrass planted there to slow the process of erosion. We got very close to fucking, the juices of one sparking at the fingertips of the other.

A shout came from the top of the bluff. Two people rolled, out of the higher fog, down the gully. They bounced off us and then we all slid in a tangle to the bottom of the cliff. In the soggy eelgrass Casey still held my dick like a talisman in her hand. Her pants were around her knees, her ass white as flour. Rin was doubled over, laughing, and then I was giggling and so was Casey, while a Volvo person Rin probably planned to suck off looked at the three of us with something like horror on his face.

The feel of memory and its shimmer of second remove bring up the sharp suggestion of Rolling Rock. I look at my watch and decide, with real regret, that I don't have time for a beer at the Squire.

Anyway Bucket probably would not let me in, for a number of reasons.

I forage through the cab and find not one bottle. I am going to have to restock both truck and boat.

People

from *Notes on the Ecology of Cape Cod* (Salt Marsh Press, Falmouth)
by Irwin E. Zeit, Ph.D.

Geologically speaking, Cape Cod was the farthest outpost of the empire of glaciers, and since its creation the sea has inexorably sought to diminish what the glacier built. With the predicted rise in sea levels due to the Greenhouse Effect, scientists believe the entire peninsula will be washed away by the end of this millennium.

In terms of human population, however, the progression has gone the other way. Since man first walked west from the Bering Straits to set foot on the Cape and islands approximately 5,000 years ago, the peninsula's population has almost always grown, sometimes at an exponential rate.

The first inhabitants were an Algonquin sub-tribe, the Wampanoag, a peaceful people who subsisted on the ample local supply of deer, turkey, oysters, quahogs and berries, as well as garden maize. By the time the white man came, these Indians numbered at most between two and seven thousand on Cape Cod.

The English zealots who first colonized the Cape were followed by farmers and fishermen in quest of a better material life. Many of them came from the West Country, and it may be that they flocked to the Cape because it resembled the low harbor hills of Barnstaple, Falmouth, and Truro. The English bought some land from the Indians, but mostly they got rid of the original owners by unknowingly importing disease, or killing them on purpose, as in King Phillip's War of 1670.

The next discrete wave of immigration was a result of the Irish potato famine. The Irish emigrating from their starving island moved south from Boston or east from Rhode Island. They were held in contempt by the English, who flocked to join the Klu Klux Klan and set up roadblocks on the Old King's Highway in the late nineteenth century to screen out Celtic migrants. Other immigrants targeted by the Klan, in Falmouth, Mashpee, and Barnstable especially, included Cape Verdean Portuguese; many of these were Portuguese-African mulattoes who had come over as crew on whaling ships. Later, "Red Finns," socialists fleeing the secret police of Czarist Russia, which controled eastern Finland, arrived in West Barnstable. Roadblocks and prejudice could not succeed in keeping the immigrants out but with the collapse of farming after the Civil War, the means of sustaining many of the Cape's inhabitants also collapsed, with population declining from 36,000 in 1860 to 26,000 in 1930. From 1930 on it grew again, reaching the 38,000 mark in 1945.

After World War Two, however, the nature of immigration changed. The consumer economy had weakened ethnic identities and the new immigrants were defined largely by what they did and bought. Now retirees came to Barnstable County from Boston, Worcester, Rhode Island, and the Midwest. The tourism boom catalyzed construction and retail jobs, that in turn attracted people looking for work. From 38,216 in 1945, by 1960 the Cape's population had almost doubled, to 70,286. From 1960 to 1980 it doubled again, to 147,925.

In the 1980s the decay of the inner city and the growth in telecommuting brought a wave of urban refugees who lived on the Cape and worked in or for the city economy. Between 1980 and 1990 the Cape's year-round population grew by 26.1 percent, from 147,925 to 186,605. The size of the influx put increasingly severe strain on the natural and economic infrastructure of the region, causing tensions and policy dilemmas that continue to this day.

It is estimated that by the year 2025 the year-round population of Cape Cod will have topped the quarter-million mark.

Chapter 13

The Price-Shoppe shindig is scheduled for the main hearing room at town hall. This is a white place in the basement with a cheap zinc conference table at one end. Folding white metal chairs are lined up on three sides around a freestanding mike for those who want to testify or just bitch.

The room is bright with people when I slide in, keeping spectators between myself and the table.

I still do not know why everyone expects me to be here.

I feel all of a sudden as if a dozen people have been plotting to get me into this room at this minute and I have not a single reply prepared for questions I cannot imagine anyway.

I almost back out at that point.

No one pays me any mind.

After a while, standing against one wall, sheltered by a folded white screen used to cut this room into sections for smaller hearings, I calm down.

The meeting has just started. The chairman is Luke Poyant. He rustles papers and checks the minutes of every meeting for the last six months. Old Virginia Gomes sits beside him in a flowered blouse, watching people with eyes that are alert as a chipmunk's.

Thatch Hallett, dressed in a tweed jacket, jeans and snakeskin boots, is folded in the front row of public seats to the right of the conference table. His lawyer, Grealey, and Skull sit on one side of him; his wife sits on the other. People say Roya Hallett was born in Iran, and she certainly looks it, with dark eyes and skin permanently tanned. People also claim her family has money. But she never takes part in Thatch's business deals, and seldom goes out in public, and I wonder what she's doing here now. The weimaraner lies under Thatch's legs, muzzle on paw, carefully eyeing Poyant.

Jack Sibley squirms in his metal seat directly behind them and I nod to myself, because it is so obvious: Jack has something going with Thatch on the Price-Shoppe deal.

Ten minutes of procedure follow. A young woman in business clothes and hair cut in a suburban bob bustles through the rear door, followed by a camera crew. The crew's equipment reads "Cape 11 News." Someone says her name: Michelle Meyer. Her lights murder shadows in the room. Everybody perks up. She has a tight figure and eyes clear and blue as a swimming pool. Poyant sits straighter and pays attention to his timing.

Finally he announces "Item four. Now this is an advisory item only. The Cape Cod Commission, uh, they'll present their response to a proposed change in the Price-Shoppe variance off of Marston's Road." He squints at the camera. "This is not normally allowed after a Development of Regional Impact permit was issued—except here under paragraph forty which says, in case of new evidence of significant impact," he points into the audience; "is that what CCC is saying?"

A man with still hands and a tie with seagulls on it nods. "Which we have," Poyant continues.

"Duly noted," Virginia croaks impatiently, and waves at the seagull tie.

The CCC man stands up. He holds a map over his private parts. He has short graying hair and a nervous squint. He opens a chart of traffic flow patterns around Route 28. He hands out copies of Price-Shoppe's environmental impact assessment. He points out test sites on groundwater circulation charts. Some of those sites are where Thatch asked Rin and me for permission to drill.

Thatch's face is the color of bubblegum. He whispers to a man in a business suit sitting behind Grealey. The suit opens his briefcase and passes Thatch a document. It's pretty clear where all this is leading and I can feel people tense, waiting for the punchline.

There is only one lens of fresh water, the CCC man explains. His voice is stronger now. He points to three places in South Chatham where population density exceeds six hundred per mile. So much water is being drawn out of town well sites there that it creates a vacuum. The vacuum has started drawing brackish water from Stage Harbor into the aquifer.

He pauses. The cameraman leans forward, the sound boom moves in. The CCC man reads from his notes. "In light of the increased capacity requested by Price-Shoppe Enterprises Inc., the Board of Commissioners of the Cape Cod Commission will consider designating the area from Oyster River west to Sulpher Springs Pond as a District of Critical Planning Concern, making it subject to stricter standards than when the initial DRI was approved."

Everybody in the hearing room lets out breath in relief because the story will go ahead now. The area he is talking about includes the Price-Shoppe property. Thatch Hallett leaps up like he had springs in his ass. Grealey grabs his elbow, walks ahead of him to the mike. He draws his cell phone, fools with its buttons.

Watching Thatch heightens the unrest in my stomach. It clamps up sharply, then releases. I remember it doing this when the Coast Guard stopped me. Maybe it wasn't the canned vegetables, I think. Maybe it has more to do with loss of control.

"The chair recognizes Roger Grealey," Poyant states pompously. The lawyer ignores him.

"I would like to clarify this a little," he says, looking at Michelle Meyer. "The Cape Cod Commission wants to make this a DCPC area under the establishing statute and under paragraph D. Is that right?"

The Commission man nods.

"So I want to point out—for the record—that construction has started, it started last month, on the Price-Shoppe center?" He folds the cellphone and packs it in his pocket. "My clients—Price-Shoppe Enterprises of Sioux City, Iowa, and Thatcher A. Hallett Construction Incorporated—they have graded the land, they have obtained construction permits from this town. They dug test wells, they have water withdrawal permits from the State D.E.P. Mr. Hallett has built foundations and started work on a ninety-eight-thousand-square-foot building. You are clear on this?"

"That's a real point." Poyant nods seriously. The suit gets up and hands Grealey a note. Grealey stuffs it in his pocket without reading it. "Already we have one point three million dollars down on the land and another eight hundred and thirty thousand in construction costs. Mr. Hallett has put his assets on the line for this project."

Much of the audience goes still. Money is always the source of drama here and that's a lot of drama. "So you understand we *will* fight this?" Grealey sits down. The Commission guy nods understandingly but he only earns thirty-five grand a year and I can tell those millions make him nervous.

Todd Kiernan stands up. He slicks his hair for the camera. Everybody knows what Todd is going to say because he is a real estate broker of the type that likes to call itself a "real-tor" and those people are all buddies of Thatch.

"We're long past the days," he begins. His eyes, like the lawyer's, keep darting back to Michelle Meyer. I do not blame him; she looks a bit like the waffle-knit woman. I wish now I had called her back. "We're long past the days," he repeats, and clears his throat, "where everything has to be, you know, us against them; developers against conservation people. What we all want is, like, a balance. But we still have over nine percent, way over average unemployment here in the winter. Uh, and I just wanted to say that." Thatch, Jack Sibley, and a dozen others clap. A woman stands up and starts to speak.

My gut knots up again, harder. Now the pain comes not from the stomach but lower down.

Poyant interrupts. The woman did not identify herself. She says she works for the Association for the Preservation of Cape Cod. Stumbling a bit, she continues. "I agree with the balance idea. But you have to understand, the foundation of the economy here is tourism. You make this area look like suburban Boston, I mean visually—well, nobody's gonna want to come here." She brushes back her hair. She has big hands, for a woman.

"And then all of a sudden you have ninety-five jobs at Price-Shoppe, but there's two hundred people out of work, in the restaurants, and the Main Street shops."

"Tree-hugger," Thatch whispers loudly. The woman's face goes as pink as his. I bend over slightly, leaning against the folded screen. This posture relaxes the muscles in my gut, leaving some slack around whatever bothers them. The discomfort fades.

". . . we saw what those developers did after eighty-nine, after the crash," the woman is saying. Her voice almost breaks because she is so wound up now. "All the developers who made millions and they were always going on about how we had to create jobs for people here. Suddenly you couldn't find those guys with a microscope. Not here. They were all in Boston, or the Bahamas. But the people who worked for them: *They* were in Hyannis, lining up for unemployment."

Thatch's eyes have gone pale as windows but he says nothing further. The suit, marking points with a gold pen, whispers to him at length. The woman sits down, reaching for her handbag.

Grealey stands up again.

"I know Mr. Hallett has been trying to acquire additional rights, water rights, next door. I'd like to address a question, a purely hypothetical question, to the Commission, if I may: What if he were to buy these rights—would that be enough to destress the aquifer?"

Poyant whispers to Virginia Gomes. My gut rumbles. I wish I had some Maalox.

"You're referring to, uh, Marston's Hollow?" Poyant asks.

"Yes. Parcel number four eighty-eight, to the east of the Price-Shoppe property."

More rustling of plans.

"We would have to verify the assessment," the Cape Cod Commission man says.

Thatch speaks up. "It's a hundred and forty gallon a minute yield." His rough voice carries beautifully in here. "We did six test drills."

The CCC man pauses.

"The report says, you need two hundred. The Price-Shoppe property has a hundred and thirty-two."

"So that would be enough?"

"That might be enough," the Commission man concedes, "but it doesn't address the traffic. When they double-barrel Route 6—"

"You said *water* was the main concern," Grealey points out.

"No, I—"

"Let me phrase it this way. If we got the rights to that

water, would the other concerns mean you'd go ahead with the DCPC?"

"I'm not sure," the Commission man says, "I'd have to consult with the board," but his face is rigid and everybody knows what he's saying is, No.

"I don't understand." Poyant puts both his hands on *Rules of Order*. "You own the land, but you don't own water rights? Then who does?"

"Erin Lopes Cahoon," Virginia Gomes tells him. The assessors' book is open in front of her. One brown bony finger stabs at the page. "Oliver Lopes Cahoon."

"Is either Erin or Oliver Cahoon here?" Poyant asks.

From my casual position against the screen I look up at Virginia Gomes. I wish now I had not come. My gut hurts less now but I want to leave more. I want to run hollering out the door and up the stairs and out of town hall.

I pull myself upright.

Virginia, who knows everyone, spots me when I move. Her finger points right at my face.

"Would Mr. Cahoon care to let us know if he plans to sell the rights, and we could conceivably get this issue resolved right here an' now?"

"Well," I mutter. The TV lights hot as sunburn on my skin.

"Come up to the mike, please?"

I am walking. People move out of my path. The motion relaxes my stomach a bit. I stand in front of the mike.

"Well," I repeat.

Someone yells "Louder!" I hold my bad arm in; this is a habit I never lost. Sweat prickles on my forehead. Lean closer to the mike, which takes my voice and turns it into something more hard and metallic than me. "We decided not to. I mean—"

The faces staring at me seem pale, without feeling. Tight, winter New England faces; sour economy of cranberry, pitchpine, and salt.

A sadness bubbles without warning inside me. It is not gas, it lies higher than my intestines, around the lungs and heart. I think, These people could feel warmth; they are theoretically capable of shouting with joy or screaming in despair. But they have been trained to control such extremes.

I have no idea if the sadness I feel is for my neighbors, or myself who am so like them.

The lens of the video camera does not blink. Michelle Meyer has lips like a tautog. Luke Poyant holds his *Robert's* like it was the Puritan bible: black-bound, bare of mercy.

"I, ah, we got an offer," I say finally. "From Thatch Hallett, here. But Erin—my sister—and me, we didn't really want to."

"Another tree-hugger," someone whispers loudly. It's a fellow behind Sibley. He looks around for approval and nods in satisfaction at the muffled agreement.

"I'm not a tree-hugger," I snap back. "I have—me and Rin, we just have personal reasons."

Nobody says anything.

"I don't *like* tree-huggers," I continue. The APCC woman closes her eyes tiredly.

Poyant remarks, "I think maybe we should tone down the level of discourse here? Todd talked about balance—"

"But you realize, if you don't let go the rights," Virginia interrupts, "then you may stop this development—this important development for the area, maybe it's not perfect but there's a lot of jobs and money?"

"I guess," I tell her.

"You want to conserve the land?"

I stare at Virginia. People say she is a nosy old bird but Harriet likes her and Harriet never tolerated a fraud.

"I don't know," I tell her. "I never believed in that. I never liked the conservationist talk and especially, ah, I never cared for that mentality. You know, you get your piece of the Cape, then you want to close the bridges so trashy people can't come in and buy land around you and bring down the price of real estate."

I bent forward into the mike without being aware. I stand up straight once more. It is important to look calm now, for Michelle Meyer; for Thatch and Sibley. Roya Hallett stares at me; her eyes are black as a dead TV screen. Thatch smooths his beret down and asks softly:

"Then why doesn't he sell? It's a good price. His father didn't want the land—" Thatch keeps looking at Poyant but he is addressing me. "You can't do anything with it. What the hell you gonna do with the rights?"

"Frank—my father—he gave us the rights. He wanted us to have 'em."

"You just wanna stop this." Thatch looks at me directly. His eyes are the color of Sterno flame now. "You put your spoiled little idea of nature, your, your virgin wetlands in front of people. But people got to live—*you* got to live."

The weimaraner lifts its head, smelling something. Maybe it's my panic. I wonder who let Thatch bring a dog into town hall. I brought Eb when I was renewing my family shellfishing license and they threw his ass right out.

"Well you don't wanna get personal, Thatch," Poyant says.

"It is personal, for me," Thatch replies. "You all know that. It'll get personal for him, too—he stops this, and some people don't have jobs come January—they're gonna remember why. They'll remember Ollie Cahoon, and who he is."

I want to throw that right back at Thatch. Anybody with any guts would cut him down now. People lean forward in delight because the story is to end on climax.

Looking at them I no longer feel sadness. Their tightness is hostile. For the right price they would watch this town get paved over from Pleasant Bay to the Harwich line.

I sense now that the massive tension in my digestive tract has been a symptom of mysterious labor, and suddenly here is its product; not gas or shit but anger, shining like black chrome, propagating itself in lines of strain from my asshole all the way to my mouth, exerting force on the contours of my brain.

My mouth opens. I will tell Thatch exactly what I think. He doesn't care for the land, he doesn't care for the people either. Quick money is his goal and—

My jaw won't work. The colors of my rage turn this white room dark. My arms have gone so tight they hurt my shoulder where Ricco twisted it.

During my year in jail I learned the danger of this rage. I trained myself to separate it out, just as I did last night with the Coast Guard—spread it fiber by fiber and then methodically fasten each fiber down and out of harm's way.

Take a long breath.

"I don't have to answer you," I mutter at last.

"Louder!"

My voice goes high and vibrates like a violin.

"I don't have to answer to *anybody*!"

I push the mike away and stride toward the exit. Shoulder spectators to one side. Bang against the Betacam tripod. Michelle Meyer presses herself against the wall, holding a notebook to her breast. "Jesus, man, watch it!" the sound man exclaims.

The door whispers shut behind me. I walk ten paces down the hallway. Leaning against the wainscoting, I slide into a squat. Sweat has soaked my tee shirt. My breath comes hard.

With the kind of clear detachment you get after physical release I understand this truth:

Thatch knew exactly what would happen today.

Not only that, but he went around telling everybody what I would do. Which accounts for the way people have been acting.

Like Sim Pierce. Sim works construction in the deep winter, if there is extra work.

Price-Shoppe is extra work.

I am blind-sided by an urge to go to Marston's Hollow and check if it is still there. That is not rational but when I feel threatened I check the things that depend on me. I go to my boat when a high wind is forecast to make sure the mooring lines won't chafe.

I take Sam for ice cream after the doctor gives him shots.

I visit Marston's Hollow during Fourth of July weekend to make sure no tourist built a bonfire around the flower-apple tree.

It is full dark at this hour so there is no point in going to the Hollow now.

My scalp dries. I remain in the hallway another minute or so. Voices rise and fall, rise and fall beyond the doors of the hearing room.

I should go back in there, I think; but the voice of anger is tired now.

It never sounds as strong after the first effort.

I look back down the hallway toward the hearing room. The dark shape of a squatting man is reflected in the glass door of a different committee room diagonally across the hall. For a splinter of second I wonder who that twisted figure is. The immediate realization that the man is me brings relief so strong it almost makes me laugh—because I look funny, no two ways around it, hunched on the floor like a worshipper in some weird cult dedicated to tying yourself into knots.

I get to my feet carefully.

My stomach makes noises, but it was only the travails of starch after all, and has little to do with undigested rage, or the coldness I sensed earlier.

I use the men's room anyway. Then I go straight out the fire exit to the stairs.

Chapter 14

In the morning I have the beginnings of a head cold.

I can tell it will not be a big deal because it does not have that feel of real weather building up behind. Just a dripping nose and itchy throat.

Sleep has eased the tension in my stomach and replaced it with a zinnia delicacy.

Hooker's stove has gone out and it is chilly and damp in the cabin. I do not feel like a cold shower. I grab clean underwear and row to the pier.

The truck starts on the first try. I drive around a bit while the cab warms up. I tell myself I am looking for Eb, although so much is going on in the front of my brain that I probably wouldn't see him if he walked right in front of me.

The sky is mostly overcast, the clouds gone the color of cavalry swords after a long campaign. They march tiredly to the east. I have a feeling, as I sometimes do when things go wrong on the boat, that all the little details I fucked up in my life, the people I pissed off, the maintenance chores I delayed, are ganging up on me in a way that has suddenly become dangerous.

Just like at sea, when you forget to check a seacock in the spring, and that does not matter till you get caught in a blow, and you have to run the engine hard for hours, and suddenly the saltwater intake hose splits and the valve won't close and boom! you've got three feet of water in the bilge and seven-foot seas and you are a razor's width away from capsizing, which happened to me once.

The hearing is not a serious thing in itself. It's the pressure that bothers me. You cannot live in a town like this if everybody is mad at you. The way people get by is through knowing who to see to get a trawl door welded cheap, or let you slide on insurance here, or have the gang at the dump look out for an old outboard for the quahog boat. That kind of thing.

When you live on the edge, as Cait and I do much too often, it is the people, only the people, who keep you from going over.

I spot a floppy tan dog Eb hangs out with at the lighthouse. A lemon-colored Volkswagen with the Portuguese flag painted on one side and a gay-pride rainbow on the other trundles by on Cedar Street, going ten miles an hour. Manny's profile, the long nose ahead, the gray-feathered hair astern, is clearly visible. I do not wave because he never looks to one side or the other while driving, just aims dead ahead down the yellow line.

On Bridge Street the dogcatcher's truck flies by doing forty and I figure I should give the animal-control officer a call. I buy groceries for the boat at Hamblin's and two six-packs of beer for the truck. Then I head for Queen Anne Road.

*   *   *

The Kitchen scene on a gray morning maybe five degrees above freezing in early December is as normal as it gets.

Walter, collapsed in a wicker armchair, listens to Manu Di-
bango, watches the cooking channel. A thick joint fumes in
his blackened fist.

Rin soaps the baby's peach-colored back in the sink. Harriet, zipped into her neoprene rowing suit, stokes up on coffee and Old Golds to fuel her through the morning kayak.
Outside the windows, next to the sink—the one off-key
note—wind-burned forsythia bloom, yellow symptom of
climatic heartburn.

Today the Kitchen smells of heating oil, bacon, coffee,
and Johnson's no-tears baby shampoo. Rin says, "Cait says
you should call her," and laughs. I don't ask. Deep wrinkles
appear by the side of her mouth when she laughs. She always
had those wrinkles, even when she was a kid.

The shower water is hot and it reams out my sinuses. I
find a bottle of reds and a box of Maalox in Rin's tampon
bag. I eat three of the forsythia-colored tablets. Their lemon
flavor reminds me of Easter cookies.

I ring Cait from the downstairs phone after I have tow-
eled off and dressed. She picks up on the first buzz.

"Hi, where you been? You at the Kitchen?" Those are her
words, but her voice contains far more information. She is
upset, furious, confused, in roughly that order.

"What's up?"

"Give ya three guesses."

"Sam."

She takes a sip of something, most likely herbal tea. She
stopped drinking coffee four months ago. It was, she decided, a passion that might weaken her heart.

"Your son. You know what he did?"

"Cait—"

"He wasn't at Ethan's last night. They didn't go to hockey
together. That was a story he made up. You know what he
did?"

I let it come.

"There was a call from the dog pound. The mutt was

there, of course. They weren't gonna let him out without a fine and I said I wasn't gonna pay it, he's your dog. So your son takes your chaincutter from the workshed and bikes over there after dark with Ethan. Martha is furious at us, by the way. And he cuts the fence and takes the dog. *And* he lets out another twelve dogs that're all runnin' around town now."

My lower jaw hangs a little. I don't know if I am angry or sad. I do know, as the words sink in, that I am kind of impressed.

"We-e-ll—"

"I been on the phone all morning. And guess who was here?"

"I—"

"Sergeant Bearse. The juvenile officer."

"Did he—"

"He says the animal officer won't officially report it. Probably. Long as we pay for the fence. *And* three hours overtime for the dog catcher. There's a letter from the bank," she continues as if this was the same subject, which in a way it is, "registered."

Cait winds down. I tell her I will pick Sam up at school. She wants me to ground him. When I ask to talk to Billy she hangs up.

Rin and Harriet think Sam has balls. They do not offer to help with the dogcatcher's overtime. Harriet goes rowing. Rin says, "Least you could do is argue with her." She thinks Harriet is too old to row. "She could tip over, in this cold water, and that would be that."

"You can survive," Walter says. "Twenty minutes in fifty degree water."

"Why don't *you* tell her?" I ask my sister.

"She doesn't listen."

"That's the thing," I agree. "With Harriet, you can't gumption her into things she's scared of. And you can't scare her out of the other things. Anyway, it's for a good cause."

"The MSPCA." Rin sniffs. Her face is long. She sticks

her thumbnail in the gap between her front teeth and sucks. Zappa looks at me and says something like "Audubon."

I drink coffee, mop my nose, flick the TV to weather channel. The jetstream curves out of Canada into Ohio like a snake dragging its belly across a furrow. The cold air, riding south on the snake's back, loops around in a half circle that includes most of New England. The wind, still blowing twenty-five, is supposed to dwindle; the barometer, rising slightly, stands at 29.98. Tomorrow, more clouds, northeasterly fifteen, snow possible.

I should be fishing today. I have got to go tomorrow. I call home again and this time the machine answers. Cait is screening.

I leave a message for Billy, anyway.

At two o'clock I tell Rin I am going to fetch Sam and she asks to come. Randy borrowed her car and she is getting cabin fever here.

Sam walks out of the Middle School behind a tumble of boys heading for the yellow row of buses. He spots the shit heap, shambles over without enthusiasm. He brightens, though, when he sees Rin. My son squeezes between us, shoveling piles of junk behind the seat. His books spill onto Zappa, who snoozes seriously at Rin's breast. Looking around to ease past the buses I catch sight of Casey Ryan watching us from the Middle School portico. I grin at her. I think, for a moment, she is not going to smile; and then she does, with the kind of "*Jesus*, Cahoon" look she always gives me.

As I turn left down Depot I wonder what to say to my son. I look at him as he chatters about anything except last night. It seems like, at age nine, he spends far too much time avoiding subjects. The curve of his cheek, the arc of his eyelashes appear babyish to me. He wears a nylon jacket that reads "Mondo Destroyers." He carries a Power-morph schoolbag that he didn't own last time I saw him and I get a cold feeling because this is the first tangible symptom of our living apart: that my son should buy a new book bag without my being aware.

His basketball shoes are blown out and his hair needs a trim. But I have not seen him in a few days and I do not wish to start right off criticizing him.

At the corner of Munson he leans way forward and says "Rin, look—" pointing—"there, that guy in the Subaru, he's dressed up like a chicken!" Both of us peer around but don't see him. We are heading up 28 now toward Queen Anne Road. The impulse I got yesterday comes back.

"Let's go to Marston's Hollow," I say.

Rin agrees, popping her gum. Sam shrugs. He would have preferred going to Denny's. He has the sense not to say so.

The road between 28 and Oyster River has been widened for construction trucks. A cement mixer roars the other way, almost forcing us into the verge.

The dirt road into the hollow is the same. Every bump and rut evokes in the small of my back a wince of recognition. We park in an elbow of meadow where cranberry trucks used to load.

When we get out of the truck into the wash of wind, the quiet that used to greet us like a kindly grandparent is gone, replaced by noise from construction over the hill.

I have not been here for a month or more. The shadblow, burned by the hurricane, astonished by wind, are still in bloom but their ivory blossoms are turning the color of mud.

I feel bad for these trees; they are like a woman in love, coming out with her most tender confessions, being frozen by one cold comment from an indifferent man.

The long turning has stolen other colors. The gaudy leaves of swamp maple have gone ochre and gray, mimicking colors to come.

From the russet and green of the old bog a flock of starlings, foraging for the few berries that still grow here, rises at our approach, a pixelated crowd of treble bitching. They fly to the island in the bog's center and thicken the branches of the flower-apple tree that just last month was also pink with false spring.

The lance-leaved violets are shrunken and dying. South of the bog, the salt-meadow grass has taken on the colors of cheap jewelry. Its gold highlights shadows between the platinum trunks of scrub oak, the black-green of pitchpine, the deep scarlet thickets of poison ivy.

Yellow jackets buzz around us. Their presence this late, like that of the forsythia, is a product of the last hurricane. The high winds knocked over shallow-rooted locusts where the wasps were getting ready to hibernate, and the combination of homelessness and a profusion of sweet sap from broken trees drove the yellow jackets wild with the false intimation of spring.

Sam swats at them with his Power-morph bag.

Rin folds Zappa in her serape.

A truck backfires over the hill. The starlings take off again, northward, eastward, twittering. Sam ambles toward the creek that leads to the marsh. Rin follows him. I skirt the bog and walk up a deer path over the hill. The sounds of construction become more distinct. Bulldozers creak and roar, hydraulic hammers pop.

I am used to this noise, living on the Cape. Even so, when I get to the top of the little hill my breath stops for a second or two. The gently rolling stretch of second-growth wood that was here a month ago has vanished. What I see now is a perfectly level field of brown mud that seems to stretch for miles, although I know from the hearing it is 650 feet by 540 with 475 feet of frontage on the road.

Men pray to giant fetishes set in a vast altar of concrete in four lines straight down the middle of the field.

Or that's what it seems like. When my eyes get used to the pattern of activity I realize they are nailing up forms for what will be concrete pillars for the discount superstore. The forms are hollow within their hollowness, for electricity and plumbing. The workers pull strands of cable out of the narrow cores and leave them raw in the sun.

A cement truck with the words "Kiernan Concrete" stenciled on the side pours gray slush into smaller mixers. Two bright yellow Caterpillar graders worry and reverse, worry and reverse, shoving twenty-foot-high leaching tanks into position near a trench. The smooth steel pistons of the graders' shovels are cold and merciless as a scalpel. The iron oxide soil looks like the cut flesh of a huge cadaver. I guess Thatch is not going to halt this project just because the Cape Cod Commission raised objections. The sourness of diesel smoke hits my nose, a friend, an enemy; these machines are close cousins to *Hooker*'s power plant. I wonder if they too have problems with injection pumps.

On the far horizon of cleared land a man on a palomino rides perimeter. The weimaraner forages in his wake. The camo beret stands out against a panel truck's side. Men in anoraks walk up, holding clipboards. The horse frets prettily and Thatch quiets it down. A hunting rifle is stuck in his saddle holster. Thatch comforts the animal as he listens to the engineers' reports.

Stakes prick the outside plan of this construction. The Price-Shoppe stores always have a theme. This one, I read in the *Stranded Times*, is meant to resemble the castle of a Bavarian king. It will have towers and crenelations and ornate fountains.

I retreat sideways down the hill, fading into the woods like a Hollywood Comanche.

They staked out bales of straw across the slope in a long revetment. The sandy soil is washing away despite these measures; every rainfall sluices more of it into the bog and the marsh beyond. I kick at scraps of Tyvek blown over the hill from the development, and push through the deepening sedge. As I move the sounds of machines are absorbed by the trees and billion grasses.

I soak one of my boots in jumping the tidal creek. By the

time I catch up to Rin and Sam the noise of the Price-Shoppe site has become a low murmur, weaker than the gibberish sough of wind in eelgrass.

The sun comes out. Pale spills of it light embers in the shallows to the east. Sam walks down a sandy spit on one side of the creek—it is half tide, and he can do that—scaring what killifish have not yet moved deep for winter.

At night a pair of barn owls that live on opposite sides of the creek hoot at each other across this water like housewives gossiping across an alley.

"North owl" and "south owl," Cait used to call them.

A blue heron panics. It takes off down the creek, desperately trading height for speed. It drags its legs in the water, croaking its old-codger croak. The bird looks like a bad Pentagon project, a bomber that will not work at twenty million bucks a throw.

Rin shows me a bra she found hanging on the apple tree. A B-cup at least. I am not paying attention, though I notice its size. The quahog boat I used for jigging and clamming lies dragged up in the spartina.

Sand has halfway buried the skiff Rin and I used to paddle around in when we were children. The skiff lies beside the work boat, to one side of the path. Her planks are cracked by the sun, and the green and red colors of her paint have faded to antique hues. Her strakes are light, silvery and cracked now so she looks like part of the beach: a skiff-bush with woody berries that blend into the dusty miller and beach plum.

My sister and I used to float that rowboat down the creek and around the clam flats all summer.

Frank was on the shoreline in those days, cigarette permanently stuck in his mouth, eyes too far to see.

Watching us drift, seeing us follow the minnows the way Sam does now, as the warm southwest wind ruffled our hair like a mother who wants to smother her child with kisses but limits herself to that one light touch.

Later Sam paddled his own skiff as Cait and I dozed on the little dock in front of the shack that still stands at the creek's end. Thatch has not knocked it down because it is tangled up in the working rights Rin and I still control.

More herons come here than used to, but the clams along the creek are sparse and the scallops pretty much gone.

The sense of constriction comes out of nowhere. Before I know it my throat is hard as concrete. The snot was flowing pretty well enough before. Now it runs like tapwater.

Tears build up. I hold them back, blinking. When I was very young, Frank would look at me with irritation if I cried. The irritation had changed to a poorly concealed contempt by the time I was Sam's age.

If I was happy, though, and he was in a good mood, we would work on the shoreline together and then he was fine company.

I turn away into the beach plum, holding one nostril shut while I blow mucus out the other, pretending to examine the old skiff, though she is good for nothing now, not even kindling, she is so rotten.

The constriction eases.

After a minute I follow Sam and Rin to the shack. I am amazed by my earlier reaction. I twist my thoughts away deliberately. In the twist I remember the hearing, and its taste of confusion, the tangled currents of people.

I suppose there is a link. Maybe the scale of what is going on next door finally got to me. It is hard to resist a force that can level a half mile of woods and build the skeleton of a ninety-eight-thousand-square-foot discount shopping center inside a month.

Also there is no point. Because even if Price-Shoppe does not fly, Thatch will build something else—condos, another strip mall. Something that needs less water, generates less waste, slips under the radar of the environmental cops.

But whatever it is, it will be too big for the hollow. The

charm of this land lies in smallness and detail and it will not survive the proximity of such scale.

Thinking in this way seems to cut the power of what I felt earlier. At any rate, by the time I get to the front of the shack, while my nose still runs, my throat works fine. Rin and Sam are sitting against the cracked-shingle wall, sharing a Mars bar.

I stop, astonished once more.

Sam—Power-morph action fan, nighttime liberator of hounds—examines one of his books spread open on Rin's knee.

My son, who disdains all activities that remind him of being the age he is, listens placidly while Rin reads aloud from the book I saw splayed by his bed the other night.

This is what Rin reads:

Abner Hersey and the Assembly of Saints

from *Children's Tales of Olde Cape Cod* (Olympia Imprints, Yarmouth Port)
by Wendy Rose Adams

Before the revolution the best doctor on Cape Cod was Abner Hersey.

He lived in Barnstable and was the only man who would ride up and down the Cape to tend to the sick. He was irritable, cheap, and stubborn to boot. He was frightened of disease, and terrified of death. Summer and winter he wore a great, felt-lined cowhide coat and huge cowhide boots. On his head was perched a white wig, and, on top of that, a red cap. When he visited his ailing clients he rode in a high black carriage devoid of windows or openings save a hole in front through which he would groan instructions to his horse. This was a huge and irascible jet-black mare that bucked at the coaxing words of other men and responded only to the curses and complaints of her owner.

Children shrank from Abner. Strangers, upon seeing the black rig, stepped quickly into the woods, thinking, This surely was how the devil would travel when he came to the peninsula.

Abner Hersey, for all his complaints and bouts of anger, loved certain things. He loved the sixty acres of his farm. He fenced them well and fertilized the sweet meadows and did not allow them to be overgrazed by cattle. He loved his horse, which he called Cleo. He was fond of his manservant, Edward Childs, who prepared his potions. And he loved Hannah Allyn, the daughter of a local squire, whom he had married late in life. She was a gentle, quiet woman who quickly learned to steer around Abner's moods and humors.

Most of all Abner loved his little daughter, Mary. When Mary spoke or smiled the man's irritation dissipated, and he performed whatever task she asked of him with good humor and grace.

When Mary caught smallpox he labored for ten days and nights to save her.

When she died he locked himself in the stable with Cleo and groaned and raged for a month.

After Mary's death Hannah stopped speaking. Every day in warmer weather she went to the little grave and put a flower on Mary's stone. In cold weather she put there a sprig of evergreen. After the first month Abner came out of the barn and started doing his rounds once more. He was cheaper and more irritable than before. He also worked twice as hard, especially when tending the young.

When the revolution came, Abner refused to join the supporters of independence, whom he considered to be a bunch of loud-mouthed, drunken upstarts. He attended three meetings of loyalists, or Tories, and spoke at each one. Unfortunately, each time he stood up he solemnly addressed his audience as "fish." "Fish," he would begin, "I wish to inquire if ye have seriously considered the Stamp Act resolution . . ." At the third meeting the Tories expelled him from their society.

Hannah dulled her grief with the routine of Mary's grave and the work of taking care of Abner and tending to her own mare, a nervous and delicate roan. Edward Childs grew stooped and gray mixing nostrums and ministering to Cleo. One day, exhausted from his labors and angered by the horse's stubborn ill will toward him, he picked up a shoeing hammer and hit Cleo in the forehead. She dropped to the floor, dead. Terrified, Edward ran to fetch Hannah. Abner discovered his dead horse in the stable that evening. In his grief, he went to Hannah; but before he could speak a loud knocking came at the door, and they heard a familiar cry: "Doctor! Doctor! My child is ill!"

Hannah took Abner by the hand and led him to the stable. Trembling, she hitched her roan mare to the grim black carriage. "Go," she said. It was the first word she had spoken since Mary died. Then Abner got in the coach and drove off, following the desperate father. And Hannah, watching him leave, reflected that she and Abner finally had made a life together. It was not a life of happiness or particular joy, it was filled with sadness and small angers. And yet, she thought, it was a useful life. Despite their losses, and in the face of his fears and irritations, they had learned how to take care of each other and the people who came to them for help. It was enough.

And she went back to the house to comfort Edward.

When Abner died Hannah returned to her family. In his will, Abner stated the people he loved would live and die without his aid but he had found a way to keep his farm safe forever. He left his sixty acres to the thirteen Congregational parishes of the Cape, to be administered till the end of time by a council of deacons that came to be called the "Assembly of Saints." The profits from the fields would purchase bibles and physicks for local doctors. As added insurance—so Abner warned in his will—every hundred years he would come back to Barnstable and see how his land was being kept up.

The deacons were no saints, however. Nor were they good farmers. They overgrazed Abner's fields, never fertilized, and let the fences rot. They met every year in Crocker's Tavern in Barnstable on December first, the night of Abner's death. They spent the profits from his land on ale and food. And so, inevitably, the profits dwindled. Twenty years later there was no money for books. Fifty years on, the next generation of "saints" had even run out of money for ale. By the time the hundred-year anniversary came around, they long ago had obtained permission from the General Court to sell the ruined fields to the highest bidder, and the Assembly of Saints was no more.

On December first, one hundred years after Abner died, Crocker Tavern was quiet. The saints, and their descendants, were long dead. Only a single client, the great-grandson of a famous revolutionary politician, was awake in the taproom. At midnight he heard a loud knocking at the door. Upon opening the door he saw a huge black horse hitched to a closed black carriage standing in the cobbled forecourt. A long, agonized groan issued from a hole in the carriage's front.

The horse turned and galloped, faster than the wind, down the Old King's Highway.

The man staggered off to wake his drinking companions and tell them what he had seen. But he was a well-known drunk and a spinner of tall tales, and nobody believed him.

Chapter 15

"Can we go to Denny's now?" Sam asks.

"Christ, Sammy."

He glares at me.

I blow my nose. Either it has gotten colder or I have grown chilled, sitting here. "Come on," I tell the boy, "I want to talk to you."

He looks at Rin. He uses the kind of stare under half-lowered lashes that Caitlyn uses when she does not want to do something but knows she has to.

"There's a better story in that book," he says, attempting damage control. "It's got *pirates*."

"Typical guy," Rin says, and flops her breast free for Zappa.

I climb down from the porch and walk some distance down the beach. It's not really a beach—the sand is covered by eelgrass—but you can walk on the high-tide wrack where seaweed and sedge are piled up thick and matted as a rug.

Cans of soda, candy wrappers, and tampon applicators litter the weave.

Sam kicks one of the cans behind me. I sit down and he strolls by, hands in his Mondo jacket. He circles. Finally he sits, looking at the flotsam.

Gulls complain and bicker.

"I know what you're gonna say," my son announces.

"Oh?"

"Yeah. You're gonna say I was stupid, and everything."

"No kidding."

He looks up at me. His eyes are soft but his gaze is hot and steady.

"I didn't *try* to break anything! He's my dog! Even if he spends most of the time in your truck."

"You know we got to pay for that. What you did. The fence, and everything."

"So?"

"So it's going to be expensive. And it's going to come out of your allowance, some of it anyway."

"That's not fair! *You* let him get away."

He looks back at the shack as if hoping for support from his aunt. I sigh.

"Eb gets away all the time," I tell him. "You can't always blame me for that. Anyway, you let out a dozen other dogs, too. They want us to pay for the dogcatchers, runnin' around chasing all those mutts you let out."

He peeks at my face. I am careful not to show any trace of a smile. "There's rules, rules you got to obey, Sammy—"

"Yeah, but Mom wouldn't get him out of there. An' I didn't have any money 'cause my allowance is so small and I couldn't call you or nothin.'"

"Anything."

"*En*-ee-thing. Anyways you woulda done the same thing if he was your dog!"

Sam takes a stick and stabs a horseshoe crab shell repeatedly, the way Yakusa assassins do on Power-morphs.

"That pound is there for a purpose," I tell him after a beat or two. "It's to keep dogs that run away, or dogs who are lost, so they don't get hurt."

"He *hates* it in there."

"That's not the point."

"He's my dog, and he hates it there!"

The mucus is dripping down my lip again. I take out a tissue and blow. My teeth chatter delicately, and my throat hurts. I catch sight of the heron standing on a point of marsh. He looks like a thin man stooping to examine his reflection in bright water. It does not make sense that the scallops should be so scarce here. The tidal flow is good, not too fast for shellfish. The bottom is a fine combination of silt and soft sand. But the spat do not settle any more and if they settle they don't grow. Some say it's because of golf course and cranberry fertilizers and others say it's silt from all the developments washing into the marsh and nobody knows for sure.

Quahogs, too, are not as plentiful as once they were, although that has more to do with the fishing pressure from all the former longliners who took to clamming year-round.

The golden grass looks the same as it always did, and the metal hues of sea and sky have not changed since I was a boy. It seems to me that despite the changes underwater this place is like a museum because it preserves exactly the conditions of my past. If it were not for my knowledge that time has gone by it could be me sitting there instead of Sam, and Frank dressing me down for breaking the windows in the Moyers' dockhouse. My mind shines a quick flash of the doctor in Sam's book galloping crazily into the dark in his black carriage. There is no connection I can figure out between my thoughts and this image. Maybe I am getting a fever.

"Shit, Sammy," I mumble. "I didn't really mean I disagree with you."

He does not look up, but he stops stabbing the crab.

"I broke rules all the time, I never really wanted to hurt anything, either."

"Ethan says you're hurting people 'cause you won't sell the hollow. He says, everybody wants you to sell, but you won't."

"We don't own the hollow," I say in a voice with no energy in it. "Just the rights."

"Whatever."

Neither of us looks at the other for a while. I feel suddenly as if the strength I once had for this kind of exchange is simply not there anymore.

Maybe, I reflect, it was never there. This endless give-and-take, this long-term economy of raising a kid, is so much harder and more complex than fishing. And I am no longer sure I have the grace and endurance even to make it fishing.

Finally I say, very softly, "Maybe I will sell. If Rin wants to."

He is staring at me now and I am the one avoiding his gaze. He has that cocked head look, he learned it from Eb, that shows he is puzzled. I cannot tell if he really disapproves or not. I stare over the water again. The sun is quite strong and in its glare the reeds and shallows are converted into a blur of black and silver. Frank and I used to rake for quahogs in the mouth of the creek and if I wanted to I could see us in that blur, the tall figure scratching at the bottom, then retrieving the rake with his long steady backpull. Frank twists the rake upside down, shaking clams loose from the basket on the end, casts the rake forward again. The shorter figure glances sideways from time to time to see how he does it.

It could be Frank did the smart thing. It could be he realized he just was not made to be a good father, so he cut his losses, and ours.

What that means, as inevitably as the waxing of moon makes the tides stronger, is that I should follow his lead: get out of the way of my boy's growing up.

I blink sand from my eyes, and the memory of Frank and me is broken up by the break in actual vision. Turning from the water, I notice how the golden aster took over the sandy ground between wrack and creek.

There will always be a detail of wood or marsh or water on this shore that is gentler than the connections of family. In this knowledge lies a solid comfort.

The snot is coming faster again and my throat hurts worse and that is a concrete pain, not the abstract smart of shame, or memory.

I get to my feet, groaning like Abner Hersey. A Caterpillar diesel revs in the distance. I wipe my nose on a jacket sleeve, pull the watch cap lower around my ears, and grab Sam by the collar.

"Come on," I tell him. "Let's go to Denny's."

Sam wriggles free. He does not like me to touch him. "Do you really have to take my allowance?" he asks. Picking up the horseshoe shell, he wings it thirty feet into the cold green tide.

A gull dives to check it out then rises, screaming cheat, against the wind.

NOAA weather forecast

This is the December seventh extended forecast for waters from the Merrimack River to Chatham, Massachusetts, up to twenty-five nautical miles offshore:

General outlook: The jet stream is expected to curve southward from Ontario over the next three days. The high pressure system currently over New England will move out to sea early this morning, followed by an area of low pressure. A depression currently over the southern plains states will be moving westward at the same time. It will be prevented from curving north by an Arctic high now over the Rockies and also by the direction of the jet stream.

Offshore forecast for New England waters from the Northeast Channel to the Great South Channel including the waters east of Cape Cod to the Hague Line:

Winds northwesterly, ten to fifteen, seas three to four feet; becoming south then southeast later today, increasing fifteen to twenty, seas four to six feet. Visibility diminishing to less than one mile in snow.

Reports from offshore buoys:

Isle of Shoals; temperature eight, wind northwest twelve, water temperature forty, seas two feet.

Southeast portion of Georges Bank: temperature nineteen, wind unvailable, water temperature unavailable, seas unavailable.

Chapter 16

The Blizzard

68 degrees 57'W; 40 degrees 22'N

41 degrees 11'N; 69 degrees 01'W

The tide is not right for leaving the fish pier until four thirty Friday morning.

My stuffed-up head slows me down and Billy is late at Larry's. Then I have trouble getting through to the operators at NMFS. I cannot leave without calling the fisheries service because if the Coast Guard sees me out there they will automatically report my numbers and the feds will check me against their log and if I am not marked on that log they will pull my license.

But everything else goes smoothly and somehow we get aboard *Hooker* and drop the mooring and it isn't four twenty yet.

We barely make it out of Aunt Lydia's cove. Once we hit a

sandbar and get stuck hard enough that I have to reverse the *Hooker* off.

It is very cold. NOAA radio says higher temperatures associated with the low have made it to New York but in the meantime the mercury here has dropped to eighteen degrees.

Brash ice has formed in the shallows. It looks like faint glass pudding as it gets stirred up by *Hooker*'s screw.

This kind of weather I should take seriously. This weather says I should go to the Kitchen, brew cocoa and watch *Oprah* reruns till I pass out in Harriet's armchair. It is just no goddam *fun* when the mooring rode is so swollen with ice that I have to pound it thin with a baseball bat to pull it out of the fairlead.

But I keep moving, going through the motions of leaving harbor. Partly I do this because we are broke and I still have not paid the power company. I have not made the boat mortgage payment either, though the check Johnny Norgeot is holding for me will cover that and more.

Partly it is greed or, more exactly, the lust for the ease that money brings. I want to earn a check like last time. That is why we are heading back to the 706 line.

Also, I have got to admit, I like fishing.

As long as the shit does not get too deep I like going over the bar and seeing land get thinner and thinner till even the standpipes are gone and nothing but ocean surrounds me.

I like getting out where there are no phones and you don't have to talk or do anything but deal with your boat and the sea and the weather.

Some of the Chatham skippers keep cell phones on their boats now. Up to fifty miles offshore they can call the plumber or wife or girlfriend as they sit in a wheelhouse and drag the bottom of Georges Bank.

There is no way I am putting a cell phone on *Hooker*. I prefer not having anything to do with shore for one or two days.

Even this morning, the second day I have woken up separated from Cait, I don't feel as bad as I could because the simple motion of water has cut the effect of separation.

It's as if the waves' amplitude and wavelengths worked in exact opposition to the frequencies of the mind, damping pain by simple physics.

The bar is no trouble. The swells are oddly regular and smooth as mercury. You would never think that within half an hour they could grow to the size of trucks or small houses. I was working on the boat in Aunt Lydia's once when that happened. The wind whipped up suddenly and when Ray Crosby tried to sneak in a wave came out of nowhere and knocked his boat sideways. Then the next wave rolled it over.

Sim Pierce saw it happen and got on channel sixteen right away. He was used to Chief Downey and the way he could get the rescue boat over the bar inside fifteen minutes. But the Chatham Coast Guard station had been shut down a month or so before. He was unable to raise the Province-town station at all.

Sim and I both tried to find him but we couldn't even locate his boat.

By the time the Coast Guard found Ray's body he had two lobsters and a clutch of crabs fastened onto his intestines.

At eight we pass the "BB" buoy. Gilbert's dragger is working off the ship channels, running down the tide. We do not talk on the radio.

By nine thirty we are off the sixty-fathom wreck. The fishfinder shows some echoes but nothing like what I saw last time on this ground.

The thermometer stands at twenty degrees. Sea smoke coils off the waves and winds around the boat. Wind takes the mist overhead and separates it into strands and then braids the strands back together so that it looks like we are being covered by fuzzy, rat-colored macramé.

By ten we have made two haulbacks east of the wreck. We are rewarded with an average catch: no gray sole, a box of ocean dab, a few lobsters, and one jet black creature about two feet in length with dead eyes and a long thin boom sticking out of its head. It has a huge, underslung mouth with many rows of teeth and transparent fins. It takes me a few seconds, after the initial shock, to recognize a ceratioid angler. This is a fish that usually lives at 200 fathoms and deeper.

A lot of codfish again. We keep fifty poinds. I make sure I pitch the rest personally, but as I am sliding them out the gate Billy shouts, "Wait!"

I lean on the gaff with one arm and hold onto the gunwale for added support. "Don't even think about it," I tell him.

"You tole me they'll die anyway."

"Yeah?"

"So, what's the point?"

"The point is," I say wearily, "we don't get a two-thousand-dollar fine like last time. The Coast Guard—"

"I know about the Coast Guard." Billy jerks his hair back. "But we could eat some. They wouldn't know. The Coast Guard, I mean. And it's such a waste—we always *waste* everything."

"You want to cook this?" I gaff a big market cod and slide it toward him fast like a hockey puck. "Here!"

I guess I do it rudely. It is not only the hair toss in Billy that reminds me of his sister.

"I only wanted," Billy says quietly, "to make some chowder."

"Be my guest," I tell him. "Only cut it here, now, and throw everything overboard you're not gonna cook."

And I go forward.

* * *

We run south of the wreck now and make several good hauls of low-rent skate. When men who can work together tackle a job they tend to acquire a rhythm and despite the recurrent irritation between us Billy and I are just starting to do that. I handle the winch and net and he sorts the fish into different checkers and knocks ice off the decks with the Louisville Slugger. He steers while we are hauling back or while I am gutting catch or handling the doors. We are both dressed in layers of sweatshirts, long underwear, ski socks, hoods and oilskins, but it is so bitter out there we have to come in and huddle by the wheelhouse heater at intervals.

I got the coal stove going, too, and the below-decks is warm enough.

I steer after the fish are cleared and Billy tends to his chowder. I bought spuds and onions when I went supply shopping and he boils some of each. He cuts up the fish into rough fillets and then cubes the fillets. He adds some razor clams and sea scallops that rattled out of the cod-end last haulback and it is all starting to smell pretty good.

Even out here the sea is calm. The barometer is steady at 29.31, the low pressure over us weak and departing. The wind is northeasterly, not northwest as NOAA predicted. Four-foot swells roll greasy as Muzak out of the north.

The sun breaks free of sea smoke around noon. Half blocked by clouds, it shines in patches, and the division of light splits the sea into two distinct countries. One is a friendly place of clear green-white waters with yellow in them too.

The other country, the one that cloud obscures, is mean and blue as a state trooper's eyes.

The gaps between clouds dwindle and vanish. The light loses its clear division and becomes diffuse and vague. It feels like it has been filtered and qualified and the sea reacts to it the way a child would to love similarly questioned and made conditional.

The sea turns dark and sullen now and the swells hump up a little. The tension of this withholding is great; Billy and I keep looking at the dense, low haze now restricting our horizon. Petrels zip in and out of the swells as if evading the weight of sky.

The snow begins just after one. Immediately I feel release.

It's as if I was expecting bad news and now it has come I can deal with it. Both of us, sorting fish, work faster.

Checking the instruments I find these readings: barometer 29.08; it has gone down 0.09 inches in two hours as the low pressure zone steps on the coattails of the high. Engine-oil pressure 33, main-gear 159, which is normal. Cooling-water temperature 260, a touch elevated though not dangerous. I suspect this is due to our running the engine and the winch fairly hard over the last few hours. Or maybe we are sucking in a little ice.

The first flakes of snow are solid and small, the size of air-rifle pellets, and they sting our faces the way BBs might. Within twenty minutes the flakes change, becoming bigger and lighter and more populous. The water loses its hard quality and goes a soft gray-green in color, like ginger-ale bottles filled with milk.

Visibility drops to a quarter mile. The ocean around us seems not to disappear but to become a different place, a land of forgotten words, of half-remembered travels that go on and on even if you cannot follow them with the eye.

I spend more time with my face in the Furuno. The edges of its rubber mask leave lines on my cheeks.

Billy comes up with mugs full of chowder. I am not looking forward to this food because I do not usually eat what I am fishing. The stink of fish is everywhere, I don't need the taste of it inside.

But the chowder is good. Billy used to work at a yuppie seafood restaurant in Boston and he learned more than he lets on. He is pleased by the fact that I finish two mugs, and writes out his recipe in the logbook.

Poor visibility brings people closer. I have noticed this before. In a pea-soup fog, guys who in good weather don't even look at each other will talk and ask questions with interest.

Now I run *Hooker* farther south, bring her around and drag north to just short of the wreck, then turn and repeat the process. In the wheelhouse, Billy and I talk occasionally about the boat and the snow.

During our fourth run north, he shows me a thriller he is reading. It is called *Asia Rip*. It's about how the Fulton mob wants to kill a New England fisherman who found out how they rig the price of fish. This is so obvious it amazes me that someone bothered to write a book about it.

Billy switches from the Mafia to the French secret service. I tune out as he explains how the French hired the Gambinos to kill JFK so GIs would stay in Vietnam. Billy's conspiracy theories are nothing like Caitlyn's New Feminism. His theories are usually hostile, crawling with deep and secret enmity, whereas Cait's lock into a fuzzy pinkish cosmos where everybody would love everyone else if we would just craft a virtual marketplace that allowed men and women to deal honestly with each other.

Yet both are built on a deep need for something to explain just why they cannot make their world do what they want it to do.

When Cait obsesses on a book that says women are flying horses, torn between seeking a rider, and soaring free among the structures of the Web, it is not because she fully believes this hogwash. Rather, it is because it puts order in the tumble of thoughts and emotions inside her head. Just as the checkers keep separate for Billy the different sizes and species of fish he knows nothing about.

The tug is soft at first. Quickly it grows more insistent. It pulls me out of that line of thought as fast as if someone had thrown a bucket of seawater in my face. *Hooker* hesitates, and gently loses way. I yank back on the throttle. Too late, I check my watch. The boat rocks in the long swells, the trawl warps shiver tautly in the wake.

"Fuck!" I yell.

Because I was thinking about Caitlyn and flying horses and Billy's stories, I forgot about the sixty-fathom wreck.

Hooker was dragging steadily northward all that time,

eight minutes and an eighth of a mile past when we were supposed to haul back. Now the otter trawl is hung up on the remains of a ship the chart lists as having sunk in 1927.

I check the Loran. *Hooker* is two hundred yards off the ship's coordinates. The wreck comes thirty feet off the ocean bottom here.

The fury is like a stone in my throat as I go aft. I wind the legs in gently, letting the winch pull *Hooker* backward toward the hang. Snow drives directly into my face. Our ass-first motion causes the swells to slop messily over the after deck, washing away the slush that accumulated there. My nose runs without restraint and I mop it with the cuffs of my gloves. Eventually the hawsers are at a fifty-degree angle to the horizon and we are close to sitting on top of the wreck and still the net does not give. We are hung up good.

I let out another twenty fathoms of cable, put on the brake. I give her hard starboard rudder and a quarter power and swing the boat around 180 degrees. The south-trending current helps us around. Then I wind the winch until we are almost on top of the hang again.

Still nothing gives. Billy stands by the wheelhouse door, smoking. He wears a slightly amused expression, as if it were funny to see me all steamed up, which I suppose it is. I let the current carry us south once more, then reverse toward the wreck. Eventually the legs are leading almost straight down into the swells. I am doing the equivalent of untwisting a caught string and the net does not move at all. I imagine dead seamen, their bony jaws awful as they wind my otter trawl around the bollards of their drowned vessel.

Idiotic. It is only the memory of *Commando* that fills my mind with such garbage.

I keep tension on the Hathaway as I think about what to do next. Holding the brake with my left hand, resting my right on the cheek of the drum. The winch thrums with effort. The diesel chuffs easily. The snow makes circles and spirals as a light wind blows it around the blue-gray of snow-sea fading to blue-gray of snow and sky above.

The hum of winch drops a register. Just like that. And the drum starts to move. A slack loop of steel cable lies down flat over the tip of my right hand where it rests, stupidly, on the arc of the drum.

Of course I am still wearing gloves. The gloves are a little long for my hand and the cable only nips my fingernails. Even that hurts like crazy.

The problem is that three fingers of my right glove now are firmly caught under the coiled cable. Sixty fathoms down the net is finally free and the drum is turning fast. I cannot pull my hand out because the glove has a tight wrist-band.

Within five seconds half my body is thrown over the winch and my left hand no longer can grasp the brake lever.

"Brake!" I gasp.

Billy stands there, the cigarette hanging out of his mouth, but he does not react. My whole body now is arced over the top of the winch and my hand is being pulled underneath, into the gap between the drum and the steel brace that holds it. That gap is wide enough for my arm but not the rest of me. If the glove does not rip immediately the best that can happen is, my shoulder will dislocate.

If the glove does not give at all the winch will tear my arm off as easily as you would pull off a well-roasted drumstick.

With the arteries severed in one arm I will have maybe five minutes to live. The fear explodes in my brain and in the light of that explosion my missing of Cait seems a tiny thing, wolf turned to dog by a change of light.

I yank with all my strength and scrabble at the cable with my weaker hand. I am too far away from the brake lever now to touch it with my fingers at all. Swinging my legs over the winch, quite gracefully, I kick at the lever, and miss, and topple off the drum to the deck. The force of the fall badly twists my right arm. And that twist, combined with the panicked pulling of what is, after all, my stronger arm, finally winds the wrist cuff the way it needed to be twisted.

My hand slips out of the glove, as if somebody simply let it go, a scant three inches from the brace.

I lie on my back, grunting for breath. The snow falls on my face and eyes and into my open mouth. My right shoulder is hot with pain and so are the fingertips on that hand.

The shoulder moves, though. The fingers will be okay. Billy leans over me, saying dumb things. I get up, groaning. My hands shake as they jam the winch brake down hard.

The legs lead at a forty degree angle, dripping weed-covered from the crowded snow, the blackened waves.

"Jesus, man, I'm sorry," Billy keeps repeating. Finally I yell at him to shut up. I start the winch again, real slow, and wind in the legs till the doors rise dripping to their blocks.

I move like an old man on the slushy deck as I go aft to hook the doors home.

*　*　*

The net, when it comes back, has one big three-cornered tear, maybe six feet by five, in both belly panels. This is not bad, considering. I tell Billy to jog the boat on a course of 010 degrees while I fetch twine and shuttle and mend the hole.

My brain feels kind of empty. Under the emptiness I am fuming at myself.

"*That*'s what fuckin' happens," I mutter, "*that*'s what happens."

That in fact is what happens when you let your mind wander onto shore stuff while you are screwing with winches and fishing gear. I know it is my fault and my fault only.

It has only been three days since Caitlyn kicked me out of the house. If I am not careful I will start blaming Caitlyn for the winch and Billy's uselessness and I will get madder and more vulnerable to something else going wrong with half-inch cable and three hundred horsepower.

Hook, loop, retrieve. I drag toilet paper from my pockets,

blow my nose, watch the white shapes of tissue float into the smaller white forms of snow.

The Gardner thuds without falter. A couple of pilot whales cruise by on the periphery of our silvered world: black arcs that do not roll among the green arcs that do; they leave our world as casually as they entered it, bound southeast.

It feels less cold than earlier. I check the radar and go back to fixing the net. The gray light turns pewter with turquoise details, like a Navajo bracelet. The turquoise goes a deep purple and then black. Finally the snowflakes look like sea-return on the radar screen, a sizzle of white noise against the dark.

The third time I go to the radar I check the engine water temperature. The sense of security, of having some control over object and motion, which was slowly drifting back to me after the winch incident, sluices in a rush from my body.

Three hundred and thirty-five degrees: well into the red zone. I hit the fuel-kill switch. The diesel thuds lower and sinks into silence.

I do not say a word. Billy looks at my face and keeps his mouth shut. The most likely explanation is that something jammed the cooling-water intake. It could be weed or ice although I have seen little of either out here. I dig out tools, go down to the engine room and unscrew the water filter housing. The filter is clean. I unhook the seawater intake hose between water pump and cooling jacket and yell to Billy to turn over the engine. When he does, freezing water sloshes into the engine compartment, with good pressure behind.

I kill the engine at the throttle. I pick up a flashlight and walk out on deck, slipping a little on the snow. The fish are still in their checkers. It was a crummy haulback, mostly slime eel. I lean over the transom, watching the exhaust. It is almost full dark now and I have to switch on the flashlight to find the exhaust port. Hot water, wound among cloudlets of diesel vapor and steam, drips into the waves, illuminated by the yellow beam; but what's bad is that the exhaust creates a sheen on the broad swells the color of grackle feathers that runs all the way along our wake into the blizzard.

When I go below again and pull the engine oil dipstick the top of it is coated with a brownish emulsion. There is water in the lubrication system. It was not like that this morning when I checked the oil before turning her over.

I sit on my haunches down there, my winch-wrung shoulder resting against the Gardner, soaking its heat into the nexus of pain. Trying to ignore what I cannot avoid. Feeling the failure of the engine mesh with the other failures occupying my brain until they have grown together like tendrils of honeysuckle.

Finally I climb back to the wheelhouse. I pick up the mike, increase the volume, using my left arm, which aches less than my right. Hold the mike to my lips.

I cannot do it. I put the mike down and ask Billy for a butt. He hands me a Merit and takes one himself. My fingers shake a little as I hold the cigarette. Two of the fingernails on my right hand are turning puce in the chartlight. The smoke goes in like leather sex—brutal, gentle. My lungs feel full in a way they have not since I last smoked, in the Kitchen.

"We got to get a tow, man." It comes out phlegmy, like the exhaust.

"Got to call the Coast Guard."

Billy looks out the window. It is so black now that all you can see is snow flying in the glow of decklights.

Living darkness.

"Got to do it," I continue.

"Whatever," Billy says.

"Don't *wanna* do it," I tell him.

He looks at me, narrowing his eyes against his own smoke, then looks away again.

"It's not your fault," he says, "if it's the engine."

I shrug.

"Not stopping the winch," Billy continues, "now *that* was my fault. I was just, like, frozen."

We both stand there, caught in reluctance.

"I look at you," Billy continues, still not looking at me. "You are really clueless in some ways? I mean, you don't know how to handle people; but you don't panic."

"Nobody panics with things they really know," I tell him.

He throws his hair back. That, and the way he mentions these things without looking at me, reminds me so strongly of his sister that I get a weird sense I am talking to another version of my wife. Maybe this is a male zombie of Caitlyn that looks different but you can see, from the telltale gestures, Billy is identical underneath.

"All I know is welding," Billy continues. "I always liked stainless steel because it's stronger than other things. And it won't rust easy. You know where you are with stainless. But everything else—"

He sucks at his cigarette.

Somehow what he says makes it easier for me to do what I have to do.

I pick up the mike again and take another drag of cigarette, blowing out the smoke in a solid column.

"Fuck," I say loudly, and key the transmit button.

* * *

The Coast Guard responds. So does Bill Gilbert. I do not want to take a tow from Gilbert. Part of me would rather stay out here and drift. That's how stupid pride is.

But Gilbert is eight miles northwest of here and he is willing to pick us up after he resets his last gillnet in about two hours.

I check the chart. I figure I can run the engine fifteen minutes at slow every hour, enough to hold us in the same position against the tidal current.

With luck Gilbert will charge less than the Coast Guard forty-two footer, which would have to come all the way from Provincetown.

He shows up a half hour after he said he would and passes

the towing warp without comment. His boat, the *Loaves and Fishes*, looks like a wedding cake with all the snow iced over her foredeck and wheelhouse roof. He pays out seven fathoms of tow line, which is about right. He takes up the slack—and *Hooker*, which was drifting and rolling broadside to the oily swell, turns into the wind and starts moving once more.

The snow, from falling almost straight onto the boat, regains its whirl and dance as we are pulled through the blizzard and saturnic water.

Gilbert calls us on the VHF and asks if we heard the transmission. I ask, "What are you talking about?" He says somebody put out another radio message last night claiming he was *Commando* and he was sinking.

Gilbert's voice has that tightness that means he is angry.

I light another Merit and pace up and down the wheelhouse as I smoke. Billy makes cocoa. Twice more he tries to apologize for not hitting the winch brake. Both times I blow him off. The reason I do this is partly because, yes, it was his fault, on the face of it; I told him about the brake lever, and he did not pull it.

But he is a new hand and cannot be expected to fit reflexes to knowledge this soon. So it is not his fault. Anyway I just growl "Forget it," a little impatiently; which, as it turns out, is a mistake.

The nav light shines over the chart table on the scrap of paper holding Pig's number in Vermont.

I wonder if it is snowing in Vermont the way it is snowing here. I wonder if Pig has found snow-pussy.

I pick at the cheap veneer peeling off the wheelhouse panels. Old tide tables, calendars, and business cards—from hook dealers, winch dealers, net dealers—are tacked in drifts to the bulkheads.

I pull them off one by one and drop them in the trash sack.

After a while the wheelhouse really starts to get to me. The place usually feels good—I said this before—because of all the instruments and charts and the knowledge they imply. However this knowledge is valuable only if you use it to go somewhere. If you cannot—if, worse than that, you become dependent on someone else for movement—then everything in here becomes, not a totem of power, but a sick reminder of how much you have lost, of how impotent you are. The scoreboard of failures is still lit inside my head, racking up the count like goals from the "visitor" team.

There are other failures. But Caitlyn and Sam and the engine are hardest because I cannot spotlight the reasons for them. What has broken the internal jacket of my engine is as serious and unknown as what broke the internal lock of my family. I do not know if it is the "fuel" problem Doomo talked about, or Bucket, or something that is not there in our lives, the way an absence of oil will cause an engine to seize. Yet the effect feels fatal, to engine, to braid of kin. And this knowledge is so scary that all of a sudden I feel like Billy, frozen near the winch brake while the wild machinery prepares to tear something soft and alive into its spurting and separate components.

My cigarette burns an eighth of an inch from the filter. I drop it in a cold cup of coffee and bum another off Billy. I throw on gloves and oilskin and go out on the afterdeck. I lean on the port gallows frame and stare into the night, filling my eyes with the silent movie of snow.

The smoke rolls in and out of my lungs as if I had never quit. Without the roar of diesel I can better hear the noise of our passage. The night, the cold seem to magnify sounds louder than I ever have heard them before. *Hooker's* wake sings and chuckles. The swells wash sibilantly toward us, echo slightly in the trough, make surprised sounds as they find a hull in the way, and rush aft in turbulence, out of earshot.

And all around the snowflakes fall, hissing very softly as they touch the water, a billion Arctic birds dying every second as they plunge their cold hearts into the relative warmth of the Atlantic.

Water

from *Notes on the Ecology of Cape Cod* (Salt Marsh Press, Falmouth)
by Irwin E. Zeit, Ph.D.

Before the population explosion after World War Two turned their landscape into an increasingly straitened suburb, Cape Codders treated groundwater the way Americans traditionally treat any natural resource—as a wealth bequeathed to them at birth, and in such plenty that they might shamelessly exploit it, and never pay a tab for the service.

Folk wisdom once had it that such a sandy, porous peninsula could not possibly support so plentiful an aquifer. Local legend, in an interesting parallel to the region's glacial birthing process, averred that the Cape was fed by a great underground river running south from New Hampshire. In 1917 an Eastham eccentric named Nye C. Nickerson set out to prove this theory by dumping 1200 pounds of orange dye into a mainland stream. He must have been gratified by the results, for a week later, ponds as far as Mary Dunn Road in Barnstable had turned faintly orange.

It was only in the 1960s that the Cape's giant surge in population began seriously to affect the water supply. The damage came to light when some of the most delicate of the Cape's fauna were poisoned by the dumping of raw sewage and other runoff, as contamination forced closure of shellfish beds from Bourne to Eastham.

At that time, most towns had installed piped-water systems yet over a third of all residents still relied on untested private wells.

In 1966 a study by Orleans hydrologist Arthur Strahler posited that the Cape, if not fed by one river, nevertheless indeed relied on a single pool of fresh water for its drinking needs. That pool, or "lens," consisted of a web of "domes" and "sub-domes," linked like capillaries through porous subsoil across the Cape, and resting on denser saltwater lying underneath. A federal study subsequently confirmed Strahler's hypothesis, and Barnstable County was officially designated a "single-source aquifer" in 1972.

But increasing concern could not keep up with the damage. The quadrupling of the year-round population since WWII—and a doubling of *that* in the summer months—constituted far too great an insult. Again, wastewater was the prime vehicle of damage, for sewer systems were, and are, confined to Hyannis and Barnstable, and Cape Cod relies largely on private cesspools to treat its flood of effluents. In the seventies, contamination of freshwater ponds by fecal coliform bacteria became a routine news item during tourist season.

Other sources of poisoning existed. Cranberry bogs required pesticides, and those pesticides leached straight into the water table. The proliferation of lawns and golf courses added a cocktail of noxious grass fertilizers to the area's hydrology. Over the thirty years of Cold War, personnel around nuclear BOMARC missile sites and other facilities at Otis Air Force Base and Camp Edwards routinely dumped jet and rocket fuel and other industrial solvents that sank into the water table as well. Concern mounted when studies suggested that cancer and birth defect rates in adjoining towns stood higher than average. The military reservation was declared a "Superfund" site in 1990, but cleanup of its 70 dumping grounds and the eleven "plumes" of toxic groundwater emanating from them continues to prove problematic.

Human contamination, it became evident, was not the only issue. As the millennium dawned, officials started to shut down wells sunk close to the shoreline in Chatham and Mashpee during the summer months. This was because high demand had pumped the wells very nearly dry, creating a vacuum that was filled by salt water intruding from either the sea, or from the saltwater pool underlying the aquifer.

Regulations, such as Title V septic plans and water-zoning, were implemented to tackle hydrology problems from both the quality and quantity angles in the 1990s. At this writing, however, it is unclear how successful these attempts will be, while population growth continues at a pace unabated since the administration of John F. Kennedy.

Chapter 17

Vermont

41 degrees 42'N; 69 degrees 56'W

44 degrees 09'N; 73 degrees 07'W

We cross the bar inbound just after eleven thirty. It is two hours before low tide and the sea is still soothed by snow but the swells have grown. They are five feet high now, rolling out of the southeast. And the tide is pushing against the wind, out of the harbor, which always pisses off the water.

Already by the second channel buoy the waves are rising in odd rhythms and shapes. They loom and subside to a jazz beat, resembling dromedaries, baked Alaskas, the open maw of a mythic animal, all fangs and slaver against the glow of Gilbert's range light.

Once, off the Nauset dogleg, when we are taking the swells on the port bow, a wave twisted by the shallows comes at us the other way, from the port quarter. We are pushed faster than our towboat, down the slope of the bandido wave for ten seconds. Although I am steering as carefully as I can the wave surprises me and *Hooker* almost gets away, turning sideways like a cowed dog ready to roll over for the greater hound.

I spin the wheel fast and catch her just in time. In the snatched instant before the rudder responds fear blows into my gut, fast, familiar, filling easily the space dug out for it by the terror of that winch.

Past the fourth buoy the waves calm down. Gilbert has no trouble pulling us through the rest of the shallows.

Billy and I unload at the pier next to the *Loaves and Fishes*. We have to pull the boxes through ten inches of wet snow and the poor footing makes this tricky work.

Johnny Norgeot is in a bad mood. A Coast Guardsman from the Provincetown station came around asking questions about VHFs. They think one of the Chatham boats transmitted the fake *Commando* Maydays. "Nobody here would do that to Flickie's family," Johnny says. "I mean, that's sick!" He gives me a check for last trip that is a little disappointing because prices took a drop yesterday. Nevertheless it will cover the fines and the mortgage payment and leave something on top.

I put off dealing with Gilbert while we get rid of the fish and Billy hoses down the afterdeck and I call NMFS to tell them we are back. Now he offers to tow me to the mooring without my having to ask. We accomplish the task in silence. When he slides in close to pick up the tow warp I look sideways at his figure outlined in the wheelhouse door.

"Hey," I call. "Gilbert?"

No answer.

"So what do I owe ya?"

More silence, broken only by the slow Thwank! Thwank! of his exhaust. Finally he says "Why don't you give me twenty bucks fer the extra fuel. There's some time involved, obviously, but I ain't gonna charge you for that."

His tone is snide and superior as usual. I do not react to it.

Maybe his tone is normal and I am dumping on him the contempt I usually feel for people who rely on other fishermen to get them out of trouble. Maybe he holds me in contempt because I am not a Jesus jumper like he is. Anyway he has the right to feel superior, because of having to tow me in.

"Listen," I say, "thanks. A lot."

"Don't worry about it."

His diesel burbles. The *Loaves and Fishes* fades into the bruise of snow, headed for her mooring in Ryder's Cove. In this silent harbor with land hidden in falling softness it feels like I am living in an abandoned house surrounded by strange water. That is not a bad feeling. I shut down the boat and turn in.

Thinking about the engine keeps me awake for awhile. Thinking about the *Commando*, which Johnny reminded me of, keeps me awake a little longer. It is true, what Johnny said: Nobody I know in the Chatham fleet would pull a prank like that when there is family around hard-mourning those people.

My head is still stuffed up and the cabin is cold and for a good forty minutes I toss on my bunk, wondering if I will sleep at all tonight.

Then the exhaustion in my body hits the kill button.

* * *

In the morning I row in and call Doomo. Flurries switch on and off in a sky the color of broken promises. Sea, beach, and land have been turned into a lovely and subtle geology by the blizzard, a kind of cross-section of ice age and sediment whose epochs are flagged by the different colors; white, taupe, violet.

Cream, russet, and midnight blue.

Doomo is in his workshop. He grunts when I describe what happened, as if already he has guessed what it is. His tone says, fixing it will be expensive; it will take a long time.

He will come down after lunch if the roads are clear.

As I hang up I notice somebody took another can of spray paint to the ice shed shingles. Beside the "COMMANDO LIVES!" a single word is scrawled, like an invocation, in blue letters three feet high.

remember

I excavate the truck from its cerement of snow, using one of the dinghy oars as a shovel. The truck fires. I drive it to Larry's. The roads are a disaster. Cars lie buried in drifts and a tree took down a power line on Route 28. The windows of town peek like nosy housewives from behind blue-white drapes of snow.

The doors at Dorene's Bridal are blocked with blown drifts. The mannequins on each end of the central window wear scarlet.

It is an open secret in Chatham that Dorene's Bridal is a front for a call-girl service and that the dress colors signal to initiates which girls are available and when. I am not an initiate and can only speculate as to what kind of girl might be for hire and how one would go about meeting her in a blizzard.

Jeb Flick, the town plow driver, has sideswiped a whole row of Swedish cars on Main Street. Jeb is the brother of Flickie, the skipper on *Commando*. He swears the plow does not heat right and that is why he has to warm up with Christian Brothers while he drives. Maybe his presence on the road reminds others of what happened because when I get to Larry's two gillnetters are yelling at each other about the last *Commando* transmission. One gillnetter's friend couldn't have done it. The other gillnetter says he could.

I hide behind the *Stranded Times*. One of Chatham's three remaining longliner skippers is in the court reports. He was picked up for OUI two nights ago in Eastham. The judge gave him one year's suspended sentence.

An editorial quotes an expert in cabin fever. She claims people on the Cape in winter suffer from a pathological fear of leaving the peninsula. She calls it *"misopontia,"* from the Greek word for "bridge," because you have to cross a bridge to leave here. Like most *Times* editorials, this one refuses to come out either for or against the issue for fear of offending advertisers.

I slap the paper down on the table. I suffer from many of the Cape maladies but misopontia is not one of them. I would love to leave the Cape right now. Just thinking about getting out of here is like warm June sky in my chest.

My head is clearing up. The hot bacon and eggs make me feel more optimistic. The two gillnetters stand and shove each other around. One smacks the other in the mouth and before you know it seven men are pulling and cuffing at each other in the gillnetter corner of Larry's.

I do not get involved.

Instead I go to Cape Fishermen's Supply and charge a package of up-to-date flares. I buy six more tubs of Might-E-Foam to line the rest of *Hooker*'s hull. As I roll the tubs to the checkout counter, I notice a box marked "Northstar Marine Radios" and a bill of lading that lists "EPIRB" and "VHF," one unit each. EPIRB means Emergency Position Indicating Radio Beacon, VHF is the frequency used by most fishing vessels for short-distance radio traffic. The box is addressed to "Ferguson Flick, FV Commando, c/o Cape Fishermen's Supply."

"That EPIRB got here a little late," I comment.

Trish is on duty at the cash register. She looks up from her coffee. Her stare is sharp and she cuts me with it for a few seconds before looking down at her java again.

"Fucking criminal," she says finally. "That's what it is: fucking criminal."

I watch her as she rings up my purchases. Trish has been dealing with fishermen too long to get bent out of shape easily. She puts her coffee down hard, and it splashes across the desk, and she curses.

I load the tubs into the back of the truck and lash them

down so they don't fall through the holes. Then I drive to the bank.

Only the middle parking lot at Fuller's Landing has been plowed and I have to climb over drifts five feet high to get to the Chatham Bank and Trust island. Inside I deposit the Down-Cape check in my boat account. I also fill out a slip for our family account. I reflect, as I do this, that our separation has already been set up for us. Cait has a household account into which I pay money. I have a boat to live on by myself. I wonder if this is a coincidence, or rather a reflection of a separation that already had occurred and was just waiting for an excuse to acquire its own, independent form. I write another check for last month's boat mortgage payment. The counter bimbo taps it into the terminal, and pauses.

"There's a hold on this account."

I look at her blankly.

"I just put money in."

"No, I mean the mortgage account."

"What does that mean?"

"I'm not sure." She gives me a look blanker than mine. "Uh, I'll find out, if you want."

She goes into an office, comes back, and asks me to check with consumer loans. When I get there Mrs. Snow is on the phone. She smiles at me, tells the phone she'll "take care of it." She twists around to glance at Vaitsos' door, and twists back.

"Ollie," she says softly, "you were thirty-eight days late on that payment."

"That's right." My good fist gets tight. I do not want to deal with problems on the mortgage now. It is just one area I do not need problems in. I tell her this.

"They—we—have the discretion. To reassess the mortgage at that point." She looks down, says nothing. I say, "So what happened?" Mrs. Snow remains silent. She picks up the phone, punches four buttons.

"Somebody put a hold on it," she says, still not looking at me, and hangs up. "But I, I can't get hold of him right now. So this time, I'll just run it through as if nothing happened. Okay?" She looks up now, and smiles. Her eyes are cloudy with trouble. I do not ask her about the trouble.

I do not want problems with this now.

She taps seven numbers into the computer, which pips out a slip in return.

"You'd better make the next payment early," she says, and now her eyes are clear again. "Just to be sure. Have an apple."

"No thanks, Mrs. Snow," I say, "I appreciate it."

"You always pay, in the end," she says. "*I* know that."

I wonder sometimes if Mrs. Snow had a crush on my uncle and that was why she was always so nice to me when I was a kid.

I do not want her to get into trouble because of me.

I think about that on my way through the lobby. By the time I get outside a crack has appeared in the clouds. Through that break the sun sends a cypher of light that awakens the trillions of crystals sleeping in the conspiracy of frost that Fuller's Landing has become. The sham aesthetic of the development is taken over by the glitz and dance of snow.

The monstrous statue of Fuller appears forlorn under its white padding. It looks as if he only wants to free himself from the pompous lock of bronze and go sledding. The sounds of winter are all around. The hard air makes them clear and hard as well: the zing-crunch of snowshovels, the rumble-scrape of plows; all are solid within the shell of fourteen inches already fallen.

I think, once more, of Vermont. It is as if the thought had been building and building, like snow accumulating on a ridge, until it gets so heavy it must break off and slide into the valley.

I could go see Pig.

That tone in Doomo's voice means a day or two of waiting at least.

I have no obligations at home since Caitlyn kicked me out.

The idea of leaving connects to the feeling I got reading that piece in the *Stranded Times*. Misopontia. The opposite, I suppose, would be "the lust for bridges." Or maybe it was the *Times* piece that sparked this line of thought.

Whatever the origin, it feels like I was suffocating in a sealed room, and someone just thrust open the window.

Today is Friday. I will pick up Sammy and we will drive to Vermont for the weekend.

A gust of pure excitement blows me up one of the biggest drifts of the parking lot, and I ski down the other side on the worn soles of my work boots.

I lose my balance and land on my back at the slushy bottom. As I get to my feet I spot someone standing in the stillness of observation at a second floor window in the offices across from Fuller's statue.

The figure is large and straight and wears a camouflage beret tipped at an angle.

Thatch Hallett stares at me as I wring the soaked cloth of my work pants and I stare back at him and neither of us moves a muscle to acknowledge the other.

* * *

I am still hungry, despite the bacon and eggs I just ate, so I buy a guacamole and hot pepper sandwich at the Box Lunch. On my way back to the pier I stop at Cabbages and Kings and look through their collection of H.O.-scale trains. It is not a big collection and the trains are not cheap and Sam has most of them already but for thirty-six dollars I buy a Canadian Pacific shunt engine I am sure he does not own and that will look pretty good wrapped under the Christmas tree.

At the pier the dinghy is pulled up differently from the way I left it. A note is speared soggy on the port oarlock.

You can't run an engine like this. The vibration cracked the oil cooler. I can
replace it by Monday if you want (I changed the oil for you).

    Lars

    PS: *GET A NEW ENGINE. I can't be responsible for this one.*

Lars is Doomo's real name. I stare over at *Hooker*. Riding to her mooring with the cargo of snow on deck she has the snug look of a scoter duck with its head tucked under its feathers.

It dulls the shine of snow to look at my boat and know she needs something I cannot give her without money; and also to know I can't make money without what I cannot give her.

I call Doomo from the payphone and ask him if he thinks I can make another five trips once he replaces the oil cooler and he refuses to say yes.

With the profits from five moderately good trips I could put a down payment on the GM diesel. Maybe the Scituate outfit could arrange financing on the rest. I tell Doomo to go ahead and replace the gasket.

I hate making do with boats. You cannot go offshore on the cheap. You end up cutting corners and using poor materials and eventually they fuck up on you. And, as I said before, they never fuck up one at a time; they wait for the worst situation and then break in a string. And suddenly you are swimming in forty-degree water fifty miles out, wondering where the hell the process started.

The sun fades, reappears, fades. It starts to snow again. A volley of hard flakes rattles against the ice-shed wall. One of the Down-Cape fishboys is trying to scrub away the graffiti with paint thinner. Around the letters, the mineral spirits have stained the white shingles a very light robin's-egg color.

Turning from the water, I go into the culling shed and borrow Johnny's phone.

I reach Pig on the second try.

* * *

Taking a trip is both easy and not easy. It is easy because once you have really decided to go you will do it, one way or another.

It is hard because, just like the ocean, a trip will never take the form you expect, but twist and change shape and make you change with it.

Maybe that is the point of traveling.

Sam cannot go. He has hockey practice all weekend. Caitlyn tells me this in the kitchen as she makes dinner. Her hair has been trimmed and someone fashioned tiny braids at the back, with little beads strung on. She cuts up chorico and onions for kale soup. I get the feeling she was going to invite me to eat but now I am heading out she won't ask.

She wants me to take Eb, who is barking his head off on the run outside because he knows I am home.

I am not certain Pig will appreciate Eb's coming.

The house is tidy. Most of the old magazines have been thrown out. The four books stacked neatly on our kitchen table are entitled *The E-Tailer's Declaration of Independence*; *Woman Scorned—Witches and Healers of Old New England*; *Dancing at Dark [A novel of the Reagan Era]*; and *BroadBand: A Guide to the Economics and Philosophy of GyNET*. A shelf over the kitchen sink holds vials of herbal tinctures. Billy and Fleetwood sit bolt upright in their armchairs, watching *Seinfeld* reruns. Fleet chuckles nonstop. The smoke in that room turns life ochre.

I call George. Paula answers the phone. She says, "George isn't in," and hangs up without saying anything further.

I fetch a box of Maalox from upstairs. A hand loom Caitlyn bought three years ago but never used lies half assembled in the hall.

And she bought a new pair of ballet slippers. They lie in a silver Fayva box, open on the bed, cradled like eggs in a nest of thin pink paper.

I examine the shoes. They are bright scarlet, with little tufts of red lace on the front.

"You dancing again?" I ask when I get downstairs.

She jerks her head, swinging hair out of her eyes; she never gets her hair trimmed short enough. A box of Raisin Bran is wedged under one elbow. She sticks her hand in the box, takes out cereal, tilts the cupped palm over her mouth.

"I'm taking a class at Dance-Mania."

She chews the Raisin Bran. I can tell she expects me to be critical because we need the money more than she needs ballet lessons.

If I mention that, of course, she will say the same thing about the skiing.

"You getting back into it?"

"It's for the exercise. You know. Healthy mind in a healthy body, et cetera."

She puts down the cereal box, tries not to grin.

"They're doing a dance version of *The Heidi Chronicles* at Wellfleet Harbor Actors' Theatre. I thought I might audition. Figure, if I'm gonna make a complete fool of myself, I might as well let people get a chuckle out of it."

Suddenly I do not want to go to Vermont. I want Caitlyn to ask me to stay. I want her to finish making the kale soup so we can eat it together and talk about things other than hockey or Sam or money. Afterward we can go upstairs and hug for a while and then make love, slowly, while the snow starts up again like a story told in pale installments till it buries the pines outside our window.

"I'm glad you're back into dancing," I tell her. "You were good."

"I was not good."

"Yes, you were. You were—you were like a bird, flying, when you danced."

"You coulda been a poet—"

"I'm not kidding, Caitlyn."

She stops what she is doing and glances at me.

"Well, thank you. Thank you, sir," she says, but she doesn't smile or anything—in fact the corners of her mouth turn down, and for a second I think she's about to cry. Instead she looks at her fingernails, which are red as her ballet slippers. The beads in her braids are red and black and blue.

Those braids make me feel the same as when I saw Sam's book bag: left out, because my family is doing new things while I, like all the other strangers, only find out about them later.

"You know," I tell her, "I think maybe we should work a schedule, where you take time off. To dance, I mean a couple mornings a week? If I'm not fishing . . . I could hang out with Sam, or he could go with Harriet."

The corners of her mouth are level now. She looks at me as if I were a breast of chicken whose "Buy before" date was yesterday. Then she stares at her fingers again.

"You mean, if we were back together?"

"Yeah. It would be better that way. We both need time on our own."

"And you think a couple mornings will do it?"

Something fibrous has come into her voice. I cannot define it. It reminds me of something rather different—when I pressured her to make love, in the days when she still agreed to. I went inside her but her body had not consented. She wasn't hard inside but she was not soft either. That never stopped me, as I recall; yet it did not feel as good as when the lust was shared.

I always felt, afterward, as if I had lost something important, and could not remember what.

"I know it's only a start," I tell her, "but we can start with little things. Maybe bigger things will come later."

Caitlyn bends her head to one side. She keeps her eyes on her fingers. Then she smiles, a smile like dark chocolate, not completely sweet. It reminds me, poignantly, of Casey Ryan.

She turns, touches my arm. The fiber has gone out of her voice when she speaks next.

"Ollie. You won't give up."

"You're really not goin' with Bucket, are you?"

"What do *you* think?"

Her body, which was almost still, suddenly shakes loose, taking movement into the curves it adopts. She swivels, gathers the sausage and onions in her cupped and joined palms, and dumps them into a stew pot.

She washes her hands, sets the timer and flips her scarf off the coathook.

"You going or staying? I need to pick Sam up."

I nod. I know Cait's tone when she has put something behind her. "See ya," I say.

"See ya. Wait," she says, and picks up one of the books off the table. "I got this for you."

I look at the book. *BroadBand.*

"Drive carefully," she adds. "Huh?"

* * *

The snow is tapering off by the time I finally leave Chatham. The Cape is not used to real winter and Route 6 has only been plowed twice or three times at the most. The highway is like a trail in the Yukon wilderness. The trees bend double from the weight of snow. They bear giant amorphous white fruit where the blizzard has gathered in crooks and crotches. The cars inch along in a slow freight of red lights on thick and floury rails.

Driving as the flakes hurl themselves at the headlights feels like being pulled by its billion arms into the belly of a giant albino squid.

Eb sits on the seat junk. He holds the tennis ball in his mouth. He snuffles out the cracked window at the smell of highway salt.

His own smell is better. I suspect the dogcatcher hosed the dead seagull off him.

I placed the beer in back, wedged on a panel of spare netting just behind the cab, where it will stay cold yet remain accessible.

Now I crack the rear window and pull out the ride's first Rolling Rock. I will space the beers by stages, like Loran waypoints: one before the canal, one after Boston, one in Concord, one in White River Junction, at the Vermont line. Enough to relax, not enough to lose reflex.

There is an art to driving and drinking, as there is an art to travel.

The love of art is warm inside my joints.

The PAVE PAWS radar looms in a space between flurries just before the Sagamore Bridge, like a Cold War ziggurat in the uncertain light of a moon that is close to full.

Across the Canal the roads are clear. I play highway music on the tape deck: Black Flag, Dead Kennedys. I reach Waitsfield around midnight and, following Pig's directions, drive a windy but well-sanded road over a mountain pass to a village built between two frozen rivers. At twelve forty I pull into the driveway at the address he gave me. This is a small cottage in a row of similar cottages squeezed between the snowplow drifts in front and a loom of hardwoods behind. I park behind a red Toyota and go inside.

Pig and another guy and a tall woman are half passed out on a floral print convertible couch in the living room. Dry heat pumps in ample waves through floor registers. The three of them wear only underpants and T-shirts. Pig says, "Hey animal!" and hugs me, but he is really stoned and I am really tired from driving and beer, and we don't get much beyond that.

He shows me a tiny room with a camp bed and a cheap reproduction of a J. R. R. Tolkien print. A boxed set of *The Lord of the Rings* sits on a bedside table. Pig does not mind that Eb is here.

That heating plant is really efficient. Even in this side room the temperature must be eighty degrees. The whole cottage smells of propane and old socks. I take Eb for a walk and feed him Kibbles. In bed, I listen to the dog lick his balls for a couple of minutes. I find Cait's book and open it to a page where she has outlined a paragraph in yellow.

The GyNET Group supports New Feminism ideals in that it does not believe in demonizing men. Rather, by building a network of independent female investors and entrepreneurs, artisans and dealers, retailers and clients, we seek to foster the minimum level of independence that will allow us to recapture control over our economic lives, for both ourselves and our partners.

"Sounds good to me," I mutter. The bit about investors sets me wondering if GyNET might somehow offer a way to finance a new diesel for *Hooker*.

I read another paragraph. It discusses the concept of "false-myth partnership." According to the book, it's what happens when two people "partner" emotionally, but remain together for the very economic reasons that end up making their union a burden.

I close the book, a feather of unease in my chest. I recognize it as a version of the twinge I got when I saw Caitlyn's miniature braids earlier tonight: the sense that something is going on here that I do not understand; that I am not even close enough to see until it has already happened.

I asked Cait what she did when she first got the job. Typing in data, sending e-mails, she told me, cold-calling potential members. But I never asked her what she thought about GyNET, or what the point of working there was other than to earn extra money.

I wonder for the first time if my wife is doing something important, and I have not the slightest clue what it really is.

I put the book on the floor. I don't feel like reading anyway. I close my eyes. The white lines of blizzard and the yellow lines of highway stream behind my eyelids as if all along they had been connected to a spring-loaded drum pulling them into my head and now they have to be wound back into the night before I can relax again.

It feels weird to be here. My mind is still tied to *Hooker* and the diesel; to Caitlyn and her books and her tiny, beaded braids.

My body, however, is being pressed down by gas heat and the fatigue of highways. Sleep comes much faster than it did on *Hooker*.

Chapter 18

Black Diamond

44 degrees 31'N; 72 degrees, 54'W

I seldom—with one exception—recall my dreams.

This is true only when I wake up at my own speed.

If I get woken up, the debris of dreams smashed by rousing me so quickly tends to confuse my vision.

In a social anthropology course I took at UMass I learned this fact: The Masai believe you should never wake a man suddenly. They believe his spirit is free to leave when he is asleep and often will go hunting without him. If the body is woken without warning while the spirit is hunting, the spirit will be unable to get home in time.

I do not believe in spirits, but here is an idea that feels accurate.

I get woken up that first morning in Vermont. My eyes snap open to a figure wadded in ski parka and scarf. The figure is slight and shakes me by the shoulder. Although part of me knows this cannot be Caitlyn another part of me believes it is. She wants me to come back, I think, although what she said in the dream was not so specific. It was the *way* she said it—how she glanced at me first, then looked at her fingers again.

"Cait?" I say thickly, "—what?"

She quits yanking my elbow. Her hair, except for the roots, is the color of straw. The parka is red. Her eyes shine green in annoyance.

The dream colors fade. The anger feels familiar but this is not my wife. Nor is it the woman I saw half undressed on the couch last night.

My guard dog wags his tail. He buries his long nose in her crotch. She fends Eb off impatiently, although you can tell by the way she does it that she is used to dogs.

"Look, I'm sorry," she says. Her voice is quite a bit lower than Cait's. "But that's your truck out there, or whatever it is? It's blocking me in."

"Ah."

"It's my one day off?"

I flail around, looking for my jeans. She leaves. The outside air is so cold it is like a different medium: tungsten perhaps, in a gaseous state. The truck will not start. She leans her head against the neckrest of the Toyota while I blast ether into the carburetor. When finally I get the shit heap running and out of the driveway she doesn't even wave. I look after the woman's car. Its muffler is louder than the truck's.

She was pretty, I think, in an Irish sort of way.

Eb leaps in the thick snow, growling and carrying on. He jumps into the cleared road, takes a deep sniff of air, and starts loping downhill. I haul him back inside before the idea of Eastham can cross his small mind.

The dog's fur is matted and covered with burrs. He has had no real attention in a week. I comb his fur with a brush from the truck and ruffle up his jowl skin some. He grins oafishly. I feed him Kibbles.

No one else is awake. The sun loiters behind a purple mass of mountain and pine behind the cottage.

It has been a long time since I woke up in somebody else's house. I have to sniff out shower and coffee maker. Today the place smells of booze as well as propane and socks. The glass protecting the Tolkien print is smudged with coke stains. A Weber grill and a dismantled snowmobile lie like abandoned expeditions in the mounded snow beyond the kitchen window.

A barn, much older than the cottages, with a cupola and dark blue shutters, is framed in the limbs of a thick oak. A stovepipe steams beside the cupola.

The silence outside is like a living thing. The state road is not much used. I had forgotten what it was like to live without either sea outside or construction.

The girl in the Toyota woke up early. I am dressed and primed with coffee by eight thirty. The lack of noise in the cottage emphasizes the space around me.

It also seems somehow to isolate my actions, and in that isolation they appear to me bizarre, and without cause. I have to think about what I am doing here. I am not a fervent skier. I'm here because Pig invited me, and also because for days I have been worrying about a lot of different issues without making sense of them. It is likely that one of the deepest reasons for my presence in Vermont is I wish to take a break from worrying about the deep reasons for what I am doing. On that note I take Eb for his morning walk, then tie him up in my room with water, Kibbles, and Frodo.

I write Pig a note and leave.

To reach Mad River you run across farmland up Route 17, then over the pass to the ski area. Past the stretch of cottages and the Twin Rivers Market and over an iron bridge, cows graze and woodsmoke rises from trailer homes and cow barns. Then the woods take over. I drive through six miles of birch, oak and spruce. In a thin gorge, outcroppings of granite are cut by the frozen embroidery of a stream. Snow lies unbroken between the trees.

A small excitement like an unexpected wildflower blooms in me after a few minutes of this. The feeling comes, not only from being somewhere different or from going skiing, but from the road itself.

Perhaps the feeling is not so much excitement as a negative—a lack of depression. Because I am so used to Cape roads where every curve unfolds into a further stretch of ruined wilderness: another copse leveled, another ranch-house built, another marsh filled in, another mini-mall lifted into the flinching sky.

Every single day of my life I have driven the roads of home and felt my mood sink a notch as a plot of checker-berry, or a pond, or a clear view of marsh, was disappeared by construction.

I began setting deadlines when I was fifteen. When that field goes, I used to say, I am leaving the Cape for good. When that acre of scrub pine becomes a condo, I'm on my way.

The field went, the woods went, and I never left.

This Vermont road has no construction. This road barely has cars—in five minutes I have passed only one, going the other way. Within that absence—and in the corresponding presence, uncompromised, unsoiled, of real space—something that was forever being pushed down inside me is allowed to rise, like the earth underneath a log pile, when all the firewood has been taken away and it finds itself in the spring completely free of weight, and full of the joy of weeds.

*　*　*

At the Mad River Glen ski shop I rent a pair of Rossignol Combis with Salomon bindings adjusted for an intermediate level of expertise.

I ski all morning.

At first the militarism of downhill skiing—the sheer energy required to heat the lodges and feed the skiers and haul them fifteen hundred feet up to assault a mountain in twelve-degree weather—makes me nervous.

A ten-knot breeze funneling up the glen causes me to wish I had something denser than fishing sweaters to ski in. Watch cap and shore jackets are okay when you can pop into the wheelhouse to warm up at will but this is a Saturday, and the lift-line is ten minutes long, and my body cools fast with immobility.

The lift line contains Volvo people who look at my clothes as if they smelled old pollock.

Maybe they do.

My right shoulder is sore where I sprained it over the winch. My left arm still aches a little where Ricco twisted it.

But going up the chair lift is like a repeat of driving up the mountain road. I am hauled from the noise and people of the base into an immediate silence, a museum of snow and forest broken only by the white swaths of ski runs and the rhythmic squeak of cable wheels when the chair passes under a pylon.

The sky is clear. A looping low has stalled over the Appalachians, and dry Arctic air washes the country clean from Minnesota to Maine.

The sun cresting the eastern hills appears unfiltered, a coin of burning gas hovering almost too close for comfort.

The college kid riding beside me complains repeatedly that the last snowfall barely covered rocks and roots. They do not make enough artificial snow here, he adds. The ecologists say snowmaking takes too much water from the river and everybody believes them. I don't answer. Pretty soon he shuts up, and knocks his fiberglass boots together for the balance of the ride.

Each branch of every tree at the summit is flash frozen in a sheathing of ice that catches the rays of sun and refracts them in all directions and colors.

I take it easy this morning. I learned to ski at college: mostly at night, down the baby slopes of Mount Tom. That was fourteen years ago and I have only skied a couple of times since.

My legs are scared into memory after the first hundred yards. They recall under duress how to bend at the knees, and hop a little coming around a turn. My body overall remembers how to use the bad arm, swinging the left pole in a shorter arc, using my thighs more on left-hand turns. The stiffness in my shoulders is evoked as I use them, but only in historical ways, like muscle souvenirs of the Squire, or the Hathaway winch, that will not impede control.

I warm up a little after the first couple of runs, down Fox and Lark. I carve decent parallel turns back and forth across blue runs like Quacky and Porcupine. I avoid the expert slopes marked by black diamonds on the trail map.

After an hour my confidence has returned to the extent that I can relax a bit. I lean cautiously into the turns, enjoying how the skis' sharp edges carve into the hard powder; working on the rhythm, the rise and fall of ass, the back and forth of weight; pushing the ski tips downhill at the beginning of a turn, pulling the heels up at the cusp, as gravity pulls me down and around.

Circles started are half completed. The tension in that first half arc generates power to start the next.

On a lift of mogul the soles of my rented Rossignols lose, for one second, the worried bonds of earth. Then I power turn, hard and heavy, driving my knees around and through the valley between the bumps.

And fall. The college kid was right—there is not much of a base here. The broad, gradual slopes are good but I find that where the trails narrow and steepen the combination of traffic and gravity has ground away the snow cover and I hit rocks.

Not pebbles, either. Big black New England rocks. Granite so hard a glacier could not grind it down with fifty thousand years to do the job. Close relatives of the boulders that tug at my nets under the waters of Western Georges. Where the snow survived it has been compressed into bottle glass by the traffic of skiers all following the same path down the chute.

My passage through a run called Chipmunk is typical of that terrain. I come into the second chute leaning back more than I should out of bodily fear, and skid slightly as I turn left across ice. Hidden as it is by a large mogul in the black shadow of trees, I never pick up on the thin tongue of rock that bisects the trail.

The skis, moving too fast over ice, come to a dead stop when they hit that rock. My center of gravity, too far uphill, abruptly is catapulted in the opposite direction, so that I wind up crashing on my thigh and right shoulder and sliding all the way down the frozen chute to where the ground levels off once more.

After my second fall I decide to go down to the main lodge for a break. I am wicked out of shape. My knees are trembling by the time I reach the lodge. To breathe this hard air hurts my lungs. My feet, locked in the unyielding shell of ski boots, ache terribly. My right shoulder hurts worse.

I buy a hot chocolate at the buffet. I sit in the damp and generous heat, unbuckling my boots, watching, a little enviously, as families clomp back and forth in half opened snowpants. I am especially jealous of the dads who smoke. I spy on them as they observe their kids from the deck, holding low-tar butts out of the icy wind.

I should have insisted, with Caitlyn. I should have ordained that Sam skip hockey this weekend. He would love this mountain. For some reason I focus on the image of him listening to Rin as she read the story about that doctor. I am still surprised he listened all the way. In those surprises I see him growing up—paying attention to the ground beneath the surface.

I finish my hot chocolate, buckle up, go outside. A hand taps my shoulder and points as I wait in the double-chairlift queue. Someone yells "Hey!" Turning, I see a red parka, yellow hair, eyes with a flash of green to them. She is two twists of queue away: the woman who woke me up. She ducks under ropes separating the middle portion of the line, where I am standing, from the tail end where she was.

"Hi," she says lightly.

She has a ski-jump nose and a mouth that changes shape with ease. Her grin contains a flavor of request. I am supposed to pretend I was waiting for her, to justify her jumping the line.

"Pattie," I announce, obligingly and loud, "you're late." For the hell of it, because it is called for, because I am in a new place where no one knows me and I can do what I please, I lean over, put my right arm around her shoulders, and kiss her on the mouth. She stiffens, then relaxes.

I let go.

We shuffle our skis together as we are pulled into the vortex of the lift. We sit in the double chair like two worshippers in hard church pews, being uplifted in the temple of forest. She says, "Thanks."

"No problem."

"Sorry about this morning," she continues.

"It was good for me," I reply, "to get up early."

She glances at my face. Her eyes are cool.

"You're the animal, Pig said."

"Pig says that."

"You're the draggerman."

"I'm the draggerman," I agree, neutrally.

"My youngest brother works on a dragger. Outta South Bristol. I'm staying with my older brother."

"Gary?"

"No."

"*Pig?*"

She nods.

"He never told me he had a sister."

"One sister. Three brothers."

"Wow," I say.

What I'm really saying "wow" about though is how little Pig told me about himself—how little fishermen know about one another generally. You take solitariness for granted on a boat and it's not till you go ashore and bump into some new and crucial personal detail about a guy you've been fishing with for months or even years that you realize how weird such solitude is.

She laughs without amusement.

At the top of the lift she skates off. She wears jeans under her parka and her ass is hard and it turns in a curve that is graceful as a breaking wave. It shifts right, left, right. I am sorry to see her go.

Then she brakes, next to a sign that reads "Upper Panther." A black diamond is painted under the name. She waits for me to catch up. Her eyes have lost their coolness.

"Yuh wanna do this? It's a good run."

"Sure." What I would like above all is watch her move over the hard-packed powder, over the ice and rocks, weaving from the rough ground a verse of grace and sex.

We do Upper Panther. It is not that much harder than Chipmunk. I only wipe out twice.

We do Slalom Hill. She cuts her turns beautifully, bending well down, then leaping like a deer into the follow-through; but afterward she brakes too hard, as if suddenly frightened, the way a deer would be, by the abandon of that leap.

I have far less control, and ski faster, so we match up. On the rides uphill we exchange baseline data. She has been working in Augusta and is signed up for paralegal school in Bangor. She took the winter off to ski bum. Now she is not sure she wants to go back to school. On the third chair she opens a pack of Camel Lights.

"Yuh mind?" she asks.

"Only if you don't offer me one."

"Yuh smoke?"

"No," I tell her. "Give me that."

There is a way people blow cocaine. It's the same way my truck burns air in starting. They mix it with ether and set fire to it and smoke the precombustion. It feels good to ride up that chair with the cold mountain oxygen as a base and also with the growing sense of pleasure from having a pretty girl beside me. To taste the sugared abrasion of tobacco with a girl who has no history to tangle us up provides a lift more potent than crack. I suck the fumes deep, deep into my lungs, and hold on.

When I let them out they make a column that is doubly thick, from cold, from the residue of burning.

"Ahh," I say.

"First one of the day," she agrees.

"You know the one about the guy who's banging his head against a stone wall? And someone says, 'Why are you doing that?' and he says, 'Because it feels so good when I stop.'"

"Is that how you feel about smoking?"

"No," I tell her, "it's how I feel about skiing."

Her laugh is rough, almost a guffaw. If her eyes were not so green it might bother me. The sun bears the sheen of electroplate and the pines are of more or less of the same hue as her pupils. The snow is a soft blue and the rocks are solid and without fault.

All textures are correct and the Cape, where textures are not so simple, seems far away right now.

* * *

We drink a couple of beers in the main lodge after the lifts close. The place is hot with overdressed bodies. A fire snaps in a fieldstone hearth. The TV shows the women's downhill in Wengen, Switzerland. Christmas lights flash rhythmically against the windows. Behind them the mountain hardens to purple.

My body feels like it was put through a washer's spin cycle twice. Every part of it aches. The fingers I hurt on the winch throb harder than when I first pinched them. Even my eyebrows ache. My inner tissue is so parched it takes three beers just to ferry a drop of humidity as far as my bladder.

By that time she is gone. She has to check in at work. She waitresses at a motel restaurant on the other side of Waitsfield. She gives me a kiss on the lips, fast and dry as a sparrow's peck. I ask, "You skiing tomorrow?" and she says, "Maybe in the afternoon."

"I'll be on Upper Panther," I offer quickly. "Anyway I'll see you at the house?"

She smiles, her thoughts already departed. Disappearing in the crowd, she tosses her hair sideways to free it.

They all do that, I think.

Her name is Rachel. I say it softly but out loud, and even as I say it I can feel myself go kind of hot because two hundred miles away Caitlyn is working at her job and she gave me to understand she is not seeing Bucket.

Even if she lied about that, what I am thinking about Rachel is potential poison on its own account and death to the honesty we once had together and which is the oxygen our family breathes.

But I am not here to think about Caitlyn. In fact I am here to *not* think about Caitlyn. I am separated from my wife and my boat.

I am here to ski and drink beer.

I lean forward to claim the bartender's attention.

On the screen above the bar a girl's hard body, locked in a red synthetic suit, rotates on a forty-foot jump and plummets, helplessly, into the orange mesh of a safety fence.

Chapter 19

The Rock 'n Rolls I left in the back of my truck froze overnight.

They turned into a yellow-white ice far too plentiful for the thin glass to contain and exploded outward. The shattered green glass still curves around the frozen beer, trapped by the paper label, the cardboard box. The green in the Rolling Rock glass reminds me of Rachel's eyes.

On my way back to the cottage I stop at the Twin Rivers Market. It looks like an old-fashioned grocery store with beer signs in the windows.

Inside, the store has been taken over by a convenience chain. The original floorboards are still in place, worn by generations of women buying thread and kids negotiating for string licorice and men come in for gossip and tobacco. Shelves that once held dollar nostrums and garden trowels lurk dark and empty behind a half-completed chipboard wall. An electronic sign bearing the name of the chain is propped reverently on sawhorses, waiting to be set up and hooked to the grid.

Bright refrigerated shelves in front contain three types of soda. Around a Vermont State Lottery machine, racks of journals advertise the betrayals of soap-opera stars. A refrigerator is devoted to the national beer brands and a couple of Vermont boutique brews that are twice as expensive. I slide out three six-packs of Rolling Rock.

I get a feeling while I wait in the checkout line that I could just walk out of here without paying for this stuff. Of course they would call the cops but in fact nobody would really care. And the reason they wouldn't care is, nobody really owns this. Not the beer or the breath mints or the tampons or the Quik Pik lotto tickets. It all comes in semis from a warehouse somewhere and the money that pays for it leaves in trucks that go back to the warehouse, and humans have nothing to do with it.

GyNET would not approve, I reckon.

I do not steal the beer. The fancy of it sets my heart beating faster, but I know from hard experience that this is not a danger worth courting.

I wait my turn, pay, get in the truck, and drive over the bridge to Pig's cottage.

I drink all evening with Pig and Gary and Gary's girlfriend, whose name is Samantha. I try to see traces of Rachel in Pig. All they have in common, it seems to me, is their Maine accent, their beer and Merits, and a slight lift to the brow that makes their eyes look vaguely tilted.

The hours go by and we all get shit-faced.

Rachel does not show up and does not show up and the light roil she put in my surface tension smoothes back down.

Pig feeds Eb Cheetos. While Samantha is in the can he tells me there is not a lot of snow-pussy around yet but he is seeing a girl at the Mehuron supermarket who loves to give head.

Gary overboils spaghetti and adds a can of Chef Boyardee

with onion powder and tabasco for sauce. A feast like this calls for wine and I make another trip to the convenience store for two-liter bottles of Spanish rotgut and a pint of Fleischmann's peppermint schnapps.

Samantha plays mostly Jimmy Buffett on a huge chromed boom box: middle-of-the-road stuff that hunches me grouchy on the sofa. Gary unfolds a square of *Newsweek* containing half an ounce of blue-white powder.

"Aright," Pig cries; licking his mustache, he moistens toilet paper and wipes down the Gollum print. We snort the lines through shortened soda straws. It is mostly crank and novocaine so we who already feel little pain are further anesthetized. The speed of this evening increases to ninety frames per second. The tobacco craving grows large, the drug saps my will to resist. I smoke one, then two more Merits cadged from Pig.

Now I physically cannot sit still for this music. I fetch tapes from the truck. Everyone energetically pogos for a side of Black Flag, arms flailing, making the cottage tremble.

When the speed is all sweated from her bloodstream, Samantha switches back to Jimmy Buffett.

Punk is "devil's music," she tells me.

I do not react. I sense that I cannot argue with Samantha because there is not enough pinned down inside to argue with. This is true of Gary too. How can I argue with cut drugs and dwarf fables and odes to barbecued shrimp?

How can I wrestle a hopelessness that includes no frame of reference? Even Pig bases his existence on the dark assumption that he can do no better than what he always has done.

Yet I owe it to Punk to protest.

When I was fifteen everyone except George saw me mostly as the boy with the withered arm who could not play hockey. Music was no help because on all sides lay the barren front beat of disco.

One day I heard the Ramones on the college station: a

dark groove with a bass that shook buildings. It contained a commitment to attack anything as long as "normal" life was the first casualty. There were no freaks in Punk—or, more exactly, freaks were respected because they were *not* normal. The gift that Joey Ramone and Johnny Rotten passed on to me was an identity of sorts. It was not healthy, but it beat what I had before.

Watching Samantha and Gary subside into the sofa reminds me very strongly of the kids I went to school with—that sense of loss, of waiting for a tow, as if they had no power to move in their own direction.

Like my boat when her engine is stilled.

I have to say this for fishermen: They usually are going somewhere, even if it's in the wrong direction.

In that, fishermen are punk rockers.

* * *

I sit on the end of the couch with a coffee mug of peppermint schnapps. Working on my breath for when Pig's sister comes back. But I do not think of Rachel now. Out of nowhere I am oppressed by a need to call Sam and Caitlyn, although it is much too late and even if I did get through, Cait, on hearing the buzz softening my speech, most likely would hang up.

In the echoing spaces booze has excavated in my brain I find that my last encounter with Caitlyn scared the shit out of me.

I can take it when she gets mad. She blows up and says it's all over and after a while we get down to what is really wrong. Even when she made me leave three days ago it was because she was furious at my getting into trouble at the Squire.

But last night was different. Last night she was calm. She did not even complain—as she had every right to do—because I was going skiing when money was so tight.

And yet, she did not want me around. This is like the difference between screaming at your kid because you are angry, and doing the same thing deliberately, for punishment. It means you have thought it all out, and weighed the options.

It means you have a policy.

I know all about policies. Frank made policies, when I was young. If you lied you got two slaps of the hairbrush on your ass. If you were fresh it was only one. He was never cruel or unfair, and that was the problem. The reason he could be so fair was that basically he didn't give a shit.

That's as far as the deep thoughts reach while the coke scans bebop, then shifts to ballads and then fades gently from my head.

Pig reminisces about *Hooker* for Samantha and Gary. He paints garish pictures of me and him bringing in hundred-weights of whale cod over the side. He is lying and knows it and of course he knows I know. I get the feeling he wants his friends to understand why he invited me. His eyes are pink and his moustache is wet and for some reason this bothers me although I never worried about it on *Hooker*.

I take Eb for a walk. The air is so cold it hums and the stars vibrate in the dry air. The moon, hiding behind the mountain, pisses velvet shadow on the ridge.

I have overdrawn my energy account by the time we return. I climb into the tiny bed and pull the blankets over me.

* * *

The next morning my teeth ache from grinding them all night. My thighs are sore and the winch shoulder is hard to move at first. Despite the excesses of the previous evening, however, I got a reasonable amount of sleep.

The red Toyota is not in the driveway and I figure, that's that. Rachel has a boyfriend she spent the night with so I might as well forget that fantasy.

Relief lies solid in the thought.

My lungs are tight. I taste tobacco in my mouth and this is like a torn ticket, something that permits a return to the show, the whole drama of matches and softpacks and filters and lighting up.

I think sadly of the months I spent fighting cigarettes to where I wanted as opposed to needed them.

Try not to dwell on that. A hot shower softens my muscles to where they can work without complaining. Coffee does the rest. I am on the mountain by ten.

The wind is strong and although it is a little warmer than yesterday, maybe fifteen degrees at the top, the cold feels more powerful.

The snow is packed and the ice extensive. My legs are uncertain this morning, their bloodstream memory of cut and slide abraded by fatigue, and a tinge of caution.

So much can go wrong on a hard mountain.

Despite my caution, or maybe because of it, I keep falling victim to the same one-two feint as yesterday: the slide sideways down ice, followed by a stumble over a grouting of rock.

Every three runs I break to drink hot chocolate and watch what Pig calls snow-pussy. A woman in the cafeteria looks like the waffle-knit model. Her husband resembles the surgeon in a soap Rin watches. They have a five-year-old girl with a thick French braid and freckles. All three wear expensive sports gear and move without reference to anyone else.

The husband smokes: long breaths of dun-hued vapor, curling into the freezing air. You have to smoke outside, it's a state law. I watch him, envy rising hot as acid in my brain.

My stomach is tense from Gary's food. I buy a pack of Maalox and eat three of the tablets and feel better.

I wrote off Rachel this morning but as the day rolls past noon I understand that, where the memory of yesterday's skiing seems to have faded from my tissue, something has crept in to replace it—a decision. My limbs and stomach already aim toward skiing Upper Panther after lunch.

I suppose my dick had a hand in the decision too. It has not been getting much attention recently, even from me. A bad prospect is hope enough for my dick.

I soon discover that I am going to need more than a bad reason to ski Upper Panther. The ice there is thicker and more plentiful than yesterday. Clouds obscure the sun most of the time. The occasional flurry comes horizontal, vindictive. It feels like the mountain itself is spitting at me. The light is correspondingly flat. In that flatness granite lurks, gray against the gray. I pick carefully around the moguls. My legs tire fast. The vapors of schnapps and red wine return to the corners of my vision.

And that is where she shows up, in the corners, the periphery, hissing to a stop on a patch of packed powder, upslope, showering me with shavings.

"Hey."

"Hey. I wasn't sure—"

"Well." She shrugs. "Here I am."

I look at Rachel standing there. Through the hard air she looks back at me without deflection. This is the sense I get of her—she is here with no holdback. What you see is what you get.

Dots of green shine like radar targets in her pupils.

We ski all afternoon. We drink hot chocolate. I manage not to bum cigarettes off her on the lifts. Toward the end of the day my legs start to wear out. Because I am unable to finish turns with the power required I take two bad spills, one after the other. Both are on left-hand curves.

Finally as I move too fast down Slalom Hill I hit a mogul and lose control. I brake left, cross-slope, waving my arms stupidly in the direction I would prefer my center of gravity to move, and slide, once again, into a patch of rock.

The usual occurs. My skis hang and trip me up. Both my safety bindings let go. I flip sideways onto my right shoulder. The inflamed muscles burn fiercely and I yelp as I slide down the ice. The slope is steep here and for a while it feels like I am actually accelerating.

When finally I come to a stop I am on my back, head downhill. Watching the snowflakes fall as lazy and irresponsible as the ones over Western Georges. Coughing as an occasional flake slips down my windpipe.

She kneels beside me. Her breath is sweet with chocolate and tobacco. When she is sure I am not hurt she retrieves the skis. I sit up, groaning. She kneels on the snow, running her fingertips down the Teflon soles of my rented Rossignols, feeling the deep grooves left there by the compound fractures of mountain.

"Jesus," she says. "I think maybe you've had enough."

I say, "I think maybe you're right."

* * *

We drink at the base lodge, standing by the lustful fire. The beers slide down with the usual approximation of bliss. Looking around me, at the men and women, mostly young, all holding bottles in their hands or tilted at their lips, I remember how Sam would stop crying, as a baby, the second Caitlyn put him to her breast.

Beer gurgles into my stomach. My body burns with a good ache. I am drinking with a pretty girl. I have skied down a mountain of ice and survived. Everything is possible and nothing has happened.

For a moment I feel as relaxed and peaceful as Sammy must have felt in the first six months of his life.

It starts to snow again, lightly; against the deepening cobalt of the slopes the snow makes a kind of silver foreground. Rachel was on the early shift today so she is off tonight, and when the base lodge starts to close down and I ask her if she would like to go somewhere else she says "Sure," with no big weight to it, and suggests a steakhouse down-valley.

The place is a typical ski-town joint with booths and varnished pine tables and Christmas lights shining along every surface. The list of burgers runs one and a half pages down the menu. I think of Sam, who loves hamburgers, and wish, on a number of levels, he was with me now.

I start talking about Caitlyn.

The openness in this woman creates a debt. I have no wish to blur or hide among the perfect hygiene of these mountains.

"We've separated," I tell her, "she kicked me out. But not really."

Rachel says nothing.

"I mean, we're still close. Whether she still—likes me, or not, I don't think she even knows yet. I'm not sure she can tell.

"There's a place," I continue, "you have to get over, to get into Chatham Harbor. It's a big sandbar. The tide splits into different currents there, and with the right wind the waves get so confused they don't know which shape to take and they end up looking weird, like pyramids or—anyway the point I'm making is, sometimes at night when I can't see the markers, I think I've already gotten over the bar, and the currents are normal again. And I stop paying attention to where I am; then the Loran numbers change the wrong way. And I know that, never mind what I think, I'm still being pulled by it. The current."

"I'm sorry," she says, "I have to make a phone call."

She stops among the counter crowd to talk to a couple she knows. The men aim eyes at her. I drain my beer, gritting my teeth, feeling the back of my neck warm up. With all my so-called honesty what I was really trying to do was impress her. I am acting like a teenager. How open I am, how poetic I talk. The perilous currents of Chatham bar. *Christ!*

She apologizes when she comes back. Something she had to do, she would have forgotten had she put it off.

I order a "South of the Border" burger with chili and bacon. I scrape the beans off with my knife when it arrives, remembering how my stomach reacts to food like this. The meat is greasy and overcooked. I eat everything, including the beans.

The run of beers evens the jag of hangover. Taking short hits off her Merit keeps me awake. The tobacco hunger is not fierce right now. She tells me about Maine. She says plenty of woods are left in the hills behind Union. Locals can afford to buy land there, as long as they stay ten miles or more from the sea.

She is planning to move to Union next summer.

"What about school?" I ask.

She shrugs. "I can get work. There's a legal aid place in Bath. I just want to live in a place I like.

"They're good people," she adds. "Yuh know where yuh are with them." She gives me that green look, direct as a traffic light. "You'd like it there."

"There's good people," I answer, "on the Cape." I finish off a beer so far down the series I have no idea what number it is. "But things have been changing—I mean, people get lost." I glance at the TV. A McDonald's commercial features Disney elves. "I never see my friends lately. I'm not even sure we're still friends."

"You keep friends, on the mid-coast," she says, spilling half her beer. "Yuh got to."

"My best pal, George," I answer. "I hung out with him all the time. He practically lived at my house, growing up. But I never see him anymore."

"Yuh got to have a place," she says. "People without a place are hollow."

I mop up the beer she spilled.

We last until ten. Both of us have gone a little loopy with fatigue and beer and trying to be as clever and honest as possible.

By the door of her car I touch her arm. She swings slowly around, into my shore jacket, lifting her face to say something. The Christmas lights cross her forehead. I cover her mouth with mine.

Here are codes that need no translation.

She opens her lips, puts an arm around me. We stay there a long time, balancing into each other's cheekbones, teetering a little on the ice of the parking lot. Her tongue is warm and strong and tastes of Merits.

The cottage driveway is empty of cars. Eb barks monotonously inside. She finds a bottle of wine and we drink a glass each and then take Eb for a walk.

Eb is trembling from being cooped up for so long. I tie a rope around his collar. Four times he drops his tennis ball in the snow. The fifth, he loses it for good.

The moon drains cold light through a sieve of branches. When we get back to the cottage she takes me by the elbow, unlatches a door I have never seen open, and pulls me into her room.

* * *

I turn the light off when we undress. Her bed is too soft for two people and gravity draws our bodies into odd shapes.

She turns the lamp back on, covering it with her sweater. In the aqua light I focus on her eyes and the smallness of her breasts and the freckles summer left behind on the tops of them. The freckles remind me of Sam's cheeks; I shut that thought away fast. She removes my watch cap. Her pubic hair, dark against pale skin, looks like bare trees on a snowy hill. Her skin reddens where I touch it. I think, Maybe the need for heat, in this country of ice and rock, is what lies behind our speed in coming together.

She fumbles for a rubber. When she pulls me on top of her I feel like I am at the summit of a slope, a blue run like Chipmunk maybe, or Quacky, long but wide enough for easy parallel turns at the top.

Then with only a tiny twist I am inside her. We start to move. And of course the way we move is like skiing, lifting to shift our weight up, against gravity, so that we can attack the slope from a different direction. Then pressing down, deep into the trend of snow, of slope and mountain beneath.

I see the run in my mind's eye. The blued snow, the evergreens, the gray sky. As the slope steepens, we carve our turns with added care, aware of gravity, of green ice in the heart of moguls—the thick pain of falling here. I run my hands down her back. Both my palms fit over the hard arcs of her buttocks. She is very warm and that heat thins the space between us. Rachel's skin is smooth as dry powder snow freshly fallen on a firm and even base. I cannot keep myself from following gravity down that snow and before I let myself go, I already have gone, turning less as speed increases—taking off, over the final mogul, into the frozen air.

She moves for a while under me, then clutches hard enough to hurt, but does not cry out or otherwise let me know if she has come or not.

Under the bed, Eb sighs in utter boredom.

I raise my head after a while. Looking at her closed eyes in the lamplight.

"You must be nuts," I whisper.

"What?"

"Me. My wife," I add lamely, "an' everything."

She turns her head sideways. "It's *because* of your wife. It's because you're clueless—"

"I'm not clueless." Irritation surfaces, a broken-off knife blade behind the frontal lobes.

"Like one of those Boston guys in the woods," she continues, "in hunting season—always going too far, yuh don't know where you are."

I shift my weight, giving my left arm a break.

"You can never find me again unless I want you to," she adds.

I think that one over for a bit. The knife blade disappears, absorbed in the shallow hope she offers.

"You think you'll want to?" I ask finally.

She rubs her nose.

"Don't talk," she says, "not right now. I like things like this. It's safe. Or half safe, anyway."

"Is there such a thing? Half safe?"

"Shhh."

I am thinking of *Hooker* now. Her half-useless engine, her emergency flares too old.

Rachel turns off the lamp. I fit my breathing to hers, as she does to mine. Then the rhythms change, and fall out of synch. She rolls to the side and puts her face in the crook of my neck. Her breath, deep now with wine, is soft as a vole's. The rubber slips off and I catch it and drip it onto the floor, where Eb promptly eats it.

I circle my arms around her body. Sleep tracks me, a zealous scout; and the closer it gets, the more I feel Rachel change beneath my hands—the elbows and knees, the buttocks and back that in the course of fucking were so unquestionably hers, become something else. They become pieces of a body whose sole connecting principle is the fact that it is not Caitlyn's.

Slowly, even as I try to avoid it, every inch of Rachel defines itself by how it is not my wife.

I suppose guilt is the engine here, and regret, that I no longer can touch Cait in the easy way in which I touched this stranger; but it is a weird sensation, based on skin rather than more complex emotion. As if my flesh had changed—gone soft with the loss of Cait.

Changed in myriad and most subtle ways to become a grief of skin, an epidermal lack.

I try to remember only Rachel, I think of her skiing. The first time we skied together I thought she moved like a deer and in my head she still has a lot of the deer in her.

Half of her surging forward with power and force. Half of her holding back, playing it safe, looking for a place to land that will not put those thin and vital legs at risk.

I get up to piss. I eat four Maalox. When I come back, looking through the frosted glass, I notice a light on in the converted barn behind the cottage. An old woman, very thin, is silhouetted in the top window. She is seated in a rocking chair, she is rocking back and forth, the shadow where her eyes must be aimed directly at our window, at Rachel's bed, where she watched us fucking.

Chapter 20

The Cod

44 degrees 09'N; 73 degrees, 07'W

The cod return to me that night.

It's my old dream, with a few minor changes.

I am down there with them again, in a kingdom of green jewel set in fault lines of jade light.

The cod are mostly whale cod. Somehow the hegemony of green does not affect the brown and gold and silver of the fish. They shine with an inner flame, separate from the water, their stripes and shades lacquered and smooth like sunset on a winter marsh.

The king cod is down there also, great presence in a slow school, flicking his tail in rhythm and assurance as he follows sand lance through a field of big rocks.

That is one difference. The bottom is much more cut up this time. Rocks existed here before, but now they are larger—quarter hills, whole cliffs, and jagged too. No way I or anyone, even the draggermen who fish the harder ground, could shoot a net in here.

Another difference is this: Although before the cod moved in vectors dictated by their prey, now they proceed, slow and steady, in their own direction. I am not sure if they are breasting the tide or following it but for the first time ever in the cod dream I have to swim to keep up.

The effort does not matter, I have no requirement for rest or air. I feel the same toward these fish as I always do. I need them so I can live, they must live so I can kill them. In a strange way, they need me to kill them to define their life.

Tonight, however, a component of danger arises, as if the cod know my life is threatened, or their life is threatened. It does not matter which because if one goes, so does the other; we are species endangered by the same stress. The sadness that surges at this thought is not a personal one. It lies less in the loss of myself than in the destruction of this dependency.

The bottom shallows. A bulk that is dark and does not move looms out of the murk on a wall of boulders. Its flat side denotes a surface made by man: a fishing vessel, thickly decorated with barnacles and algae, rising from among the huckster fingers of a bank of kelp. Ghost-fishing gillnets and potwarps and hung-up otter trawls wind like haunted-house props from the vessel's superstructure.

The king cod stops beside me. His mouth opens. His goatee sags. I think he wants to tell me something, but his eyes are only amazed by the fate of fish and the responsibilities of the school.

He turns, fins easily around the kelp, over the wreck, and disappears into the glassy tide.

The others follow him.

I let them go. I cannot bring myself to get closer. On the transom of this sunken boat I will see a name and know the doom of which the fish were certain. And while part of my brain is sure that this is *Commando*, and that finally I have found Thatch Hallett's wreck, another portion is equally certain it is not.

And that when I swim past the stern, I will recognize the red-leaded doors, the oaken gate, the slick panels of Bruno fiberglass.

And I will see, as I swim by, the words, *"Hooker,"* and the home port "Chatham" underneath, painted on the wreck's transom in black letters.

Chapter 21

Plumes

44 degrees 09'N; 73 degrees, 07'W

In the morning I wake knowing two things: I am in Rachel's bed, and she is gone.

The odd clink travels from the kitchen, wrapped like a present in mountain silence.

A plow goes by, subtly shaking the cottage.

Eb stirs and groans. I think of Sam, opening his eyes, realizing Eb is not around, the way I am made aware of Rachel by her absence.

I shake my head, recalling the codfish, to clear the taste of strangeness. The sky above the mountain has flattened with dawn and the sea is very far away. The window stands empty in the barn behind.

My stomach feels soft, unclenched.

I put my clothes on fast.

Rachel eats poached eggs, fiddles with the coffee maker. Her hair is bound tight in a ponytail and she wears waitress shoes. Makeup dims her eyes. She smiles at me, keeps doing what she is doing.

The TV is on. I click around and find the weather channel. The low over Appalachia, which carries strong winds on its leading edge, wants to travel north. The jet stream, still curving south, checks it over West Virginia. Right now the TV predicts light westerlies in southern New England, partly cloudy. I could sneak a trip in, if Doomo has finished.

I will have to fit in a trip to pay him.

I can listen to the radio on the way home and decide before the bridge for sure.

She brings me coffee.

"Yuh leavin'?"

"Uh-huh."

"Write me?" she asks. "I'll give you my address."

"I'll know how to find you, then."

"It's just a P.O. box."

She offers her mouth. Her tongue darts between my lips, snaps back.

"Maybe I'll come to Maine," I offer.

"Cool," she says. "Bye." And leaves. Just like that. I can hear the busted muffler of her Toyota past the bridge. My stomach feels warm and thin at the same time. I strip the bed, take a shower. When I come out Pig is on the couch, watching *Good Morning America*. He clutches a can of Miller in one hand. His face is tight and low on color. He does not answer when I speak.

I take Eb for a walk. I count out forty bucks for expenses. Pig grunts and continues to stare at the show but he takes the cash. A little kindle of anger starts in me, because what happened with Rachel is none of his business, assuming that is what bothers him.

It was not snow-pussy with me.

When I tell him goodbye he says, "Yuh pretty good at using people, aren't you, Ollie? Just using 'em for what you need?"

He still does not look at me. He sits on the couch with his pink eyes and wet moustache and nothing at all left between us to talk about anymore.

I fetch my dog, get in the truck, and head up the mountain toward Mad River Glen.

The anger at Pig is soaked up by the woods. What's left is a mild regret, because you can fix this kind of problem if you maintain contact, but that contact is gone for Pig and me.

He would be a fool to come back to Chatham now, unless he wanted to work in a restaurant.

I drop off my Rossignols at the rental shop. They keep the deposit I left, to pay for damage to the soles. I stop in Waitsfield for coffee and a sandwich and a pack of doggie biscuits for Eb.

We reach the highway just past noon.

* * *

The drive is easier by day. The mountains trend eastward. The complexity covering their slopes has no boundaries. Trees become branches, branches twigs, the detail as small and pliant as you care to follow it. The overall effect is of an infinite delicacy, argent without end. Blue, pewter, cream hills. Icicles tear like sharks at the eaves of gas stations. Forests of birch, of green-black conifer roll under the shit heap's motion and behind. Flashes of the dream float through the coral of my brain, how it felt to swim like that, warm and deep with large and harmless fish.

My brain more often sketches details of Rachel, the corners of her mouth, the ploughed furrows of hair. To touch her pubis in memory, the softness like liqueur at the center.

I loosen the crotch of my pants.

How she stroked my arm, my left arm, measuring the difference.

"Was it an accident?"

"No."

"You don't want to talk about it."

"I was born that way."

"Thalidomide? It doesn't bother me, Ollie."

"Good," I told her, "'cause it's not like I had the choice."

She keeps touching it. Cait used to do that too. I have met two types of women: the ones who kind of like it, perhaps because it lessens the male threat, making me vulnerable the way they are. And the ones who hate it, for a slew of reasons, take your pick.

Rachel liked it.

"We lived near Otis Air Force Base," I told her finally. "They dumped shit in the water. Rocket propellant. JP-4, ethylene dibromide. Cleaning solvents.

"The Cape's water table goes south and west, in that area—in little streams, only underground. Frank—my father—his house was in Forestdale, near Snake Pond, on one of the biggest plumes. Nobody knew, back then. My mother thinks that's the reason. A radar station, too, it could have had an effect. But the doctors weren't sure. There was some leukemia in babies; a couple had deformities. I mean, it might be genetic."

I feel my left arm with my right hand. It does not seem so bad today. Thin and three inches shorter, but I could work those ski poles fine.

I think perhaps I should move to Maine. In Maine plenty of people are as screwed up as me, because of cousin fucking, and the chemicals from paper mills.

Maine has room to move and roads like Vermont where you can drive for miles and miles and never see a development.

My bad arm feels warm, probably because it has to do all the driving while I feel it up.

In my gut, what I believe is this: It is warm because it did not bother her. Because she rubbed it with fingers light and soft as snow in air twelve degrees above zero.

They are cleaning up the plumes now. Eleven in all, from the Otis dumping sites—the Air Force landfill, the BOMARC silos, the avgas pipeline—all the way to Forestdale and Cataumet. They are sinking well holes along their length.

Giant pumps are being built. They will suck the foul water, millions of gallons worth, spin out the heavier elements, scrub what is left, then pour it back, clean or at least not poisonous, into the aquifer.

Frank hated it. Harriet told me, one night the Wolfschmidts got the better of her restrictions. He would look at my arm as if it were a symbol of all his failures: his son, his work, his marriage. "It wasn't your fault he left," she added thickly, "he didn't talk to me the months I was pregnant with Rin, either.

"Finally he went out to get a pack of Marlboros and I didn't see him for six years."

On the seat beside me Eb recurls, drops a tennis ball in my crotch, puts his snout on top of that. Each eyebrow lifts in turn as he watches me drive.

Eb's eyes are moist and gooey and dark brown and when he feels happy they water a little. Leaving my bad arm to drive, I clear the mucus from the corners.

He farts, but the smell is not so bad. His muzzle holds more gray hairs than the last time I noticed. I rub his ears gently as we follow the highway south.

AA MEETINGS

SUNDAY

UPPER CAPE—AA discussion (no smoking), 7:30 a.m. Civil Defense Room to rear of Falmouth Town Hall, Falmouth; AA speaker meeting, 9:30 a.m., DeWitt Clinton Lodge, 175 Main St., Sandwich; AA speaker meeting, 10 a.m., cafeteria at Falmouth High School, Gifford Street, Falmouth; AA discussion, 3 to 4 p.m., Pause-A-While Drop-in Center, 159–161 Worcester Court, Falmouth; AA discussion, 6 p.m., Otis Air Force Base Day Care Center, Old Hospital Road; AA discussion, upstairs at Old Firehouse, Water Street, Woods Hole; AA speaker meeting, 7:30 p.m., cafeteria at Barnstable County Hospital, County Road, Pocasset; and AA speaker meeting, 8 p.m., First Congregational Church, Main Street, Falmouth.

MID-CAPE—AA discussion, 7 to 8 a.m., Masonic Hall, Old Bass River Road, South Dennis; AA discussion (no smoking), 7:15 a.m., Burger King, Route 134, South Dennis; AA speaker meeting, 11 a.m., cafeteria at Barnstable High School, West Main Street, Hyannis; AA beginners meeting, 5 p.m. and AA discussion (gay), 6 p.m., Barton Auditorium, Bay View Street, Hyannis; AA beginners meeting, 6:45 to 8:15 p.m., West Dennis Community Building, School Street, West Dennis; AA speaker meeting, 7:30 to 8:30 p.m., West Barnstable Community Building, Route 149, West Barnstable; and AA discussion, 8 p.m., Methodist Church, Pond Street, Osterville.

LOWER CAPE—AA discussion, 7 a.m., Drop-in Center, 14 Cove Road, Orleans; AA discussion, 7 a.m., Unit 8, 336 Commercial St., Provincetown; AA discussion, 9 a.m., Universalist Church, Commercial Street, Provincetown; AA discussion (no smoking), 10:30 a.m., American Legion Hall, Main Street and Monument Road, Orleans; AA discussion, 5 p.m., Club Dry Dock, 42 Bay Ridge Lane, Orleans; AA beginners meeting, 6:30 p.m., 96 Bedford St., Provincetown; AA discussion for women,

7:30 p.m., Club Dry Dock, 42 Bay Ridge Lane, Orleans; and AA speaker meeting (no smoking), 8 p.m., Church of the Holy Spirit, Orleans.

THE ISLANDS—AA discussion, 6:45 a.m., Martha's Vineyard Hospital, Oak Bluffs; AA discussion, 8 a.m. and 9:30 a.m., AA big book discussion, 1 p.m. and AA discussion, 8 p.m., Drop-in Center, Gouin Village, off Vesper Lane, Nantucket; AA discussion, 11 a.m., Martha's Vineyard Hospital, Oak Bluffs; AA speaker meeting, 3 p.m., Grace Episcopal Church, Woodlawn Avenue, Vineyard Haven; and AA discussion, 7 p.m., Sacred Heart Parish Hall, Oak Bluffs. NOTE: Calls may be placed to 775-7060 for help or information on closed meetings.

AL-ANON/ALATEEN
SUNDAY

Al-Anon newcomers meeting, 9:30 a.m. and Al-Anon discussion, 10 a.m., community building, Barlows Landing Road, Pocasset; Al-Anon discussion (no-smoking), 9:45 a.m., Conference Room 1, Lobby of Falmouth Hospital, Ter Heun Drive, Falmouth; Al-Anon meeting, 10:30 a.m., Pause-A-While Drop-in Center, 14 Cove Road, Orleans; Al-Anon 12-step meeting, 7 p.m., Community Services, Vineyard Road, Martha's Vineyard; Al-Anon discussion and Alateen meeting, 7:30 p.m., Bourne United Methodist Church, 37 Sandwich Road, Bourne; and Al-Anon adult child 12-step meeting, 7:30 p.m., Burger King, Route 134, South Dennis. Information: 394-4555 between 10 a.m. and 3 p.m.

OVEREATERS ANONYMOUS
SUNDAY

Discussion, 10 a.m., doctors' lounge, Martha's Vineyard Hospital, Linton Lane, Oak Bluffs. Information: 775-9306.

NARCOTICS ANONYMOUS
SUNDAY

Discussion, 8 to 9 a.m., Pause-A-While II, 159–161 Worcester Court, Falmouth; 12-step discussion for women, 4:30 to 6 p.m., 336 Commercial

St. (upstairs), No. 8, Provincetown; discussion, 7:30 to 9 p.m., Bourne Manor Nursing Home, Route 28, Bourne; and discussion, 7:30 to 9 p.m., Federated Church, Main Street, East Orleans. All meetings non-smoking. Information: 778-6166.

Chapter 22

Shubael's

41 degrees 43'N; 70 degrees 03'W

41 degrees 38'N; 69 degrees 46'W

By the time I reach the bridge I have listened to a dozen forecasts and they all say pretty much the same thing.

I am starting to believe in the stability of prediction, in the constancy of numbers, the thousands of temperature and isobaric readings channeled into met stations from Idaho to Newfoundland—a truth: that while the Appalachian low has started to twist, and move northward riding winds of forty knots and more, the jetstream, together with high pressure in New England, will keep it south of New York City. It will stir up the Jersey coast a bit but north of that we will have moderate winds from the southwest then south, and a fishing day.

I have reasons besides money for going fishing now. In a few hours Rachel, and that cold sharp air in Mad River, and the clean feeling of going over the bridge, will have started to lose texture in my mind. Already I can feel the letdown begin. Doing nothing will make it worse.

I do not wish to see Caitlyn now. I do not want to look at Caitlyn with eyes that only a few hours before touched on Rachel peach-soft beneath me.

Obviously I have a treason of body to tackle here and a betrayal that rots what was good between us the way water seeping will rot the tough pine of a boat's deck. But what would be worse, to her, is that I turned my back on our grim compact; that I escaped, for a while, the drowning clench of marriage, and looked on something that gave me hope.

Caitlyn might cut me some slack on the fucking.

The hope she could never forgive.

I call my buddy George from a rest area in Yarmouth only fifteen miles from home. His number comes easily to mind because I just talked about him to Rachel.

Paula answers. George is not in. Lightly I say, "Just thought I'd ask him if he wanted to go on a trip early tomorrow." For ten or fifteen seconds Paula does not respond. Then she says, "I don't think so, Ollie. In fact, he don't want you to call him anymore. You know you always bring trouble for him."

"Wait a minute, Paula," I say, "it's not like—"

She interrupts me.

"He lost six months of his life because of you."

Silence for a beat. Finally I say, "He made his choice. Anyways I did four months more time than him."

"Only 'cause you slugged a guard," she says, and hangs up. I blurt "Bitch!" in surprise mostly because Paula and I always got along before. Staring at the sky, which has filled with long, regular clouds like bars painted the color of Fanta by the setting sun.

In a way it's good Paula said that. The anger it causes sops up the milk of guilt inside me. When I call Cait she answers on the second ring. My chest thuds with the knowledge of what I have done, but in formal questions no lies are necessary or detectable.

She tells me the check I gave the phone company bounced. Also, Doomo finished the cooler job. I work out tides in my head. The ebb will start around twelve thirty A.M. so we can leave, at the latest, at three. If we leave by three I can fit in five hours of sleep before going out.

"After I drop off the mutt at the Kitchen," I tell her, "I'm going to the boat, and we'll head out early."

She hands the phone to Billy. I tell him to meet me at three at the pier.

When I hang up the phone I feel as if merely by talking to her without telling her what happened, I said something hateful to Caitlyn, although I know there was nothing noticeably different in my tone.

I cannot blame Paula for saying what she did.

Every sign on the highway now, every village mentioned—South Dennis, Harwich Port, Brewster—seems to darken in memory against the burnished image of Vermont.

If I play the Ramones loud enough I cannot think about cheating or anything else. I am moving fast when I get off the highway at Exit 11. A clutch of cars blocks the ramp at Route 137 and I slam on the brakes to avoid hitting them. More cars are stopped by the overpass where a large mass condenses in the dimming light. It is a strange shape, alien, like a chunk of meteorite, something I cannot recognize. In the wake of sunset it looks black.

I pull over and climb out of the cab, muscles stiff, confused by a halt in movement so close to resolution.

Walking closer I realize the object is a big animal, sprawled sideways on the asphalt. A horse, still saddled and bridled. Seeing it spread out in a way you never see with horses makes it appear twice as large.

A girl sits against the bridge railing. Her shoulders tremble, and she lowers her face against the people around. One leg is stretched out at an angle that is not right and she clutches at her knee with both hands but that is not why she is crying, I can tell even from a distance. She stares at the horse, saying its name over and over. "Starlight"; her breath says it, the name phrased in vapor. "Starlight."

It's a chestnut animal. The left hind leg is broken cleanly above the fetlock.

The horse whickers softly, moving its neck and head only. Behind me, Eb barks. The girl's sobs find an echo in my stomach. A man checks her knee with fingers that know where to go.

"There anything I can do?" I ask a geezer in a billfisher. "They called fer the rescue squad," he replies. "They're gonna have to put that horse down.

"It's a goddam shame," he continues, pointing at a white Subaru sedan with a dent in the right front rocker panel. "He says he didn't see 'em against the sun, but I ask you."

The Subaru looks familiar. A young Cape Verdean leans over the girl, clutching insurance papers. He asks nervous, pointless questions. I walk around the Subaru. The driver's side door is half open. A huge rubber chicken mask, with neoprene coxcomb and a fat plastic beak, lies deflated on the faux leather of the passenger seat as if it had died and its soul taken wing like a bad poem. A stack of yellow fliers spills onto the road, and I pick one up.

COMING SOON

DUKE OF CHICKENS

fried and barbecued chicken house

Nye Road, Chatham

"WE DELIVER ANYWHERE"

* * *

The Cape Verdean, the Duke of Chickens, has straightened. He watches me with eyes as unreadable as those of the horse, or the chicken mask.

From the south, the shrill yip of a rescue truck increases with the wind, and that is a bad sign, though I do not realize it yet.

* * *

We leave harbor without fuss. The pier is deserted. Most of the boats are moored and shut down. This makes me nervous.

NOAA weather radio, however, says what everybody else says. The Georges Bank weather buoy is still broken so they have no readings for that area. The Appalachian low is starting to tighten into a strong winter anticyclone, but the jet stream will lock it down well south of here.

Medium southerlies, it is predicted, will kick waves to six feet over shallow ground.

The NMFS ladies, when I called them at two-thirty, told me most of the Gloucester fleet was in port, but that was because they used up their hours.

I have another one hundred and ninety-two hours of legal fishing left before New Year's.

It is fairly warm, in the mid thirties. The wheelhouse barometer reads 29.17. With the diesel burner on, the wheelhouse is hot. I follow on radar the bright dots of high-flyer buoys that the harbormaster places to mark the ever-shifting channel over the bar. I switch on the autopilot between buoys and go through the logbook, examining notes on tows I made over the last two months, looking for ground a little closer than the 700 line, in case the storm comes north and we have to run for cover. I decide on a wreck by the sixty-fathom countour almost due east across the shipping lanes from the "Rose and Crown" buoy. We got one pretty good haulback there last fall, and it is far from the closed areas.

Though these are poor criteria for choosing a fishing ground, I reflect as I stow the parallel rulers. When I was hooking, I had been doing it for so long, I knew what I was doing so well, that it got so I had a gut feeling of where the cod would be in every season, at each change of tide or wind or temperature of water.

More often than not, I was right.

We cross the bar at 03:20. The seas twist as the currents search around the shoals for a way to go. Even by starlight I can make out their movement. Where the currents meet, instead of making waves, they slide under each other like snakes, leaving a scabrous sheen. It is hard to believe a mere four feet of water lies beneath the keel.

Billy is in a good mood. He reads me an editorial in the *Stranded Times* about the fisheries council. They are talking about further restrictions on the allowable days of fishing. The newspaper sees in this some good, some bad.

Billy puts away the paper, opens his bag, and takes out a coffee cake he baked. He insists that I look at it where it sits proudly in its nest of Saran Wrap. He has drizzled sugar icing in the shape of *Hooker* in the center.

"I figger," he says, "this kind of work, it's good to eat good food."

Billy wears a knife at his belt. Caitlyn bought it for him. It is shiny and has a handle made of exotic black wood. The sheath includes a hole for a four-inch stainless steel marlinespike. This is a yachtsman's knife, of limited use on a fishing vessel.

I tell him it's nice.

Billy warms up the cake and explains exactly how it would suit the Bohemian Grove conspiracy for New England fishermen to go broke. I watch the radar and stare out the dark windows at perils I could never spot in time.

Around six o'clock something coats the very edges of the mares' tails and then the crests of the swells with glow. The sun comes up a half hour later, cold and hard and the color of drowned flesh, over Cultivator Shoal. For a few minutes the small-angled light digs out the sides of waves, making them seem bigger than they are, enormous moguls or small mountains even. And the proximity of other mountains, in time if not in space, and above all the recent body memory of rhythm—the deep kneeling into troughs, the light lift as I shifted weight, tucked my heels up so I could point the tips of my skis into the hollows between moguls; the long slow pull into valley as I slid deeper into Rachel—are linked with actual movement in me now.

Hooker's stern is kicked upward by a swell. I lift my heels a bit. As she rushes into the next wave I lean forward, my hands coaxing her wheel in the right direction, pressing my knees into the instrument bulkhead, and there is a whisper of coming as she settles into the curdled foam, a glimmer of Rachel's eyes in the greenish spray around the starboard bow—a sense of shift, behind the knees, behind the stomach even as I remember how, in the aftermath, Rachel was defined by difference—a compendium of lines that did not fit or mesh with Caitlyn's.

I never understood why Cait stopped making love with me. Obviously anger and boredom can build up to a heat and weight that will stop things. Too much heat will expand and seize up any machinery, no matter how well oiled.

But we used to fuck well, with a healthy hunger. And surely, if Caitlyn was too full of heat and rage, she could change things: alter the mold, force the O-rings; get out? Not sit in immobility and weight for the sake of anchoring her conspirator in the same bitter form.

Check the instruments. Water 120, engine oil 36, main gear 162, fuel, half a tank; all as it should be. The engine runs evenly. The barometer reads 29.15. All these readings take place in the shallow rhythm of perception. The deep memory runs on like good diesel beneath, for what is in my mind now is familiar and good. It has its own course and momentum.

Caitlyn and I started living together the autumn I broke up with Casey. I was renting a shack in the woods between Shubael's and Micah's ponds. She was doing the choreography for *South Pacific* at the Orleans Repertory. Only three weeks off probation and I had figured out banging nails was not for me. I started quahogging a little and mostly jigging off the old clam skiff that ended up in Marston's Hollow. I would putt out to Crab Ledge and pick up a box or two of mixed groundfish over the course of a day. No big bucks but my overhead was almost zero, just fuel and jigs, surgical tubing and monofilament, beer and food and the shack's rent, which was low.

I did not go to sea every day. As the light shrank slowly into winter, and the swamp maples put on and then slowly shed costumes that turned gaudier with every frost, it was easier to lie abed, letting the woodstove convert the stored heat of catshit oak and pump it into every corner of our shack. Watching Cait, her dark hair disciplined with elastic. Long body sheathed in leotards and draped in torn sweaters, she performed her breathless rhythms across the cedar floor. "Six-ha, seven-ha, eight; bend, jump, and ha-one, ha-two." Bloody Mary is the girl I love. We read the *Weekly World News* out loud to each other. "*Titanic* Lifeboat Found—1 Man Still Alive!" "Scientists Probe Two-Headed Secretary!" Caitlyn rolling up her pillow on one shoulder to mime one head taking dictation from the other. Touching each other in the hot darkness with Cortez fingers. Our bodies full of surmise, and slippery with desire.

That winter was cold and the harbor iced up. I was unable to go fishing even when I wanted to. By spring we were so broke we could not afford to buy food. We ate regularly at the Kitchen and waited for the alewives to run up Muddy Creek so we could catch them in dipnets as they leaped and wriggled, desperate to spawn, against the flow. On the day they first ran we fried up pounds of roe and ate it together in bed and made love afterward with the eggs of a million uncompleted herring rounding out our bellies.

Of course no one expected it to continue forever, and we moved out of the shack that summer, but goddammit! There is enough of the pond left in me to want to hold her at night, when darkness veils the props of what has happened since; to touch Caitlyn in ways that bring out the pond in her.

Those days are eleven years gone now but the memory of them is strong and clear as tidal current inside me. It smashes against my continuing wonder, that Caitlyn asked me to leave: that we are living apart. The distress from that collision has nowhere to go. It swells up, liquid yet tough as engine parts, building on the shallow ground in my chest. I pound my fist against the throttle housing so hard that the r.p.m. increase by three hundred, although I never touched the lever.

The spray crashes high over *Hooker*'s bow. She is banging a little harder now. The mogul waves are higher, sharper.

I pull the throttle back again and shut my eyes tightly to scrape those images off the inside.

I am tired but that is no excuse. The last time I day-dreamed like this I missed the tow deadline and hung up on a wreck that tore both bottom panels of my best net.

I open my eyes, and go below to check the fuel pump.

Chapter 23

The waves keep growing. By the time we have crossed the shipping lanes they are coming funny—it's not so much their shape that is odd, but their direction against *Hooker*'s course. Checking the compass and squinting at their silvered backs I reckon the seas are running a little east of south now, and so is the wind.

The wind started shifting a long time ago, I realize. It brought ambulance sounds from Chatham center, which is east of south from the highway.

The barometer reads 29.05. It has dropped .10 inches in two hours.

I look for the sun, pressing my cheek against the wheelhouse glass to find it. It is no longer the hard ball it seemed earlier. Muscled clouds flex out of the south, preceded by a mist that sucks out the warmth and direction of light.

I flick on weather radio again. No change.

We shoot the trawl, steering 105 down a ledge of rock and gravel off the sixty-fathom contour, 100 yards west of the wreck. We are almost beam-to the swells and wind on this course. The crashing of wave against hull fills the wheelhouse and I cannot hear Billy's yakking. This in itself is an indication of the turmoil outside. So is the fact that I am steering by hand. The auto cannot cope with seas this rough when we are towing.

By the time we are halfway through the tow the wind is coming full southeast. I do not jump to this conclusion. The wind is not unitary, it takes time for all the different gusts and riffles to line up in a new direction—but when it becomes obvious, the chrysalis of fear slowly awakening in my intestines opens into a higher life.

A wind backing east at this time of year is never a good sign. And a backing here, with an anticyclone known to be lying south—frankly, it sucks.

Because it means the low pressure area, against all predictions, has started to veer north.

And that means *Hooker*, instead of riding out the ruffled outskirts, is positioned to suffer the psycho rage of a full storm. For this will be a late fall nor'easter, an Atlantic anticyclone. Cruelest and most violent, the serial killer of storms. It could be coming after us with ninja moves in anywhere from two to six hours.

I turn up the radio and wait for a change in the forecast to back up my observations but it is the same looped recording it has been for the past four hours: wind southwesterly fifteen to twenty on Nantucket Shoals; and then the notice for the broken weather buoy.

I figure now the absence of buoy data has something to do with it. They are not usually so wrong for so long.

"Billy," I call, pulling back on the throttle. "We gotta go home."

"It's blowin' up a bit," he replies.

I glance at him. Billy is staring at the hard waves, balancing easily against *Hooker*'s motion.

"Christ, man," I tell him, "you're starting to sound just like a fisherman, you better be careful or I'll hire you for good."

Billy says "Yeah, I'll be the winchman," but he smiles as he says it, so wide I can see his molars, and I smile back, we are both grinning at each other like trick dogs for a moment until the fear squiggles in my gut again and I tighten my focus on the situation at hand.

He takes the wheel. I winch in the net. This work is harder than it used to be. I have to hang on with both hands against the rolling. Hooking the doors in is as jolly as any pastime that involves playing with three-quarters of a ton of iron swinging unpredictably in a thirty degree arc.

When I wind the cod end up it, too, swings wildly and in a manner that might be dangerous for the boat if we had any weight of fish in there.

We do not. Skate, pout, maybe a quarter box of gray sole, but I cannot bring myself to toss them, just open the fish-hold hatch and scrape it all down.

No need to worry about ice since we are going straight home and the temperature is only thirty-eight anyway. I dog the hatch solidly and hook the safety chain to the doors so they cannot swing off their blocks. Billy falls off course a little. Slices of dark water are carved off the bow as we roll, and chute back to the after deck till my seaboots are shin deep. The wind howls Arab songs in the antennas. It cuts through the seals in my oilskins, letting the rain in. I am damp by the time I go forward.

In the wheelhouse with the door dogged shut it's a lot quieter. I check the Loran, then the chart, mark our position and plot the quickest course home. I may have to revise that if the wind gets much stronger because then we will have to steer more according to waves than to honor a line I drew on paper. Already I must reduce steaming speed to avoid pounding *Hooker* too hard.

Also if the wind comes much further east we will have to take the longer route through Pollock Rip Channel to Stage Harbor because the outer bar would kill us with waves coming right across it from the ocean.

For a while, though, I believe we got away with it. As I fill out the catch report I am writing memos to myself in my head. The memos read the same as always: Idiot, you did it again. You let everything slide until the bank was the spear's point to a long haft of pressures. And because you cannot miss that next mortgage payment you can't take a day off when the weather looks dicey. And then *you* are the asshole out there in a nor'easter when the engine quits and all they hear is the last pathetic whine of the loser you have become.

The Mayday with a deadly flatness to it. The silence that continues after and forever.

At 13:40 we are abeam of the GRS buoy, the green of its Racon beacon staining the radarscope in our direction. The wind is dead southeast now. The waves are bigger but manageable at lower speed. The radar shows no traffic at all. On the VHF, an oil rig support skipper tells the Coast Guard he is steaming for shelter in Johnstown.

The engine runs well, its meter even. Billy smokes his Merits in the wheelhouse, cupping them in the usual way, in the shelter of his chest, between drags. The wiper on the starboard window whines and slaps, whines and slaps.

At 14:45 NOAA weather radio finally revises its forecast. The snake of jet stream straightened out unexpectedly. The low is moving north. A winter storm warning is issued from Watch Hill, Rhode Island, to Chatham, including Nantucket Shoals and Southern Georges. "Thanks, guys," I mutter, watching foam hiss down the starboard side of the deck while the green-black water underneath it slams like small artillery into the cabin trunk. It is not NOAA's fault; their marine weather division gets almost no money compared to the aircraft side of things. The bulk of the money always goes to aviation.

I read that in *National Fisherman*.

At 15:52 I record this log entry in a scrawl that zigs as the waves thud on the bow and zags as they rock under. "41 degrees, 38.3 minutes N; 69 degrees, 46.8 minutes W; position approximate (Loran skipping). Course 306 speed @ 3 kn. Waves 10–12, wind ESE 40 gusting 50, barometer 28.99, very heavy rain. Course to Pollock Rip—"

That is all the log reads because I cannot figure out what to do next. The Rip channel is tricky and full of crosscurrents. I am a little nervous about going that way with the Loran skipping. The channel buoys, however, are eight feet tall and steel and the radar should pick them up with ease. I hear sheets of water being whipped onto the cabin roof and over the scanner rotating obediently on its plinth. The Furuno may not for long survive such treatment.

Yet the bar has become even more of a marginal proposition with the wind hauling in this direction.

I say nothing to Billy. I reach into his breast pocket and take out a Merit and he lights it for me without saying anything either. The zinc-colored sun slips between rashers of rain and in that fast shine I notice the tuna harpoon has been torn from its lashings. I completely forgot it was up there.

I think of Manny the time he came with us tuna fishing, the summer before last. Standing in the pulpit, trembling with excitement and pride because, though he winged one fish with that harpoon, he nailed another hard beside the dorsal fin.

For a moment the memory washes over me. All one afternoon we chased a smoking line with the sea greasy and flat as a diner griddle. My uncle red as a fry cook from exertion. Manny's grandfather was only cabin boy on a whaler, yet my uncle always talked about it as if he were heir to a proud guild of harpooners. While we trailed that fish he was flushed with the images of all the men he had ever hoped to be.

Eight hundred and eighty-two pounds of bluefin at four bucks a pound.

Maybe we should try Pollock Rip.

I take a long drag of the cigarette and grind it out. The barometer now reads 28.96. Moving to the chart, I double-check the Pollock Rip course. And then the engine hesitates.

It is the old symptom—the rhythm falters, like a piano player suddenly unsure of where he is in the music. It slows down a bit, speeds up, too fast; then holds, at slightly lower r.p.m. than before.

Memory at once is washed away. The sense of "I" goes too. Fear has grown without awareness. It swarms out of my gut like Hollywood assassins.

"Take the wheel," I snap at Billy. "There, zero-one-five degrees, see?"

My knees do not support me well on the companionway. I hang on hard to the engine room bulkhead because the rocking seems worse down here. The fuel pump is hot. So is the manifold, where it joins the engine block. Billy says nothing after I take back the wheel but he keeps looking at me. I can tell he is scared and trying not to show it. I wonder how much fear I am showing. He extracts a cigarette, then presses it back into the pack.

"Ah," I grunt. I can barely hear myself over the smash of water. "Don't worry about it," I add loudly. "That pump keeps runnin' for hours. It's not the cooler, like last time."

But we have no choices left now. The Pollock Rip route will take four or five hours in this weather and never mind the Loran issue. If we lose power in Pollock Rip we will not be in much better shape than if we lose power over the bar.

And the bar is only an hour and forty minutes away unless the waves get bigger.

"The bar," I continue. "It shouldn't be too bad yet. Wind's still mostly out of the south."

Of course the waves get bigger. It must be blowing near fifty now. We come into shallower water near Monomoy and the circle of which all waves consist finds footing on the sand four fathoms under and hoists itself a little further into the air.

The shape of the shoals changes the direction of the swells. They are coming almost due east here. We cannot hold even a northwesterly course anymore because the waves would climb *Hooker*'s side and roll us. I have to steer in doglegs, first northeast, then west-nor'west, attacking the swells on the starboard bow or riding them as they come up our starboard quarter.

The clouds and haze have been steadily absorbing light so that when night falls it does not come as an event but as just another step in the deterioration of visibility.

The rain increases in volume. It is so thick it sounds like a rush, like heavy canvas being continually ripped. Darkness makes all sounds louder. The rain and the crash and wash of waves and the faltering roar of diesel all come across as an obscenity of noise. It's the way I imagine war must be, the madness of mechanized violence translated into decibels.

The waves through the laboring wiper now appear only as an affirmation of dark, a feeling of cold weight, of lightlessness. While we steam northeast the blackness rises and rises to starboard, over the bucking slope of *Hooker*'s bow, higher than seems possible, and higher than that. Now *Hooker* hesitates.

Like a horse getting ready to take a jump, she is pushed back against the haunches of her prop. She twists, surges upward. Then, as if we, on the horse, were a rider suddenly reaching the top of an unexplored mesa, the blackness breaks up around us into smaller sable ridges. The boat shudders, cants to starboard; her bow smashes down in an explosion of froth and rainwater; and she is surging down the far side of the wave, surfing for what feels like a minute, the goddam swells are that big.

This kind of movement is hard to control. On a northeasterly course I have to steer her thirty degrees off the angle of the waves' attack to split their force between the side of the boat and the bow. I goose the throttle when the bigger waves come. That way we will not get pushed backward and broached.

I cut our speed well down when we are running west-nor'west and the waves, coming from behind, surf us into the night.

Once when I do that the fuel pump falters badly, and the diesel almost dies. The bow swings far to one side and we roll thirty, forty degrees. Billy is thrown against the port bulkhead and I hang onto the throttle housing so as not to fall. The surf at the waves' top strikes us so hard the hull booms like a bass drum and shudders in every strand of matting.

I should be worrying about the hull. I should be thinking about the cavities down there where the foam shrank and the ice maybe formed, caves where stress accumulates and finds nothing to resist its power.

I do not think about it. There is nothing I can do and only so far I can think. The mistakes are all made, the decisions taken. In this fact lies shame, and anger, but also a bitter peace.

Anyway, on that last wave, the engine picks up again. I pull the boat back on course and she straightens up quickly. Ten minutes later the radar shows a blip to port that must be the first channel buoy.

I should turn immediately toward it but now I hesitate. How I feel about the bar is too dark and strong for considered action. All the stories I heard since I was a kid—all the times I got lost in there and the waves turned to hard chaos around me—combine into a pattern of thought that is far from objectivity.

I want to turn tail and run from the bar as fast as the engine will move; I want to go in this second and beat the bar at its own sport. There are no half measures here.

This is exactly the way I felt the first time I met Caitlyn, at the Squire. It seems odd, but also makes perfect sense, that I should have the same reaction to something so all-encompassing and lethal as I did to falling in love with Cait.

I send Billy below for the sea anchor. While he searches for it I switch the VHF to channel sixteen and key the mike.

"Chatham Coast Guard, Chatham—" I stop, because no one is in the Chatham station now, only empty rooms and the spectres of dead transmissions.

"Coast Guard Provincetown," I correct myself, "Provincetown, this is fishing vessel *Hooker*."

The wind is loud enough that I cannot hear the static. With the visual component nearly gone this storm has become an animal of body: the constant tension of thighs absorbing the up-down pitch of waves, the pectorals compensating for our whiplash roll, ears blocking out the wind's shriek, the rain's rip, the smash, wash, smash of swells—the adrenal glands squirting out potion to compensate for fear and the multiple-choice possibilities of death.

I try Provincetown once more, then Brant Point.

A voice puts words into the mouth of noise.

"*Hooker, Hooker*, this is Swear."

His carrier wave dips and climbs against the lament of wind.

"Swear?"

"Yeah."

"You got water in the parlor yet?"

"Up to the sofa, Ollie. How's it with you?"

"I'm about a mile off the breach. Engine's slipping a little. I just wanted to let somebody know, I'm coming in."

The boat falls, lifts like an elevator. We are coming up fast on the bar. The VHF carrier wave fades in and out, in and out, quick as Punk. I push hard on the wheel and goose the throttle as another big one surges. Something slams on the after deck, like a metal hand pounding for entrance.

A piece of gear has come loose.

Billy returns, holding tight to the hatchway, the sea anchor looped around his shoulder. Yank the throttle back now as the bow dives. This is a bad trough, and solid water explodes against the windows. The wheel kicks in my hands. A crack appears on the port-side glass. A stream of water spurts through the after door. My stomach feels empty, scraped out like a pumpkin by the steel spoon of panic.

Open the throttle against the next onslaught. Key the mike. My hand hurts where the wheel hit it. My voice trembles.

"Swear. This is *Hooker*, listen—"

"Ollie, this is Swear base."

My uncle's voice.

"Ya go back outside now. Swear is callin P-town now, OK? The 48-footer come pick yah off. That bar's gonna be crazy, over."

"I can't. Fuel pump's fuckin' up. Over."

"Ollie, yah listen now."

"No time, Manny."

Silence for a while. I think of *Commando*, the in-out quality of the transmission I heard. Swear's transmission has the same rhythm. Maybe all emergency transmissions have a similar frequency: sentences and clarity chopped to pieces while the entropy of disaster gains hold and will not let go of small patterned things, like high-frequency radios and boats. I hear traffic on Sixteen now, stuff I cannot catch. Manny's voice says, "Okay, I'll tell him." Then he comes back to me.

"*Hooker*," he says, "the *Crazy A's* is off of Pollock Rip now. They can't tow your boat in those waves—"

"Got that."

I twist the wheel hard, my stomach willing the boat over a wave that in the end is not so bad.

"He says, meet him at number one buoy, he'll pick ya up."

Crazy A's. Phil Amaral. We will be back at the sea buoy in ten minutes if I turn around now. Then perhaps an hour of jogging against the storm until Amaral shows.

Even if the injection pump quits all the way I can put out the sea anchor and drift with our bow to the waves and we should be OK.

My stomach relaxes. I know we probably will make it now. We do not have to be swallowed by that iron water slamming against our hull. We do not have to continue fighting like this, struggling to hold a line on a chart, killing ourselves to get over this wilderness of shoal into a port that is always dying with the weight of ocean, alone and terrified as always in this place.

Because Phil Amaral is out there, and the *Crazy A's*, and they can take us off the bar and off this damaged boat and ferry us into the shelter of Stage Harbor.

The wheel will not turn in my hand. I decide to force it; my brain will not send the command. The wheel is stainless steel with nylon string braided around it for grip. Usually I turn it without thought, as if it were spliced to my sinews, feeling the cables tense and slacken, the big bronze rudder funneling water into force.

My wheel, my prop, my boat.

I pound my fist against the throttle housing. The r.p.m.s do not change. My knuckles feel like they have been stove in. The absence of bulkhead to keep the rage at bay allows it to wash out away just as suddenly.

Key the mike, buying time. Sucking on my knuckles. Balancing the bow between a wind that has gone frankly nor'east and waves that lag behind, from the east.

"Manny, gotta think about that."

"Go back out, Ollie," he says urgently. "Go back. Ya hear me? Ya won't make it over the bar now."

It comes down to *Hooker*. I can barely see her bow against the rain and waves. This is a body thing again—in the warmth of the wheelhouse I feel her against me, the way I used to feel Caitlyn after we had made love a second time, the boundaries between us confused and lessened.

Every move of her, the way her flat ass lifts to a wave and her deep skeg keeps us on course as we are carried forward and her hard chines cut safely into the next swell is more familiar to me now than the motions of my wife. The thought of abandoning this boat is like the idea of leaving Sam, or Eb.

My friends are few enough. I cannot afford to let one go to the storm.

I grip the mike hard and click the transmit button without meaning to. I know *Hooker* is not the only issue. I have to think of Billy. My first responsibility is to the crew of this vessel, not to the hull itself.

I decide, again, to turn back.

The compass light shines bloody. The Loran numbers jump. If we can make it another two miles we'll be all right. Two miles only; forty minutes at this speed.

I am sick to the tendrils of my heart with abandonment.

"Billy. You wanna get off? There's somebody to take you off."

"You gettin' off?"

"No. I'll stick with the boat, but you go ahead."

"I'll stick with you."

"You get off," I almost shout, "I think you should."

"Nah."

"You sure?"

"Sure," Billy says.

I key the mike twice.

Click, click.

"Manny," I say abruptly, "thanks, but we're comin' ahead."

He doesn't react, other than to say he will stand by. The VHF returns to noise.

I hang up the mike. The thing that is loose aft bangs again. The boat's glass booms with the force of it. My stomach is tensed once more. That tension is familiar and in a weird way the familiarity makes me feel better.

"See what that is, Billy?"

He is already looking—switching the deck lights on, clearing mist off the after window. In bright worklight the rain looks like aluminum, hissing in flat milled panels out of the hysterical night.

"It's the otter board. The left—port—one."

"Is the chain loose?" I yell.

"I guess."

"I mean, did it break?"

"I don't know. No. I can't really see. No."

"Fuck," I yell. If the block is all that's holding the cable it could easily jump off and go overboard on a big wave. If that happens, the door goes too and in the violent dance of waves the still-tethered door will inevitably stove in the hull, or at least foul the prop. And then the same thing will happen to us that happened to Ray Crosby.

"I'll hook it up again," Billy yells.

"No," I shriek at him, "Billy—"

Wind invades the wheelhouse. It rampages wolf-like through my charts and instruments. Suddenly an inch of water is sloshing on the deck.

The aft door is open. Billy is gone.

I strain toward the door, trying to steer and watch the waves and watch Billy at the same time in the damp sparkle of deck light. This is how men die, experienced men, and Billy is not experienced. He has not a clue of what that water can do. I see him wait for it as *Hooker's* stern comes up, not a big one, and the wave explodes over the transom and the starboard side and sluices across the afterdeck. Then he is running low at the port gunwale, grabbing hold of the gallows frame. His oilskins glisten against the lights, the metal rain, the darkness beyond. He grabs the securing chain, leans forward once, twice, trying to move in time with the wild swings of that door; then, leaning well outboard, tries to hook it into the brace on the door's inboard side.

He misses the first time but he has the right idea. Only he is much too high up the gunwale for this weather, holding on with one arm crooked on the steel as he leans forward to aim the hook again.

I turn to the forward windows again, watching the night alter as we surf down the wave's back.

Look aft. Billy holds the chain fully extended as the door swings toward him. He is very close to securing it.

Forward, as we level out in the swell's trough. I bring the

r.p.m.s down. The waves are much shorter in the shallows and they are adopting the flaked shapes of confusion. This is where the tide divides into different currents, and the waves must react to the split. When we crack into the bottom of the trough it is like hitting a cement floor.

Look back.

Gone.

Water swirls uncluttered, black and white and green around the empty deck.

Not gone. A shoulder, dark clothes, emerge like reefs out of the foam beside the portside gallows.

The port side door, secured now, throws itself against its restraint of chain.

Without wasting time in thought I fumble the autopilot switch to "on" and run out the same way he did.

Hooker takes the next wave by herself, hesitates, cants across the crest. I pray she doesn't broach. If she broaches in these waves we will capsize.

Knee-deep in freezing seawater I wind a fist around Billy's sweater and my bad arm around a stanchion. The water pours over me, cold—so cold it makes me want to let go. That kind of violence is just too much. It's like an army of bad cops, there is a whole ocean of it this bad, dark and hard and endless and we might as well go quietly.

A tongue of wave yanks me away from the gunwale, prying my hand loose. I am washed on top of Billy. Something slams me against the winch, smacking my ear against the steel.

The bow cracks into the following trough.

That deceleration washes me back again, and half over the wheelhouse coaming. My boots, full of water, are heavy, but I race them to get purchase—hauling Billy by his sweater all the way over the coaming, into the wheelhouse, as the boat tips to port.

I scrabble to my feet and fall against the wheel. Push the throttle to redline, and hard starboard rudder to keep from broaching. A wave looms to starboard. It is ragged and tall; it seems separate from the rest of the surf. The foam at its top looks like monstrous fingers reaching for me and Billy. In the space between I see a mouth open, roaring. It reminds me vaguely of myself, when control has gone and nothing works in my head but the will to scream and damage. Foam slaps the side window and cracks one of these too.

The fuel pump falters, picks up once more.

Just let that pump keep running another ten minutes, I think. Let it keep running, and I will do something drastic in return. Like never cheat on Caitlyn. Never let anger gain control over my words to her.

Course of 30 degrees to buoy three. The Loran jumps every couple of seconds now. No sign of the buoy on radar. I do frenzied math in my head, factoring speed, time, and deviation since the last buoy, coming up with maybe four minutes ETA at the next.

The wind yowls higher than ever, and leans *Hooker* to port. Something snaps on the wheelhouse roof. The boat hesitates, more than water could make her. Her port-side chine drags against the sand. Then she comes free.

I wedge Billy with my leg, practically standing on him. Water from the open door froths over the coaming and sloshes around the 'house. The boat pitches like her bow had been kicked upward by a giant boot. I lean my body into the wave and wrestle the surf for control of my rudder. The terror has gone from my stomach now—it's as if the bar is too big even for terror, it has taken over me and the boat and Billy too and there is nothing left now but the action it demands of us. Jamming my face in the Furuno mask I am amazed by the vicious sea-return. I stare at the screen a full half minute and see nothing that makes sense. When I look at the compass again we are fifteen degrees off course.

I swing the wheel wide to port.

The engine revs, dips, revs again.

A wave cracks, not hard, on the port quarter this time. If my math was right we should be past the third buoy now and if so we have a half mile of shoals to the north and somewhat east of us and they are taking the brunt of the storm now and we are *through*.

Billy groans below me. His arm flops against my left boot.

The Loran's display reads "SEARCHING ... SEARCHING."

I pay attention to compass and time past the next two markers. I have to steer carefully because we are in shallow water and the waves retain their funny shapes. They come from three directions and sometimes open up so wide that for almost five seconds we are running through calm water between the crests.

"Ollie," Billy says.

The waves past the sixth marker, though still sharp, are only half as violent. *Hooker* now moves more like a boat than a piece of flotsam. I look at the subsidiary blackness of waves and the glow of the lighthouse touching us every ten seconds with its yellow gesture. The "dangerous bar" warning strobes weakly. For a second a great soapy love for Chatham harbor floods my innards. It is like what you feel for a woman who rages and criticizes, and then opens her arms and takes you to bed.

Harbor is always a function of risk.

I slow the engine, flick on the auto, and kneel beside Billy.

One arm is hooked around my left boot. In the meager shine of the compass light he looks like a piece of sailcloth torn off and come uncoiling in the backwash. His face shines against the dark water still sloshing inches deep in here.

"Ollie?"

"You OK?"

"Ollie."

"I'm here. We're almost in. We made it."

"I can't feel my knees."

The wind is still loud. I am shaking violently from being cold and wet and afraid. I know Billy means something different—his knees were where they were supposed to be, when I hauled him in.

"You look fine," I tell him at length.

"I can't feel my feet either," he says, weakly. "The door hit me—hit my neck."

I try to make out his neck. With only the binnacle light for illumination I cannot see it clearly. The shaking stops for a few seconds.

Some news you cannot slake by trembling.

The engine rhythm dips again. The interval between dips is shorter than before and I figure the storm somehow has accelerated the fuel pump problem.

Billy's eyes are shut, in fear or pain.

The change in my boat's rhythms affects me not at all.

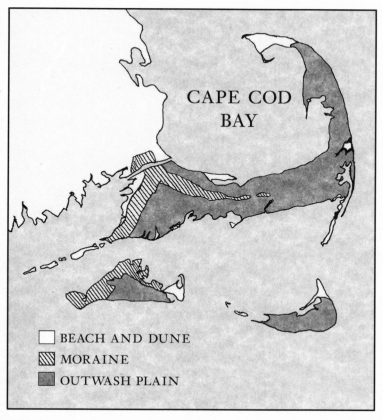

CAPE COD
BAY

BEACH AND DUNE
MORAINE
OUTWASH PLAIN

GEOLOGIC STRUCTURE OF CAPE COD. *Courtesy Elizabeth Orr.*

Chapter 24

Life support

41 degrees 42'N; 69 degrees 56'W

41 degrees 38'N; 70 degrees 16'W

Ambulance lights stripe the night as we approach the fish pier.

I called Swear again as soon as we were out of bad water, and he must have phoned the fire department first thing.

The waves are high, for Pleasant Bay, and I have to steer fine to bring us in. The wind blows dead on the pier but I do not worry about the gelcoat, just lay *Hooker* starboard-side-to along the portion of dock forward of the *Mary Anne* barge. The wind jams us hard into the pilings.

A thin figure in a lumber jacket stands like a heron on the bulkhead. I throw Manny a spring line. When he has it secured I use slow forward and port rudder to keep the boat in place. Now the engine runs without missing a beat.

The EMTs climb backward down the slick ladder. Their

sacks of equipment swing like counterweights. I have laid Billy flat on the wheelhouse deck. They touch him carefully, asking questions full of ease and friendliness. I know this is all professional and fake but it makes me feel better and Billy responds to how they say it as much as what they say.

"It was the trawl door," I tell one of them while he dials his cell phone. "It hit his neck."

"Yeah, we got that."

He turns toward me. I recognize the guy who wanted to operate on Jack Sibley's balls.

"You don't have to do anything here," I ask him, "right?"

"Nothing we can do here."

It should feel better to know he won't attempt to cut. I cannot feel anything yet. Perhaps it is the guilt making my body like Billy's; nothing but emptiness below the voice pipe. That and a tiredness that underscores every move, because of wrestling the wheel for six hours.

Now I have nothing to wrestle.

They slide him onto a collapsible board and wrap a shiny bag around both him and the board. Then they belt the package into a fiberglass stretcher. A handful of people gawk over the pier edge now. They haul Billy delicately. An EMT guides the stretcher from the ladder. It is weird to see Billy going up the pier like a box of fluke. "What's it look like to you?" I ask the would-be surgeon, trying to keep my voice steady.

"Can't tell yet. He's got some feeling though."

"You mean, he's not paralyzed?"

"We're taking him to CCH," he says, "they'll take good care of him."

He leads me into the wheelhouse and hands me insurance forms to sign. Then he goes up the ladder. By the time I tie up fore and aft and kill the engine the ambulance lights have been swallowed by rain and no one is left on the pier.

Voices thread into the night outside the Down-Cape buildings. The words *Commando lives* stand out clear and black against the ice-shack shingles.

Someone spray-painted the wall again.

The culling shed is full of people who are not talking loud when I open the door. Not a fish in sight, only the washed-down concrete. Manny, Swear, and Sandy Southack stand near the door. Erin and Harriet mumble by the office. Johnny Norgeot comes out of the back with a coffeepot. Rin wears a purple slicker with a lump inside that is Zappa. She walks over, puts her arm around my neck, and drags my head to breast level. My watch cap slips off.

"What're you doing here?" I mumble into her cleavage.

"Harriet called me," she says, "when the wind came up. I called Manny."

"It's not his fault," Johnny says, pouring coffee. "They screwed up on the forecast."

"It's gusting to fifty-eight," Manny objects, "there was mare's tails all afternoon."

"A good seaman can't rely on the forecast alone," South-ack announces in his radio voice. Rin swings around.

"What do you know about it, Sandy?" she asks.

"He just shouldn't of gone," Southack replies, his jaw sticking out. "I didn't mean the injury was his fault; he just shouldn't of gone."

"Then it was his fault, a little," Manny says, "he shoulda known," and drops his cigarettes on the cement.

Harriet lights an Old Gold. I put my good arm against the wall. My inner ear still compensates for the rocking and pitching and the floor of the culling shed feels like it is flexing gently under my feet.

"Gotta go to the hospital," I tell Johnny.

"Don't drive in this?" my mother asks.

I look at her and laugh, too loudly. Even Harriet, after a second or two, sees the irony, and her lipstick cracks.

"Glad ya made it, Ollie," Johnny says, "anyways." He hands me a paper cup.

I call Cait on the office phone as I sip my coffee but only the machine answers.

I leave no message.

Cape Cod Hospital, when I was born there, consisted of one ivy-laced brick building, built when Harding was president, where Harriet's GP had visiting rights. He did not charge for my birth because he had delivered Harriet and Doctor Higgins never charged for the babies of children he had delivered.

Now it is a four-story building with multiple wings, each of which dwarfs the original structure. It has a big endowment and a folk reputation for making people sicker than they were when they went in. It is affiliated with Falmouth Hospital and maintains links with a ten-state HMO network. Brightly lit "pavilions" stretch right and left to absorb the Cape's different vectors of agony: speed, alcohol, old age. Cancer and AIDS.

Medically speaking, it's the only show in town.

The emergency room is quiet but the grandmothers volunteering at reception cannot locate William Sturges in the computer file.

After five minutes a supervisor unearths him in the neurological "queue." I ride the elevator four floors up. A nurse tells me to wait in a bright room with orange squares on the walls. From the nurses' station a radio whispers classic rock.

I call Caitlyn again from a pay phone. This time she answers. When she recognizes my voice her own takes on a layer of caution. I tell her Billy is hurt, that he has damage to the neck.

She says nothing. I can feel her freeze down the line. The rest of our conversation is like novocaine. She will drop Sam at the Kitchen and drive down.

I tell her where to find us and ask her to be careful on the highway and she hangs up while I am talking.

Billy is her only brother. Her father is dead and her mother lives in the cryogenic belt of Arizona. Billy is the only family that counts.

People magazine, the July issue, fills my pupils with colors and font. I absorb none of it. Eventually a youngish woman in a tan business dress shows up. She has a brown square face with a prissy mouth and pretty eyes set close together and broad shoulders. Her hair is cut short. Her name tag says "Dr. Chakrapani, Neurology." I get the feeling she never uses the stethoscope slung around her neck. It is there to prove she is a doctor.

We shake hands and she makes sure I am related to Billy so she can talk to me. She gets me to sign more insurance forms. I feel okay, signing, because *Hooker* still has workmen's comp. It was a condition of the boat mortgage. Otherwise I would probably have let it drop with the rest of our insurance.

Guilt comes then, for feeling such relief, when Billy is so badly hurt.

When the paperwork is out of the way she says, "We are still assessing the damage. The bad news is, there is no way of telling right at this moment how much trauma the vertebrae suffered. The backbone," she explains, glancing at my seaboots. "The fifth and sixth sections were cracked."

"And the good news?" I ask, staring at the orange squares.

"The good news is, we do have some response. He is coming off the CT scan now." Doctor Chakrapani grips my knee hard. I am convinced she got through med school on a swimming scholarship. "You can go see him in a minute or two."

The Soul Survivors play "Expressway to Your Heart."

I sit in an orange chair and watch the "No Smoking" signs. I want to steal a pack and light up two cigarettes simultaneously. I grasp the armrests with both hands. Inside my head I am still rolling and pitching over Chatham bar. I can hear the mad-dog scream of wind and the slam of waves and the treacherous ritards of my Gardner. Through all the din I feel the tremble as that trawl door bangs against the gallows.

A nurse walks up, cocks her head. "Listen," she says, "he's

gonna be *fine*." She leads me down a corridor that shines with flattened light and points into a curtained cubicle.

The first angle I have of Billy is the mound of his knees and then the triangle of his nose foreshortened over a blanket. I never noticed that one of his nostrils is pinched almost shut. He needs a shave. I stand beside his head and the eyes move but the top part of him has been velcroed into flesh-colored plastic forms so he cannot move anything else.

"OXYGEN IN USE. NO SMOKING," a sign reads.

"Billy."

My tongue is dry as dust. I have to repeat his name.

"Hey," he whispers.

The usual machines throng this end of the cubicle. A clear IV tube plunges into a bandage on Billy's wrist. An EKG beeps. A little green TV screen records the regular square-roots of systole. Boxes of latex gloves and masks are stacked on a shelf. Another screen hoards three belts of sine curves. Everything separates here, I think: systole from diastole, alpha wave from beta wave, plasma from hemoglobin, fluid from fluid.

In that separation is a terrible loneliness.

DO *NOT* RECAP NEEDLES

BIO-HAZARD

SHARPS

"I'm just—I'm sorry, man." Waving my hands helplessly against the hardware. I had no intention of saying this but the words are strong in me. "I did this—"

"Ollie?"

I take a deep breath. "The doctor says you have response."

"It's not—your fault." He talks quite strongly, and licks his lips. "It din' have anything to do with—"

"Does it hurt?"

"Don't change—subject."

"Okay. But it was—I mean, I shouldn't have let you go for that door. You were so quick."

"Did it—" licking his lips again—"to myself."

I say nothing. Watching him makes my teeth grind together so hard I can hear them.

"Remember the winch?" he asks.

"The what?"

"The winch." He licks his lips. "The winch. You know—"

"You mean, when I got—"

"You got caught."

"Yeah."

"Well, shit." His eyes roll. He wants to move, and can't. My body twists a tiny bit, trying to turn in the direction he wants to go. "I felt like such a—*ass*hole. I couldn't even move when your glove—"

"Man, you can't worry about that."

"But it's why."

"Well, you sure as hell saved our ass this time. But we shouldn't have gone out. We just—shouldn't. You were a good deckhand there, man."

"Shit." He's looking at me again. His eyes are clear as a child's. "That doctor. Is she French?"

"No." I smile. I feel like crying. "I don't think so.

"Billy," I add, "you're gonna be—"

I stop. This is what people say on TV just before the actor croaks. You're gonna be *all right*.

"I'm gonna be here," I finish. "Caitlyn's comin' too."

"Caitlyn," he mutters. "You know she threw out—her Christmas doll."

I wonder what drugs they are pumping into him. He grins weakly, as if he guessed what I am thinking.

"Every Christmas," he continues, "she got a new doll. Cannibalized the old one. Took its—good clothes. So the new one looked perfect. You can't—*fight* her.

"Call Fleet?" he continues after a moment.

"Sure. You need anything?"

"Coors? Cigarette?"

The Merits are in his shirt pocket, folded neatly over a chair. I take out the packet, expecting it to be waterlogged. It is only slightly damp. I remove one of the drier cigarettes. "I'll smoke it for you," I tell him.

***

They used to have smoking lounges in Cape Cod Hospital, but not anymore. After leaving a message for Fleetwood I go downstairs and stand outside with a couple of Salem-sucking pediatrics nurses under the ER canopy, in the curled wind. Filters litter the sidewalk. A sign proclaims Cape Cod Hospital to be "a smoke-free campus." The tobacco tastes both necessary and dangerous, like an IV. I look at the sodium glare of Hyannis staining the rain the same color as the fourth-floor waiting room. There is no feeling here of the emptiness of sky you see offshore. Many more stars are visible at sea. The space between them is much more full of emptiness. Or maybe not emptiness, but reduction past all boundaries and the obstacles they impose.

The shame in me now tastes just like when I fuck up offshore. That is the closest comparison I have—when the Loran goes crazy and I am in the middle of shoals at night and I did not keep track of my dead reckoning. Time, distance, and deviation gone unrecorded. That is when space itself turns lethal. And so, through that laziness, those omissions, I become deserving of all that can happen; and anything can happen, under those conditions.

My stomach aches with the tension of hours. I feel it with one hand; it is hard as a trawl cable. My chest muscles are taut as well. It feels like the ache has moved upward with all that tension.

Like my whole abdomen now is reacting to an iron absence, something nonspecific but rigid as hell.

My lip drags downward with what I'm thinking.

I suck a last drag deep into my lungs. The poison reflex engages, and I cough, and grind the stub into concrete. This is what I want: the reminder tobacco brings, that the body can only take so much bad freight before it changes something at the level of cytoplasm. A tiny message in that darkness, rewritten into gibberish, then multiplied and multiplied until it has eaten the body up. I walk over to a nurse and cadge a second cigarette. We light our butts, two feet apart. The minty smoke tastes cold and chemical. The nurse is pretty in a rounded sort of way. She turns toward the door as if sensing my assessment.

I turn with her, waving the cigarette for attention.

"Excuse me—"

She squints into the rain.

"Do you know Doctor Chakrapani?"

"The—the neurologist?" I have a feeling she was going to say "black," then thought better of it.

"That's right. She any good?"

The nurse looks at me, cool as her menthol.

"She's real good," she says at last. "She was in pediatric neurology for a while. Not so great with kids, but—"

She throws her cigarette away then, and goes inside.

I look into the sky again: at the furious spin of rain; taking shorter puffs, willing myself behind that orange, into the dark vortex of the storm where the void inside my body would be as nothing against the vacuum of weather. Where my carelessness would not even be noticed by the wind. For a while my chest tightens more.

Then the smoke relaxes it, closing the easy path to relief.

I throw the cigarette into the wind. Behind me, the hospital throbs with pain and machines that never stop. Even if the power shuts off they have backup generators that roar immediately to life.

It feels like my boat to me. Perhaps all life-support systems have the same feeling, that sense of duty, to go steadily onward through the night, the destination does not matter, the quality of life is immaterial, all that matters is the simple aim of keeping an organism alive until morning.

I take the elevator back to Neurology.

* * *

Fleetwood comes in a half hour later. She is pale and does not wish to talk. I remember she hates hospitals and any hint of broken skin.

Fleet fainted once when the first teenager was murdered in a *Friday the 13th* movie. She cut her forehead in falling. She came to in the theatre's rest room, took one look at her face all gory in the mirror, and passed out again.

This happened three times before she finally was carted out.

She checks in with Billy, slips me a can of Coors, and leaves. Hiding the beer under my chair, I forget about it immediately.

* * *

Caitlyn arrives ten minutes after Fleetwood.

She wears her cape-like coat and the scarlet ballet shoes. Both are soaked. Her black dress is muddied at the hem. Her hair is wild with storm and amid that riot her little beaded braids are tangled like Christmas-tree ornaments. My wife's cheeks glisten with rain. I am sitting with Chakrapani, who leafs through the CT printouts. The neurologist stops talking when she spots Cait. Nurses approach, asking her name.

The three of us go through the printouts. The dose of digital information washes through us like an enema. Chakrapani is guarded, optimistic. Her fingers stab at patterns marked by nerve dyes. "There may be damage we cannot detect," she says, "but what this says to me is, he may be able to walk, with some impairment, a lot of therapy also. He may live normally. I want to send him to Boston," she continues, "to fuse these vertebrae."

I wonder, staring at the printouts, if the nerve dye staining Billy's spinal fluid came from the dogfish Amaral caught. Wondering about that is a way not to think about what the doctor really said.

Chakrapani walks out more quickly than she came in. Caitlyn makes her nervous. I know Caitlyn is distrustful of foreigners. If the foreigners are not white she is even more suspicious. This is not racism so much as lack of familiarity, assuming there is a difference.

Caitlyn makes me nervous. I watch her get to her feet and smooth her hair in the glass of a print. The seascape has nothing to do with J. R. R. Tolkien but it reminds me of that print in the cottage in Vermont.

I think: I sleep with someone else and not only do I forget about Rachel inside twenty-four hours but I forget what that change in me could do to others.

It is like taking out a knife and cutting someone and then you go ahead and make coffee without noticing the blade or the blood on the formica.

She takes a deep breath. Her breasts push against the leotard under her dress. I figure she was at the dance studio earlier. She flicks something out of her hair. She is wearing the braided silver necklace she bought in Salem. Looking at her neck, at the delicacy of that shell-colored arc, reminds me of Billy's injured spine. Following the curve lower, to the small of her back, to the swell of hip where she carried Sammy during his first months, triggers something different, a surprise lust. I feel myself harden, and lift my knees to hide it.

The radio advertises a boxed set of Buddy Holly tunes.

"You don't have to stay," Caitlyn says. "I mean, I'll stay now. You should go back."

"You said Sam was at Harriet's."

"I know. He's upset. I told him about Billy."

"Was that a good idea?"

"Billy's his uncle. He has a right to know."

"Well, I need to stay."

She turns. Her shoulders drop. This is not defeat—it's the opposite with her. Like the way *Hooker* settles into the water when she starts to really haul that net across the rocks.

"I don't want you here, Ollie."

It is none of her business.

"Please, Ollie. Just be with our son?"

"He's fine, at the Kitchen. Don't do this to me, Cait."

"Do this to you," she says. Her lip pulls to the left. Her eyes seek out the print again. She twists the ring on her middle finger. It is shaped like a pentagram: a Wicca symbol.

"You did this to yourself, Ollie. *You* did. Harriet told me what happened. You did this to Billy."

"I'm not mad about it," she continues. "I know it's dangerous, on a boat. But can't you just respect what *I* want for a change?"

I sit motionless. I still see no need for movement. My dick has gone soft again. She turns quickly, picking up her coat. She smoothes it, with no wasted motion, and folds it over a chair.

"You have to look at yourself," she tells the coat. "You have this stupid ethic. I used to think it's a male thing, but now—I think it's just you."

"You're going on again, Cait."

The Standelles play "Dirty Water." The last time we fought at night the TV showed ballet. The music is loud for a neuro unit but we will not dance this time. I find no comfort in ritual here. The muscles in my gut lock up, relax. She takes off her sweater, drops it over her coat.

"I'm going on again." She talks normally, as if we were in a restaurant, discussing the hors d'oeuvres. "You know, the thing I figgered out, in the end, is—you love this." She waves at the orange walls. "Hospitals. You love being here. Death and, like, drama."

"You're nuts."

"Well, maybe not hospitals, but you love emergencies. Like, fishing is one long potential emergency. The talk is all emergency talk. That's why you love going offshore. You love living your life like every day you're gonna have to escape something dangerous again. You have this idea it proves you're brave or something. But you are wrong.

"Because anyone can be brave in an emergency, Ollie. Or almost anyone."

She walks across the waiting room and sits facing me. Her face is pale and her eyelids, dark. Part of me wants to go over and hold her like she was two years old. Part of me wants to hurt her with blunt, violently swung verbs, because of what she is saying, because she is saying it at all.

"An emergency dictates what we have to do, and it's over fast. Like tonight. You don't have to think about yourself. You don't have to think about Billy. You just make sure he gets good doctors, and good care."

She leans her head against the wall behind her. I think, Billy cannot lean like that anymore. Because of me, surgeons will fuse his vertebrae in the same way Billy welded lengths of stainless steel rod.

She closes her eyes. Her fingers move, marking phrases. Her words are low yet very clear. This is a secret of both inflexion and content. She no longer uses the recovery language, the hazy connections of Dr. Hinckley.

In a funny way, Caitlyn too works well in emergencies. When the drama is sufficient, she drops the ersatz thrill she must import to other situations—the fancy scrollwork of codependency and air. At such times her own logic comes back and it is a tool as sharp as my treachery and she wields it more accurately.

"What really takes guts," she says, "is what comes after. Sticking it out. Year after *year*. Waking up every day, every fuckin' *hour* of every day. To keep a level . . ."

She swallows hard.

"Keeping people safe, all the time. Giving them enough to make them safe. I mean, what if Billy is paralyzed? Who's gonna take him to the bathroom? Who's gonna change his bed? *That's* courage, Ollie. *That* is guts. And it ain't gonna be you."

"Not even GyNET?" I ask and, in asking, react to the wrong part of this. Her eyes flick back and forth at mine. I lower my gaze. The piece of flower she pulled out of her hair earlier lies by my right boot. It is not a flower, though. It is a twig of golden aster, a bushy weed that grows in halfway places between marshland and the sea.

"Don't." She replies without anger. This is the awful strength in her words, that she has no need of my reaction to make them true. "I'm talking about what I *feel*. I don't need GyNET for that."

I stand up abruptly. I should not have said anything about GyNET. Only a few hours ago I vowed to put distance between myself and that kind of rage.

I pick up my jacket and watch cap. My chest is so tight now it feels like my lungs and heart are cramping up. I am sick of how my insides react to strain.

"Where you going?"

"To the Kitchen. Where you wanted me to go."

She watches my fingers adjust the oilskin.

"I don't think we should see each other for a while, Ollie."

"We're already separated."

"I mean here. I'll take care of Billy."

"You already said that."

"I want you to promise not to come."

"No way."

"He's going to Boston. I want you to take care of Sam."

"Sam's gonna want to see you," I say.

"I'll see him. I can take care of both of them. That's *my* courage, Ollie."

"And us? What about us, in all, in all that bravery?"

I look up at her without flinching. This time she lowers her gaze and slumps into the plastic seat, and the exhaustion in her face settles with her.

"I don't know," she whispers. "It used to be, you went out,

and then the wind would pick up, and I was so happy when you were okay. Or the times we had no money. The drama, Ollie.

"But one day, I just got tired of it. It was like, this wasn't my show, anymore."

I look at her for another moment. Her eyes are closed now. I think, She has no idea if I am there or gone.

And then she says, very softly, "I bet you never even looked at that book."

It takes me a few seconds to figure out what she's talking about.

The book she gave me before I went to Vermont.

BroadBand.

Turning, I leave the room, and the woman dressed mostly in black stretched out among its overdose of light.

Wood

from *Notes on the Ecology of Cape Cod* (Salt Marsh Press, Falmouth)
by Irwin E. Zeit, Ph.D.

The scrubby woodlands lying to the sides of the Cape's highways, and between the houses and built-up areas, are now referred to as "undeveloped" or "natural." Yet such country is but the last stage in a process of intrusion that by ecological standards has been as fast as it was violent.

The first stage came directly after the creation of the Cape's glacial geology, approximately 20,000 years ago, when the glaciers receded and the climate warmed, allowing first, the growth of a form of sub-Arctic moorland, rich in bog life; and then, a boreal forest consisting primarily of dwarf birch and northern spruce.

The second stage was a product of the interglacial epoch in which we still live. This, a northern temperate forest, was described by John Brereton, who accompanied Bartholomew Gosnold on the first European expedition known to have reached the Cape and Islands. Brereton wrote of "high timbered oaks . . . cedars straight and tall; beech, elm and holly, walnut trees in great abundance . . . hazelnut trees, cherry trees, sassafras in great plenty."

In fact what Brereton saw was not virgin woods but a balance created by the Algonquin tribes who inhabited the region. These tribes always cleared a small percentage of the forest by controlled burning, turning mid-altitude acreage into maize plots and destroying the brush around big trees higher up so as to hunt deer and turkey with greater ease.

Then came the English farmers. They arrived with varied kinds of Christian beliefs but one type of agriculture, based on iron ploughs and draft animals; on clear-cutting the entire forest to make way for fields and pasture. Their agricultural impact on woodland was compounded by the need for fuel for heat and by the use of firewood in industries such as saltworks, lampblack manufacture, shipbuilding, and glassmaking.

Here was the third stage in the Cape's ecology. Unfortunately, the white colonists went too far in their uses of the resource. By 1847 Edward Hitchcock, a geologist, could write that the lower Cape looked like "the depths of an Arabian or Libyan desert." Almost all of Cape Cod was fields, exhausted by constant cultivation, eroded by the sea wind. The only woods left were in relatively inaccessible places, like Sandy Neck or the islands of Wakeby Lake. The deer and wild turkey had long ago disappeared.

The consequences of the third phase proved dire. Erosion washed away topsoil and dug deep gullies in the land. Belatedly, Cape Codders initiated conservation measures. But a certain economy had created these conditions, and only the destruction of that economy could reverse them.

What halted the third phase was the collapse of New England farming after the Civil War. In the second half of the nineteenth century 58,000 acres were left to run wild in Barnstable County. From Appomattox through VJ Day, an army of second-growth woods crept back and took over the fallow land.

These woods were very different from the forests the Indians knew. Instead of high timber, the ground was covered by contorted pitchpine, low, brushy scrub oak, stumpy black cedar, weedy locust—plants that made poor firewood but were tough and resistant to salt wind. As the trees came back, so did the deer, but not the turkey. They had been hunted to extinction throughout Massachusetts.

The fourth stage was and is a creature of the post–World War Two boom. After the war the peninsula turned into a leisure machine fueled by the '50s surge in prosperity and population, and playground structures were built to serve it. The Mid-Cape Highway opened up the peninsula's length to the heady independence of the motor car. Tens of thousands of houses and motels were built, with supermarkets, dry cleaners, banks, gas stations, malls, restaurants and other structures put up to accommodate their occupants. The second-growth woods were cut back, again and again. The reserve of space that had allowed the deer to return dwindled to acreage protected by conservation trusts. When an effort was made to re-introduce a nucleus of wild turkeys on Cape Cod, the only adequate space left turned out to be a semi-poisoned tract in Falmouth and Sandwich, reserved by the Department of Defense for rocket launch pads, and practice-bombing by the U.S. Air Force Reserve.

Chapter 25

The wind is less strong and its gusts are more erratic on the drive home.

Sometimes the clouds part to reveal a moon that is a rotted ivory, like the eyeballs of a road-killed possum. The soaked landscape hides from that light in banks of mauve shadow. The snow of three days ago is disappearing fast, melted by the warm engine of the nor'easter. What remains lies across the country in hollows or plow ridges, like rib bones.

It is one o'clock in the morning by the time I get to the Kitchen. Walter and Rin are still up. Reruns of *Nogales Home Cooking* flash primary colors across the screen.

A vaseful of storm-fooled forsythia on the table die vainly to match TV's fast attraction.

Rin's ex-husband, Randy, dozes in Harriet's chair. The crook of one arm protects his head. Black beard hairs curl around the elbow. The Wolfschmidt bottle stands within easy reach.

"Sam's asleep," Rin says, "in the pink room."

Upstairs I dig a half dozen Maalox out of my sister's tampon bag and eat them all. Sam's blankets are banked in ridges like the snow outside. His feet lie halfway across Eb, who is curled clockwise on the bed. The dog looks up, guilty as hell, but I let him lie.

The bald kangaroo lies on the floor. I tuck it under the blankets beside them.

I sit on the bench downstairs and watch TV without seeing much of anything. Walter fetches the single malt from his cellar cache and pours me a shot. A Mexican chef wants to know if we have ever tasted real *chicharrones*. Rin wants to know how Billy is, and I tell her.

The Maalox calms my stomach down. It loses some of the rigidity it acquired in the hospital. My chest still feels cramped.

Part of this, I realize now, comes from wrestling that wheel in the storm; but part of it feels like the ache in my stomach has packed its bags for some reason and moved upward into the cavity around the lungs where all the major tracts come together.

The whisky has no effect on the cramp. My head still believes it is climbing black swells and surfing the curl on a lobster boat. I stick my legs out and hit a cairn terrier and it does not bark or react.

Rin leans underneath the table, feeling the dog's throat.

"It's okay," she announces. "He's snoring."

Randy, who is only half asleep, giggles. He came by to steal vodka two months ago when Rin was in Boston for a concert. Harriet was smoking and drinking Wolfschmidt and reading *Glamour* as usual at the table's head. In order to suck up to Harriet and in this way find out where the vodka was hidden, Randy patted the dog at her feet. The terrier did not move at all.

"How's Ryan doing?" Randy asked.

"Oh, he's about the same," Harriet said, in a voice that quavered somewhat.

Randy touched Ryan once more. Rigor mortis had set in and he was beginning to smell.

I feel this dog with my fingers. His fur is warm.

The hope.

Walter lights up a joint and Rin bogarts it long enough for Randy to get annoyed. Behind the sweetness of grass I can smell fresh dog piss under the table.

It is no coincidence that we find shelter here, I think.

Because we are all so screwed up in this family, and maybe the reason we let ourselves get screwed up was, we had someplace to come to where we would not get turned away or even criticized much.

Only what I did last night is not just a screw-up. It is not reckless marriage or bad birth control or busting open the penal code. What happened to Billy smashed the information in him; it broke channels that made his body work.

I have a deep feeling that, even if he functions again, there will always be messages inside him that do not get through.

I can think of nothing sadder than lost messages.

I need to get out of here.

The thought is sudden, and strong as a bad odor.

If I am ever to become a man who does not threaten the information in others, I need to leave the places that until now supported my reckless navigation.

The Kitchen, the Cape. My own house even.

It comes to me at this point that talking to Caitlyn was like seeing somebody you worked with who just took another job. You are glad to see each other and then as you try to make conversation you realize ninety percent of what you had in common is gone.

The Mexican cook, dashing *aguardiente* into a panful of chicken, starts a flash fire that almost takes out his eyebrows.

Walter wants to pour me another whisky. I shake my head.

In the laundry hallway I dig up some sheets. I filch a couple of reds and more Maalox from the tampon bag and retreat to my old room.

Zappa snuffles in his crib. The bed rocks under me for an hour or so before the reds finally kick in and I go under.

*　*　*

Sam and Eb wake me at six thirty. The dog covers my nose with slobber. Sam, always less physical, sits at my feet. I read to the boy for half an hour or so, averting my rough face from his smooth one so the morning breath will not gag him.

I give him an update on Uncle Billy and he is worried for a minute and intrigued for five by the medical details. Then he has to find his school stuff and all other thoughts are scattered, like starlings by a backfire.

I call the hospital. The fourth-floor nurses tell me Billy was transported to Boston. This is the new shift and they don't know which hospital. Someone thinks his sister went with him. There was no change in his condition.

Sam leaves with not enough time for the bus but as usual he makes it anyway.

Afterward the house seems to sag as if he had sucked all the energy out with him. The wind died overnight. It is fairly warm. The sky, though cloudy, seems cleaner than it has been in days. Eb long ago ate all the cat food. He farts so badly I have to put him in the truck.

Rin shambles in, nursing Zappa, tying her pajamas. She switches the VCR to cooking shows she taped yesterday while watching soaps on other channels. *Heart-Healthy Frying*. An attractive blond cook debates the fat content of canola oil. The magentas of television are too warm, the cyan shades too cold. It all feels like poison to me against the spotlessness of sky seen through the windows.

I have to get *Hooker* off the pier. The thought of my boat with her engine gone and the Loran useless and the wheelhouse windows cracked contains a shade of arsenic as well.

Anyway I probably will have to sell the boat and the rights to Marston's Hollow also to pay for Billy after the workmen's comp has gone. The policy only covered fifty thousand dollars, which will fund all of two days in a Boston hospital.

A shard of fear pricks me now. For all we have been living close to the edge moneywise, we never completely went over before. But the papers I signed last night will break us.

Boiling water meets Nescafé. Watching the liquid swirl brown around the cracked mug as I stir seems to sharpen, make more accurate, the feeling that touched me last night.

If I lose *Hooker*, it truly is time to leave the Cape.

Events have spun into a vortex, like seawater from the thrash of a prop, like coffee under the rotation of my spoon. And out of the funnel so created something solid has formed and lodged in my decision centers.

"I'm gonna move off-Cape," I tell Rin. "Soon as Billy's taken care of, I'm outta here."

She looks down at Zappa. Morning Madonna. Her face is soft, at rest. On the tube, the debate has finally gone against canola.

"Where you gonna go?"

"I don't know. I been thinking about Maine." I sip at the coffee. It is flat and at the same time bitter. I look for milk and find only skimmed.

"What about Sam?" Rin asks.

"I'll see him weekends. It's not that far."

"It's such a tragedy people don't eat hush puppies," the blond cook says seriously, "when all it takes is a few simple precautions."

"And when's this s'posed to happen?" Rin asks, popping a can of Tab, watching the cook.

There is nothing to keep me here, I think; not today or tomorrow or all year. It is time I stopped fooling myself that I pull my weight as a father, at least on a day-to-day basis.

Even now I only see Sam on weekends.

Cait will have to let him spend vacations with me in Maine, if we stay separated.

My breathing accelerates as I realize that, in leaving, I could let things subside into a more natural equilibrium. Cait and Sam would have an easier routine, uncomplicated by my comings and goings. And between vacations and long weekends I could end up spending more, and more useful, time with my son than I do now.

"Might even go up today, after I see Billy. Just overnight, with Sam, take a look around. He can skip one day of school."

"You can't go today."

"Why not?"

"It's the critter row."

"Oh." I put my mug down. "Well, tomorrow then."

"Take us with you? Far as Dorchester."

I look at her again. There is too much peace in her face. Poor Southack, I think, without malice.

"Sure."

"If you go."

"I'm gonna go," I tell her. "And I'm gonna see about selling the rights to Marston's Hollow, if that's still OK by you."

"Clean sweep," my sister says, "huh?"

"Clean sweep."

"Fine by me," Rin says.

Harriet comes down in her sweat clothes. She looks a little tired but her movements are deliberate. She arranges Old Golds, Nescafé, *Stranded Times*, in an order appropriate for morning. In the living room she switches on the CD player. Mel Torme winds into Christmas affect. *"While in thy dark streets shineth,"* he sings. Mel draws "shineth" into four different syllables. Rin stares at the living room door, her face long.

"Leave her alone," I say. "Anyway you can't stop her now."

"Oh, I know," my sister replies. "I let her make her own mistakes. She lets me make mine. We agreed on that long ago.

"But I'll miss her, Ollie—I'll just miss her. You know."

No one has taken a shower yet so the hot water is plentiful. I stand in steam for ten minutes. My mind feels flat as television, as Nescafé, but my body seems to resume its familiar relief, its arcs and angles, under the flush and scald of water.

When I get out, Rin tells me Caitlyn called. Billy is at Mass. General. She will stay with him overnight.

She'll call again later.

*   *   *

The critter row always starts at the fish pier because plenty of parking is available there for the crowds of spectators who never show up.

I go early, to find Johnny unloaded my boat for me and towed her back to the mooring.

A panel truck marked MBL trundles from the loading bay, loaded with live dogfish bound for Woods Hole to get the glands around their assholes cut out.

Hooker turns slowly to the breeze at the northern end of Aunt Lydia's, looking absolutely unchanged, as if what we went through yesterday had no more effect on her than a shift in wind direction.

Suddenly and for no good reason I feel proud of *Hooker*. I never checked the flange in those waves, but the hull held. In any event she did not break up or take on water even.

I guess that Might-E-Foam worked.

What I am really thinking is: She came through for me. When it came down to the pinch she got us safe to harbor.

She might not have made it without Billy. I see him again in my mind's eye, clutching the gallows as the door swung wild against the swells. I blink my eyes hard to wipe out the vision. I get out of the truck to tramp back and forth along the beach. My chest is not as rigid as it was in the hospital but it's still harder than usual. This makes sense because the feeling of tension, of holding something in, is as strong as it was last night.

I wonder casually if that is the secret to hardness in general: that it must be based on an absence.

It takes far more effort to keep a shape when there is nothing solid inside to mold it around.

The MSPCA van shows up at ten A.M., on time. Then a couple of friends of Harriet's arrive. One of them is Virginia Lopes. A *Times* stringer wants a press release. "We don't do anything without the official release," he announces.

Walter, Manny, Harriet and Rin arrive together. The MSPCA lady makes an announcement that is eaten by the wind. Manny and Walter and I hump the kayak off Harriet's Ford and carry it to the water's edge. I look at Pleasant Bay. Surf left over from the storm, like an assault battalion that never got word of withdrawal, froths at the cut in the barrier beach. Whitecaps litter the bay inside.

It is going to be a hard pull.

For the first time in fourteen years of critter rows I feel nervous. Too much can go wrong in a life. Thinking about what Rin mentioned, a week ago: the health concern, the impact of stress on delicacy.

I mention this to Manny, expecting support. Manny likes bad news, dire predictions. This time he surprises me.

"She'll be okay," he says. He turns to face me, pulls me by my weak arm and kisses my cheek. His cheeks are more stubbly than mine. He smells of K-Mart cologne and vodka.

I stare at him. His eyes are light brown, and a little runny.

"Christ. You wanna loan again?"

He squints.

"No. I don't want no fuckin' loan.

"I just see you're sad, an' that's it."

"Yeah," I say, not agreeing.

"Yeah," he repeats, glaring at me.

* * *

After Harriet has rowed off I drive around town but the clouds of Christmas lights and little whiffs of *Adeste Fideles* coming off Main Street accentuate by contrast the gray thoughts in my head. I feel as if everybody is looking at me and pointing:

There's the guy who stopped the Price-Shoppe.

There's the guy who made me unemployed.

There's the guy who went out in a nor'easter and got his mate paralyzed.

Rin says the *Times* had a news brief on Billy. Everybody knows, by now.

Eb does not care. He just likes being in the truck with me. I rest one hand on his coarse fur as I drive down Barcliff to Main.

At Dorene's Bridal the dresses of the mannequins, every one of them, are sequined and green.

I get locked in behind the Coma Club bus on Old Queen Anne. Two men are trundled in wheelchairs from a hospice into the yellow bus.

I wonder, if things go wrong, whether Billy will end up like them, hunched in an aluminum frame.

I am ready for a beer now. I rummage around, then remember that the last Rock 'n Rolls froze in the back in Vermont. I stop at Hamblin's and buy a six-pack and twist open a bottle. The skunky smell itches my nose but the beer changes nothing inside.

The monster "cottages" of Fuller's Landing loom out of the landscaping with their usual lack of warning. I stash the bottle and park near Fuller's statue. He stares at the hill of plow snow in the middle of the parking fields. For the hundredth time I think, he looks nothing like Fuller.

The statue resembles me more than it does Thatch's son.

The Hallett Construction office is in the biggest "cottage," one street over from the bank, on the second and third floors. It contains rubber trees and glassed-in offices and wall-to-wall carpeting exactly like Chatham Bank and Trust's. It is quiet and smells of carpet cleaner.

The portraits all depict Thatch's projects. One is an aerial view of the Price-Shoppe land right after he cleared it. The photo includes Marston's Hollow. I can make out the clam shack, the quahog skiff. The hollow looks the size of a Band-Aid compared to the vast scrape of the development.

I should fix up that old skiff, I think. Then I shake my head, because I am going to Maine, and I sure as hell don't need to waste time on that skiff if I am going to Maine.

The secretary tells me Thatch is not in. She says Mr. Stubb will see me.

Mr. Stubb is Skull.

After a few minutes he comes into the reception area. His baggy suit and worn Oxfords look out of place amid the twenty-five-year-old surveyors in sports clothes. He points with his clipboard toward an office, and leaves again without saying a word.

I examine the computer terminal, the filing cabinets in the designated office. I feel like I need to go to the bathroom and I know that if I did nothing would come out. Skull's homburg and Antartex hang in a corner like a spare carapace. A cheap veneer nameplate on his desk reads "Nickerson Flick Stubb III."

Flickie's uncle, I think. Or maybe he's his great-uncle. Either way, I had forgotten Skull and Flickie were related.

When Skull returns he has Todd Kiernan with him.

"What's he doing here?" I ask Skull.

"I handle all Mr. Hallett's realty transactions," Todd replies.

"He's our real estate consultant," Skull corrects him, softly. "I'm assuming you changed your mind about those rights?"

"Maybe."

"Maybe means nothing," Skull says sharply. "I don't have time for 'maybe.' Do you want to sell the rights or not?"

I look up at the old man's face. I don't believe in lawyers but it would be nice, just once, to have someone who was paid to be on my side.

I wish Thatch were here. I do not want to go through this twice. The recessed neon glares off Skull's pate. The lines in his face are deep, like the gullies of an eroded mountain.

Eventually I tell him, "Yes."

"And you would sell them to Hallett Construction, in partnership with Price-Shoppe Corporation?"

"I guess. Whoever."

Skull makes a note on his clipboard. He glances at Todd, smoothes his five hairs into place, pulls out his calculator, and hits a few keys.

"Did you have a price in mind?" Todd asks. I quote the figure Steve Vaitsos mentioned. Skull taps that in without expression. His eye sockets from this angle look like test-drill holes. More than ever he resembles a skeleton. The real estate man crosses his legs.

"One thing," Todd says. "Do you yourself still own these rights?"

My eyes are focused on Skull but this question draws them to the younger man. Todd strokes his lime-green slacks over one shin.

"I only heard," he continues, glancing at Skull. "There was some problem with the bank?"

Skull leans back, placing the calculator on his desk.

"That was resolved," I tell them, and clear my throat. "They made a mistake."

"Well, good," Todd says. "I mean someone told me yesterday, but."

"Did you speak to Vaitsos?" Skull asks sharply. He is talking to Todd.

Todd crosses his legs in the other direction.

"Have you talked to Grealey?"

"Uh," the younger man says. He has one of those personalities that know no active verbs.

Skull draws his breath in all the way. He stares at me for at least ten seconds. His stare is not friendly and it is not hostile either. The glasses magnify his pupils by a third. They are gray and faded, like the skin of a water mammal, or the color Pleasant Bay turns in a fog. I wonder briefly how Harriet is doing. The Strong Island part of her route should be all right, but going down South Beach she will have the wind broadside.

"I'll discuss it with Mr. Hallett," Skull says finally. "Mr. Grealey has to sign off on the legal aspect. I can't make any predictions, but I am sure Thatch will want to talk to you further about this."

Getting to his feet, he grasps my left elbow hard.

I look at him in surprise. Skull is not the kind of man who touches.

It seems odd that both Skull and Manny want to feel up my bad arm on the same day.

Skull drops his hand, sniffs, and looks away.

After I leave Hallett Construction I sit in the truck and finish my beer. Then I walk into Chatham Bank and Trust and straight down the corridor to Consumer Loans. The woman behind the reception desk wears her blond hair cut in a bob and is twenty-two years old at most.

"I'd like to see Steve Vaitsos."

"He's not in now."

"I see," I say, although there is much I do not see. It seems weird to be in this bank, for instance, and not see Mrs. Snow at her usual place. I don't think I have ever come in without spotting her, if only from a distance. I ask where she is and the girl looks at her computer screen. This is what she does instead of saying "Um," although she says "um" anyway.

"I think Mrs. Snow took, like, early retirement. Um, is there anything I can help you with?"

Maine, I think.

I want to go to Maine.

The things and people I rely on already are gone. The codfish are gone and Caitlyn is gone and soon Marston's Hollow will be gone also.

I return to the truck and open another beer and it has the same effect as the first, which is zero.

* * *

I hang out in the Kitchen for the rest of that morning and early afternoon, trying to get hold of Billy. The number the MGH switchboard gave me does not answer.

At three thirty I drive to the middle school and ambush Sam between the portico and the buses. He looks around to see if anyone is watching and sneaks fast into the cab.

Eb does his whirlwind imitation, losing his new tennis ball, streaking Sam with drool. The boy yells at him and hugs him at the same time.

"You *always* do this," he tells me angrily.

"Harriet's coming in," I reply, "it's the critter row today."

"Oh, *god*," Sam replies, "I don't believe this, it's so *queer*." He hunches down to make sure no one spots him on our way out of the parking lot.

I drive to the fish pier. Only the MSPCA van is there. Eb curls up with his muzzle in Sam's lap.

"Wanna go to Maine?" I ask Sam.

"Whaddya mean?"

"Tomorrow."

"I got school. I got hockey practice."

"Screw hockey practice. And you can miss school for a day or two."

Sam looks at me in surprise. He would not mind skipping school, or hockey, but he has never heard a grown-up suggest it before.

"I *got* to go to practice. And I got homework. Mom says, you shouldn't say that."

288

"What?"

"Screw."

"I told you, you can miss one day. You can bring your homework, do it in the truck."

He thinks about it, staring out at the bay. His eyes in this light shine with the hidden glimmers of old oak. Something hurts in my chest. I wonder if I might be suffering from angina. Christ knows I have had enough stress and fatigue recently. That can cause heart problems.

"I want to see Uncle Billy in Boston," I add. "We can go to the train section in the Museum of Science on the way."

He glances at me. He loves the train section.

"Can we go to Denny's?"

"Sure. Or Burger King—I'm not sure if they have Denny's in Maine." For the first time the excitement of potential travel—of going to a place where you don't know if they have a Denny's—surges in me: guiltily, because I should not be excited, when Billy is strapped into a bed with numb legs, and machines that parse him into discrete elements, and people who wake him every two hours to stick sterilized metal into his flesh.

Harriet is late. Manny, Rin and Virginia Gomes show up. A Range Rover with 'roo bars, and a rifle rack holding a 30.06, parks by Harriet's car. Thatch Hallett gets out, adjusting his beret. I think, Already he has tracked me down, but he does not even look at me, just says something to Virginia Lopes and stares across Pleasant Bay with the rest of us.

Thatch's dog, Jesse, trots to the water and barks at the waves. Eb jumps at the window, bruising his nose against the glass. I remember Harriet saying she and Thatch dated in school. The concept of that seems as bizarre as anything I have ever heard.

It is also strange to look at Thatch and realize that soon we may have nothing to squabble about. It feels worse to think that Thatch has won—that I will give him what he wanted, the way everybody does.

Ordinarily that thought would bother me so much I might try to do something about it.

But things have changed. I am leaving Chatham and what Thatch does or does not do with the land will have no impact on me. This is like suddenly realizing that your feelings for a certain woman are gone so you don't really give a goddam who she sleeps with anymore.

Part of me hears myself saying this as if it were someone else trying to convince me.

Part of me feels good because from now on I don't have to waste energy fighting.

Sam and I take Eb for a walk. The sideways light of afternoon picks out the colors in the salt marsh framing Pleasant Bay. The dying spartina looks like lost assay, brass wires and rods of lead and billions of tiny amber ingots shimmering under fathoms of light. Some of the beach-plums, still confused by Gisela, are in the last stages of their bloom.

Purple stains the oak branches. The pines are black-green, white-green. The bay is gray, and washes into mauve with distance.

Eb finds the dead seagull immediately. Before Sam and I can react he rolls on top of it and shakes his legs in the air. His lips pull back and he grunts in pleasure.

"*No!*" Sam and I cry together. I grab his collar. Sam takes his tail. The dog rolls, digging all four paws into the beach. The herring gull is so corrupt it is flat. Just an outline of gray feathers and white bone and a yellow beak with the single red spot. "Gawd!" Sam yells, "Eb you stink, gawd!" But he is laughing because Eb looks so foolish guarding his flattened, sandy carrion.

We haul the dog slowly down the berm. Eb stops fighting and trundles on his own toward the water. We let him go.

He stands in the low waves for a few seconds. Then he ducks his head and peers underwater. After ten seconds he surfaces, a rock wedged in his teeth. He trots out, shakes himself, deposits the rock safely above the high tide mark, and goes back to repeat the process.

My son sinks to his knees, watching Eb. I sit beside him in the cold wind. Without further thought I grab Sam and pull him on top of me, poking him in the armpits where he tickles easily. His body twists and rockets like a bag of snakes and this forces my body to understand how long it has been since we did this. "Don't," Sam gasps, "don't *get* me, Dad, cut it *out!*" so I quit tickling and just hug him and Sam stops struggling and for at least twenty seconds it's all like it's supposed to be as we lie there in the wet sand, in the stink of dead herring gull, while Sam catches his breath and my chest feels like it wants to open up and suck my son inside to protect him forever.

* * *

At four a quahogger's skiff comes around Minister's Point with the blue wedge of Harriet's kayak balanced on the culling board. My chest drops into my ankles. I run toward the landing. Then I notice the purple of my mother's exercise suit, upright beside the quahogger.

I stop, feeling foolish.

"There she is!" someone shouts.

"She didn't make it," I say.

"So what," Rin replies from behind me.

"So nothin'."

"She didn't have to finish," my sister adds. "They pledge a buck a mile, is all."

"Granma," Sam shrieks suddenly, "you *rule!*" Out of nowhere his face is alive with pride.

There are times I cannot figure the boy out.

When my mother steps off the skiff we crowd around her. She is pale under the ruins of her Prince Matchabelli. Her careful perm has melted into a peroxide rat's nest. Her eyes are pink with salt and bright with triumph. She hugs Sam, coughing, holding her cigarette clear of his face.

"Eleven miles, twenty-two pledges at a dollar a mile," the MSPCA woman says, looking at the pledge sheet. She doesn't smile or anything. "Two hundred and forty-two dollars."

"Better than a kick in de teeth," Manny tells her. He grins so she can count the teeth left in his mouth.

Thatch stands behind Harriet, making her look small. He gazes out beyond Tern Island where the water, in the lee of North Beach, is slick and lustrous as oil.

I take Sam to the house, to get clothes for him and dog food for Eb and to leave a note for Caitlyn. A registered letter that she accepted for me lies pinned by a box labeled "Introduction to JavaScript" on the kitchen table.

Her computer has a new screensaver. It's the outline of a female form, blue on a green background, dancing alone from one corner of the terminal to the other.

The letter is from the bank. I put it in my back pocket without opening it.

CB&T always sends me registered letters.

I am navigating in the front of my brain now.

In the back lie Billy, and Caitlyn, and Marston's Hollow. A taste of Rachel is left also, like the awareness of your salad at lunch, a hint of onion perhaps; but this trip has nothing to do with Rachel.

I have no intention of going near her area even though she is moving to the mid-coast somewhere, near Union.

This is a different sort of trip. It will be clean of women and the promises they invoke.

I plot the fastest route to Portland on the Triple-A road atlas from Cait's bookshelf.

Chapter 26

On my second night at the Kitchen after the storm I wake up at four in the morning.

The reds I took last night make my eyes feel soft. Otherwise I am far from sleep.

Zappa snuffles in his cot and as I listen to him breathe it appears to me that the darkness of this room is a scale model of the darkness surrounding our lives.

In that black absence only doom has direction. The children of light, like Zappa, Sam, like Billy even—delicate as cobwebs—will be ripped into air by the first heft of pain.

Flawed boats, men of compromise.

No hope exists, none at all. Caitlyn is gone from me. Billy will never walk again.

Only habit shuts the hatch against our suicide.

These are night thoughts. The fear they hold is real but

in this place without an edge to vision their connections are flaccid and uncertain.

To cut them to size I go down to the kitchen and turn on the TV.

The edges of TV, too, are vague, but despite or because of this it works as analgesic.

I read all of Harriet's perfumed magazines. Darkness becomes a liveable gray. Another J. Crew catalogue, latest of the Christmas specials, crowns a stack of similar publications. The waffle-knit woman stares at me, indifferent in four-color separation.

I wonder what I ever saw in her.

It got colder overnight. Walter tramps to the cellar. Heat pipes clearly transmit the *whank* of iron on iron. The room grows warm.

A circle of soiled sunlight forms on the wineglass cabinet. The TV, from being the focus of life in this quiet house, dims into mere electrics.

The circle of light, descending, turns the frost on the windowpanes into a dozen miniature Tiffany's exhibits, and part of my brain appreciates this, and part of it doesn't give a shit.

Sam is up and dressed by eight. He leafs through Powermorph comics with his Corn Chex, absorbing the frames fast as a videocam, hoping I forgot his bath.

I would like to get an early start but Rin is not ready. She yaks on the phone to Randy then takes a twenty-minute shower which uses up all the hot water.

It is eleven by the time her bag is packed and Zappa is changed and fed. Walter says flurries are coming through. Harriet worries about our driving north. Her face sags from exhaustion. I agree silently with Rin that maybe it is time our mother gave up the critter row.

She will be sixty-five next September.

I dialed the Interflora franchise while Rin was packing to order flowers for Billy. In the middle of the call I remembered our Visa account has been maxed out for four months. Now

I unsheath my filet knife, go into the garden and harvest for-sythia. The frost earlier cut short their growth and they are right on the cusp when their petals are about to brown, as the shadblow's already have done. I gather an armful, three-foot branches of sunshine-made-stick, and stow them, wrapped in an old, dampened sheet, in the back of the truck.

Then the shit heap will not start. My starter-fluid can is dry. Walter loans me a can of ether.

Anyway we get on the road and it is not even noon. Cirrus clouds ride flank to that high-pressure mass. Zappa cries for the tit. Rin gives it to him. I slip the Ramones into the tape deck when we get on the highway, and take the tape out immediately. I am not in the mood.

I am not even in the mood for beer, although I secured my ride supply out of habit. Along with the ether, Walter let me have a six-pack of English ale, which I stashed in the back with Eb.

Route 6 reminds me of driving to Cape Cod Hospital.

It brings to mind earlier vectors as well; and one in partic-ular, and the disaster that launched it, powering my life like a rocket booster.

The highway fades in my vision, or rather it is the same highway but where my memory is concerned it is a quarter past ten on a sharp cold February night thirteen years ago. I am driving a monkey-shit brown '73 Chevy Impala sedan ninety miles an hour toward the canal and fear gnaws at my insides as if I had swallowed a coyote and the coyote was starving.

* * *

"Slow down, man," George is yelling. His forearms are braced against the dashboard.

"We just got to get beyond the bridge," I tell him.

"They'll stop you for speeding. That won't do us—"

"He saw the car. I know he did."

"It's only the town cops, for now."

In the glow of the speedometer George's face looks the color of old scrimshaw.

"I can't believe you *did* that," he says. "I can't believe you just walked *in* there."

Something in me shouts excitement, shakes its fists in the air; but the panic, because founded on hard limits, is greater. On the back seat lies a shotgun Frank left behind because it was so rusted the firing pin would not cock. A BB pistol, a plastic Uzi and a realistic-looking kid's rifle that shoots darts with rubber suction cups are piled alongside.

George and I started drinking at breakfast that day and we got into the peppermint schnapps by mid-afternoon. Around eight P.M. we were feeling pretty lethal, what with the schnapps and being twenty and broke and not having gotten laid in a while. It made sense, in that skewed context, to load up on dangerous items for the cruise to Provincetown.

"Nobody gonna mess with us," I told George. "None of them chickenshit Portygees."

"Nobody," George said.

"None of them uptight gay boys."

"Nobody."

"None of them loser townies," I continued, and a knot of anger grew in my chest as I said this, because I had run into Frank on Main Street the day before and asked him for a loan.

Frank turned me down, but that was not what made me mad. It was the way he did it—bored, cold-voiced—as if I was just another loser to him.

Just another guy without the gumption to get a job and hold it.

In Provincetown we spent what cash we had at the Governor Bradford but were not through with drinking yet. At the Orleans rotary I said, "Let's go into Cumbie's and get some dough."

"Oh, how you gonna do that?"

I unrolled my watch cap, pulling it down over my face. I could see fine through the mesh.

"How do you think?"

"We could do it," George whispered, laughing softly into the neck of the Fleischmann's bottle, which was empty. "That Tyler would shit his pants."

"Chickenshit."

"Totally."

"Wouldn't really count," I said, "with fake guns."

"Shit." George laughed so hard he was rocking back and forth to absorb it. "Cut it out, Ollie."

But I steered us into the parking lot and stopped the car in shadow. That was the trouble—I was sober enough to make some of the right moves yet drunk enough not to stop.

And there was that piss-off I had felt earlier. It had not steamed off with schnapps. In the long slide of a good high I ignored the sectors in memory that figure time, the uncertainties of data, and the margin of error you must allow, for navigation.

"You ain't gonna do it," George said confidently. He had an uncle who had done time; he knew real toughness. "No way."

I leaned back instead of answering and grabbed the shotgun. Got out of the car, staggering a little. Smeared dirt over the rear tag. I could see it all happening before I did it, me walking in there with the *Miami Vice* moves. Chickenshit Tyler, raising his hands, the stink rising from his pants as he handed over the cash. I saw it clearly, and knew it must work this way.

And it does, it almost does, as time advances in the convenient neon. Chickenshit Tyler and a client raise their hands. Tyler throws a hundred and eight dollars into a plastic bag. But he does not shit his pants. And he is silhouetted against the plate glass, watching, as we skid back onto Route 28, the brown Impala with the unmatched retreads gripping the tarmac and away—

Time retreats, then and now, till all chronologies meet, one mile from the bridge, where my truck rolls at this moment; where thirteen years ago three state police cruisers waited, lights out, for the Chevy hurtling like a rust-sucked vampire out of the awesome Cumbie's caper; and we come together in a panic of crouching troopers, a screech of sirens, a cusp of whirling, blue-red lights.

* * *

"Slow down," Rin says, "you're goin' eighty."

"Yeah," Sam agrees, "I feel sick when we go this fast." He throws down *Power-morphs: The Slow Beauty of Kango*.

I drag my foot off the accelerator. My palm is moist on the wheel. I take a deep breath. Why George didn't get out, after that stunt—just tell me to pull over and let him walk— I still do not know.

I would never have ratted on him.

I wipe one palm dry on my jeans.

The scrub pine rolls gently by on either side, concealing the strip malls of Bourne. All this was glacier once, and those hills, the wave of sand the tongue of glacier built, and left behind when it retreated. The hole that fear dug out when I rode with George evokes and makes more real the void that hurting Billy left.

I shift in my seat to roll that void in ways less painful, but the hollowness, like all good hydraulics, rolls to match my movement.

I touch the concave section below my sternum, making sure the organs work all right. My heart beats, a little fast maybe, but its timing is solid and steady.

The highway curves and swoops toward the canal. Providence, New York left; Plymouth, Boston right. The Upper-Cape Price-Shoppe, built to ressemble Buckingham Palace, looms over the canal's eastern shore.

Then the soar of bridge, lifting us over the black ribbon of water, and a lone Turecamo tug churning conscientiously to the east.

Nothing, I think vaguely. Nothing at the pith of me.

Through that void, as through a lens, I see only the

green of pine, the gray of oak, and a smear of dark blue, to the north, where Cape Cod Bay meets the white clay of Manomet.

"Read you a story?" Rin offers, holding up the *Cape Cod Tales* book.

"You took that!" Sam accuses.

"You left it," Rin answers, "in my bag, when we went to the Hollow."

"It's boring."

"I thought you liked it."

"I only like the good one. The one about Mom's family."

"So I'll read that one."

We round the rotary and chug onto Route 3. The pages lisp. Rin's voice starts stubborn and high against the mindless hum of Goodyears spinning north.

The "Witch" of the Whydah

from *Children's Tales of Olde Cape Cod* (Olympia Imprints, Yarmouth Port)
by Wendy Rose Adams

In early Colonial days the connection between the West Country of
England and Cape Cod was strong, for many families from Devon and
Cornwall had settled in Barnstable County. Thus, after a Devon man
named Samuel Bellamy sailed his old sloop to Boston with a cargo of
Jamaica rum, he made for the Cape, to stock up on supplies, and to give
his crew a rest.

Samuel Bellamy had sharp dark eyes, long black hair, a fast tongue,
and a fancy, ebony-handled sailor's knife. He had an eye for adventure
and a plan to salvage gold from a sunken galleon off Tortuga. He also
had an eye for pretty girls.

One night, after a fine supper of cod cheeks and ale in Higgins
Tavern, in Eastham, he took a walk through the Judgment Lot nearby.
At the meadow's end he heard a girl's voice raised in song. He traced the
sound through the woods to a hollow by a small brook. In the center of
the hollow was a hillock. On the hillock grew a flower-apple tree. It was
spring, and the tree was in bloom with its white and pink blossoms that
looked like Spanish lace in the moonlight. Under the tree sat a girl
dressed in a long robe of blue wool. She had hair the color of pieces of
eight and eyes as blue as the Atlantic. Her name was Maria Hallett.

Sam Bellamy sat down beside her. He fell under her spell, and she
under his. For a month they courted and then, because he was a ship's
captain and his sloop had business elsewhere, he sailed south, promising
to return for Maria when he had salvaged the galleon's cargo.

But salvage is a tricky business. Sometimes the wreck one seeks is not
where the chart says it is. Even if one finds it, the cargo often has been

scattered, or buried too deep in the coral. After a year of fruitless effort, Samuel Bellamy ran out of money and patience. His men talked openly of mutiny. So Bellamy did what many had done before. He ran the black flag up his mast, and turned pirate.

In Eastham, meanwhile, Maria had given birth to a child with dark hair and eyes like his father's. Because she was not married she bore the baby in secret, and took care of him in John Knowles' abandoned barn. Despite her care the baby froze to death one cold March night, and Old Man Knowles caught her burying it by the marsh. She was tried for adultery and negligence, and locked up in Eastham jail.

But Maria was too wild to be held by a village jail. Again and again she broke out to walk the dunes by Nauset Beach, searching the horizon for Bellamy's ship. The villagers grew weary of chasing her. Many of them were fearful of Maria by then, because of her wildness and because when free she took off her robes to sing and dance in the hollow by Judgment Lot. Someone said she was a witch who had sold her soul in exchange for magic powers. After a while everyone believed this to be the truth.

Eventually they left Maria alone, and she built a shack of driftwood in the dunes behind Nauset Beach. There she weaved cloth from the wool of lost sheep, dyed with wild cranberries and shellfish and tree bark. The patterns were so beautiful that people suspected the devil had assisted her in this work as well, but that did not stop them from giving Maria bread or ale or whatever she needed in exchange for cloth as blue as the sky or as red and cheerful as the trees by the ponds in autumn. On the rare occasion a traveler passed down the beach, Maria would ask for news of her lover. And one day news arrived, because Bellamy was now known up and down the Colonies as "Black" Bellamy, a daring and ruthless buccaneer.

It was early fall by then, and two and a half years since Samuel Bellamy last laid eyes on Maria Hallett. During that time he had taken a half-dozen fat, slow merchantmen off the Virgin Islands. In a rare calm off the Carolinas, Bellamy chased down and captured a London ship named the *Whydah*, whose holds were full of ivory, gold dust and indigo dye. Now Bellamy turned the *Whydah* north toward Cape Cod, for he intended to make good on his promise to Maria Hallett, and pick her up on his way to Devon. Once in England he would bribe the King's officials into granting him a pardon.

It was not to be. Bellamy took his last prize, a pink named *Mary Anne*, laden with Madeira wine, in Nantucket Channel. It was the evening of Friday, April 16, 1717. Shortly afterward the wind veered east. Both the *Whydah* and the *Mary Anne* found themselves blown northwest toward Cape Cod and the roaring breakers of Nauset Beach. They tacked and labored, they set anchors, but the storm increased in power. By the time the sun came up both ships had been driven into the shore and broken under the terrible hammer blows of surf. Timber and bodies littered the beach for miles. Among the wreckage walked a tall woman with golden hair and haunted eyes, dressed in a long woolen robe as blue as the sea.

Nine men came ashore alive from the *Whydah* and were tried for piracy in Boston. None of them was Samuel Bellamy.

Chapter 27

The constancy of Maria Hallett

42 degrees 17'N; 71 degrees 01'W

By the time the story is over we are passing the Plymouth County House of Correction.

Trucks toss wet salt on my windshield. Periodically, because the washer does not work and the wipers are old, I have to crank the left window down and pour Windex on the outside glass.

Sam and Rin are silent. Zappa slurps greedily at the other tit.

The breath of traffic shakes us, dulls our eyes.

"I thought she was seeing Bucket," I say at last.

"What are you talking about?" Rin says.

"Caitlyn." I point at the book. "That's where she was when Billy got hurt. That's why I couldn't get hold of her. She was dancing around that fuckin' tree!"

Rin fills her lungs with air, and lets it all go.

"I never know what you guys are talkin about," Sam complains.

"Don't whine," Rin tells him, "it's got nothing to do with you."

"Nobody tells me nothin'."

"Pretending she's a goddam witch." I pry up a piece of dashboard with my thumbnail. "I saw the dress, I saw the slippers. I saw the *loom* for chrissakes. I still didn't get it. She had marsh grass in her hair. She went out nights." I yank the vinyl strip free and drop it on the crowded floor. My jaw twists with tension. "Two weeks ago, when she told me she went to the Squire—"

"It's the busy season for witches." Erin's voice is light.

"You did it too?"

"She asked me to. I said no. I'm not a witch. No matter what Randy says."

"Miss Ryan said witches aren't real," Sam says. "They're just, like, symbols, of what we're scared of."

"Miss Ryan *would* say that," I tell him.

Clouds shake hard sleet onto the roof. Opening the window and dumping Windex makes my hand numb and sets Zappa crying from the noise and cold air.

"That bra," I pick up again, when the window is closed. "The one we found in the bog. It wasn't her size."

"Ellen," Rin says.

A state police cruiser flashes past, a long gray-blue predator, going too fast to notice our lapsed inspection sticker.

"So what *do* they do? Just dance?"

"Just dance," Rin answers, glancing at Sam. "I think we should change the subject."

"Nobody tells me nothin'," Sam repeats.

"Nobody tells me *anything*."

"Whatever."

Caitlyn in her red ballet shoes, spinning around that apple tree under the moon. Stainless light shining on breasts, on naked hips. I should feel shock, and a kind of G-man delight, because I figured out what happened.

I should be relieved, because she was not flirting with Bucket at the Squire.

Rin stares wistfully at the Independence Mall. Sam is back to Alien Power-morphs. The bald head of his kangaroo lolls from his backpack. I wonder, what the hell am I doing moving to Maine, when Sam will stay on the Cape?

It is all very well to swear I will come down from Maine every weekend but in practice it won't happen.

Sam will have other things to do, and so will I. It is just too far away.

Even Rin and Zappa are traveling no farther than Dorchester.

And something turns in me.

Direction, the concept of it, falls apart.

Every voyage must have compulsion behind because there is nothing so dangerous as leaving shelter. Yet when I look to find the compulsion powering this trip, it is gone. Just like that; like a set of keys you know you put on that table, but that simply are not where you left them; and which could not have moved, but somehow did.

My teeth hurt from clamping. I relax my jaw.

I hardly know anyone in Maine.

So what am I doing leaving George, who stayed in the Chevy with me and did six months on the Hill (six more suspended) because of it? Who backed me up against Jack Sibley and his nailbangers?

A meanness surfaces within my head, tight Yankee reflex against an optimism of heart.

And what do you have to show for that? it asks. A buddy you never see?

There is Johnny Norgeot, I tell the meanness, a little sadly. Not a great friend, but he always helps me out. He was glad I made it back after the storm—the only one who said that. And what else is there, when you get down to it, but a kind word against the wind?

A fish wholesaler, the meanness replies contemptuously.

Fuck you, I tell the meanness, and pay more attention to the traffic, which thickens as we near Route 128.

Rin wants a beer. I stop the truck in a rest area and get two Bass Ales out of the back.

Then hesitate.

Part of me wants that beer the way Zappa wants the tit. Another part of me is too busy with thinking to put up with the slide and vagueness of booze.

Eb tries to lick my cheeks off. I shove him away, and replace the second beer in its cardboard rack.

Past 128 the Pru, the Federal Reserve, the John Hancock building, poke their clustered silver spikes from the bed of horizon. Out of nowhere comes the image of Maria Hallett, sitting in the doorway of her shack, watching the horizon for Bellamy. But the *Whydah* sank, and the *Mary Anne* was crushed on the ravenous bar for Sandy Southhack to find, maybe, three hundred years later.

Bellamy was drowned on the same shore that almost got *Hooker*.

Bellamy never came back.

Maybe it is because the lens of void inside my ribcage magnifies the drama along with everything else but that fact seems to me the saddest I ever heard.

Sadder even than Billy, lying under one of those towers up ahead as clean men and women test the purity of his spinal fluid.

"Jeez, Ollie," Rin says, "speed up can't you, we're only going forty."

"I get sick," Sam points out, "when you drive this slow."

"Goddammit," I yell, "I'm thinking." I speed up though.

"I'm doing it again," I ask Rin, "right?"

She looks at me. She knows exactly what I am talking about.

"I don't feel so good about this," I continue. "I mean, if you just abandon things you care for, 'cause they're not perfect, 'cause you're not perfect—just leave 'em *behind*—it must mean, you don't love 'em very much. Right?"

"I don't have a problem with that," my sister says. "You do what you have to do."

A P&B bus blares at us from behind.

"It's what Frank did. All my life. I thought I was better than Frank." In third we accelerate better. Shit heap rattles like a can of old nails. The tubs of Might-E-Foam bang around in back.

"I mean, what it comes down to, you're jiss fucking over your own people. Right?"

"Zzysygy," Zappa says, and spits up.

"If you're trying to tell me, here," Rin says, wiping the spit-up with a paper towel, "what *I* should be doin', then you're, like, way out of line, man. Totally way out."

"I'm not necessarily."

"Oh it's easy for you." Rin's face goes long. The lines around her mouth are tense. Her eyes burn my face like Coast Guard searchlights. "You got your boat. You always had your boats—clamming, fishing. You always go back to that."

"It's not what you think, the fishing."

"I know about the fishing. But you'll stick it out. It's what you are, Ollie. Don't you know how jealous Caitlyn is, of that? Don't you know how powerful that makes you?"

"I don't—"

"Why d'you think I let you boss me around? Ever since we were kids, playing in little skiffs."

"Rin, I—"

"You got that *trade*, Ollie. You got the water," Rin says, looking straight ahead now. "What I got, I got men. That's what makes *me* powerful."

"But Caitlyn has a job. And she has her dancing."

Rin blows breath out of her nose hard to indicate what she thinks of Cait's dancing.

"She could do it again," I say, although I know what Rin will answer, which is that dancing is a young woman's game. She knows I know so nobody says anything more except for Zappa, who says "kazoo."

At last the P&B bus passes, throwing gravel at our radiator, its diesel roaring frustration. The driver shakes his head in pity as he goes by.

* * *

We arrive in Dorchester twenty minutes later. The house Rin is looking for has three Harleys propped by the garage. A stocky man with a crew cut, leather pants and dark glasses grins widely and kisses her on the mouth.

Rin parks Zappa with the guy while I haul her bag out of the back. She stands in front of me, eyes narrowed, hands on her hips.

"You're not going to Maine."

I love that gap between her teeth. She looks about eight years old with pockets bulging from shoplifted fireballs when she smiles like that.

"I don't know," I grunt. "I guess maybe not."

"Da-ad!" Sam yells, from the truck.

"We'll go to Boston," I tell him quickly. "We'll see Uncle Billy."

"And the train section?"

"Yup."

"And Denny's?"

"And Denny's."

"You're a better man than me, Charlie Brown," Rin says, and, taking hold of my head, drags it down to her cleavage. She shifts her grip, trying to hug me all the way around, but cannot connect around my chest.

An irrational conviction grabs me, that I have become thicker in the upper body.

It's as if the decision I just made neutralized and then built on the assorted vacuums that migrated to my ribs after

Billy was hurt, giving me more mass than I had an hour ago—although how this would translate so quickly to fat and muscle I do not know.

The biker turns away, removing his dark glasses.

My sister lets me go, eventually. I pick my watch cap off the driveway.

"What about you?"

Her face is round again, and pink with excitement.

"Oh, you know me, I'll always come back," she says, glancing behind her to make sure Zap is all right in the biker's arms.

"See ya, Rin," I tell her.

"See ya." She goes over and messes up Sam's hair.

"Cut it out!" Sam yells.

I get in the truck and edge into the cluttered street.

The last I see of Rin, she is holding Zappa high in the air while the biker, diving between her arms, French kisses her with the endurance of a sponge diver.

NOAA Weather Forecast

This is the December fourteenth extended forecast for waters from the Merrimack River to Chatham, Massachusetts up to twenty-five nautical miles offshore:

General outlook:

The jet stream will flow westerly over the weekend. The high pressure system currently over New England will continue to dominate the area's weather for the next two days. A low pressure zone now moving across the central plains will enter western New England early Monday.

Offshore forecast for New England waters from the Northeast Channel to the Great South Channel including the waters east of Cape Cod to the Hague Line:

Winds northeasterly fifteen, becoming north fifteen, seas four to six feet; diminishing ten to fifteen, seas four feet.

Reports from offshore buoys:

Isle of Shoals; air temperature twenty, wind north twenty, water temperature thirty-nine, seas five feet.

Southeast portion of Georges Bank: air temperature unavailable, wind unavailable, water temperature unavailable, seas unavailable.

Chapter 28

Sam and I stop by MGH but the reception woman says visiting hours are over for neuro-ICU. I tell her we are family. She looks at her screen and says no one is allowed up. The patient has refused visitors and calls. "The patient," I ask, "or his sister?" and she smiles, using her mouth only.

I do not argue. I figure I can always come up again, once I have straightened things out with Cait.

I am going to stick around now.

That decision is strong in me because I just made it and the problems are not yet clear and I think: Maybe that strength will touch Caitlyn, by its force and shining novelty.

Although it is weird to imagine her upstairs in this gray tower and I cannot talk to her or see her even.

We ask the reception woman to deliver the forsythia. She says it's against the rules. We leave the yellow branches propped by the main door so someone else can use them.

Then we go to the Museum of Science and, after that, a Denny's in Milton, and then we are well into rush hour.

Somewhere around Duxbury the truck's heater quits. I check the radiator but there is still plenty of water. Maybe the hot water intake is jammed up. I drag an old sleeping bag from behind the seat and fold it over my legs and Sam's. By the time we reach the canal it is freezing in the cab and Sam presses his whole side into mine to keep warm.

We get back to the Kitchen just after eight o'clock. Harriet offers to defrost soup for me but I am too restless to hang in the Kitchen tonight. As usual the planes of highway and the long red wires of brake lights have been burned into my eyes. Movement draws out a further need for movement.

Northeasterly winds, fifteen to twenty, the weather channel says.

Sam falls asleep. I drive around town. Eb fastens his nose to the window crack and sniffs. I believe I reached some kind of personal watershed with what I have been thinking today and this ought to be mirrored in my surroundings but the town looks just the same. The CVS arcade touches me because I remember the movie theatre that was there when I was a kid. The whalebelt boutiques piss me off. The windows of Dorene's Bridal shine brightly. Tonight the mannequins wear purple.

I wonder for the thousandth time what the color means, and if the place really is a call-girl service, or if people only wish it were.

A bluehead pulls out in front of me, speeds up to 15 m.p.h., riding her brakes. Her Crown-Vic carries the "Environmental" vanity plate with the right-whale flukes. She turns right down Crowell without signaling.

The strip malls past the Route 28 rotary impart a deadness, as if they carried a virus of plastic that might reach out and cover my eyes with clear film before I had time to blink them free.

All this is thin reaction, I tell myself. What's important is, the absence of drive in the pith of me—this new aversion to departure.

"I'm staying here," I mumble, trying the feel of those words against the tongue. They do not taste differently but just saying them makes me feel odd—half disappointed, but also half excited, as if that decision in itself might open doors into hallways of thought, places I would never go without it.

I pull a U-turn at the A&P lights and drive back down Main Street to the alley leading to the Squire parking lot. The lot is almost full. The only space left is at the end, almost in the bushes.

I sit in the cab for a few minutes, wondering if I really want to go into the bar, watching my breath form and vanish against the windshield. Eb pushes his nose into my hand. I rub him behind the ears. I gave him a hose-down yesterday but he still bears a flavor of seagull.

I do not really want to drink. I would like to warm up, but for now the sleeping bag keeps hypothermia at bay.

I could use a cigarette, but it is not so urgent a desire.

Simply breathing inside the Squire will slake that craving.

The reason I will enter that bar, I decide finally, is to confirm the decision I made.

I want to tell Bucket, and George if he is around, that I am going to fight it out here. I might not say anything specific but simply being inside in my usual stance will serve as affirmation.

I need to read, in the movements their bodies make, in words of greeting or rebuff, the rightness of this act.

I walk in the back entrance.

The hot air enfolds me like a fat man's hug.

Frank is not in his booth. Manny and Swear whisper over the table by the Power-morph video game. They do not notice me. I do not seek them out.

I walk to the front room. When Bucket catches sight of

me he puts down the rag with which he is polishing a glass and pads in my direction. I raise my right hand, palm out, talking fast.

"I wanna come back in man I know I fucked up—"

"You fucked up."

Bucket's eyes are pink with smoke. His beer belly lolls under a Squire tee-shirt. It seems ludicrous that I ever thought he slept with Caitlyn. That was bad imagination, a function of anger. Although I am not making up Bucket's lack of welcome now.

"Anyway." I spread my hands. "Up to you?"

Bucket examines his glass, and rubs a soap mark away with the edge of one thumb.

"Shit, Ollie," he says finally, "you can come in." He looks at me, eyes narrowed, and adds in a lower voice, "I heard what Sibley said.

"Only next time—go outside?"

He keeps looking at me, waiting for agreement. I nod. He nods. He gets me a Rock 'n Roll. I worm into the crowd, feeling through my clothes the body warmth of the place. "I never did ecstasies as *suppositories*!" someone yells.

The Rock 'n Roll tastes like it always tastes. Jeb Flick whoops at some joke he made. It bothers me that he can laugh so easily when his brother drowned two months ago.

It should bother me that I am in the Squire listening to Jeb laugh when my mate is in the hospital with his legs not working. But I do not turn around and leave.

No sign of George. Fleetwood is slumped in one of the booths with a Coors bottle and a shot glass empty beside her. I move around the sides of the bar, looking for a clear section on which to rest my elbows. A girl in a white turtleneck goes to the ladies' room. I take her place, leaning on the polyurethaned oak, into the altar of drinking, indifferent to sacrament. I am not thirsty yet.

The level in my bottle is almost unchanged.

Things truly must be new and strange.

Sandy Southack, across the bar, cadges a drink from Bucket. "I'll be flush next week," he says.

"Uh-huh," Bucket replies.

Beside Sandy a knot of Jack Sibley's nailbangers stare at me and square their shoulders. I stare in return and finally they get bored and go back to their bottles. Their lips curve over the neck's rim and their throats move in the oldest rhythm of all.

The rhythm reminds me of Zappa; and it reminds me of how I felt in Mad River, when I drank beer in the lodge with Rachel.

Someone large shoves himself between a whalebelt and my left shoulder. I smell perspiration and swivel fast, always aware of the nailbangers and the hostility they hoard.

Sim Pierce, bulky in his gillnetting sweatshirt, blocks the Christmas lights.

I examine my beer. Sim says, "I'm sorry about Billy Sturges. I jiss wanted you to know that."

"Yeah," I say.

"He gonna be okay?"

"I don't know."

"We almost went out that night," Sim continues. "I'm glad we didn't."

"You see Wayne Ojala," I say, "tell him thanks for me."

"He was standing by." Sim strokes his beard. "He's a good guy, Wayne."

"He's a fuckin' gillnetter."

Sim rumbles. He lifts a finger. A beer appears before him.

"Just wanted you to know," he repeats and, picking up the fresh bottle, starts to leave.

I touch his elbow. He turns back halfway.

"You were pissed at me, 'cause of the hearing."

"A lotta people were," Sim says after a beat. "Thatch is gonna hire thirty, thirty-five more carpenters . . . You're gonna sell anyway, what I heard."

He looks at his beer, waiting for confirmation of what he already knows.

"Thatch," I begin, "makes one kind of work." I don't know why I cannot simply answer Sim's question. "You could work for George Peters," I add.

Sim has large hazel eyes, always surprised looking.

"He got work, this winter?"

"He's doing that development down my road. You know, the open-space plan?"

Sim shakes his head.

"What makes you think George is hiring?" He turns away for good this time, pushing me aside without meaning to, leaving a hole the whalebelts do not fill.

That is when I understand Sim cannot get a job with George. He is not a good enough carpenter.

George pays well and his work is year-round and he gets his choice of people.

One of the whalebelts hands me a crumpled letter. It carries "CB&T" printed blue in one corner and the green-white stickers of registered mail. I recognize it as mine. It must have ridden in my hip pocket since yesterday until Sim dislodged it in leaving.

I replace the letter in my pocket. With a thumbnail I strip the soaked label off my beer bottle. I feel bad, thinking what I did about Sim. I also feel good that we are talking again. This half bad, half good way of being is probably how it will continue for me if I stay here.

Maybe what I am trying to arrive at is a balance. Friends you never see against guys who do not like you much but help you anyway. A strip mall here, a plot of scrub pine untouched beside it.

It just does not cost that much more to build with space around.

One of Sibley's nailbangers holds his cigarette cupped the way Billy does.

I take a big swig of beer. I do not wish to think about Billy right this minute. I check my back pocket, out of reflex, making sure the letter is still there. I take it out and bend it back and forth as it it were tin and this might soften it. Then I edge my thumb under the flap and rip. The paper inside is black with big letters spelling out the kind of words that hit your stomach a half second before they touch your head.

require the bank to foreclose on the second conveyance, secured by mineral, water, fishing and hunting rights on a property located

I slide the second page free.

to foreclose on a floating balloon note as secured by a fishing vessel, known as *Hooker*, currently moored at Chatham, Mass.

I pick up my beer bottle and put it down again. My face feels hot. Moisture rises warm in my armpits. It is a gearbox kind of warmth. The high temperature comes from meshing, when milled steel engages with steel, imparting torque.

And the whole linked assemblage starts to spin, slowly at first, then, as it comes up to speed, bestowing movement, and a necessary direction.

Mrs. Snow did not take early retirement.

Mrs. Snow was fired because she allowed me to make late payments on these two notes.

No factual basis exists for this calculation. All I know is, in the core of me, where the value of "um"s and soft evasion make their own inexorable two-plus-two, I have grown certain it is true.

I push away the bottle and stand straight, looking for a horizon. But there is no horizon in the Squire.

Todd Kiernan thought I had lost the rights to the Hollow. Todd handles all of Thatch's real estate business. Thatch is a director of Chatham Bank and Trust.

No bank is going to repossess a clapped-out and unsalable fishing boat unless it has a compelling reason to do so.

Removing my watch cap, I let the smoke cool my head by evaporation, but the calculations I am making do not rely on body heat to reach their sums; like a diesel engine they generate their own fire and grind on independently.

Thatch must have pushed the bank to pressure me on the mortgages. Because of that pressure, I got nervous about making payments.

Because of being nervous I took a chance on the weather. Because I took a chance, Fleetwood has no one to drink with and is passed out alone in a corner booth at the Squire. And Billy is in MGH instead of lying on the brown couch drinking Coors and outlining to his friend the deepest evil of Jacques Chirac.

My fault. In the egotism of penury I end up using people. Pig said that.

But the penury is not something I want or court and in this case the risk it caused was not induced by me.

My lungs ache. Maybe the smoke in here is finally swelling my bronchial passages. I shift around, looking for a better stance. Heat is strong in my stomach too, as if I just ate warm soup, though all I have had today is a bowl of cereal and a Denny's quarter-pounder.

Crying Johnny whangs one chord, then a second. "Why you look at me like dat," he wails, "why you look at me like dat?" The whalebelts pogo in place, jerking a half-beat behind the bass. "You make me so nervous, honey—I put out the baby, changed the cat."

I think of Thatch the way I saw him last: staring at Pleasant Bay as if all this land and the waters around it were his to do with what he pleased.

I pick up my beer bottle and put it down, too hard, against the counter. A whalebelt glances at me nervously. Bucket looks up, unsure of provenance. My right fist is tense as seasoned maple around the glass. I want to break something with it; I want to take my bottle and crack it over the bar and know in that facile destruction, in the jade green glass smashing into a thousand sparkling fragments, the damage I might do elsewhere.

My chest truly aches now. I am breathing in gasps and still not getting enough oxygen. I take a couple of longer breaths. Abruptly I let go of the bottle.

Flex the fingers of my right hand. Twice, three times.

This anger can be divided, the way all angers can. I can take Thatch and the harm he has caused and split it all into smaller parts, into the steel-wool surface of his eyes, into the anomaly of drive behind that surface; carving it even smaller, more specific, into a tiny recall of the man I met, when I was a kid, the couple of times I went to Fuller's house for birthday parties.

I grasp the Rolling Rock bottle again and lift it to my lips. My fingers use only a little more force than is required for that small action. I have to unclamp my jaws to swallow. My breathing is deeper now—though the tautness in my chest, like a large, elastic bubble lodged under the sternum, is more noticeable than ever.

I can divide this anger. I know I have that power.

What I seem to lack right now is the desire.

I swallow beer.

The thought arrives without warning, like that radio transmission from the *Commando*, sent by someone different but with message nonetheless.

I am running away from Thatch.

I sit back in my head and watch that thought. Sucking at the beer more frequently than before because taking mental bearings like this makes me thirsty. The harder I watch, the less I can navigate. It makes me uncomfortable, when I cannot navigate with the kind of care such activity deserves.

"You *e-e-evil*, woman," Cryin' Johnny howls.

I treat myself to three more deep breaths and my chest feels better but the heat is really getting to me. Maybe it's all the thought. I adjust my watch cap and take a long swig of beer but neither of these here-and-now actions weakens the connections thinking made.

Sweat oozes off my forehead. I pick up the bank letters and look at them again. The black Gothic lettering is so flat and officious, so full of the cowardice of institutions.

You cannot kick a bank in the balls. Yet I have no clue how to fight a bank and I certainly do not know how to the fight the men who hide behind a bank's polished counters, or the lawyers they hire to protect them.

I tear the foreclosure notices into squares four inches across. A gesture of impotence; the rage of the little man. Even if I stay on the Cape there is nothing I can do to fix my failures. That does not stop me from ripping the squares into two-inch pieces and then making confetti of those and dropping the entire mess in the ashtray.

I leave money on the counter and go out the front exit so I don't meet anyone I know on the way.

The air outside freezes the sweat on my skin. I walk through the alley, back to my truck.

The cab is cold as the night. The engine fires right up. Eb likes the taste of sweat on my face.

Anyone would say I had tried my best. I fought as hard as I could for as long as I could and quit only when there was no choice.

I drive out of the parking lot and turn left, going where my thoughts already have traveled.

Chapter 29

Night vision

41 degrees 39'N; 69 degrees 59'W

The dirt track that turns off Marston's Road twists, not according to the desire of Frank, who cleared it, but rather to follow the path of least resistance, avoiding glacial boulders and the bogs where marsh streams pool.

Junk rattles in the shit heap's back; empty beer cans, the boxes of Might-E-Foam I still have not removed.

I have always liked the way this road takes the dips casually off-center, making my truck list to one side, forward, to the other side, and back.

The first time Harriet took me to the Barnstable County Fair she bought me a ride on an elephant. The animal was ancient and slow but riding it felt like this, and ever since then I have made the association when I came down this road.

The moon, a thin arc clipped from its northeast limb, peers from small tight clouds through the top of the truck windows. It travels between fingers of oak and brushes of pine, now to the right, now to the left, till its chromed light seems to crinkle out and cover, first the expanse of sedge at the northern end, then the whole of Marston's Hollow. I shut off the engine. Water drips steadily. I figure now one of the baffles came adrift and blocked up the heater box.

Trees strum the wind. Eb whimpers to get out but I will not let him.

I do not want to have to chase him if he tears off after a raccoon or something.

Later I will understand that, in this small thought, I already had caressed the outer skin of intent.

I shut the door quietly and trudge into the clearing.

The shadows of the low woods reach for the bog island and miss. The island is bathed in moonlight and the flower-apple tree is etched in that light, black and crooked against cold sheen. Besides the wind there is no noise. Even the owls are silent.

Caitlyn dancing around that tree, the black cape flying. I have a small feeling of how it must have been for her: the sense of barriers broken when she came at night to accomplish this act without sanction.

I know she took her clothes off when the wind was warm. Ellen and my wife, two long white characters burning by force of magic against the belly of darkness, singing spells from $9.98 Wicca books she purchased at the health food store in Orleans.

Now, soft as a woman soothing her child, comes the voice of the north owl, threading vowels together in somber lullaby among the darkest pines.

His mate answers, farther south, by Oyster River.

I walk by the side of the bog, toward water. At night the shack seems in better shape, the way it was when I was a kid, when Frank kept it up. He spent a lot of time painting and shingling it and repairing ice damage to the little dock, in the days when he still owned the land itself.

He taught me how to shingle one summer, handing me materials as I perched nervous on the slope. Start at the bottom, left to right, following the slat he had nailed above for a line. I liked the tin "silver dollars" we employed to pin the tarpaper down. I kept some in my pocket for months after, feeling wealthy. The flat cedar smelled sweet as Froot Loops and the hammer was like growing up, too heavy in my hand.

In that at least he was patient, and a good teacher. I felt proud by the end of the job, the way kids do. As if already I had learned a skill, something that could grow into a trade and finally a place in the world where I needed no one to protect me anymore.

He must have cared for this place, he must even have loved it, to put so much work in. I do not remember him working much at anything else once he quit working for the town. I try to remember why he sold it, why he hung onto the rights. Probably the stronger reason was money, since we were always short. Maybe he kept the rights because he could not bear to give it up entirely.

And maybe he gave us the rights so we would have something left; if not possession, at least a share in the land he once had loved.

The thought transfers smoothly into this—I should let Sammy shingle up the old shack.

I remember then, consciously, what my unconscious mind is still trying to ignore.

The land is finally gone.

With our water rights in hand Thatch can build his project. He can even fill the cranberry bog, under the revised wetlands law, as long as he digs out a corresponding "bog" on land he does not want. Even if he doesn't build here, he will figure out some way to use it.

And he will tear down the shack, first thing.

Whatever happens, Sam and I will never come back here. We no longer can rely on it, in the mind's eye, as Frank intended, as a place that remains: a refuge.

I get the same wince inside I got at the Fishermen's Supply, only higher up now and multiplied—that sense of missing something ahead of time, though the thing itself is spread out alive in front of me.

It is not a comfortable sensation. It expands that sense of hollowness at the core. And it makes me about as flexible, and as resistant to danger, as all things formed around emptiness.

Clamping my molars hard together I walk around the old bog. I head uphill at the northwest corner, over the hay-bale glacis of the development, until I stand at the fringe of the scrub pine, looking at what Thatch has built.

The last time I saw this strip of land I was surprised at the scale of the project. Now a savor of awe rises in my mouth as I gauge what has happened since.

The basic skeleton of only a week ago lies clearly carved from darkness by security lights hung on poles around the perimeter. It has been heavily fleshed out in concrete and plywood. Twelve rows of pillars support a mezzanine that has to be a third of an acre in area. More pillars will be raised beside and on top of the first set. The completed building will add up to four floors, forty thousand square feet in area and almost fifty feet high.

They are going to build four more buildings around that.

From the second level the frameworks of high, round towers rise at each corner. Three more protrude from the roof's center. The towers, too thin for real use, rise over the main building by another thirty feet. They carry pointed tops—in imitation, I suppose, of the castle the architects copied.

The towers will house air-conditioning units and ventilators.

I cannot move. Nothing in me has the courage to try. The size of this project does to me what vastness is supposed to, in churches, malls, government buildings. It reduces the individual, makes him powerless before the sales pitch.

That is when I realize how vain was my urge, a scant twenty minutes ago, not to turn away from this.

Because the fact is, you cannot fight something this size and win. It is too big. One man can only punch at such enormity, bruising his knuckles, getting arrested for disorderly conduct.

Too much money lies entrenched here, money backing money, and corporate perqs and pension funds and insurance tie-ins and tax incentives and co-op advertising meshing back and back into the power grid of America, until finally to commit a crime against one means attacking America, and you wind up broken, or in jail; or at best, merely irrelevant, the way you started.

My stronger fist is tight in my pocket. I do not know if this is because of rage or cold. I get a sense that in the short time since I left the Squire the temperature has dropped rapidly. My left arm feels numb. Taking my right hand out, I rub the stringy muscle.

Now, under my heart, light and easy, like turning on the tube, comes the expectation of retreat. The rest that comes when holding your ground no longer helps. Abandoning the situation—just leaving the challenge be—is the only option left.

There is no shame in giving up against such odds.

The north owl cries behind me. His two-part hoot is only a little louder than the wind, and it sounds in roughly the same key, maybe three notes higher, like a chord.

When all the lights of Price-Shoppe are switched on the owls will move, for eight acres' worth of neon is too bright for nocturnal hunters.

The security lights hurt my eyes, the way they would shock the retina of a barn owl, causing him to turn, take wing into the dense air of night.

But I do not turn. The thin cold light seems to continue its trajectory, bright, merciless, through my optic nerve, into the center of me. It looks for a hard object to bounce against, finding nothing.

I did not abandon *Hooker*. (A knot of toughness lies in the thought; it is too small to reflect light.) Yet to fight Price-Shoppe, or Thatch, requires more than not giving up. I would need to multiply my own tiny power a hundred, a thousand times, until it matched in strength the girders of this bizarre palace.

Like the hydraulic rams of those bulldozers, asleep in a corner of the development. Such rams exert a strength fifty times greater than the force required to extend the first piston.

Or like something I used once, an industrial trick that turned a weak and solitary action into a force to shatter steel.

It seems odd that no guard is here. Probably the cops drive by when nothing else is going on. I remember, as I squint against the lights, that the multiplication of force I am thinking of was recent, and associated with *Hooker*.

It could have been the Hathaway. That winch almost broke me. But I do not think it was the winch, whose power I am used to and can usually control.

The perimeter lights only partially penetrate the building's mass. They illuminate the outer columns—the hollow supporting framework, with the small square at the top from which writhe the color-coded snakes of electrical cables—wriggling out of the tight space, the long flange at the center of these supports.

I walk slowly down the hillside, stumbling a little in the brush, my night vision wasted by the lights.

I skirt the bog, moving slowly as ever, listening for owls. Now inside my head a small film plays of myself at work: my hands pouring catalyst into a tub of Might-E-Foam, aiming the mixture into *Hooker*'s flange, where it grows to a hundred times its own volume, pumping in streams like vanilla milkshake from the escape holes I drilled.

"That stuff will blow up steel, you don't give it room," Doomo said.

The hands switch jobs. They drag the tub up a ladder, pour it into the opening at the summit of a Price-Shoppe column, block the hole with some of the scrap plywood lying all over the floor.

The columns are of Kiernan concrete. I could fill a dozen of them with the Might-E-Foam in my truck. There are no other escape holes in the columns. Even though the concrete is armored with re-bar the pressure in that meager space would be too much. Every one of them would explode outward, like beer bottles left in a truck bed on a night when the mercury sinks well below freezing.

I see myself ahead of time, on the ground, watching that concrete come apart. I remember watching myself, thirteen years ago, just before I ran into the convenience store with Frank's rusted shotgun.

The forward vision bothers me because it implies, this is just as stupid a move.

Don't do this, I tell myself. Don't do this.

I make my way diagonally to the dirt track, and walk to Marston's Road.

No headlights mar the dark, no cars or trucks are parked on the verge. Night vision returns, blackness burning wide in my pupils as I complete the circle and back to the shit heap. Eb whimpers pitifully in the cab.

My chest feels both heavy and light as I lift out the tubs of Might-E-Foam, with the clear bottles of catalyst taped on the side, and dump them in the gorse beside the truck.

Chapter 30

Might-E-Foam

41 degrees 39'N: 69 degrees 59'W

I straighten for a moment after I lift out the last tub, getting my breath back, although this is not heavy work.

Here is what I am thinking: I could load all this stuff back in the shit heap.

I could drive away.

After a while I bend down and pick up one of the tubs. It is a little heavy for my left arm. It holds, though, under the nub of elbow. Picking up a second, a bore of strength comes into my chest.

I am not drunk tonight, I am not doing this for booze money.

I am not turning my back on this.

That is what it comes down to: I am not turning my back.

Emergency thinking at its finest, Caitlyn would say. Yet I am nothing if not an emergency type. I am short and sharp and angry in my attention span. I can only be what I am by acting as I do. And if my love is the same way—if it relies on others, as Cait contends, to pick up the pieces, to cover the long gaps between—well, there is nothing to be done about it.

If I get away with this, I promise silently, I will pay more attention to the long run. I will focus my emergencies, be true to their implications. I will tend to Billy, and to Sam.

I will have no truck with abandonment.

Yet already I know my standing fast will be as on a fishing boat, where you cope from crisis to crisis, and keep what course you can.

I hump the two tubs to the place where shadow ends, at the end of the woods by the Price-Shoppe site. Two more trips to the truck and the whole load is hanging at the edge of Thatch's project. Only wind stirs the evergreen, the threatened beachplum.

I move faster now, shuttling the tubs through the lit perimeter, into the fetal mall. The smell of new concrete and wet plywood pricks my nose, reminding me of the months I worked on construction sites before I went fishing in the skiff.

A wooden ladder leads down a hatch to the vastness of cellar. I haul the ladder out and over to the central columns.

This work reminds me of when I was banging nails. Casey caught the brunt of my boredom in the days I did this kind of work. As I hump loads across the building site I reflect that leaving her to wait in her mother's house while Caitlyn and I escaped to Shubael's was not the worst betrayal. The worst cheating was on myself, because I would never see what course Casey and I might have taken; never know the colors and shapes our friendship could have adopted over time, or how she might have changed, within the forms of it.

The tubs are lined up now, one for every pair of columns, two rows of six beneath the central towers. Breathing sandpapers my throat. My hands shake a tiny bit. Sweat tickles the spine.

Nonetheless it is easier to go through with actions already painted in your mind. The sundown cast of the nearest spotlight gives me light enough to work by. I drag the ladder to the column farthest from Marston's Hollow. In this I will work backward, toward escape.

The top of the big drum is secured by a plastic zipper, which I yank off in one twist. With my fillet knife I cut away the tape holding the plastic bottle, and slice off its top.

Squirt the catalyst into the tub. Stir the mixture with a plywood stick.

Then I grasp the tub under my right arm and climb the ladder. The liquid, in catalyzing, warms my elbow.

At the level of the wiring hole I brace myself against the rungs and carefully lift and tip the tub until its raised spout pokes into the hole. I drain half the tub into the column. It gurgles like a kettle filling.

I bring the lightened container down with me and move to the next. On this column the roof, close overhead, prevents my lifting the tub all the way to empty it; but ninety percent of the foam is gone.

It is not as easy as I thought to find a piece of plywood of the right size to block those two holes. Panic surfaces as I trot from scrap pile to scrap pile. How long did it take the catalyst to work on *Hooker:* Three minutes? Five? Eventually I locate a stack of two-by-eights cut into squares under a bandsaw. I haul an armful of these to the columns and roughly wire them in place with strands of cable, two in each hole, butted one on top of the other against the columns' inner flange.

They only have to hold until the foam fills the space inside. After that, pressure will keep them in position.

The next three pairs of columns are a matter of routine. The adrenaline and work keep me warm. In the convection of heat a fine optimism perkles upward. Even if the columns do not break, this foam will surely crack them, making the structure unsafe. Price-Shoppe will have to rebuild. The cost will shove this project into an unprofitable zone.

The town will buy the lot and make it public land, a park.

As I drag the ladder to the first of the fourth pair of supports a crack fractures the wind. A hollow bang follows immediately.

A slab of concrete, maybe four feet by two, lies on the deck by the first row of columns.

A waist-high glob of foam moves beside it, wide as a fishing boat's diesel—wobbling and enormous in the release of pressure.

My heart bangs as I scale the ladder again.

Only two more pairs to go. I finish that column and start on the next. Another crack sounds down the row of supports. And another. A groan, as if the building had gas, comes from the roof overhead. I wonder if maybe I should clear out of here, in case the whole roof comes down. I see myself lying under tons of sub-code cement. The vision is so strong that I do not notice a light cadence of hooves. And I don't see the horse where he has drawn it to a halt, peering intently into the shadows where I hold on tight to my tub of power.

"Hey, you! *You* in there!"

I jump, almost dropping the tub. Adrenaline expands like Might-E-Foam in my system.

The thing to do is, ditch the foam and run. Now. Only right at that moment comes a really big bang as one of the columns in the fourth pair blows apart. I watch it become rubble, with little bits of cloud attached, in my angle of sight.

In that hesitation he spurs the palomino close to the edge of concrete. Thatch seems big, even from this distance. His beret shines under the moon as if he had dusted it with glitter. He wears an army desert jacket and high boots. The dark shape of Jesse lopes back and forth behind the bigger animal.

He pulls the rifle from his carbine holder and aims it one-handed at what can only be shadow-form on shadow-ladder in the darkness under that deep roof.

His left hand gropes behind him, and springs light, a tight beam, following the ladder till it pours brightness across the top half of my body.

"What the *hell* do you think you're doing?" His voice is almost quiet. He is reluctant to believe what his eyes say is going on. "Jesse," he adds, "go"; and the dog bounds across the drainage ditch, onto the foundation, to stand growling at the foot of my ladder.

I lower the tub. I do not think Thatch will fire that gun but the extra adrenaline has set my knees to shaking. I hold the ladder tightly with my good hand. The urge to jump and run is gone. Perhaps this thing of value that kept me on-Cape in general is happening here in the particular, when staying is easier than escape.

Or maybe I am not so sure about Thatch's reluctance to shoot. I squint into the flashlight beam.

"Ollie," he says, in that same calm voice. "Ollie Cahoon."

The light unpins me and moves down the line of columns. In that accusing finger of glare, I examine the destruction I have caused.

Half the columns are blown out. Long scabs of two-inch-thick concrete lie on the ground, or hang outward from the columns, suspended by tie rods.

On three columns the destruction of concrete has revealed a rusty span of I-beam running from floor to ceiling inside.

Glare returns.

"What are you doing?" he repeats, more loudly. The horse shifts at the sound of his voice. He shifts the rifle to compensate, so its hard length stays sighted on my face. "Why are you doing this? You know we'll only build it again."

I squint harder through the shine. It is tough to say something real to a half-invisible man.

Jesse barks to let Thatch know he is doing his job.

Faintly behind the wind, Eb yowls in answer.

"I can't let you do it," I say. "I know you got the bank, and Price-Shoppe, and the town. They're all with you, Thatch. But not me." I clear my throat.

I am scared. There's no way around it. I do not want to get shot, or go to prison.

Again the finger of light probes the cavities of his mall.

"But why?"

"I said at the hearing. Because—"

"The tree-huggers," he interrupts. His voice, though louder than before, remains cool. "You selfish little prick. *This* is what people want. *This* is—"

"No. This—"

"This is what people here need!" he interrupts, and the rifle wavers for a split second, then steadies. "We're not gonna hurt your lousy fish, your lousy little quahogs. But this—"

"That's not what I was tryin' to say." I clear my throat again. Jesse' growl deepens, and he stands on his hind legs, sniffing.

"It was my land," I continue. "My father left us the rights."

"Get down, Ollie," he says. "Get down now."

"He left us the rights so it wouldn't be destroyed."

"I said—"

"But you know about sons, and fathers." And in the perversity of what I am trying to do my voice grows louder. "You did the opposite, with Fuller. You turned the Cape into mall jobs—Price-Shoppe jobs. *That's* what you gave Fuller. And because of that, he left the Cape."

Thatch says nothing for a good twenty seconds.

"And when he died," I continue, less strongly, "you tried to make it up to him, with Fuller's Landing. You didn't see, the whole time . . ."

The palomino shifts again. The rifle tracks neatly.

"I come over here." His voice is low once more. "I see somebody, somebody wrecking this building. I can't see who it is. He threatens me, he's holding something, it looks like a gun."

"Thatch." My voice is not strong at all anymore.

"I don't have any choice."

"Thatch?"

"Do I?"

"Thatch—"

The wind gusts gently.

For a brief piece of time I think the roof caved in. The force is so big, it makes me fly.

The sound that follows is too loud for a thirty-ought-six. I land on a pile of scrap ply and all the oxygen is blown out of my lungs. I end up sprawled on my back, half on the scrap, half on the concrete floor.

Price-Shoppe's roof stretches away into the distance above me, a little out of true maybe but still whole, and endless.

My chest is warm, and aches. Otherwise I don't feel much of anything. I hear the dog panting, loud as a diesel. I decide to roll over. Suddenly my strength is one of the things I do not feel anymore.

My head hurts where I banged it. My watch cap came off in the fall. I lift my head an inch or two. It takes great effort. Jesse stands three feet away, looking back at Thatch. Thatch reins in his horse, which is kind of trotting in place, nervous as hell from the shot. The muzzle of his rifle points downward now. He says "Heel" and the dog pads toward him. He drops the rifle in its holster and climbs off the palomino.

I lean my head against the plywood. Some feeling is gone, some is enhanced. The warmth grows in my ribcage. This is not the vague absence that has been bothering me over the last couple of weeks but it is not good sensation either—the colors of it are purple and brown, warm and cold, thick with pain and thin with a kind of nerve refusal, as if my body were cutting off contact with certain areas.

Like Billy, I think. I can't feel my knees.

A crack sounds above and to the left. It is probably not a bullet, because my body is not flung anywhere. Dust and foam spatter around me. A gob of foam lands in my left eye. A cloud half the size of a longline tub settles on my chest, spoiling the view. It feels cool against the rise of warmth in that region. It is less soft than it looks. Its consistency is somewhere between shaving cream and styrofoam and it is getting harder all the time.

Thatch's beret looms over the top of that cloud. The shadows and planes of his face shift as he kneels beside me. He plays the flashlight over my chest foam. The bubbles shine against the dark.

"You stupid little prick." He almost whispers it. "I didn't want to do that."

My eyes watch him carefully. My brain wants him to stop yakking and get on the cell phone for an ambulance. I lick my lips so I can make that point. As usual he interrupts me.

"You stupid prick." It is not an insult anymore, it is almost a phrase of pity. He touches my forehead. His eyes wink in the reflection of light. He slowly smoothes the hair across my forehead. His fingers feel cold. In that slowness, in that chill, I can sense the dearth of anger in this man. I draw a breath, to get air for speech, but my chest hurts so badly now I have to stop.

He rises abruptly and disappears behind the foam.

"Thatch?" I whisper.

The wind moans, subsides. My legs are really cold. So are my arms, both of them, the good and the bad. I try to move them. This hurts my chest intolerably.

The cloud in front of me, the foam over my one eye, seem to darken. The roof, the columns, the woods beyond are being shorn of light. The owls will have left, they do not like loud noises.

Forms lose their edges, their hard edges.

Shadow grows. In that blackness I see a lot of green, like the sea at a certain depth, where most of the reds and blues have been screened out and only the emerald shades are left. The movements my hands and feet make now are circular, small; dog-paddle. My breath is so short as to constitute osmosis, or close. The emerald blackness washes over what is left of the Price-Shoppe site.

In that gloom, as usual, they wait.

The codfish.

The silver brown of their scales shines strongly. I understand now that those colors, part of the sea, cannot be canceled by water. They swim patiently, without emergency. Now my own efforts are powerful and I can follow them along the platinum shoal.

The king cod moves beside me. His glowing eye follows my movements. He fins without effort, leading me and the school together.

This is the first time I can remember the fish making noise. It is indistinct and low, rising and falling, like women singing in the next town.

The goatee of the great cod drops then lifts as he scoops up crab, sandlance, baby eel—always keeping course.

The bottom changes. Sand becomes gravel, then rock; big sharp slices of boulder, granite and mica and rounded slate, piled up where the wreck lay earlier, *Commando* or *Hooker*; it does not really matter, never did.

This is the place where no dragger can shoot its trawl.

The hardness of that bottom is absolute. Yet still we swim in that single direction. And the gloom advances, overtaking the green shades, the color of Rolling Rock bottles, and Rachel's eyes; and then the brown and silver tones of my codfish, and finally even the textures of this terrible ground.

* * *

I have no idea how long we swim like that. Navigation is not possible in utter darkness.

At some point light stains the cruelty of this sea. Blue, white, red dots flash on the periphery, like the northern lights I saw from *Hooker's* wheelhouse, two weeks ago, forever.

The voices are not fish, nor women either, and I miss the softness in those earlier tones. Words are built out of nothing. Pain comes from the water again, in currents, in tides. I look for the codfish, but they are far away now. Only a shadow within shadow marks the school; a quick flash, of umber scale, of brazen eye, among the columns of night. Then even this is gone.

A sadness so great it seems like it could swallow the Atlantic and leave room for more opens inside my chest.

I do not want to live in an ocean without codfish.

But the words now are loud and, in their causal relationship to pain, compelling.

I open my eyes to see an EMT with a familiar face holding up a hypodermic and squirting its thin liquid into the air.

The little drops of drug, catching the blue of police lights, turn blue themselves, miniature round oceans rising, stopping in mid-air, then falling into the coldness of the dark.

Epilogue

41 degrees 41'N; 70 degrees 16'W

Far down the wind-roughened surface of bay the dragger pulls its net into a band of beaten light.

In another five minutes, if it keeps this course, it will disappear behind the main hangar of Barnstable Marine.

The lawyer, Grealey, frowns at me, then turns to see what I am staring at. He does not notice the boat and flips his cell phone again in irritation.

Silva waits patiently, though every other defendant has gone inside the courthouse. Bailiffs sniff like beagles, getting ready to shut the doors as court convenes. But Silva knows enough to wait if a lawyer wants him to.

Beside us the statue of James Otis stares out to sea, a perplexed expression on his face, as if he wondered just how he had ended up here, on a windswept hill peopled by lawyers.

Thatch stands under the statue. I know Grealey wants me

to say something definite but I have nothing to say to him at all. He is willing to wait, though. So is Silva.

As for me, I have been waiting for days. Ever since I was lying on my back on the floor of Price-Shoppe time seems to have stretched into a different substance, a thing of delay, like a hard ball of clay being pulled into longer and longer string in the ruthless hands of a child.

* * *

The longest wait was lying on that rubble where Thatch left me, waiting for the EMTs to haul me into the rescue truck.

The EMT was the same guy who dealt with Billy, and Sibley; I guess he's always on night duty. He told me later he was sure I was going to die on him. There was a lot of blood and my vital signs had dropped and I kept fading in and out. He jammed wide-bore IVs in both arms and hit me with dopamine at a rate of 700 micrograms per minute. If my heart stopped he was ready to slice me open, right there in the truck, and start open-heart massage.

But my blood pressure went up with the dopamine. It was enough to get me to Hyannis.

The surgeons cut me fast. They expected hemorrhage inside. It took them fifteen minutes to figure out that Thatch's round, a copper-jacketed hunting bullet, had not made a big hole. It had gone high on my right chest and missed the heart and lungs and major arteries. They waited to make sure my blood pressure was stable. They spent an hour and forty minutes suturing me up again.

Time in the hospital passed featureless. Hanging around for the pain killers to wear off, for my strength to come back so I could sit up in bed or roll myself to the bathroom in a wheelchair. Waiting for tests. Waiting for a GI specialist, once they discovered that acid was eating a hole in my stomach lining. The ulcer had been there for at least six months, they said.

Waiting for the cops, the ADA, to question me, and record the answers.

Waiting in jail, of course. That's what jail is for.

An angry honking from Route 6A cuts into reminiscence.

My uncle's yellow Volkswagen pulls to a leisurely stop behind the TV van. A BMW with out-of-state plates accelerates around the VW and disappears, still honking, over the hill. Two people are visible inside Manny's car and for a moment I think the passenger is Caitlyn. Then Manny and a young man I do not recognize climb out, and stand crooked from the drive.

The stitches weep into my bandages. For no reason, because I do not feel particularly sad, fluid collects at the rim of my eyes.

Now they straggle up the hill, like Otis's militia, without discipline, two men united only in their vague purpose. The young man wears a sportcoat and carries a briefcase like Grealey's. Manny points. The man heads straight for Grealey as if it were the briefcase, seeking its cousin, that led him. He says something to the lawyer, shakes hands, and walks toward me. He has watery blue eyes, a thin moustache and reddish hair that flops over one temple. His cheeks are florid, with traces of acne damage. His lips pout. Manny limps up behind him.

"Mr. Cahoon?"

The nurses at Cape Cod Hospital told me Caitlyn visited ICU when I was still under sedation. They said she stayed until my status was officially downgraded from "critical" to "stable."

She was gone when I woke up. But I would have known she was there, even had the nurses not told me, because on a bracket halfway up the IV stand was hung one of the leopard-skin elastics she ties her hair back with.

And I thought, as I stared at it, that my wife's hair is a force. She binds it with elastic and knots it with ribbons but that only seems to increase its black power. Unleashed, it flies in the face of gravity.

"Mr. Cahoon!"

The briefcase man is in front of me. I drag my eyes upward to meet his.

"My name is Barry Himstead," he says. "I work for the Provincetown Gay Rights Coalition but your uncle, Manny Lopes, has retained me to represent you in this. You have no counsel at this time?"

"No."

"So you agree to be represented by me?"

I shake my head.

The lawyer glances at Manny, who is watching the cannons.

"Your uncle warned me you might refuse." He brushes hair from his eyes. "I think we could get you out on bail, and plead not guilty on the malicious destruction?"

I want to get out of JD-1 the way a knife wants to cut. I have no idea how this lawyer can spring me without bail money. Now my uncle turns to face me. He wears his best work shoes and a yellow tie that cinches his too-large collar into wrinkles. His eyes are narrow and he shakes his head. Dandruff falls like the first flurry of winter.

"You take a lawyer," he tells me. "Why don't ya take a lawyer? They'll nail you, boy. A man who is his own lawyer," he continues pompously, "has a fool for a client."

I wait a heartbeat or two before replying. But I don't really have to organize this argument, I have made it in my head often enough.

"If the facts are there," I begin, "a lawyer's not gonna make any difference. All you can do is plead nolo and—"

". . . and kiss the judge's ass," Manny finishes. He is out and out glaring at me now. "Ya don't think I've heard that before? When you gonna stop listening to Frank, Ollie? When ya finally gonna give up on that asshole?"

I stare at him. It takes me a second or two to figure out what he's talking about.

"I'm not—"

"Of course you are." Manny shakes his head again, looks

to the side, as if expecting even now to see my father slouching around the corner of the courthouse, a cigarette drooping in his mouth. "You do it, even when ya think it's you tryin' to fight him, you do what he's pushing you to do."

"Mister Lopes," the lawyer says, nodding at Manny, "has agreed to pay my expenses. If you concur, of course."

I keep staring at Manny. I know damn well who will end up paying for those expenses.

"So what's he gonna do," I say finally. "The lawyer."

Manny's eyes open a bit wider.

"He's gonna pull out a few extra facts." My uncle points his beak toward Thatch, for all the world like a disturbed heron. When he looks back, he is starting to grin.

"It is material," the lawyer, Himstead, says. He hikes his briefcase higher and clutches it protectively. "Mister Hallett was involved in a similar incident sixteen years ago. He was acquitted, but I think I can prove relevance."

"He can git you *off*," Manny hisses. The lawyer opens his mouth to object, then closes it again.

"I could give him the same story," I point out, not very forcefully because I am feeling cold again and unprepared to fight.

"I don't think," Himstead says, "that you could prove relevance without the precedent—" he shrugs.

"Ollie," my uncle says and his smile is gone before it got off the ground, and he looks even more like a heron, an old seabird with not a lot of migrations left.

"What the hell," I say, and shrug, which is a mistake because shrugging is not something you do with a hole in the chest.

"Okay," Himstead says, and walks back toward Grealey. After exchanging a few sentences they approach Thatch where he stands beside the statue. They talk loud enough for me to make out some words. "Manslaughter . . . excessive force." And Thatch, a whole phrase: ". . . prove a damn thing!"

A bailiff pops out the door, whispers something to Grealey, hurries inside. Thatch walks toward the court-house. The two lawyers move with him, each matching his movement to the other's.

Grealey says, "No deal."

I could have done that, I think. I didn't need a lawyer for that.

But Manny when he hears this throws his head back. The spikes of hair jerk as he stomps uphill. Ramming the group like Joe Hansen riding his bow over that right whale he stands crooked and small before the vast solidity of Thatch Hallett.

Thatch ignores him. Grealey already is dialing his cell phone. Now the Cape 11 people march up the hill. Michelle Meyer leads them, blond officer in a russet skirt, holding her mike like a marshal's baton. Manny sticks a claw-like finger into Thatch's chest, in roughly the same area Thatch's bullet hit me, and warbles:

"Lou Gonsalves, Thatch boy! *Lou Gonsalves.*"

Thatch's beret stands like a memorial to an unpopular war, motionless against the brown-gray trees.

"The TV people are here," Manny continues loudly, "they'll be in court too. You hear me, Mister big-shot finance committee chairman? Ya know what I'm *sayin'?*"

It crosses my mind that my uncle is as drunk as James Otis ever was.

For a moment nobody moves. I am getting embarrassed for Manny's sake. I look around, and my eyes stop at Skull— for Skull is the only person in motion on this sharp autumn hillside.

Skull's shoulders shake within his grimy Antartex. His head is turned away from the lawyers and he raises the clip-board high as if to shield himself against the wind. His thin lips quiver.

More than anything—more than the Hollywood bullet, the soap opera hospital, the steel injury of cell bars—this fact brings home to me the strangeness and broken rhythms of the last few days.

Skull is laughing.

Bits of steam escape his nose hair. He dabs at his eyes, and catches my stare. He turns further away from people, into the sun.

Thatch mutters something to Grealey.

The lawyer glances at Michelle Meyer.

Grealey says, "I'm not doing this. There is no way it would be admissible." And Thatch says clearly, "I'm not *asking* you, John."

Behind me, Silva speaks up. "I'm gonna be responsible, heah, we're much later than this."

A whiff of applejack on his breath.

"I'll call the clerk," Grealey replies tiredly. He grips Thatch's elbow with one hand and presses the cell-phone buttons with one thumb.

Thatch takes off his beret. He grins at Michelle Meyer. The wind grabs his beautiful hair and riffles it fondly. He follows Grealey back to the statue.

I look at Skull again. His shoulders are motionless now, and bowed, holding in something that wants to get out.

Manny climbs toward my wheelchair. His eyes bulge. The red in his cheeks is almost black. The lines in his face are taut. Anyone else would assume he is about to scream at me but I know better. Manny is excited.

Manny is proud.

I shrug again, and wince.

"Lou Gonsalves," Manny repeats. "The press forgot about it. But we got all the details from the court records."

I close my eyes.

He touches my knee briefly, as if pride were a current that had to be grounded to dissipate.

"We even got a few details nobody knows yet."

"How?" I begin, opening my eyes. But I know the answer to this too. Skull watches Manny now, fingering his eyelids. Traces of smile lurk still at the corners of his mouth.

Skull and Manny have been drinking together for forty years. And Skull was Flickie's uncle, or great-uncle.

And some people figure Thatch skimped on safety equipment for Flickie's boat because his money was tied up in Price-Shoppe.

I remember the brand new EPIRB sitting by the counter at Cape Fishermen's Supply, while the boat it was ordered for lies somewhere under the freezing swells of Western Georges.

"Those transmissions," I say, a little hoarsely. "They were you, weren't they? You and your pals."

Manny just looks at me.

I peer around for Harriet. I meant to ask her how Billy is, and Sam. But now Grealey is walking back.

And I realize, from the shortness of this latest wait, that Manny's scheme might work. Not because the judge will admit Lou Gonsalves as evidence. Not because Himstead has the right Lexus files. But because Thatch has all his money tied up in Price-Shoppe and he needs to get the development approved and he can't afford bad publicity right now.

The Lou Gonsalves case is bad publicity. The EPIRB is bad publicity. And shooting the guy who stands in the way of that approval, no matter what the circumstances, might also come off as bad PR.

That's what publicity means, when something like Price-Shoppe is involved. You don't have to wait. People, even institutions, speed up to match what you want.

Lawyers call you back. Judges delay their docket.

I glance over at Thatch. He is leaning over, touching the plinth of Otis's statue. Something naked lies at the heart of that gesture. A whole mob of deep fatigues is overcoming my defenses but if I had a month's worth of sleep I could not work up the pressure necessary to hate Thatch Hallett at this point. Even the shooting does not bother me. It was something he did in anger. I know only too well how anger works.

I wonder if this is how my codfish feel, when I catch them. As if any act committed for the sake of a pure and flame-hot passion is cleansed of both guilt and vector. The hunter dies a little, the hunted is reborn. What matters is, the cleanness of the fire.

* * *

Grealey talking.

". . . ask the DA to admit a plea bargain, get this over with. In case my client, ah, mistook his intentions."

Wind gusts.

"You also understand, guns go off by accident? He would have to waive civil charges . . ."

Himstead scribbles in a notebook. I realize that this process is far from being over, and the thought makes me more tired than before. Harriet climbs the steps but the terrier yips at my wheelchair and she backs off, her lipstick stretched in apology. An Old Gold steams between two scarlet nails. Even with a hole in my chest I can still desire a cigarette.

Raising my hand, I move into decision, ready to cadge a cigarette and to hell with the doctors and their facile statistics; but Harriet has turned away already. Her head bows as she whispers to the miniature dog. She wraps it tighter in a corner of her kaftan.

I stare at Harriet. I wanted to ask her if Cait is working today, and who is taking care of Sam. I saw Sam once in the hospital; Rin brought him in.

I shift my gaze back out to sea. All the waiting has shifted my perception in other ways. I still do not wish to go to back to jail, but after a week in there I also know that I would survive. And at least I would have this view.

If Grealey cannot cut a deal with Manny's lawyer or the DA then I will do my time and come out the other end and still be looking at the same ocean. And in a way the lack of change in that view will be a comfort: as if any constancy, even one built on utter indifference, can be used to build foundation.

I still want a cigarette.

I want to see Sam. I want to see Sam, and Rin, and Eb. I promise myself, I will do what I can to make that happen.

I know, even as I repeat the vow, that anger and the coldness of solitude are forces not so easily canceled; that there will be times when I will choose the other route, and pay for that choice with separation.

Now the dragger has almost disappeared behind the boatyard buildings. Her bow is covered by the hangar's side. As I watch, the wheelhouse disappears, then her mast, and finally the wide slope of afterdeck and then she is gone.

Only the texture of ocean is left now, a light-blue roughness up close, thinning to a softer surface and finally to a deep, smooth expanse until it is cut off by the horizon and the long gray uncertainty of sky.

Author's Note

Although this is a work of fiction, everything in this novel is real, in that it is based directly on places and activities that exist and whose living nature I hold dear. To fit everything I wanted to describe into the garment of Ollie's narrative, however, I was forced to loosen the seams of reality here and there. For example, although Chatham is the principal town in the story, it is probably too built up even to consider a mall the size of Price-Shoppe; unfortunately, the same cannot be said of other towns on the Cape, like Bourne, which is currently considering an even more destructive development called Canalside. Similarly, I have here and there worsened the environmental situation, for example by tightening slightly the bycatch limits for cod, and bringing forward the apperance of salt water in the down-Cape aquifer. In other places I have retained a few details that are no longer extant but that characterized environments I knew when I was fishing; for example, although smoking recently was outlawed in bars in Chatham, you wouldn't know it from this book. Other changes: The Orleans courthouse roof, as far as I know, works fine. The rectal glands of dogfish are in fact sold by Cape fishermen to Marine Biological Laboratory for research, but while other aspects of the animal are studied to help track neural pathways, the rectal glands are more useful for analyzing processes related to osmotic balance, and renal and cardiac function. Finally, while a product similar to Might-E-Foam exists and is employed by boatwrights, I would strongly advise that it not be used the way Ollie Cahoon uses it.

Photo by C. D. Hurter

Thinking back to the genesis of a story is like digging out dry rot in a wooden boat; every time you believe you have found the core of it, and scrape that away, another patch is revealed, deeper and more corrupt than the first. Thus, I could say this book started when I sat down on an October morning in the cabin of my boat—laid up on blocks behind a rented barn in Cotuit, Massachusetts—and thought for the first time about Ollie Cahoon and his problems. Or I could say it began twenty-odd years ago when I began longlining, on a twenty-three-foot wooden launch, for cod off Chatham. Maybe it goes back to watching my father—a former officer of the French Line—pounding out stories on his manual Corona.

All of this would be gross misdirection. A good story concerns intangibles: moods, smells, the deep logic-swells of emotion, so long in period you can never gauge what wind first kicked them up beyond the horizon. In my case, I think these intangibles include the smell of pitchpine needles and clamflats where I played as a kid, and the stories of ships told me by my parents. They have to do with the people I have known and cared for on Cape Cod. They stem above all from the peninsula itself, which like a beloved woman growing older suffers the scars and wrinkles of exhaustion and neglect and yet retains—in a detail of motion, in a memory shared, in the iron grasp she has on experiences that shaped her lovers—the power unexpectedly to stop your breath, if only for a second.